HER LAST
FLIGHT

HER LAST FLIGHT

▶ ▶ ▶

A NOVEL

BEATRIZ WILLIAMS

wm

WILLIAM MORROW
An Imprint of HarperCollins*Publishers*

HER LAST FLIGHT. Copyright © 2020 by Beatriz Williams. All rights reserved. Printed in the United States of America. No part of this book may be used or reproduced in any manner whatsoever without written permission except in the case of brief quotations embodied in critical articles and reviews. For information, address HarperCollins Publishers, 195 Broadway, New York, NY 10007.

HarperCollins books may be purchased for educational, business, or sales promotional use. For information, please email the Special Markets Department at SPsales@harpercollins.com.

FIRST EDITION

Designed by Elina Cohen

Library of Congress Cataloging-in-Publication Data has been applied for.

ISBN 978-0-06-283478-2

20 21 22 23 24   LSC   10 9 8 7 6 5 4 3 2

TO THE WOMEN AND MEN WHO TOOK TO THE SKIES
IN THEIR FRAIL MACHINES AND GAVE THEIR LIVES TO MAKE
HUMAN AIR TRAVEL AN EVERYDAY MIRACLE

Fiction is the lie through which we tell the truth.

—ALBERT CAMUS

HER LAST
FLIGHT

BARDENAS REALES, SPAIN

January 1947

THE AIRPLANE LIES in the shadow of a plateau, half-buried in sand and scrub. It sits at an angle, so the right wing slants upward against the sky while the left wing sinks into the ground. The dull green fuselage is mostly intact but the tail has broken off. Only the ghost of its original paint—the red, yellow, and midnight purple of the Spanish Republic—has survived a decade of relentless white sun.

I dismount. The mule jerks his head. Possibly he senses my nerves; possibly he senses something else. When you come upon a wreckage like this, undisturbed for ten years, known only to God, you approach it like you might approach a graveyard.

The question is, what bones lie inside?

ACCORDING TO THE MAP, MY mule and I have traveled about eight miles west of the town of Valtierra in southern Navarre, in the middle of what they call the badlands. The landscape is dry and yellow-brown, a junk-yard of plateaus and gullies, lone hills and dry streambeds, carved by wind and by occasional, catastrophic water. In summer, the heat would singe the hairs from your neck, and the dry air would suck the sweat from your skin. On this January afternoon, the weather is equally arid but cold. I took care to bundle myself in a wool coat, in scarf and gloves and one of those caps with flaps that come down to cover your ears. I don't do well in the cold, you see; my blood requires sunshine to stay warm.

Not a single living creature exists around me. Only a few wisps of vegetation rise from the soil. It's the kind of loneliness that sinks into your bones, that makes you feel as if you're the only person left alive in the world. If I still harbored any hope that the pilot of this airplane might have survived this crash, might have escaped and made his way to safety—and maybe I did, because the human heart will go on nourishing these ideas, no matter how farfetched—that hope is now gone. This bleak territory could no more support life than could a tennis ball.

And it is a terrible place to die, isn't it? Out here in the badlands of northern Spain, not a soul to care or to comfort you. The airplane settles into the earth, bit by bit, and as the years turn, every trace of your existence is buried too. If my guess is correct, the man inside this French-built Potez bomber was once one of the most famous people on earth, and now he rests here in the Spanish desert, body left to rot in the sun, untended and unwept for. *Sic transit gloria mundi*.

I TETHER THE MULE TO a withered juniper bush with a handful of oats. The wreckage is about fifty yards away, and the size of the airplane surprises me. For some reason I imagined it would be larger, but then I'm used to the behemoths of modern warfare. This airplane was obsolete almost as soon as it was built, a slow, clumsy ship nicknamed the Flying Coffin by the Spanish loyalist air force, and it seems to me that you would have to be crazy to trust your life to an airplane like that.

How whole it looks, though. How almost perfect, except for the stunted wing, the broken tail. If there's one thing I can't abide, it's the sight or sound or even idea of an airplane crash, but this one doesn't look like a crash at all. It just looks like it came here to rest, in the shadow of a giant plateau, and never got up again. And the plateau hid it from human eyes passing above, and the desert made a fortress around it, and only my friend Velázquez remained to know that it was ever here at all.

I start forward. The cockpit windows are opaque, the blades of the propellers frozen in place. On the side of the fuselage, a door hangs ajar. The wind howls on my cheek. It's impossible to imagine that nobody has stood here before me, that I alone have discovered this wreckage—*you! at last!*—but that's what years of civil war and reprisal and misery will do. Things get left behind and forgotten, because nobody exists to remember them. The wind howls around you and covers you in drifts of sand until a single woman, bedeviled by the mystery of your fate, encounters some tiny clue, entirely by chance. Now here she stands. At last, you are remembered. You are found.

ON THE OTHER SIDE OF the doorway, the world is dark. I fish the flashlight from my coat pocket and switch it on, but there isn't much to see. Every surface is coated in dust. A pile of sand spreads from the entrance and across the floor—*deck*, I suppose—according to the direction of the wind that carried it. Because of the slanting platform beneath me, I feel unbalanced, not quite sound. I sweep the beam around the cabin. The space is cramped and narrow and bare, as if someone cleared all the trappings to make room for things that are no longer there. I step toward the cockpit. My pulse thuds in my throat. But the seat is empty, the dials and switches blanketed by dirt and nothing else. I touch the wheel, which is not like the steering wheel of a car but open at the top, incomplete, a pie missing a wedge. When I examine my finger, the dirt is the same dun color as the landscape around me, as the dirt that covers the windows like a curtain, blocking the light.

On the deck next to the pilot's seat, a large, heavy book catches the flashlight's beam, face down, spine broken, pages splayed. Like everything else, it's covered in dirt, but I lift it anyway and brush away what dust I can.

I flip through the pages. A logbook.

I am not a pilot—this is the first time in my adult life that I've boarded any kind of airplane, intact or otherwise—and the entries, written in faded purple-black letters, might as well be Latin. Still I pass my fingers over them. Because whose hands touched this last? Whose pen wrote those letters and numbers? In one column, the farthest left, I recognize dates. The last one is 13 MAY 1937. To the right, in the next column, reads 0522. Five twenty-two A.M.?

I set the logbook on the seat and sweep the flashlight once more around the cabin, and as I do, an object catches my eye at the rear, near the tail, tucked in the seam between deck and wall.

It is a pile of something. A pile of clothes, attached to a boot.

OF COURSE I'VE ALWAYS UNDERSTOOD that there should be a body inside the wreckage of this airplane. A desert climate like this one has the same effect as mummification, doesn't it? A set of bones might be preserved for years or decades. Still. It's one thing to tell yourself to expect this skeleton, to know that this airplane came down with a human being inside and that the remains of that person did not disappear into the air, that those remains are just that—*remains*—and not the actual person, the human being, the living soul. It's another thing to see a boot attached to some trousers, to run your flashlight beam along the outline of those trousers and see the whiteness of bone, or rather the yellowness of bone, covered in dirt like everything is covered in dirt.

But you can bear this, like you have borne all other things. You can bear this skeleton. You can pretend it belongs to anybody, it's just a skeleton like you find in an anatomy laboratory. The person who lived inside this skeleton, who animated these bones, is long dead. As for his eternal soul, if he had one, God knows it's moved on by now, out of sheer boredom.

So. Let's imagine I'm an archaeologist. Isn't that what they're called, these people who dig bones and artifacts out of the earth, who mine the soil for the secrets of the past? Say I've arrived in this morbid landscape to investigate the remains of a brand-new human species, a previously undiscovered branch of our ancestral tree. Mere scientific curiosity prompts me to step forward, to keep the beam of my flashlight trained on the boot of my subject, to observe its physical characteristics and note that it seems to be an army boot, a type of footwear with which I happen to be familiar. A large boot, sturdy, worn, desiccated, leather edges curled by the passage of time.

I drag the beam upward, from boot to trouser to tunic. The skeleton rests on its side, in an almost fetal position, except not quite so tightly curled as a fetus. Like a man who's gone to sleep in a cold place, without a blanket. A skeleton that has gone to sleep. I come to stand near its chest. The tunic isn't familiar to me, but then it wouldn't be. This man would have been an airman in the Republican Armed Forces of Spain at the time of his death, a Republic that no longer exists, a brutal war that has since been eclipsed by wars even more brutal. How quaint and idealistic the Spanish fight seems now. This fellow in his tunic, this American fighting for a foreign cause, curled up to die.

Some nerve returns to me, some guts. I've progressed from boot to trouser to tunic, I've braved the skeletal phalanges without a quiver. There's nothing left to do now but see its face. That is to say, its skull.

His skull.

I move the beam, and it's not the grinning jaw that does it, or the tufts of hair still attached to the bone, or the cap that hangs over what once was an ear. It's the sockets of the eyes. They're black and empty, staring into nothing. I sink to my knees and gasp for enough air to cry with.

AFTER I BURY HIM IN the soil next to the airplane, and mark the spot with a cross made out of some broken propeller blades—it's a shallow grave, because that's all I can do with my two hands and a makeshift spade, so someone must return with men and tools to bury him properly—I enter the cabin to sweep the interior a final time with the beam of my flashlight.

In the corner where the body lay, there sits a small leather book.

Because it's been sheltered all this time, and because the climate's so dry, this book is in perfect condition. Unlike everything else, it's not coated in dust. The leather is clean and unstained, and when I lift it and open the pages, I find that it's not a printed book but a journal of some kind, in which someone has written in a firm black hand, notes and sketches and scrappy thoughts, until he stopped, about two-thirds of the way through.

Even with the help of the flashlight, I can't read it well, and anyway it's awkward to hold flashlight and book at the same time. I move outside and stand near the turned earth, the crude metal cross, and open the book again.

Against the cold afternoon light, the words jump from the page in a hand so familiar, it's as if I wrote it myself. But I did not. This is a story I never knew, a man I never knew. The mule brays at me; I don't have time to sit and read this through. I'll slip it in my pocket and read it when I return to my room in the primitive pension in Pamplona.

But I won't wait that long to find out how the story ends. Of course not. No one alive has that kind of patience, and certainly not me. I turn to the final entry, 5/15/37 in black numbers. His last thoughts, this lone, forgotten man; the last words his fingers would form before annihilation. A single line that wobbles and slants across the page, so you must squint your eyes and pick out the letters and put them together again in your head.

GM to rescue at last thank God She will live

I set my thumb on the page and close the book.

Nearby, the metal cross glints in the sun. A skiff of sand whirls in spirals around it. What a mystery! I mean, how the devil do they do it, these tiny, individual grains? How do they swirl about in communion with each other? Create this thoughtless symmetry? Nothing is random in nature; it is all pattern, pattern, pattern.

I open the book again. The wind riffles the pages. I find my place and read the entry again. The mule brays, irritated. I place my finger under the line and trace the words while I read once more, now aloud. Still their pattern escapes me.

GM to rescue? She will live?

Rescue. Somebody came to his rescue? Then why is he dead?

And who is *She?* There *was* no she, just this single man in his airplane. No second body lies here, no female body. Besides, Velázquez said nothing about a *She*.

On the other hand, Velázquez never did reveal a single detail he was bound to keep quiet, did he? Velázquez would never have mentioned this woman if her presence here were a secret.

The wind dies briefly. The sand settles back to earth, as if it had never dared to leave, and I believe I can hear the sound of my blood as it wooshes down my veins.

Well, then. Suppose there *was* a woman on board, a *She*. A woman whose presence was a secret. A *She* who was rescued, as the line suggests, while the man who wrote the line was left behind to die. A woman who flew airplanes. A woman who meant so much to this man, this skeleton, that he would thank God for her survival, even in the face of his own annihilation. A woman, let's say, who had also disappeared during the spring of 1937—famously so—less than a month before this airplane went down. Two grains of sand, moving in communion with each other.

My God, I think.

Why did I never see it before?

I slide the leather book into the pocket of my coat. My fingers are numb, even inside the gloves. Already the sun falls, the air turns, the wind grows colder against my cheek. The mule brays once more, like he *means it*, lady. It's time to go.

I untie the mule from the juniper bush, but before I climb aboard,

I turn to the silent airplane, the cross, the dunes of sand, and fix the scene in my memory. This was supposed to be the end of the journey, and it seems it's only the beginning. The diary is like a hot coal in my pocket. *She will live.* I stick my foot in the stirrup and swing into the saddle. The book strikes my thigh. A new road stretches before me, toward some destination that is not a place but a person, a woman who's supposed to be dead but might instead be alive, be saved, according to the orisons of a dying man, preserved in this ink and leather that beats against my leg as the mule strikes off gratefully toward Pamplona.

Because here's what I know for certain about that pile of abandoned bones, which was once a pilot named Samuel Mallory. There was only one *She*.

Only one person in the world to make him invoke the name of God.

I

▶ ▶ ▶

I have often said that the lure of flying is the lure of beauty.

—AMELIA EARHART

AVIATRIX

by Eugenia Everett

(e x c e r p t)

March 1928: California

IRENE SURFED AT dawn, when the gray light coated the water but the sun hadn't yet crested the mountains to the east. For one thing, there were fewer people around, and for another thing, they were the right kind of people, people who didn't want to be around other people all the time. People like her.

Like her, they arrived in darkness, driving dilapidated Tin Lizzies held together with spit and baling wire. Like her, they parked along the roadside and carried their boards in reverent silence down one of the paths that led from the cliffs into the dunes. Like her, they dressed neck-to-foot in bathing costumes of thick navy blue serge, because that Pacific current came down straight from Alaska, bearing fog and giant gray whales; like her, they waxed their boards in long, thoughtful strokes, waiting for enough light to see by. Like her, they listened to the noise of the surf, the volume and tempo of the crashing waves, the mood of the ocean this particular morning: whether she was lazy or angry, forgiving or ruthless, bitch or saint. Some unstudied combination of the above.

Then someone stood up, slung his wooden surfboard under his arm or over his head—they were heavy in those days, enormous, carved from redwood—and started off toward the water. One by one, the others followed. They stepped delicately into the wash of spent waves. The coldness of the water shocked them, every time. Their feet went numb, their legs. Still they continued. They unslung their boards and set them in the water and set themselves on the boards, in direct confrontation with the oncoming surf. The breaking waves crashed against them as they paddled onward. Brine filled the cavities of their noses. They watched the breakers and timed each one, calculated the seconds of calm between one wave cresting and the other one building behind it. At last someone made his move. Took his board out beyond the line of breakers and turned to paddle with the current, along the current, fused his puny human momentum with the momentum of the wave below him as the bottom of the wave met the bottom of the continent and climbed upward, upward, until the laws of physics wouldn't allow any more of this suspense and the wave curled over itself and toppled, and the man either rode this wave or toppled too, depending on his skill and luck. He was joined by another man, and another one, and pretty soon they were all out there silently surfing, like a pack of dolphins, communicating by movement and custom instead of words, while the sun slowly rose above the cliffs and blinded them.

IRENE'S FATHER TAUGHT HER HOW to surf when she was eleven or twelve. This was before the war, before the California beaches began to fill with people surfing or learning to surf. He woke her before dawn one morning and told her to put on her bathing costume, and the two of them drove south from the city until they reached Santa Cruz. Just the two of them. Mrs. Foster stayed abed in their house on Balboa Street; she was by then in the last stages of the sickness that would kill her. Foster smelled a little of whiskey, but then he usually smelled of whiskey. He told Irene to go back to sleep until they got there, so she settled down on the seat and closed her eyes, but she didn't sleep. How could she? She listened to the rattle of axles and the burr of the engine, to Hank

Foster's whistle. Once or twice another car swept by, and the headlights illuminated the air, but otherwise it was as dark as night, as dark as only the hour before dawn can be.

They reached the bay at last. Foster pretended to wake her and Irene pretended to wake. She made a show of rubbing her eyes like a baby, and Foster laughed. The air had begun to lighten. She saw the stubble on his jaw, the blond disarray of his hair, the creases along his eyes and cheeks. He was wearing his own bathing costume, well used. He untied something from the roof of the car, and that turned out to be a surfboard. It was enormous and ungainly, so heavy (Irene grabbed one end of it to help her father carry it down the beach) it couldn't possibly float. But it did. Foster explained how he had carved it himself from a local redwood, under the instruction of a Hawaiian fellow who had come to California for surfing demonstrations a few years ago. He'd gone to watch—did Irene remember that afternoon?—and thought it looked so grand, he ended up trying it himself. That was Hank Foster for you.

They found the edge of the ocean. Even in later years, Irene still remembered the rough sand on the soles of her bare feet, and the chill salt mist that rolled off the sea. She remembered how frigid the water was, how it squeezed the breath from her lungs. She didn't remember the surfing itself. Probably she never quite made it to her feet on that ungainly board that first morning. But she remembered her father's strong arm, she remembered the wildness of the surf, the freedom, the understanding that they were doing something forbidden, that Mrs. Foster would be furious when they got home.

But Irene also remembered the drive back north. The morning sunshine dried her wet skin and Foster told her about the Hawaiian princes who attended boarding school in San Mateo twenty years earlier and used to come down to surf at Santa Cruz. How surfing wasn't just a sport or a hobby, it was like a religion for them, a ritual of kingship. You couldn't rule over other men unless you could master the giant waves of Waikiki and Kahalu'u. To test yourself against the ocean was to test the essence of your human spirit.

They didn't go surfing every morning, Irene and her father. But they went often enough that Irene soon needed her own surfboard, and the muscle to manage it on the Santa Cruz coastline, both of which she acquired pretty quickly. Irene was tall and athletic, a natural at surfing and pretty much any sport, really. But mostly she had human spirit. That was it, Foster used to say, as they drove north from Santa Cruz toward home, damp and exhausted. That was what made Irene such a natural. She yearned to be free of the earth.

ANYWAY, THAT'S WHY IRENE WOKE up every morning at four o'clock and drove from her small house beneath the Hollywood Hills down to the beach at Santa Monica. She was the only woman there, but nobody seemed to care. Out there, she was treated—to the extent she was treated at all—like any other surfer. Your sex was irrelevant; the only thing that mattered was to surf well. Today she surfed exceptionally well. The waves were big and slow, the way Irene liked them. She rode them for an hour or so, and emerged from the cold foam tired and exalted, like a warrior from battle. As she walked up the beach to the cliffs, carrying her heavy surfboard, she passed a man, bent down to examine something inside a clump of dune grass, who looked up at her and smiled. She recognized him. He surfed here often; first man on the water, most mornings. As acceptance went, it was a small gesture. Still, it was something. He was what she thought of as a typical California specimen: wide shouldered and underfed, earnest and deeply tanned, couple inches taller than Irene, wet hair slicked back from a hollow-cheeked face, the kind of face that stuck in your mind, that made you think you had seen him somewhere before. Every time she saw him, she thought he should eat more. She hoisted the board more securely on her shoulder for the climb up the path.

"Hey there! Miss!"

Irene swung awkwardly, bracing her foot on a firm patch of sand. The fellow stood a few feet below, looking up at her. One hand shaded his brow from the rising sun and the other hand cradled some object next to his chest.

"I don't mean to bother you or anything, but . . . well, you don't happen to be looking for a cat, maybe?"

"A cat?"

He moved his hand to reveal a small feline head, white fur and pink nose, crisp triangle ears. A patch of gray-brown tabby spilled down its forehead, and a ginger patch surrounded the right eye. "Well. Kitten, I guess. Not yours, is it?"

"I don't have a cat."

"Found it huddled in the grass there." He nodded at the nearby dune. "Must've got lost from its mother or something."

"Of all places for a kitten."

"Or else some bastard dumped him here." He turned the kitten to face him, revealing a skinny, delicate rib cage and ragged fur. The white patches were immaculate, as if bleached. The head was so absurdly large for that emaciated body. The man rubbed his nose against the tabby patch on its forehead and addressed the tiny kitten face with just enough volume so Irene could hear him. "How'd you get here, little guy? Beach is no place for you."

The kitten yawned. Irene shifted her weight, because the surfboard was heavy and dug into her shoulder, but she made no move to leave. The sight mesmerized her, the frail calico belly encompassed by those bony hands, the thick nose caressing the minuscule feline nose. Kitten in relief against dark serge bathing costume, tanned surfer's skin. From the look of that wet, heavy hair, this man had already encountered the ocean this morning. The drops still rolled down his temples and neck and forearms; the sleeves of his bathing costume were rolled to the elbows.

"He's awfully fetching," she said.

"Yeah, a real heartbreaker. What am I going to do with you, fella?"

"Can't you just take him home with you?"

"I just might."

The kitten leaned into his cheek and closed its eyes in a delirium of relief. Irene's foot began to slip; the sand dissolved beneath her. She scrabbled a bit and the kitten opened its eyes to regard her.

"Oh," Irene said.

The eyes were lighter than Irene expected, pale amber. The kitten blinked and gathered itself. In a single athletic spring, it soared from the man's grasp to the sand next to Irene's left foot and wound itself around her bare ankle.

"Well," the man said.

"Oh, he tickles!"

"That's gratitude for you."

Irene choked back a giggle.

"Say. You all right? Let me give you a hand with that board."

"No, thanks. I'm perfectly—perfectly fine—"

"You sure?"

Well. The board *was* heavy. The path *was* steep. The man *was* attractive. On the other hand, while he had that kind of face that stuck in your mind, it was also the kind of face that said he might be trouble. Irene couldn't say why. He seemed straightforward enough. Kittens adored him. His chin was sturdy and all, his smile was sincere. His voice made an easy California rumble. Behind him, the waves roared in from across the Pacific, keeping time to the beat of the universe. The kitten rubbed its cheek on the round bone of her ankle.

"I guess I'm all right," Irene said. She pulled her leg free from the kitten, swung forward again, overbalanced the eighty-pound surfboard on her shoulder and toppled back into the sand at Trouble's feet.

TROUBLE HAD A NAME, IT turned out. "Mallory," he said, sticking out his hand, when Irene's surfboard was safely secured to the roof of the Model T and they had both visited the huts to change into dry, respectable clothes. The kitten now nestled in the crook of Mr. Mallory's arm, purring like a motorboat. Irene stuck out a finger and rubbed its forehead.

"Irene Foster," she said.

"You know, you're the only girl who comes out here mornings."

"I'm no girl. Twenty years old last month."

"Still and all. Who taught you to surf like that?"

"My father."

"You don't say. Surfs out here too?"

"No," she said. "Just me."

Mr. Mallory squinted his eyes a little, like he was trying to figure out what she meant by that. He wore a newsboy's cap over his damp hair, and he grabbed the brim and pulled it lower on his forehead, while his face turned away to observe the western horizon, the grand Pacific. He tickled the kitten's chin, and it stretched out obligingly, eyes closed.

Mallory, she thought. He had a name, Mr. Mallory, and as she repeated the words in her head, some bell dinged. Some ring of familiarity.

She nodded to the kitten. "What're you going to name him?"

"I don't know. Sandy?"

"I guess that makes sense. My father used to say you should never forget where you came from." She reached out again and smoothed the fur between its ears. "Besides, it's practical, isn't it?"

"Practical? How so?"

"Why, if *he* turns out to be a *she,* you can keep the name."

Mr. Mallory looked a little shocked. He held up the kitten and peered underneath. "I'll be damned. You might be right."

"Just a hunch." She glanced to the car, because her cheeks had turned a little warm. "I'd better be off."

Mr. Mallory tucked the kitten back into his left elbow and touched the brim of his cap with his other hand. "Pleasure to meet you, Miss Foster."

"Likewise, Mr. Mallory."

"Suppose I'll be seeing you around, some morning."

"I'm here most mornings. When I can get the car started, anyway."

Mr. Mallory stroked the kitten with his large, bony fingers. He squinted at some point over her shoulder, toward the ocean. Irene shifted her feet.

"Look, Miss Foster. I . . ."

"Yes?"

"Nothing. Glad to meet you at last, that's all."

Irene opened her mouth to say *Likewise* and realized she was only repeating herself, the same bland word. Instead she said, "I suppose we were bound to meet sometime, both of us surfing here like this," which wasn't exactly true.

But Mr. Mallory nodded, just as if their meeting were indeed inevitable, and said, "I guess you're right." He turned to his car, a handsome Nash Six, canary yellow, four or five years old in Irene's estimation. Took a step or two. Stopped and turned and touched his cap again, and for some reason this image of Mr. Mallory stamped itself on her brain, tanned and sober, touching his cap while the rising sun tinted everything gold, so that ever after, when she thought of him, or when she sat in the dawn, he made this picture in her mind.

She waved and got inside her own car, her father's old Tin Lizzie held together with baling wire, and set the choke. Went around to turn the crank but though the engine turned and turned it wouldn't start. Mr. Mallory noticed her trouble in the nick of time and came over from his Nash, which had started impeccably from its automatic ignition. He opened the hood and they peered inside together.

"Spark plug's blown out," she said.

"Got a spare?"

"No. You?"

"'Fraid not. But they'll have plenty at the airfield. I'm headed out there now."

"Airfield?"

"Where I work." Mr. Mallory straightened from the innards of the Model T and smiled at her confusion, for maybe the first time since hauling her surfboard up the dunes, and Irene thought it was worth the sacrifice of a mere commonplace spark plug to experience a smile like that. He yanked down the hood and dusted off his hands.

"I'm a pilot," he said.

And that was when Irene put one and one together, Mallory and flying.

"Oh," she said. "You're *Sam* Mallory. *The* Sam Mallory."

He scratched his head and peered at the sun. "Does it make a difference?"

Irene bent down to pick up Sandy, who had escaped from the Nash and wandered across the grit to curl around Irene's ankles. "Of course not," she lied.

HANALEI, HAWAI'I

October 1947

T HE BOY SPRAWLED beside me is the kind who sleeps deep, apparently. I like that in a fellow. You can slither out of bed, dress and brush your teeth, even write him a tender good-bye note if you're so inclined, and he won't so much as flutter an eyelid.

> *Dear Boy* [I can't remember his name],
>   *That was too lovely for words and just what a girl needs. A thousand thanks for the ride out there* [he captained the boat from Oahu yesterday afternoon] *and the ride in here. I enclose a five dollar bill. As I tried to explain last night, I might allow my escorts to pay for dinner, but I always buy my own drinks. You can keep the change for good luck.*
>
>   *Yours always,*
>   *Janey*

I lay the note on the nightstand and pull the camera from my pocketbook. My companion's all tangled up in the sheets like a Bernini god, except tanned. I find an angle that preserves his modesty. The light's not terrific, but I open the aperture as far as it will go and hold myself steady.

Click.

Then I steal out the door before he starts to miss me.

AMONG THE MANY GIFTS I received from that nice young man last night, he told me where to find Irene Lindquist. I don't believe he meant to do that, but when a fellow's plied with enough drink and female companionship, his lips will loosen in more ways than one.

A good thing, too, because the rest of the locals in this two-bit Hawaiian village weren't inclined to admit she exists, let alone lives among them, even though I know for a fact that Lindquist, together with her husband, Olle, runs an island-hopping operation called Kauai Sky Tours out of an airfield five miles away. By the time the good captain sauntered through the door of the town watering hole last night at a quarter past nine—acting as if he owned the joint, and it turned out he did—I had just about given up and prepared myself to walk those five miles through the darkness to wait for Lindquist at her place of business, since I wasn't getting anywhere else fast. Tenacity, that's what separates success from defeat. Also a willingness to do what's necessary, though I admit that going to bed with this particular informant wasn't exactly a noble sacrifice, except of sleep.

Outside, the sun's just begun to color the eastern horizon. The air tastes of the tropics, a pleasant change from my previous assignment in Nuremburg, Germany, which stank of rain and human decay. This place, you'd think it never heard of war. The vegetation tumbles from every nook, streaked with flowers; the lane meanders toward the beach as if it's got all the time in the world. While the birds twitter and toot in abundance around me, there's neither sight nor smell of another human being. Just the scent of sultry flowers and salty ocean. The sound of my own footsteps on the packed earth.

Lindquist likes to surf in the morning, before anyone else is up. So my sea captain informed me last night, anyway, under a certain amount of duress. He wouldn't reveal exactly *where* she surfs, but my money's on the beach. Isn't yours? Anyway, I've already discovered, in the course of my research, that Hanalei Bay is favored territory among those who enjoy the act of skidding on the ocean. Stands to reason I should find Irene Lindquist (not her real name, by the way, but we'll discuss that later) somewhere along that sweep of sand, and it suits my purpose that we should meet at dawn, before the sea is peopled.

Now, my informant's bedroom isn't far from this beach, because nothing in Hanalei is far from the beach. Already the waves beat incessantly against my ears. Another hundred yards and the Pacific Ocean will wash up before me, and there she'll soar, Irene Lindquist herself, right across its surface, hiding in plain sight. Assuming that dear, strapping boy was telling me the truth last night, of course. Boys will say anything when you have them at your mercy. But I have the feeling this one was on the level. He has an earnest face; the kind of face I'd like to photograph, if some grander mystery weren't consuming my imagination at the moment.

AT FIRST GLANCE, THE BEACH appears empty. The waves hurtle in from the northwest, golden-pink in the rising sun, but nobody rides them. On the other hand, Hanalei Bay swoops down in a magnificent arc, and there's plenty more beach to explore. If I were a surfer, I might know where to go looking for this woman, who has surfed all her life. Where the best waves form, according to the laws of physics and geography. But I don't surf and never have. I've got my instincts, that's all, my instincts and a Rand McNally map, and it seems to me that the beach to the right ends in some kind of river mouth, while the beach to the left winds all the way around to a cliff called Makahoa Point, if I'm interpreting Rand McNally correctly, which I am. Maps and I, we get along pretty well.

To the left it is.

The sand is soft and cool, like powder. I remove my shoes—a pair

of ragged espadrilles I acquired in Spain—and enjoy the way this unfamiliar substance pools around my feet. The dawn grows bright behind
me. Ahead, the beach turns northward and narrows as it approaches
the cliffs at the tip of Makahoa Point. Thus far, no Lindquist. Nobody
at all. I might be the only person left alive after some great epidemic.
Of course, it's also possible that Lindquist has had some advance notice
of my arrival, and chooses not to expose herself to discovery. You ask
a few questions in a tiny, no-account burg like this one, where everybody's knee-deep in each other's beeswax, and it doesn't take long for
word to get around. And believe me, I understand the impulse to run
for cover at the first sign of predators. I'm camera-shy myself. Would a
million times rather stand on the taking side of the lens than the giving,
and I don't have half as much to hide as this Irene Lindquist. If indeed
she's the woman I'm searching for.

I reach the end of the beach without encountering anybody, but
according to McNally there's another beach to the left, on the other side
of Makahoa Point. Lumahai Beach, it's called, which is a rather lovely
name, I think, and somewhere I'd like to surf for that reason alone, if
I liked to surf at all. It hints of the moon, of the mysterious.

I replace my shoes on my feet and begin the climb up the rocks,
across the neck of the point, thick with trees, palms and that kind
of thing. I don't know much about flora, to be perfectly honest; you
won't find a single artful landscape among my published photographs.
Just people and buildings and machines and the odd animal, when the
subject is willing and the occasion requires it. So don't ask me what
species of tree I'm passing, what kind of branch I'm pushing aside
as I step into a patch of cleared earth off the coastal highway. A dilapidated yellow Ford sits to one side. The tire prints appear fresh. A
footpath leads westish, behind a piece of wood shaped like an arrow
that says BEACH.

I follow this track downward through the trees until it opens up to a
pristine ocean beach, deserted except for a pile of clothes near the edge

of the sand, and a person in a long, dark bathing suit hurtling down the barrel of a perfect bow wave.

AS I EXPECTED, THIS PERSON is a woman, and when she trudges to shore she doesn't look all that surprised to see me there. Her hair is short and prematurely silver above a tanned, lined, scarred, firm, freckled face that might be any age from thirty-five to sixty. I think it's strange that she doesn't take any trouble to disguise herself. Why hasn't she been discovered here before? Is it the gray hair, or the scars, or the fact that you don't expect her? You never do find what you're not looking for, even the woman at the center of one of the world's great mysteries, who was once the most fascinating, the most photographed female on earth.

She's tall, maybe five foot eleven, topping me by two or three inches. She carries the surfboard under her arm like it's made of balsa wood. She plants it in the sand and slicks back her wet hair and waits for me to introduce myself. I find I'm not nearly as nervous as I expected. Nothing more than a flutter of excitement, even though I can plainly see it's her, it is the mysterious *She*, that I've found her at last. There's no mistaking that height, those cheekbones, those sharp, hooded eyes that have regarded me from a thousand photographs, although I never realized they were quite so blue.

"Mrs. Lindquist?" I ask.

"How can I help you?" she replies patiently.

"My name is Janey Everett. I'm a photojournalist. I was wondering if I might have a word with you?"

She stares at the top of my head for several seconds. I don't think I need to tell you how disconcerting that is. She brushes a little sand from her board and says, "A photographer, is it? I can't imagine why. I never give permission for photographs. You'll find a dozen surfers more willing. And more attractive."

"Oh, I'm not at all interested in *photographing* you. I don't wish to disturb your privacy. If you want to go on hiding from the world, that's fine by me."

Lindquist lifts both eyebrows in a way that might slay some ordinary person. "I don't have any idea what you're talking about."

"Don't you? I'm amazed. You can't tell me that nobody's ever remarked on your astonishing resemblance to the famed aviatrix Irene Foster."

At the words *Irene Foster,* Lindquist flinches. It's a tiny gesture, but my eyes are trained to notice these things, the tinier the better. Poker players call them *tells,* I believe. I hoard them like treasure, because they represent the truth, they represent a subject's instant, unguarded opinion of things. And this flinch of Lindquist's tells me everything I need to know.

She is no more a Lindquist than I am.

NOW, LISTEN UP. THERE WAS a time, which many of you may recall, when you couldn't walk into a drugstore or listen to the radio or pick up a newspaper without encountering the name Irene Foster. I myself grew from girl to woman in that particular decade, when Foster was held up as a shining example of American womanhood and what she was capable of in this brave new age of ours, the age of flappers and aviation.

In those days, we had no idea what fate awaited her. Foster was invincible. Pilots around her might crash, might fall short of their destinations, might die of terrible injuries or disappear into the ocean, but you could believe in Irene Foster. Her keen, smiling face adorned books and periodicals, museum exhibits and newsreels, advertisements for everything from toothpaste to cigarettes. It got so that you almost felt sick of her, from time to time, and just when she started to fade from view, just when the public began to tire, ever so slightly, she would accomplish some astonishing new feat, break some impossible record, and you fell in love with her all over again.

Which, naturally, made her disappearance all the more shocking. There she flew, me hearties, poised for victory in the first-ever Round the World Air Derby, one final leg to go, one last hop from Egypt to Morocco, a journey of two thousand miles that was surely child's play to Irene Foster, who crossed the Atlantic for breakfast, almost. She was two days ahead of her nearest competitor—a man, of course, whose name nobody remembers—and the whole world gathered its breath to cheer her landing in Casablanca. Maybe you were one of them, standing by your radio to hear the news, to settle some bet with your pal about her final time. Whether she would break the current circumnavigation record by hours or minutes. Maybe you waited and waited as those minutes came and went, as the bulletin never arrived, as one by one the reports trickled through that Foster had not arrived in Casablanca at all.

She hadn't landed anywhere.

Maybe you were one of those who then trawled the airwaves with your amateur radio, searching for some faint signal that might be Irene Foster's distress call. Maybe you pored over maps of the northern Sahara, of the southern Mediterranean, for some likely site for an emergency landing by a pilot known for her resourcefulness in crisis. Maybe you bought the early edition every morning for weeks and read all the updates, all the editorials, all the messages of hope and determination from those pilots tasked with searching for her across the endless dunes of sand.

Maybe you finally gave up hope and turned to some new sensation for your daily dram of fevered excitement. Maybe you forgot all about Irene Foster and her doomed flight, except when some newspaper printed a wistful memorial on the anniversary of her disappearance, or when some new theory emerged to explain her fate, each one more crackpot than the last.

Maybe you figured she was gone forever, and you'd never know what became of her.

Well, I didn't.

AND NOW I'VE FOUND HER for you. All along, she was living in obscurity on some beach on the Hawaiian island of Kauai, surfing in the morning and flying unsuspecting passengers from island to island during the day.

Still, she's not going to admit all that to some stranger, by God!

She lifts her board from the sand. "If you'll excuse me, Miss Everett. You're wasting my time and your own."

I wait until she's stalked past me before I reply. I do have some regard for stagecraft; you might say it's my stock in trade. I can do with pictures what most can only dream of doing with words, and it all comes down to how you place your subject, and where, and exactly when you click your shutter.

"Am I?" I call after her. "What if I told you I've just come from Spain, and the wreckage of Sam Mallory's airplane?"

She stops, but she doesn't turn.

"Poor Sam." I shake my head. "He never did get his due. Overshadowed by his own pupil. But if there hadn't been a Mallory, there wouldn't have been a Foster. Isn't that right?"

Over her shoulder, she says, "I don't know what you're talking about."

"You keep saying that. You don't know nothing, do you? Well, that's fine. Then you won't care about the diary we found among his remains. You wouldn't know anything about that, either, I guess?"

Now she turns. Her face is like stone. "His remains?"

"I admit, there's not much left to a fellow's body after ten years exposed to the Spanish desert. But his poor skeleton still wore its clothes, and underneath it all I found this."

I remove the small leather volume from my pocketbook and hold it up against the sky.

The funny thing is, she doesn't stare at the diary, the object you'd imagine she cares about. Instead she stares at me, no expression at all. Her brow might be furrowed, or those might be the lines etched there by time and sun and worry. She's taking my measure, that's all. She's working out what to say to me, and how much, and whether I'm telling the truth. She is calculating the risk, and isn't that what Irene Foster has always done best?

Behind me, a wave crashes noisily into the surf. Lindquist turns her face to the east, squints at the risen sun, and says, "Come with me."

IN THE CAFETERIA OF THE Hanalei airfield, an ancient calico cat lies in a square of sunshine from the window, all but dead. Lindquist stops to stroke its side, and it twitches an ear in thanks.

"Nice puss," I say. "What's its name?"

"*Her* name is Sandy." Lindquist straightens and makes for the kitchen, which is open to the seating area, this being a shabby, two-bit cafeteria, you understand, in keeping with the general tone of the town. She flips on the lights and proceeds to a large electric coffee percolator, made of chrome and remarkably modern for a dump like this.

"Coffee?" she says.

"Don't mind if I do."

I follow her to the lunch counter, which runs along the width of the kitchen space, six or seven stools lined up, all covered in worn leather. Along the way, I pause at the cat, who has the air of a local landmark, and reach down to pat her head. She swats at me with a set of razor claws that draw blood from the back of my hand.

Lindquist smiles a little. "Careful. She sometimes decides she doesn't like a person."

I suck away the blood on my hand and settle on one of the stools. "Evidently."

"I find she's an excellent judge of character," Lindquist tells me, as she measures the coffee grains.

"Aren't you clever."

"You know, I'd have thought you might trouble yourself to be a little more charming, under the circumstances. I'm not likely to open myself up to some chronic bitch."

"You're not likely to open yourself up to anybody, I expect. I'm here on a bribe, that's all, and I perfectly understand the nature of our arrangement. I'd be wasting my time trying to charm you."

She raises her eyebrows and fills the percolator with water from the tap.

"Although I suppose you could just bludgeon me," I continue. "A simple, elegant solution, and there's no lack of convenient places to dispose of an unwanted body around here."

"Oh, I *could* kill you, I guess. But then I wouldn't learn much, would I? How you found Sam, how you found me. Not that I'm admitting to anything. There we are." She plugs in the percolator and wipes her hands on a dishtowel. She's changed out of her bathing costume to a white shirt and a pair of tan slacks, which suit her tall, angular body perfectly. Under the kitchen light, you can better see the scar that bubbles up from her neck to cover her jaw and ear.

"That looks like it hurt," I say. "Burn?"

"Yes. Anything else? Eggs? Toast? I always make myself a nice breakfast when I've been out on the water. And I imagine you must be hungry."

"Oh? Why?"

"No reason." She bustles to the icebox. "Except I might have heard you left the bar of the Hanalei Tavern at eleven o'clock last night, in the company of the owner."

"He was walking me back to the inn, like a gentleman."

"The inn says you never slept in your bed."

"I made it up before I left."

She cracks open an egg and laughs. "There's nothing to be ashamed of. Leo's the catch of the town, and very particular. I'll bet you had a lovely time."

I snap my fingers. "*Leo!* Of course. Now I remember."

"He'll be heartbroken. I suppose he told you where to find me?"

"Not quite. He said you liked to surf early in the morning, that's all. I figured out which beach on my own." I tap my temple. "No flies on me."

"Maybe not, but the town's buzzing, all the same."

"A town, is it? I've seen duck crossings with more metropolitan flavor."

"And just look what it's done for you. Buttered or dry?"

"What do you think?"

She takes the butter from the icebox.

When we're settled in with coffee and eggs, side by side on the leather stools before the lunch counter, Lindquist loses the banter and falls silent. The cat comes wandering up and rubs its cheek against her ankle. She reaches down and lifts it into her lap, where it curls into a snug, neat ball and closes its eyes. Lindquist closes her eyes too. Thinking or remembering, who knows. Trying to decide what to make of me.

I lean one elbow on the counter, next to my plate. "I'll bet you're wondering how I got here."

"Oh, I know how you got here, all right. You came in on Leo's afternoon boat from Waialua, causing quite a stir." She opens her eyes. "I just don't understand why anybody cares about so much ancient history."

"It's not so ancient. It just seems that way, because of the war. It's hard to believe anyone ever cared about daring pilots and their daring flights to nowhere."

"Well, why do *you* care? You're a photographer. There's no photograph here. God knows I'm no picture portrait."

"I'm not here for photographs. As a matter of fact, I'm writing a book. A biography of Samuel Mallory."

"Of *Sam?*"

"You thought I wanted to write about *you*, did you?" I wag a finger. "Everybody knows *your* story, Foster, right up until the moment you disappeared. But Mallory's been forgotten."

"That's not true," she says swiftly. Then she catches herself and drinks the coffee. "Anyway, you forget I haven't said I'm this Foster woman at all."

I wipe my mouth. "Look. If you're afraid I'm going to expose you, don't trouble yourself. If I wanted the scoop of the century, I'd have wired New York already, and every reporter and photographer in the Western Hemisphere would be bearing down on this airfield of yours like a locust army. You can keep your privacy, since you want it so badly. I won't quote you. All I want is the inside story on Mallory. I think it's time history resurrected him, don't you?"

"I don't think Sam would have cared, one way or the other. He didn't give a damn about fame or history."

"Oh? Then what *did* he give a damn about?"

Again, she bites back some piece of candor. She's on to me and my tricks, and still she nearly slips. She wants to unburden herself, I can see that. Most people do. We all carry some burden or another, pressing into that tender spot between neck and shoulder, invisible to others, which we wouldn't mind shucking off for a blessed moment. But we rarely do. To shuck off our burden is to show it to the world, and then what would the world say? The world would judge your burden, that's what. The world would judge it, and how you've carried it all these years, and whether your burden is more or less than any other person's, and what all this says about you. Sometimes you're just better off carrying the damn thing into eternity.

Evidently Lindquist feels the same way. She shrugs and digs back into her omelet. "Don't you know the answer to that already? You're the one writing the biography."

"But that's why I'm here, Mrs. Lindquist. To hear the truth from the person who knew him best."

"Me? What makes you say that?"

I reach for my pocketbook. "Do you mind if I smoke, Mrs. Lindquist?"

"Oh, for God's sake, call me Irene."

I light up a cigarette, even though she hasn't actually given permission. Gives me a moment to gather my thoughts. I toss the lighter back in my pocketbook and say, "You know something? I think I've gotten a little ahead of myself. What I should have done, right from the beginning, is given you some background. That's a nice word we have in the newspaper world, background. Means everything you really want to know about a person."

"I thought you were a photographer, not a journalist."

"I'm a *photojournalist*, Mrs. Lindquist. I take pictures for newspapers. You know, a picture tells a thousand words? That's what I do."

"But you want to write a biography, you said. Not a picture book."

I blow out a little smoke. "Not just any biography. I want to write a whole new kind of biography. I mean, have you ever read one? Start to finish? My God, they're all so dull! Just facts and figures and dry little clips from letters, that kind of thing. I think it's because the men write them. The little dears think life can be boiled down to facts, that the facts are what's important, that facts are somehow akin to truth. I'll tell you something, the facts are the least important thing about a person."

"Oh? So what's important?"

"The fictions. The lies we tell to other people, the lies we tell to ourselves. The stories we make of our lives, the heroes we fashion of our own clay. The myths of our own creation. Those are the real stuffing of a person, in my opinion. What makes each one of us different from the other fellow."

"My goodness," she says. "Aren't you a surprise."

"Oh, I'm full of surprises, believe me. Anyway, if you ask me, a biography should read like a novel, not an encyclopedia entry. All those facts get in the way of the truth. We ought to be able to see the world through our subject's eyes, to live life as our subject lived it. To feel the ticktock of his pulse in our own veins. That's truth. *That's* what I want to do."

I finish the coffee and hold out the empty cup to her, and I'll be damned if Irene Foster Lindquist doesn't just take the cup and head for the percolator and pour me another. *Irene Foster*! Like some cafeteria waitress. She presents the scarred side of her face to me, like the dark side of the moon. Nobody's ever seen those scars before. She didn't have them when she was flying around the world the last time, that's for sure. I've seen the photos of those days, believe me.

She hands me back the coffee cup. I drink it neat.

"So let me get this straight," she says. "You decide to write a biography of Sam Mallory. You go off looking for the wreckage of his final flight—"

"No, no, no. It's a little more complicated than that. It's more of a love story."

"A love story? You and Sam?"

"Don't be jealous. It's a love from afar. A love across the years, between adoring me and unknowing him."

"I'll say. You're—what, twenty-eight?"

"Give or take."

"Well, Sam would be a lot older. If he were still alive."

"Oh, but you have to understand what a *crush* I had on him! I was just a teenager when he dropped off the face of the earth. I thought he was just the *most*. I thought he had it all over that stuffed shirt Lindbergh. All those death-defying stunts he did. Those glamorous women on his arm, a different one every week. So daring, so handsome. You might say I was fixated."

"And you didn't grow out of it?"

"Of course I grew out of it. I'm not exactly the romantic type, am I? But I always had a soft spot for him. I always wondered what happened to him. As you know, he didn't so much vanish, like you did, as—I don't know—fade away? Like when somebody leaves a dinner party without saying good-bye, and nobody can remember when she saw him last." I stub out the cigarette. "Time marched on. I went to college for a bit, traveled for a bit, started selling my photographs, ended up with the Associated Press. Then the war. I got to Europe in '44, a couple of months before the invasion, and managed to land on Omaha with the second wave. Carried on through to Paris, as close to the action as I could get. Then I got to talking with this fellow who'd flown with the Republican air force in Spain, during the civil war. We had a few drinks and so on. And he told me the strangest thing, right out of the blue."

Now, I've been watching Foster's face throughout this little biographical sketch. I want to see how she reacts to my assessment of Mallory, how she reads the story of my life, abridged edition, and whether she notices all the little spaces between the lines. And of course, the last part. The Spanish air force. The war. The thing about war, if you've been in one, you never really leave it, even when it's all over and everybody goes home. A piece of you remains behind, buried in the blooded earth, and when somebody calls it back—as I just did—that piece sort of jumps to attention, if you know what I mean. And you can't hide a thing like that.

But maybe this woman isn't like everyone else, after all. Maybe Irene Foster has been hiding from the world so long, she's just buried too deep beneath her own skin for anyone to discover in some flicker of eyebrow or quiver of chin. Maybe this woman has become a Lindquist after all. She listens to me, strokes her cat with one hand and her coffee cup with the other, and when I pause, as I do now, she takes a sip and asks me to continue. What strange thing, Miss Everett? What did the Spanish fellow tell you?

"He told me that he knew Sam Mallory in Spain, that he'd helped the Republicans during the civil war. And he knew when and where Mallory's plane went down, in May of 1937."

Lindquist bends her head to snuggle the cat on her lap.

"Well?" I say.

"Well, what?"

"Well, aren't you fascinated to learn how Mallory died? Don't you want to know the rest of the story? How we found the wreckage?"

She lifts her head, and her eyes are wet. The lashes are stuck together.

"I've got a flight in an hour," she says. "I need to go check the airplane."

"Now hold on. Am I just supposed to wait around until you get back?"

Lindquist finishes her coffee, sets the cat on the floor, and steps gracefully from the counter stool. "My husband will give you a lift back into town. In the meantime, you can clean up the kitchen."

THE DAMN CAT JUST STARES at me as I wash out the pan and the plates and wipe the toast crumbs from the counter. When I'm done, I pour myself another cup of coffee and light a cigarette. The windows have steamed up, so I don't notice anybody coming until the bell tinkles on the door.

He's a big fellow, muscular, pink faced, just starting to grow the paunch of middle age. He wears the usual island costume of pale shirt and pale cotton trousers, and his hair is even paler and thinning fast. He glowers at me and growls *You're the one?* in some kind of faintly discernible Scandinavian accent, though I couldn't tell you which part.

"Probably." I stick out my hand. "You must be Olle, here to give me a lift back into town."

"What the hell did you say to my wife?"

"Me? I just told her I know who she is, and I won't call the press on her, so long as she's a good girl and tells me all about herself."

"Jesus Christ."

"I think it all might have been a little much for her, so early in the morning."

Olle Lindquist gives me the goggle eyes and slumps into a chair. Honestly, I might have expected more from him. I think a husband should stand up for his wife, don't you? Only maybe he's the kind of fellow who will punch the lights out of the man who threatens him, but can't figure out what to do with a feminine adversary. There are such fellows. This one pulls his hand through what hairs remain to him and stares at the foggy window in the direction of the hangar.

"If you want to go to her—" I begin.

"No. She'll want to be alone." He looks back at me. "As for *you*. What's your name, anyway?"

"Janey Everett. I'm a photojournalist."

"What's that?"

"A journalist who tells stories with photographs. Except I'm through with that for a while. Hanging up my camera. Dusting off my type-writer to write a scintillating, no-holds-barred biography of Sam Mallory. I figured the only way to get the real story was to go to the horse's mouth." I flick out a little ash into a nearby tray. "The horse being your fascinating wife."

"Yes, but how did you *know*? How did you find out?"

"Oh, *that* little mystery? Nothing some careful research and a few well-placed friends couldn't solve. I'm afraid I can't reveal my sources, however."

He raises a finger and wags it at me. "*You*. Are a dangerous woman."

"They *are* the best kind, you know. You should try one sometime."

Olle stands up. "I am taking you back to town in the automobile," he says, "and you are going to get on board the next boat back to Oahu, is that clear? You're going back where you came from, and you are not saying a word about any of this."

"Are you giving me an *order*, Olle? Because I don't take orders, not from four-star generals and not from you."

"Who the devil *are* you?" he asks, incredulous.

"I am Persistence, Olle. I am Curiosity." I glance to the cat and back again. "I am Heartbreak. I am Survival. I am Recklessness and Perse-verance. You can't win."

He swears. I shrug.

The bell tinkles again. A pair of men walk in, pilots by the look of them, talking some shop. They spot me right away and the conversa-tion dies.

"Morning, Olle," one of them says. "Passenger?"

I stand up and hold out my hand. "Janey Everett. I'm new in town."

"She was just leaving," says Olle.

"Isn't he a gas? Really, I'm an old friend of Mrs. Lindquist. We go way back. Can either of you two tell me—"

But I am interrupted, just then, by the howl of an engine, the scream of air. The men all look up and tilt their ears to the sky, and then some kind of signal passes among them, I don't know what, secret pilot communication, and they all go thundering out the door, bell a-jingle, and I have no choice but to thunder after them, toward some terrible emergency, some fate that has turned in an instant.

AVIATRIX

by Eugenia Everett

(e x c e r p t)

March 1928: California

S O THERE IT was, Irene's future turning on the malfunction of a single spark plug. You could say it was luck, or you could judge the hand of fate at work, or God, or whatever you believed in. The airfield turned out to be in Burbank, half an hour away on the other side of the Hollywood Hills, but Irene didn't mind. She sat next to Sam Mallory in his yellow Nash while the sun rose to her right and the hills rolled all around, briefly green after a spell of spring rain. Above them, the sky was untainted blue, a thing Irene took for granted. Soon she would learn that most skies were not so blue; that in most places, the daytime temperature didn't hover blissfully around seventy-six dry, placid degrees Fahrenheit for much of the year. For now, all Irene knew was the coast of California.

Unlike Irene's Ford, the Nash was only a few years old and had an electric ignition, a three-speed transmission, a dry clutch, a brake pedal. Why, compared to the old Tin Lizzie, it practically drove itself. It stopped on command, it unleashed what seemed like a vast amount of power whenever Mr. Mallory pressed his foot on the gas pedal. They rolled the windows down and the wind scattered her hair every which way. Irene didn't mind. She never took much care of her hair anyway.

At one point, winding north through Laurel Canyon, Irene stroked around Sandy's ears and asked Mr. Mallory how he got the scar on his nose.

He fingered across the ridge and back again. "Crackup last summer."

"Crackup? You mean a car accident?"

"No, an airplane. We call 'em *crackups*, it sounds better." Mr. Mallory was smoking a cigarette, which he held in the hand nearest the window. He took a quick drag and said, "I guess you might have heard about that one."

"Only me and the whole world. Aren't you just a little crazy, going back up in an airplane after an accident like that?"

"Sure, I'm crazy. We're all crazy, us pilots." He stubbed out his cigarette against the side of the car. "But it's freedom up there, Miss Foster. You and the blue sky. It's the future, it's the whole damned universe, right there before you, wide open and beautiful to take your breath away. It's worth a broken nose or two. It's worth whatever price God asks of you."

OF COURSE IRENE HAD HEARD of Sam Mallory. By the spring of 1928, everyone in California had heard of him. In fact, if you lived anywhere in the world and possessed a radio or a newspaper subscription, you had probably—like Irene—spent a certain portion of the past August attached to both, desperate to discover whether Sam Mallory was somehow miraculously alive on the surface of the Pacific Ocean, or heroically dead on the bottom of same.

Irene's father did not own a radio. He claimed it was because he opposed such modern contraptions on principle, but really it was because he couldn't afford one. Irene remembered listening to the radio in the drugstore instead. Of course, the place was packed that first morning, cheek by jowl with eager listeners. The press had been talking up the Dole Derby for weeks. It was the Pacific's answer to Lindbergh mania, a contest sponsored by the Dole Pineapple Company, in which pilots from around the country took off from San Francisco Bay one fine summer morning and raced each other all the way to Honolulu, Hawai'i. First prize, twenty-five thousand dollars. Second prize, ten thousand dollars. As it turned out, there was no need for a third prize, because only two airplanes taking off that day actually made it to paradise, or at least the earthly kind.

And Sam Mallory was not one of them.

Irene didn't remember all the details. She didn't know what type of airplane Sam Mallory had been flying or why exactly he had been forced to ditch the machine in the ocean, several hundred miles short of Hawai'i, in the dark of night. Something about a faulty fuel line. All she remembered was that he and his copilot—Irene didn't recall the name—had been reported far ahead of his nearest competitor when she went to sleep that night, and when she woke the news was everywhere, in thick black headlines, in chattering radio receivers:

GOEBEL AND DAVIS WIN DOLE DERBY

Smith Second; Three Airplanes Lost at Sea

Naturally, the press was not going to let this terrible disaster go to waste. Day after day, the radios and newspapers reported back from the frantic search for the downed airplanes. They found the first one fairly quickly. But the fate of the *Miss Doran* and the rather foolishly named *Icarus*—Mr. Mallory's airplane—remained unknown. Irene would stop by the drugstore on her way home from work to listen to the latest bulletins, delivered in breathless yet stalwart tones by Mr. Floyd Gibbons of the National Broadcasting Corporation. How much food and water the pilots had carried with them. The shifting weather patterns. The dimensions and capabilities of the emergency rafts carried aboard. (As it turned out, Sam Mallory's airplane had not carried a raft at all, on account of the extra weight.) The concentration of man-eating sharks in that area of the Pacific Ocean from where the lost airplanes had issued their last transmissions.

Seven days passed, eight, nine. Irene no longer stopped by the drug-store after work; it was simply too heart-wrenching to listen to Mr. Gib-bons, in a voice of attempted cheer, lay out various scenarios by which either of the two airplanes might have survived. He had discussed Mr. Mallory's history as a stunt pilot—*The man known in Hollywood for his willingness to attempt any proposed maneuver, no matter how perilous or technically impossible, even the deliberate crash of an airplane*—and before all that, his years as a barnstormer, hopscotching the country to perform for crowds of amazed corn pokes. Before even that, his stint in the Army Air Service, dogfighting above the bloody French battlefields. For some reason, Mr. Gibbons—a celebrated war hero himself—considered that this checkered history of death-defying subsistence, hairline survival, and crackerjack piloting had perfectly prepared Mr. Mallory for his present ordeal. Irene couldn't stand his optimism. It seemed naïve to her, almost disrespectful, when the man and his copilot had obviously made a meal for the sharks by now.

And then came the morning—Irene remembered it perfectly—when she arrived home from the beach to a newspaper headline so in-credible, so almost hysterically jubilant, the words seemed to overflow and run off the page.

MALLORY FOUND ALIVE!!

*Astonishing Rescue off Coast of Maui; Story of Survival Against Odds
on Wing of Airplane in Open Ocean
Copilot Perished; Pilot Starving, Sunburnt, and Dehydrated
but Otherwise in Good Health*

(When Irene read that last part, she had to wonder whether the copy editor at the *Los Angeles Times* was a man of irony or had simply lost his head.) Anyway, you heard about nothing else for weeks afterward, the interviews and the celebratory dinners; the Sunday prayers of thanks-giving in churches around the country; President Coolidge's radio ad-dress hailing the whole affair as *an inspiring example of the very best of*

American manhood; Mr. Mallory's arrival back in San Francisco by commercial steamer, aboard which the occupant of the best first-class suite had gallantly insisted on switching accommodation with the hero of the day; the parades in San Francisco and then in Los Angeles.

Then August died into September, and the ballyhoo faded into nothing as it always did, and the American man went back to his work and his home and waited for the next thrill to smack him upside the head, from the ball field or the mountaintop or the clear blue sky.

Now Irene wound around the curves of Laurel Canyon in Sam Mallory's speedy yellow Nash, approaching the crest of the ridge where the horizon was nothing but sky. She traced the arms and the delicate paws of Mr. Mallory's newfound kitten with her finger and fastened on two details about the 1927 Dole Derby that she hadn't troubled to notice much before.

The first was the *Miss Doran,* and how nobody seemed to have found any trace of her or her pilots, at least that Irene could remember. They were just forgotten in the ballyhoo.

The second was Mrs. Sam Mallory, who had made such brave, beautiful speeches during the whole ordeal about her love for her husband and her faith that he would return home safely to his wife and little daughter.

ON IRENE'S LAP, THE KITTEN stirred, raised its head, stretched its paw, went back to sleep. Irene realized she was holding her breath. They turned the last corner and the valley tumbled into view, Burbank and the hills behind it, and the ocean to the left, all of it bathed in the clear, pale, fragile light of early morning. Irene exhaled at last. They cruised down the hill through the draft, and Irene thought she would always remember this moment, this sensation of speed and freedom.

"It's like flying," she shouted.

Mr. Mallory laughed and changed gears. "Not even close."

THE AIRFIELD SAT ON THE corner of Lankershim Boulevard and Vanowen, and stretched into a grassy infinity. Mr. Mallory turned the Nash
down a gravel driveway toward a cluster of large white sheds. The one
at the end of the drive bore the name ROFRANO in black letters.

"What's Rofrano?" asked Irene.

"Fellow who runs the place." Mr. Mallory parked the car in the
rhombus of shade cast by one of the buildings. "Moved here from New
York in '22 and bought the land up to fly his own planes. Then all his old
Army Air Service pals came out and asked if they could fly there too.
Pretty soon he had a business going."

Mr. Mallory yanked open the door and stepped onto the grass. The
noise woke the kitten. Limb by limb it uncurled in Irene's lap, yawned,
and dug its claws into her leg like tiny pins, kneading and kneading.
She detached it with one hand and reached for the door handle and leapt
free—insofar as you could leap in a lean skirt of navy blue poplin, cut
a few inches longer than what was then considered fashionable—and
nearly crashed into Mr. Mallory, who had come around to open the door
for her. *Sorry,* she said, just as Mr. Mallory said sorry too. He laughed
and reached for Sandy. "Let me take that cat off your hands, hmm?
Then we'll go find you a spark plug."

Together they walked toward the row of sheds that turned out—
when you got close enough to appreciate their size—to be airplane hangars. Already a few men milled about, reeking of cigarettes and engine
oil and energy. Mr. Mallory raised his hand and said hello. The other
hand maneuvered Sandy, who was climbing his shirt to knead the skin
at the base of his throat. Together they reached the easternmost hangar
and the biplane poised beside it, catching the morning sun in a burst of
white. Irene stopped. She had never stood so close to an airplane; it was
like a mythic beast to her. She stared at the wing, which was larger than
she expected and also more frail.

"What's it made of?" she asked.

"Just canvas and wood," said Mr. Mallory.

Irene wanted to touch, but she didn't. The airplane's skin reminded her of the wing of an insect, so thin as to defy physics. If force equaled mass times velocity, how could something that frail survive the invincible wind? On the other hand, insects could fly, that was indisputable. Irene reached out and laid her fingertip on the edge of the wing, laid her hand on an airplane for the first time. But it wasn't delicate after all. It was stiff and lacquered, the same texture as metal. Soon she would learn that the fabric was coated in a kind of glue they called dope, and this was the source of the distinctive smell she would shortly encounter inside the hangar.

But all that lay in the future. Now there was only wonder.

"Shall we?" said Mr. Mallory, standing beside her, and for a moment she thought he was inviting her into the biplane that sat beside them, inviting her to fly. She opened her mouth to exclaim *Yes!* but it turned out he just meant the hangar and the spark plug. He walked around the nose of the airplane, shifting Sandy from one shoulder to the other, and Irene, still dazed, stroked the wing a last time and followed him.

The doors to the hangar were the kind that rolled sideways, like pocket doors, except these were made of plain lumber and stood wide open to the California sunshine. Inside, Irene glimpsed two small, battered airplanes. Mr. Mallory maneuvered Sandy carefully from his shirt and back into the crook of his elbow. He nodded to the machine on the right. "Training planes. Picked them up cheap from the army. That one's a Curtiss Jenny. The other's a Canuck."

"Which one do you recommend?"

"Neither."

Irene stepped forward into the hangar. The grass turned to beaten earth. The air smelled of dust and grease and wood, a garage smell, except for something else, an unfamiliar chemical note. Aside from the two of them, and the airplanes and the tools, the hangar was empty. Irene wandered between the two machines. She touched the smooth wooden curve of a propeller blade, the taut canvas skin of a fuselage, a metal strut.

"I don't see any difference between them," she said.

"The Canuck's the same plane, Canadian model. It's lighter and it's got . . . it's got . . ."

Irene turned. Mr. Mallory stood by a wide wooden workbench that ran the entire length of the building. The rear of the Curtiss Jenny stood between them, cutting him off at the waist, so she couldn't quite see what he was doing. Rummaging or something. Irene ducked under the airplane to join him at the bench. He had pulled out a crate from the shelf and Sandy stood against it, paws on the edge, to peer inside.

"It's got what?" she said.

"Hmm?"

"The Canuck."

"Oh. It's just a flimsier airplane, that's all. But it's good enough for instruction. Here you are." Mr. Mallory turned and held out his hand, which contained a pair of spark plugs.

"Oh! Thank you. I'd almost forgotten."

Irene took the spark plugs. He was smiling at her, grinning really, and with his other hand he scooped up Sandy, who was taking some interest in the boxes of screws lined up where the bench met the wall.

"Say. If you're interested. There's an air show today, starts at noon."

"An air show?"

"You know. Pilots take turns going up, showing off our airplanes, that kind of thing. Then we take up members of the public for five dollars a spin."

"Will you be flying?"

"Wouldn't miss it. For one thing, I need the dough. Flying's a lot of things, but it's not cheap. Especially if . . ."

"If what?"

"Nothing. Got a few plans, that's all. If you're interested . . ."

Irene cast a glance out the open side of the hangar, to the landing strip that baked in the sunshine. Her heart was thudding a little. "It sounds wonderful," she said. "But I should really be getting home."

"Oh. Sure, of course."

"But I'd love to. I really would."

The kitten seemed to be falling asleep along the length of his fore-arm. Mr. Mallory stroked the top of its head with his finger and nodded. "All right. Let's get you back to Santa Monica, then."

"Wait a minute. You're just going to drive me there and back here again? For your air show?"

"It's no trouble."

"It's an awful lot of trouble!"

"I don't mind," he said. "It's a pleasant drive."

"Don't be silly. I'll just stay."

"What about your folks?"

"I live with my father," she said, "and he's away right now. So there's nobody to worry about me, really. I can stay all day."

AS TIME WENT ON, IRENE would remember that day at the airfield as a series of scenes, as pieces of a dazzling puzzle. There was breakfast with Sam—he was now Sam, and she was Irene—in the cafeteria, a neat, cheap building made of stucco, set apart from the hangars, furnished with metal chairs and tables covered in cheerful red-and-white linens. They both ordered coffee and corned beef hash, topped with eggs fried sunny side up, while Sandy lapped from a dish of cream. Sam asked Irene whether she had a job, and she said yes, she was a receptionist at a doctor's office, and she hoped to enroll in a nursing course in the fall.

"Well, now," he said, "that's admirable. Why nursing?"

And Irene found herself telling Sam things she hadn't told anyone else at the hospital, or really anyone at all. She explained—or rather he dug from her, bit by bit—how she told her parents one evening when she was very young, when her mother was still alive and her father held down a respectable job, that she wanted to become a doctor. Her mother had smiled in that sarcastic way she had, but her father had nodded gravely and said she would make a good doctor, she had a calm head on her shoulders, and she should study very hard to make this dream a reality. How later that night, she'd overheard her mother telling her father that he shouldn't indulge the girl like that, it was ridiculous to imagine that Irene could become a doctor. *Why not?* said her father. He'd seen plenty of women doctors, there were several medical colleges that now accepted female candidates. Because she will want a family one day, her mother said, and then all that education would go to waste; because children had a way of demanding your attention, of diverting this abundant river of female energy and ambition into themselves.

Irene didn't remember how her father answered this, or whether she even really heard his response through the walls of the house. Possibly the conversation never even happened, she admitted to Sam, sipping her coffee, and this was only the way she remembered her parents' reactions to her ambitions, like a composite drawing, a convenience of memory. Either way, she did study hard. She took all the difficult classes, algebra and trigonometry, chemistry and physics, and graduated at the top of the class of well-bred girls in the private school her grandparents had paid for. She had just finished her first year of premedical studies at Berkeley when her grandfather died, and his estate went into probate where it was entangled by lawsuits, and there was no more money for such frivolities as college. They ended up in Los Angeles instead, she and her father, because it seemed like a fresh start. That was a year and a half ago. Her father was still looking around for steady work, which was why he was away. As soon as they could afford it, she was going to start that nursing course.

She sat back. Her coffee cup was empty. Sam had also finished his breakfast and his coffee, and he leaned on the arm of his chair and stared at her in a peculiar way, made all the more peculiar because Sandy had fallen asleep on his shoulder, sort of wrapped around the base of his neck and held there by static, possibly.

"I'm sorry about your mother," Sam said at last. "You were just a kid."

"She was sick a long time. It wasn't a shock or anything."

"Was that when your dad started drinking?"

"No," Irene said. "He drank before. But after Mama died, he couldn't stop."

Sam nodded. "So everything was up to you."

"I guess you could say that."

"Well," Sam said, stroking the cat on his shoulder, staring gravely at Irene, "I guess I don't have to ask why you go out surfing in the morning."

THEN THEY WERE BACK IN the hangar, readying the Jenny for her flight. Already people were arriving for the exhibition, people in their dozens, men and also women in their shingled hair and dark lipstick, small hats nearly worthless against the sun, but that was fashion for you. Sam explained about the engine and the controls, ailerons and elevators, throttle and rudder. "It's an old plane now," he said. "I'm saving up to buy something newer. Faster. Rofrano's designed this bird with aluminum skin and a pair of six-hundred-horsepower engines. If I had that ship I could fly anywhere."

"How much does it cost?"

"*She*, Irene. An airplane's not an *it*."

"But why female?"

"Aw, now. I'm not walking into *that* one, believe me. Let's just say it's because a pilot falls a little in love with his airplane, after a while."

They had stopped working and stood facing each other. Sam propped one elbow on the edge of the cockpit. Sandy was inside, wandering dangerously near the rudder pedal.

"What if the pilot's a she?" asked Irene.

"Now that's a good question. I'll have to ask around."

"Do you get any around here? Women pilots?"

"Course we do. I've taught a dozen women how to fly."

"Any good ones?"

"A few. If they stick with it. Just like anybody, man or woman. You have to keep flying. The only thing that keeps you alive up there is experience. At all cost, you have to fly."

Irene turned to lean her elbows on the fuselage so she could stare into the cockpit, the simple controls, the wood that Sam kept spotlessly varnished. Sandy leapt into the seat and stretched her paws against the side.

"When did you learn to fly?" she asked.

"Ten years ago. No, eleven."

"You mean the war?"

"Joined the Army Air Service in the summer of 1917. Then—well, I guess you know the rest."

By now, Irene had turned on her elbow to face him. Their arms were inches apart on the edge of the cockpit. Irene thought he didn't look at all like the press photographs, the newsreels, where he grinned at the camera like the handsome daredevil he was supposed to be. Now he looked serious. He looked grim, like he was looking back on this career of his, as an inspiration to American manhood, and didn't like what he found there.

"I'm glad you survived, anyway," Irene said.

"Yes." He turned away and lifted Sandy from the pilot's seat. "I'm damned lucky to be alive."

IN THE NEXT SCENE, IRENE stood near the lookout tower with the other spectators, the women in their short, fashionable dresses and the men in their pale suits. Sam was about to take off in his Curtis Jenny. She knew it was him because the name was painted on the side of the fuselage, *Papillon*. It meant butterfly in French, she knew. She thought that was a dumb name for an airplane. She hoped it would fly more like a hawk, an eagle, swift and strong.

A woman had come up to stand beside her. Irene snatched a glance and saw that she was petite and pretty in the way of dolls, huge eyes inside a face shaped exactly like a heart, mop of short blond curls held in place by a straw hat.

"You're a friend of Sam's?" the woman asked.

"You could say that."

"I don't mean to be rude. I saw you together earlier, that's all." The woman put out a tiny hand. "I'm Sophie Rofrano."

"Oh, then you're—"

"Yes. Run the place, together with my husband. Isn't it a fine day? Of course, it's mostly fine in California. That's why we're all here."

Irene took the hand and was surprised at the firmness of the handshake. Most women of that size, they had a puny grasp to match. "Irene Foster. It certainly is fine."

"I remember the first time I watched him fly. Sam, I mean. He found us right after we started the airfield. He'd flown with my husband in the service, you know."

Irene didn't know, but she nodded anyway. It made sense, after all.

"He'd just bought a Jenny off somebody else, somebody who'd cracked it up and quit flying, and Sam put that airplane all back together again and off he went, into the sky." Mrs. Rofrano waved her hand at the landing strip, and the airplane toddling toward the end. "I'd never seen anybody fly a Jenny like that, not even my husband. I didn't know you could. He knew exactly how to push her, exactly how much she could tolerate, exactly what she could do. Turns and loops and dives. He put her down again—it was an air show, just like this one—and he must have found twenty new students, right there. Are you one of them? Students, I mean."

"Yes. No! I—well, we surf together, that's all." It wasn't exactly a lie, after all, and it certainly sounded less awkward than the truth.

"Surf! On the water? The ocean?"

"Yes."

"Oh, that's grand. I didn't even know Sam surfed. He doesn't tell you much about himself, you know."

"I know."

"Ah." Mrs. Rofrano folded her arms. "There he goes."

As she spoke, the noise of Sam's propeller, idling in the distance, turned loud and purposeful. Irene lifted her hand to her brow and stared at *Papillon*, an unobstructed view, soaked in sunshine. The propeller whirred furiously on its nose. It started forward, bouncing like a spring on the ruts in the grass. Irene could see Sam's leather cap and his goggles throwing off rays; she thought she could see his expression, but maybe that was only her imagination filling in the details. Either way, the crowd stirred and spoke around her, *oohed* as if they'd never seen an airplane before.

And yet. Didn't Irene feel the same way? Yes, you encountered airplanes all the time in that hopeful blue California sky of the 1920s, puttering away, climbing and falling and banking, performing heart-stopping stunts for onlookers, like looping the loop and flying under bridges and wing walking and what have you. Until now, Irene had felt no more than the usual amazement at these antics.

Now it was different. Now Sam's airplane prepared to meet the sky. Now Sam's airplane gained speed and thrust downfield. In Irene's eyes, it seemed to lengthen, to suck power under its skin, to gather all that California sunshine into its wings. Irene felt the lift of its nose in her own body, the flex of its wings; she knew the exact instant its wheels came apart from the grass and the wind drew it upward, as if it had no weight at all. She followed the diagonal line of its ascent until it soared above the boulevard, the trees, and vanished into the sky, and what she wanted to do, in that moment, was not to climb inside an airplane with Sam and soar away into that vanishing sky. Was not to pilot an airplane at all.

She wanted to *become*. She wanted to become the airplane.

THE SCENE THAT FOLLOWED WOULD soon become commonplace to Irene, but on that March afternoon in 1928, everything was new. Each aerobatic maneuver drenched her in wonder, like a river baptism, in which you were plunged several times into the water and came out reborn. The steep dive that pulled out just above the ground into a graceful upward arc. The journey along the tine of an imaginary corkscrew while a trail of red smoke curled behind like a pig's tail. The climb, steeper and steeper until your heart stopped, until the airplane briefly became vertical, then upside down in contravention of everything you thought you knew about nature and physics, *just hanging there upside down,* seconds passing into eternity, then a swooping fall while your heart resumed beating and you said to yourself, *loop the loop.* Irene wouldn't remember every stunt Sam performed that day—stunts piled on stunts, and which ones she witnessed then and which ones later—but she would remember the grand finale. Everybody would.

Papillon had just completed a double loop that set off a round of gasps and applause among the spectators. Irene thought she saw Sam lift his hand and wave to them as he soared up and off, presumably to circle the airfield and return for another maneuver, or else to land. The airplane grew tiny against the sky, a white gnat, and then disappeared altogether when it crossed a cluster of cumulus that gathered atop the hills to the east. A minute passed, and another. Next to Irene, Mrs. Rofrano checked her watch and folded her arms. Several yards away stood a group of pilots and mechanics who'd emerged from the cafeteria and from their sheds to watch Sam's antics. One of them— stern, dark-haired fellow—glanced to Mrs. Rofrano and exchanged some telegraphic communication.

"Who's that?" Irene whispered.

"My husband."

"Is something the matter?"

"Oh, I'm sure he'll be back around any moment."

But the seconds ticked on, and still there was no sign of the returning airplane. One of the other men turned away and scuffed his feet in the grass. Another lit a cigarette. Irene knew better than to say anything. The silence held them together. Nobody needed to say a single word; everything known was obvious, everything unknown was better off unmentioned. Like among the surfers back in Santa Monica, you didn't talk about the danger or the possibility of annihilation, the various scenarios when somebody went missing, sharks or rogue waves or cramp or miscalculation. What was the point?

Over on Vanowen, an engine backfired. Everybody jumped, except Mr. Rofrano, who just flinched. Irene remembered what Sam had said, that Rofrano had flown in France during the war. She looked at his profile, at the nape of his neck, and tried to imagine him flying over France, dodging enemy fire, shooting down other airplanes. The most dangerous job in the war, she knew. If the Germans didn't get you, the airplane would. On the other hand, it was better than dying on the ground, in a trench, like a rat. At least you died free, you died in honorable combat, like a knight or a bird of prey. Mr. Rofrano had a large, sharp nose, and it pointed to the sky, hunting for the *Papillon*. If anyone could pluck out an airplane from the sky, it was surely this man, a wartime flying ace.

Mr. Rofrano lifted a pair of field binoculars to his eyes. A stir passed through the crowd. Mrs. Rofrano touched Irene's elbow and nodded to the sky.

At first Irene didn't see anything, just that deep, flawless California blue and the green-golden hills underneath. She squinted and shaded her eyes. Somebody swore softly. She heard the purr of an engine, but it was just another automobile passing down the road. "Where?" she whispered to Mrs. Rofrano.

Mrs. Rofrano pointed.

Irene blinked and squinted.

A tiny gray dot wobbled into the corner of her gaze. She gasped, and it was gone.

She blinked again. There it was! Like somebody poked a hole in the sky with a needle, except it was moving, it grew larger and took shape.

"She's in trouble," said Mrs. Rofrano.

"What? How do you know?"

"Clear the field!" somebody called out, and the crowd turned and scattered, even Mr. Rofrano, who ran toward one of the sheds, followed by the other men. Irene tagged after them. She stopped in the doorway of the shed as the men pulled on the yoke of the fire engine inside.

"Get the door!" yelled Mr. Rofrano.

Irene grasped the door and pulled with all her strength, so it slid all the way open, and the men yanked and yelled at each other and pulled the engine into the sunshine. Now Irene could hear the airplane, humming and sputtering. The fire engine had an enormous tank, and all four men leaned desperately into the yoke as they hauled it down the field, parallel to the wide avenue of beaten grass that formed the landing strip. Irene lifted her skirt and ran to follow them. Her scarf fell free from her hair. She ripped it off and balled it in her hand, in case they needed a bandage or a tourniquet. The noise of the *Papillon* grew louder. Irene stopped and cast into the sky, where the airplane skimmed downward at a strange angle, sort of sideways, while the wings tilted back and forth.

"It's the rudder!" somebody shouted.

The fire engine rolled to a stop, halfway down the field, and everybody just stood there watching, because there was nothing to be done, was there? This drama was about the pilot and the plane, the wind and the ground, and everybody else was just a spectator. Irene clenched her fists and her breath. She smelled the burning oil, the fear. In later years, she wished she could remember the way the airplane came in, the hundred tiny maneuvers made by the pilot to compensate for the rudder's failings, but now, her flying career still before her, she didn't know a thing about rudders and maneuvers, in her ignorance she didn't notice any of it. She stood in awe, watching the hairy descent, the swoops and skids of battle, the crump of impact, the dust, the men running, Mr. Rofrano in front of them all.

HANALEI, HAWAI'I

October 1947

W E'VE ALL GOT a thing that terrifies us. I saw a lot of airplanes
crash during the war, and I encountered the aftermath countless
times more, and still I never did get used to the sight or sound of some
machine smashing into the ground.

When you hear the telltale noise, you gird for horror. The things
modern machinery can do to a human body, it's enough to make you
retch your guts out, enough to make you die of pity. I don't know how
the army surgeons survived it. I don't understand how you could lock
up the pity and the horror into a steel vault deep inside the bank of your
soul, how you could set about repairing a mutilated limb or a split-open
skull or some devastated viscera in the same way you might repair a flat
tire, say.

In England, before the Allied invasion, I was living in staff huts
right near an air base, and just about every other day some poor chap
would ram his ship into the earth nearby. The others in the press pool
would dutifully trudge out to take notes and pictures, to point and stare
and shake their heads at the gore, but I never would. I never went to
see a crackup if I could help it, although there were plenty of times I
couldn't help it, and I faced the wreckage as bravely as I could. Also, I
had a rule not to sleep with any pilots. You might get attached, after all,
and then they would inevitably get killed, and you were left to imagine

those last seconds over and over, the certain expectation of death, your helplessness in the face of it, your beloved body strapped into a hunk of metal that plummeted toward the earth, nothing you could do but wait for annihilation. I can't think of a thing in the world more terrifying than that.

And now this terror has followed me here, to a peaceful corner of a remote island in the middle of the Pacific. It doesn't seem fair, does it? Still I follow Olle and the two pilots out of the cafeteria and into the soft Hawaiian morning. The three of them bolt toward the smoking pile of metal and drag out the body like any old piece of meat. Olle seems to know what he's doing. He arranges limbs and listens for breath and barks some order at one of the pilots. In the distance, someone's dragging out a water tank on some kind of caisson.

And I say to myself, God forgive me.

I'M GOING TO TELL YOU a story now, a story I've never told anybody. It does me little credit, but I was young and foolish, as the saying goes, and haven't we all got some old folly that tortures us?

The summer between my first and second years of college, when I had just turned eighteen years old, I worked as a secretary at a law firm in order to save money for the next year's tuition, and there was this lawyer there who ran the place. He was handsome and authoritative, a brilliant jurist, and he was also forty-seven years old and married. He acted awfully stern with me, never stopping to banter and charm as he did with the other secretaries, as if he actively disliked me, but the sterner he was the more he occupied my thoughts. At work my fingers struck like lightning on the typewriter while my eyes wandered around the office, following him wherever he went, craving some crumb of approval, wondering what on earth I'd done to earn his displeasure.

One Friday afternoon in early July, he had made all these notes on a brief and needed them typed up, and the other two secretaries—Patty and Laura—had already gone home. He said, *I guess we shall have to wait for Monday then*, and I said, *Oh, I'd be happy to stay and type it for you*. He said it was too much trouble, and I said it was no trouble at all. An hour later I was flat on my back on the Chesterfield sofa in his private office, blouse unbuttoned, virginal navy skirt up around my hips, married law-yer rocking away on top of me, and let me tell you it hurt like the dickens in more ways than one, but I didn't stop him. I couldn't, even if I'd had the physical strength for it. I was miserable and ashamed, and at the same time I felt this surge of anguished joy when he shuddered and shook and shouted, begged God and his wife to forgive him, collapsed on my chest and called himself a lost man, because I thought that must mean I had won not just his approval, but his adoration. I was loved! Then he lifted himself off and said what a whore I was, I should have stopped him. He said this even as he wiped my blood from his skin with his handkerchief. He swore me to silence, swore this could never happen again.

That night when I went home, I couldn't even look at my mother or my stepfather. I felt this stain on me. I was so ashamed I wanted to die. In the middle of the night I went to the medicine cabinet and stared at the aspirin and wondered how much it would take to kill me, and if I hadn't been scared of my mother finding me first, I might have done it.

On Monday it happened again. He told me to bring him his morning coffee, and when I stepped into his office with the cup he closed the door and kissed me. The coffee spilled. He told me he had spent all week-end in torment, thinking about nothing but me and what we had done, drunk with love for me, how I had bewitched and seduced him, this was all my doing, all my fault. He kissed me again, and I kissed him back, because I thought I should feed this thing, this love he said he had for me, this power I thought I had over him. He unbuttoned my blouse and kissed my neck, my breasts, then turned me around and laid me over the top of his desk, so that the leather blotter pressed against my cheek. When he was finished he gave me a handkerchief and told me this was our secret, that if I said a word about this to my mother, to anybody, he would cut all ties with me and I would be disgraced as a whore in front of everybody. So I didn't say a word. I hated what we did, hated myself for doing it, hated these physical stirrings that sometimes came with what we did, and yet I never refused him, God forgive me, never once said no to him, because despite all the shame and the revulsion I craved his love, or rather I wanted him not to stop loving me, because I thought his lust for me was a symptom of love, and if I stopped feeding that lust he would no longer love me. Nobody would love me!

Long story short, we carried on through July and August, and though I still sometimes went to the medicine cabinet in the middle of the night to stare at the aspirin bottle, I never worked up the nerve to swallow the pills. I figured if I killed myself, people might find out why, and his wife's heart would be broken and his life ruined, and all of this would be my fault.

At last I returned to college for the autumn term. By late September I realized I was going to have a baby. Well, of course I was! We must have fucked fifty times at least; I doubt there was a moment all that summer when my fresh young womb was not teeming with that man's sperm. I wrote a letter to my lover and asked humbly what I should do, but he never replied. I thought it would be bad form to confront him face-to-face, so I went to Mother, who promptly took me to some doctor she knew of, who solved the problem. After the thing was done, she told me she hoped I'd learned my lesson, because she and my stepfather wanted no more to do with me, and that was when I started on the road with my camera, older but wiser, armed with a few new guiding principles.

First, no matter how much you're tempted, do not have to do with married men.

Second, never allow a male member indoors unless it's properly dressed.

Third, you may lease your body to whomever you fancy, and insist on your pleasure as a condition of same, but whatever you do, in whatever bed or sofa or sunlit meadow, for God's sake keep your heart to yourself.

In time, I was to break all three of those rules, although not at the same time. We are only human, and our miseries take on infinite form.

NOW, WHY HAVE I TOLD you this sordid, unhappy story, this stale tale already told a million times by a million other women, when I have not told another living soul? Because I think you should know that I am not so invincible, not so hard and so careless as I sometimes seem. I have been naïve. I have behaved stupidly, even culpably. I have sinned and repented, I have deceived others and been cruelly deceived myself. I have been wounded so deeply I wanted to die.

But I did not die. I am Perseverance, remember. I am Survival.

And I am not so callous that I don't feel a bone-crushing remorse at the sight of that airplane wreckage and a shudder of fate repeating itself and finally a sense of loss that almost brings me to my knees, because in my grief and my outrage I've destroyed something important. I have caused this nightmare that is my own worst nightmare.

All these thoughts bear down on me in a series of instants, and in the next instant I leap forward to help with the water tank, because I don't do so well with the blood, and anyway Olle seems to be performing every necessary thing.

The slender man at the caisson must possess some superhuman strength, because he's almost reached the wreckage. In seconds, I hurtle to his side and grab the yoke and together we haul that tank the last fifty yards. The fellow drops the yoke and thanks me, reaches for the hose and tells me to man the pump, and by God I nearly lose my mind.

"You! I thought—I thought—"

"You're an idiot, Miss Everett," yells Mrs. Lindquist as she drags the hose from its spool. "Now pump!"

AS IT TURNS OUT, THE pilot's not dead at all. He has a broken ankle and a great many cuts and bruises, and Olle suspects a collapsed lung caused by a possibly broken rib. His name is Kaiko, and he's apparently Olle's brother-in-law. Olle was married before, it turns out, to a Hawaiian woman who died some time ago, and Kaiko is her brother. Everybody's related to each other in Hanalei, Olle explains.

I'm in Lindquist's yellow truck with Olle, driving back into town, because Lindquist is flying Kaiko to the hospital in Honolulu in her own private airplane. Olle doesn't trust the tiny hospital here on Kauai. Some fellow from the junkyard on the other side of the island is coming later to pick up the remains of the machine itself, which seems precipitate to me. I ask, *Don't they want to find out what caused the accident?* and Olle looks at me like I'm crazy.

"What caused the accident is that Kaiko is a terrible pilot," he says. "He came in to land too slowly and stalled. Now he's learned his lesson. Thank God he had no passengers."

"Does he usually? Have passengers?"

"Sometimes. When we're short of pilots."

"Oh, that's just terrific. And people wonder why I won't get on an airplane."

"You don't fly?"

The wind billows in drafts through the open windows, smelling of brine, whipping my hair around my head. I make some attempt to tuck it behind my ears. "Never ever," I tell him. "By land or by sea, that's my motto. It takes longer, but you see more, and you generally stay in one piece."

Olle starts to laugh. I have the feeling he's just relieved Kaiko isn't dead, and sometimes relief finds expression in hysterical laughter. I saw a lot of that kind of thing in Europe, believe me.

"What's so funny?" I ask.

"You. Fixated on my wife, and you don't even fly."

"I'm not fixated on your wife. I'm fixated on Samuel Mallory. He *was* the better pilot, after all."

That sobers up Olle. "He was better at some things, maybe. But which pilot is still alive?"

We reach the inn a few minutes later. Olle seems to have forgotten that he doesn't like me, or maybe my heroic efforts at the water pump have atoned for my sins. He stops the truck and frowns at me.

"I still want you on the next boat to Oahu," he says. "You upset Irene."

"If I'm on the next boat to Oahu, the next boat back will be carrying several members of the press. It's your choice."

He bangs a hand on the steering wheel. "Why? Why did you have to find us?"

"Because I want to *know,* that's all. I want to know *everything.* I can't rest until I do." I sling my pocketbook over my shoulder. "And I think your Irene wants to know too."

"Irene knows everything she needs to know."

"Are you sure of that?" I open the door, slide out, and slam it shut again. The window's open. I lean my head inside. "Good-bye, Olle. Tell your wife she knows where to find me."

THE DESK CLERK CAN'T SUPPRESS a smirk when I walk inside. "Miss Everett! Here you are at last. Have you enjoyed your stay with us?"

"Positively delightful, thanks."

"I'm glad to hear it."

"Although, now that you mention it, my upstairs neighbors *were* making a terrible racket last night. You know how it is. I had to sleep elsewhere, or I wouldn't have caught a wink. Perhaps you might consider taking it off my bill?"

The smirk fades. The fellow starts to stammer.

"In the meantime, I'd like my room key, please."

He turns and takes the key from the hook and a small envelope from the pigeonhole beneath. "You have a message too," he says grudgingly.

Upstairs, my room is neatly made—no surprise there—and really quite attractive, for a rustic beachside sort of hostelry. It's decorated in blue and white and if you strain your neck out the window at just the right angle, you can glimpse a sliver of ocean. You'll have to take my word for that, however. I'm frankly too exhausted to do anything except collapse on the bed and pull the envelope from the pocket of my slacks. Inside, there's a folded note and a five dollar bill. I spread the note between my two hands and hold it up against the ceiling.

> *Dear Janey,*
>   *I enclose your five bucks. The drinks were on the house.*
> *Yours always,*
> *Leo*
>
>   *PS you left something behind*

THE NEXT THING I KNOW, I'm thrown awake in a panicked sweat. My heart's chattering, my lungs panting. In my ears, over and over, plays the scream of a doomed engine followed by the metallic smash that jolts every pore. In my fist, Leo's note is crumpled to a tight, damp ball.

But this experience is not unknown to me. I know what to do when I wake in a thundering panic, when the unexpected crash of an airplane starts the process all over again. You just lie where you are and listen to your breath, you count the beats of your pulse and your respiration until they return to normal, and then, if you haven't got a body lying conveniently next to you on the bed, you rise and hunt for one.

I strap on my espadrilles and head to the Hanalei Tavern.

"So where's Leo?" I ask the bartender.

"Bringing in the afternoon boat."

I lay down my five dollar bill and ask for a pair of whiskey sours. By five o'clock, I'm good and tight, and Leo's walking in the door, whistling.

"There you are," he says.

"Here I am."

"I've got something for you upstairs."

"So I hear."

"Bill," he says to the bartender, "cover for me tonight, will you?"

WHAT I LEFT BEHIND AT Leo's place last night was my necklace.

It's not much, really. A small gold oyster shell containing a small pink pearl, strung on a fine gold chain, not worthless but not priceless, either. Still, it's got sentimental value. Leo goes to fasten it on my neck, but I swat him away and fasten it myself. Leo's got nothing to do with my necklace. That's between me and the person who gave it to me.

"Suits you," says Leo.

A word about Leo. He caught my eye on the boat from Oahu, not just because he was commanding the ship—there's something about a sea captain, isn't there?—but because he's rather beautiful. I don't think he's altogether Polynesian, but he's not wholly European, either. He has dark hair and hooded light brown eyes that turn up at the tips, and his skin is the color of wood drenched in sunlight. He's not especially tall, but his proportions are divine, and the maritime life seems to keep his muscles honed. I don't usually prey on fellows younger than me—in fact, the opposite—but this one made my mouth water, and as I said, it was no hard duty to take him under my wing last night and make him sing.

Now he regards me in the mirror, as I work the clasp of the necklace and finally catch the hook. *Suits you,* he says, when I turn around at last. He holds out his hand and pulls me back into bed. I'm wearing nothing but necklace, and he's wearing nothing at all. He stretches my hands above my head and kisses the hollow between my breasts, beneath the tiny pearl snug in its tiny shell. He asks me why my fingers shook as I fastened the necklace.

"Need you ask? A girl doesn't just snap right back to herself after a ride like that."

Leo studies me for a bit. "If you say so."

"I say so."

"Hungry?"

"Starving."

He lets me go and rises from the bed to pull on a few clothes. He says he'll bring up sandwiches from downstairs. (He lives above the bar, you understand.) When he's gone, I roll on my side and contemplate a search of the premises, but I find I haven't got the strength to lift a toe. Instead I squint at his bookshelf, trying to make out the titles, and when Leo returns, plate piled high, I ask him if he came straight here from the pier when he brought in the afternoon boat.

"Like a shot," he says.

"And this morning. When do you leave for your boat?"

"Early. A quarter to seven."

"So you haven't spoken to anybody? Just me?"

Though my mouth is full of ham sandwich, Leo reaches out to cup my cheek. "Just you," he says.

The telephone rings. He doesn't flinch.

"Aren't you going to get that?" I whisper.

"No."

"What if it's important?"

"*This* is important."

But when I reach for the buttons of his trousers, he stops me. "Hold on, sweetheart. That was my last rubber."

"That was *what*?"

"My last rubber."

"How can you be out of rubbers already?"

"Well, I don't usually need so many."

"Can't you get more?"

He laughs. "Sweetheart, this is Hanalei. I can maybe buy more tomorrow, on Oahu."

"Tomorrow!" I flop myself back down on the pillows. "Why didn't you think of that *today*?"

"I *did* think about it. But I didn't want to push my luck."

I roll away and reach for my dress. He rolls after me and takes me by the waist and nuzzles my skin. "You don't have to leave, you know. I'm not some one-trick pony."

"I know *that* already."

"Or we could go to sleep. I know how to make you sleep."

I stare at my fingers, which have stopped trembling, at least for the moment. Leo pulls, ever so gently, at my waist.

"Don't be scared, Janey," he says. "I don't bite."

"Oh, yes, you do."

"Not where it hurts, though."

I shut my eyes and force myself to my feet. As I pull the dress over my head, I know he's watching me, and I think how easy it would be, how comforting, to change my mind. To slide back into his bed and fall asleep between a pair of strong arms. He's right, he knows how to make me sleep. That's what men are for, to help you sleep, to form a barrier between you and your phantoms. If I return to my bed at the inn, I might lie awake for hours. I might never sleep at all.

On the other hand, there are dangers aplenty in Leo's bed. There is the danger I felt when he took my hand an hour or two ago and led me up the narrow back staircase to his room; the danger I felt in my own disappointment when he stopped me at the button of his trousers. The fact that I want nothing more than to fall asleep with Leo is reason enough not to sleep with Leo.

He doesn't try to hold me back, though. For such a young fellow, he's got sense. He just sits on the edge of the bed, and when I've finished dressing he stands up to kiss me good night. He has this trick of smoothing my hair back with both hands, like I'm a cat.

"I forgot to ask," he says. "Did you find Irene?"

"I did, as a matter of fact. We had a nice chat. And then we went to the airfield and watched a plane crash."

Leo's hands fall away from my hair. He steps back.

"*What?* When? Whose plane? Is she all right?"

"Oh, Irene's just fine. It was the brother-in-law who got hurt. Kaiko? She flew him to the hospital on Oahu."

"*Uncle Kaiko?*" he shouts.

The telephone rings again.

"I think you'd better get that," I whisper.

AVIATRIX

by Eugenia Everett

(e x c e r p t)

March 1928: California

THE HUMAN BRAIN does strange things in extremis. As Irene lifted her skirt and ran across the grass to the cloud of dust that obscured *Papillon,* she thought about Sandy, of all things. Who was going to take care of the kitten? Sam's wife? What if she didn't like cats? Irene's legs pumped, her heart thundered, and she wondered if she could take Sandy home herself, if her father would care, and where *was* Mrs. Sam Mallory anyway, and then she arrived at the settling cloud, the throng of men, and saw a wing tilted to the sky.

Years later, after everything had passed, Irene's fingers still turned cold at the memory of that wing. At the time, she was too shocked to be afraid. She saw the wing, saw where it attached to the fuselage, saw that the wheels had partially collapsed and that the other wing had folded neatly against the ground. None of that mattered, though. The only thing that mattered was the cockpit, and the cockpit—the cockpit—she couldn't see, somebody was climbing on the wing, it was Mr. Rofrano—reaching his hand—grasping—the cockpit—an arm—a cheer, a roar from the crowd—and *God save us all* there was Sam, Sam Mallory, shoulders straining against an oil-stained flight suit, standing on the wing next to Mr. Rofrano, waving, jumping down to the grass. People started to climb on the wings. Sam shooed them off, but he was still laughing. Irene wiped the tears from her cheeks. He was talking to Rofrano. Another man shook his hand. A trickle of blood came down the side of his face. He took off his glove and wiped it with the back of his hand, went around to the broken wing and lifted it up, and Mr. Rofrano lifted the other wing, a few other men took hold of the wings, the fuselage, and *Papillon* started forward again on her remaining wheel, headed toward the hangars, trailed by her public.

SAM MALLORY HAD A CUT on his forehead and a broken finger, which some doctor in the crowd splinted for him. They stowed the broken *Papillon* in the hangar, and Irene retrieved Sandy from the crate where they had left her, together with some newspaper and a dish of cream.

"He should have been killed," Mrs. Rofrano said cheerfully, "but he's just too lucky a pilot."

Everyone had gathered in the cafeteria—*everyone* being the pilots and mechanics, the community of flight that was Rofrano's Airfield—where the cook served up plates of sandwiches while Rofrano himself poured something that looked like whiskey from a plain, unmarked bottle. Irene had lost count of the number of rounds in Sam's honor, the old war stories, the strange, overblown laughter that seemed to come not from the whiskey, as that kind of laughter usually did—at least in Irene's experience—but from something else. Not that the whiskey wasn't helping.

Irene stuck to coffee and sandwiches. She stared at Sam, across the table, and said to Mrs. Rofrano, "I guess he learned all that during the war. How to land with a broken rudder."

"How to land with a broken anything, really. Look at him. You wouldn't know anything had happened at all, would you?"

"No, you wouldn't."

"What he needs is a real airplane. Not like that secondhand Lockheed he tried to fly to Hawai'i, but a new one with decent engines and modern design."

"I hear your husband's designed one."

"Did you?" Mrs. Rofrano plucked a piece of chicken from within her sandwich and popped it into her mouth. "I guess Sam spilled the beans about that. Well, it's still a prototype, but we like it just fine. Of course it would be ideal for Sam."

"He says it's too expensive."

"It *is* expensive to build a ship like that. Heaps and heaps of money."

"How much?"

"Thousands. More than he can afford, even with all the exhibition fees and the students and the movie stunts. That's why he entered that ridiculous pineapple derby last year."

Irene looked back at Sam, who held a cigarette in one hand and a glass of whiskey in the other. She thought how strange it was, to see the living Sam Mallory in front of her, a man of flesh and bone and three dimensions, who ate and drank and spoke and surfed and found small kittens in the sand dunes. He didn't seem to bear more than a passing resemblance to the Sam Mallory of last summer's ballyhoo.

"What would he do with an airplane like that?" she asked.

"Oh, he wants to do something big, like all the pilots, a groundbreaking flight somewhere. But the airplane's just the start of it. You need fuel, you need equipment, you need a million little things. You see that fellow over there, next to my husband? That's George Morrow. He's a publisher, crazy for flying. Word has it he's looking for the next Lindbergh."

Over the top of her coffee cup, Irene peered at George Morrow. He had dark hair, brushed straight, and slight, lean shoulders under a gray suit jacket and sharp navy tie. He was in serious conversation with Rofrano. He seemed to be illustrating some point with an arrangement of soup crackers on the table between them. His fingers made quick, impatient movements. Irene thought he looked immaculate and intent and nervous, like a man who never took a vacation. At the other end of the table, Sam leaned back in his chair and laughed aloud. He still wore his flight suit, stained with oil and blood; his hair was curling and wind-blown. The white bandage had the same effect as an eyepatch on a pirate.

"What about Sam?" said Irene. "He's a tremendous pilot."

Mrs. Rofrano leaned her chin on her hand, as if she were thinking this over, and then she raised her other hand and waved it. "George! Yoo-hoo!"

Mr. Morrow looked up from the soup crackers and stared in their direction, first at Mrs. Rofrano and then at Irene, squinting a bit.

Mrs. Rofrano moved to the empty chair to her right and patted the one she'd left, between her and Irene. "Come join us, George. I've got someone I'd like you to meet."

GEORGE MORROW SETTLED HIMSELF IN the chair between them like a pedigree cat. Down the table, Sam's laughter had vanished, and Irene, glancing his way as Mrs. Rofrano introduced her—*This is Miss Irene Foster, a friend of mine*—caught him staring warily at the three of them.

George Morrow offered his hand. "Morrow," he said. "Pleasure."

"This was Miss Foster's first flying exhibition," said Mrs. Rofrano.

"Is that so? What did you think of it?"

"I thought it was thrilling," said Irene. "I thought it was a magnificent example of piloting. Bringing in that airplane with a broken rudder."

"Ah." Morrow cast just a flicker of a glance in Sam's direction. "*Was* it broken, though?"

"Why, didn't you see? I mean, I don't know much about airplanes, but everybody said it was the rudder, that the rudder somehow broke during the flight."

Morrow had brought his glass with him. He tapped the side with his finger, lifted, drank, and set the glass down again. "Listen to me, Miss Foster. I haven't looked at the ship since he brought it in. For all

I know the rudder broke midflight, just as we saw, and Mr. Mallory brought it in by his fine piloting and the skin of his teeth. But I will say this. The public out there, the people who watch these things, what do you think they really want to see? An airplane looping the loop? A few thrilling aerobatic maneuvers? No. I'll tell you what your average spectator wants to see, in his heart of hearts. He wants to see a crackup. Like that derby out to Hawai'i, you saw what happened. Everybody living their nice quiet lives, working in some office or driving some delivery truck, they want to see something horrifying, something life or death, and the best pilots know that. The best pilots give them what they want."

Irene stared at his hand, which had lifted and settled the glass at least twice during the course of this speech, adjusting it one way and then the other. He had a funny way of speaking, an East Coast twang that spat out words like a machine gun, and like bullets the words were all precise, manufactured in advance, so you knew he had already delivered this speech many times. It took her a moment or two to realize what he meant by them.

"You can't be saying he crashed that airplane deliberately," she said.

"I'm not saying he did or he didn't. But all the money in this business comes from publicity. You've got to keep the public interested, or you won't make a dime. The books and lecture tours and racing prizes, that's all because the public wants to hear about your daring escapes and your gory crackups. You've got to do something new and exciting. If you want to keep flying, you have to feed the public."

"Feed the public." Irene rolled the words between her teeth. "But that's *your* job. You're a publisher, aren't you, Mr. Morrow? You feed the public."

"It is my privilege, Miss Foster, to *furnish* the public with inspiring stories of human bravery. Aviation happens to be at the vanguard of all that's daring and courageous in American manhood. They are the last remaining pioneers, these men, the last fellows willing to die to expand the frontiers of human capability."

"Those are some grand sentiments, Mr. Morrow. But what about womanhood? Isn't a woman capable of courage and daring?"

Morrow turned his shoulders an inch or two in Irene's direction, as if she'd finally said something worthy of interest. "Do *you* fly, Miss Foster?" he asked.

"No," she said. "Not yet."

"But you'd like to."

"Would you object if I did?"

"Not at all. I admire the courage and skill of our lady pilots every bit as much as that of men. Maybe more."

"Why *more*? Because you don't expect it?"

"No. Because there are no obstacles for a man to climb into a cockpit and learn to fly, except his own natural skill and courage. A woman who flies must battle not only the objections of certain backward elements of society but often the dictates of her own upbringing."

"Why, Mr. Morrow. Are you a *feminist*?"

"Of course I am. As every right-thinking man should be, in this modern age." He smiled at her, a remarkable display of white, square-toothed dentistry. "It's good business, after all."

Mrs. Rofrano laughed. "Everything's business to you, George."

"It's what makes the world go round. All a man needs to do is give the public what it wants, Sophie, and what the public wants now is *novelty*. It wants new heroes to worship. And if you ask my opinion, it's the age of the woman, right now." He stabbed his finger into the tablecloth. "The great story of our times isn't this Volstead business, it's the emancipation of the female sex."

"Do you really think so?" Irene said. "Do you really think the female sex is emancipated?"

"I think a woman can do whatever she wants to do, these days, whatever she dares to do. She can vote. Why, she can run for office herself. She can walk into a speakeasy and order herself a cocktail, if she doesn't mind breaking the law. She can show off her pretty ankles and drive a car and get a college degree and a job. She can race cars and fly airplanes."

"Hear, hear," said Mrs. Rofrano cheerfully.

Morrow lifted his empty glass, clinked it against Mrs. Rofrano's glass, and rose from his chair. "If you really wish to fly, Miss Foster," he said, straightening his cuffs and his tie, smoothing back his hair, "I hope most sincerely that you lay aside any reservations, any objections from friends and family, and simply do it. Now, if you'll be so kind as to excuse me, I'm afraid I was supposed to be in Pasadena an hour ago."

WHEN HE WAS GONE—AND THIS took some time, because George Morrow never left a room without shaking a least half of the hands inside it—Mrs. Rofrano slid back into her original seat and said, "Well? Are you going to follow his advice?"

Irene's coffee was cold. Her sandwich was nothing but crumbs. She looked down the table to Sam Mallory, who had long since returned his attention to the man sitting beside him. Sandy had finished her cream and found her way into his lap, one paw outstretched across his waist like a lover, and he stroked her small calico head with one hand and smoked a cigarette from the other. The glass of whiskey stood empty in front of him. The collar of his flight suit was unbuttoned.

"I don't know," Irene said. "Flying costs money."

"Most pilots I know don't let that stand in their way. They find the money, one way or another. They find a way to get in the air, whatever it costs them."

When Irene was nine years old, just before her mother got sick, she went with her parents to the Panama-Pacific Exposition in San Francisco. She saw the Tower of Jewels and the Palace of Fine Arts and all the other glittering exhibits, but what she loved best was the wooden roller coaster in the Joy Zone. The speed and the noise, the way it whipped you about. She made her father pay for ride after ride. When she got home, she set about building one in the backyard. It started on top of the treehouse her father had built, about twenty feet high in a eucalyptus tree. She nailed together wooden boards and fitted the rails to her red wagon. She still remembered the way it felt when she climbed into the wagon at the top of the track for the first time, staring down the curve to the ground. It was like the way you felt on your surfboard when a giant wave began to swell up beneath you, lifting you upward into the break, and you knew you were about to experience the ride of your life or else possibly break your neck, one or the other, no telling which.

"Yes," she said to Mrs. Rofrano. "I guess I know what you mean."

HANALEI, HAWAI'I

October 1947

MY SUITCASE IS already packed when I wake to brilliant sunshine. I packed it at three o'clock in the morning, after tossing in bed for hours, because I figured I might as well do something useful if I wasn't going to sleep. And it worked! When I climbed back into bed my nerves went still, as if the act of packing had flipped some switch inside me from on to off.

How my head aches. How stiff and sore the length of my body. I long for coffee, but that means going downstairs to face the desk clerk, so instead I wash and dress. It turns out the hour is only just past six o'clock, so I have plenty of time to make the boat to Oahu. I sit on the edge of the bed and stare at my reflection in the mirror. I'm wearing a white shirt and navy slacks, and a cardigan sweater knotted around my shoulders in case of draft. Underneath the collar of my shirt, the necklace lies against my skin. I guess I'll have to face Leo again, on the boat, but I figure he'll be busy at the wheel. When we arrive, I can slip away in the bustle, and Leo will go to visit his uncle at the hospital in Honolulu, on the other side of the island, and that will be that.

Now here's a funny thing. To think I was knocking bits with Irene Lindquist's own stepson! What a gas. What a way life has of connecting you by invisible threads with other human beings. On the other hand, how could I have guessed they were related? Leo's mother was a local girl, he explained last night as he buttoned his shirt, a native Hawaiian with whom Olle fell in love when he first arrived in Hanalei as a healthy young globe-trotting whippersnapper a quarter-century earlier. Leo was born seven and a half months after they married, or something like that. I didn't dare ask Leo how she died; at such a moment, it hardly seemed tactful. Anyway, he was already halfway out the door, rushing off to the Lindquist house to get the full story from his father and Irene, who had returned from Oahu once the doctors had stabilized Uncle Kaiko.

Uncle Kaiko. Of all the dumb luck in the world.

I rise from the bed and unlatch the suitcase. Buried between the shirts and the underwear, the small leather-bound diary has the electricity of an artifact. I smooth my fingers over the top and sides to remind myself that it's real, that Sam Mallory's fingers rested here, too, that he lived and breathed and requires some kind of justice.

The clock says a quarter to seven. Time to go.

I close the suitcase and lift it from the luggage stand. Pick up the matching leather satchel that holds my portable darkroom equipment, my notebooks, my hairbrush, my jar of Pond's cream.

The door creaks when I open it. The stairs creak too. I suppose they send some warning of my approach, because Irene Lindquist is already on her feet when I reach the foyer.

"Good," she says. "You've already packed."

LINDQUIST HAS LEFT HER BEAT-UP yellow truck at home today. Instead she's driving a fast little ragtop Buick, cherry-red, creating such a monumental draft that I can't hear a thing, and half the time I can't even see through my hair that blows every which way. We roar past the harbor. I catch a glimpse of the passenger ferry, two or three customers lined up at the gangplank, though not Leo in his sharp navy uniform, the one I tore off him yesterday evening. He's probably in the deckhouse.

The car curves up the bay and around the point, past Lumahai Beach of yesterday morning, until we come to a sprawling white house overlooking the ocean, surrounded by porches and flowering shrubs and a few clusters of mature palms.

"Nice place," I say, when she shuts off the engine.

"We call it Coolibah. You'll be staying in the guest cottage."

"Oh, I will, will I?"

"Not that I don't trust you, Miss Everett," she says dryly, "but this was the deal, remember? If we're going to be sharing secrets, I'm going to keep you where I can see you."

"*Are* we going to be sharing secrets?"

She opens the car door and removes her sunglasses. "Probably. Now collect your things and follow me."

It occurs to me, as I follow this legendary woman down the lawn to a cottage, that I have somehow lost the upper hand in this match and that perhaps I never had it at all. The cottage is tiny, and a fresh coat of white paint can't quite disguise its ramshackle character. Irene tells me, as she opens the door, that this was the original building on the property, when she bought it from some fellow who had thought to make a fortune in pineapples, and discovered too late that he had a brown thumb.

"We don't have many guests, so I'm afraid it's not all that up to date." She flips on a light, and boy was she telling the truth. There is an ancient canopy bed with a yellowing counterpane and two flat pillows, a dresser nobody wanted, a braided rug my great-aunt Mildred would call old-fashioned, a general air of dust and must. Even Lindquist looks taken aback. She inspects the interior of a Victorian wardrobe and frowns. "I suppose I'll have Lani come down this afternoon and freshen it up a bit," she says.

"Perhaps you might loan me that cat of yours, as well? I have a feeling I'm not the only inhabitant." I gesture in the direction of the baseboard, which sports a mousehole large enough for Mickey.

Lindquist pokes her head through a door. "At least the bathroom's new. Olle had the plumbers out last year, when his mother-in-law made noises about moving in."

"His mother-in-law? From his first wife?"

"Let's just say she remained a thorn in his side, even after poor Malina died. And of course she was still Leo's grandmother. Luckily for Olle, she met a man from the south shore before she could move in, and married him instead."

I run my finger along the edge of the dresser. "You know, I don't believe you mentioned a stepson."

"You never asked. Anyway, I try to stay out of Leo's business. He's a grown man. He doesn't need me meddling in his private affairs."

"Not the evil stepmother, are you?"

She folds her arms. "You know, you puzzle me, Miss Everett."

"Me? Why, I'm an open book."

"Call me vain, but I always thought that when somebody discovered me at last—and of course I knew somebody eventually would, I knew this blessed anonymity couldn't go on forever—it would be somebody who admired me."

"I admire you plenty."

"Really? Because I sense the opposite. I sometimes have the peculiar feeling that you hate me, Miss Everett."

"They're not exclusive, you know. You can admire somebody without liking her especially. Besides, I don't *hate* you."

Lindquist laughs. "What would you call it, then? Resentment? A general cussedness at me and the world?"

I sit on the bed, stretch back my arms, and cross my legs. "Nothing like that all. It's just that I've learned, in my years on this earth and especially behind the camera, not to trust the outward face a woman like you presents to the world. It's usually the opposite of what lies inside."

She nods. "Go on."

"And in any case, I'm here to learn about Sam Mallory. So you'll forgive me if I regard you as a possibly hostile witness. You've got your own reputation to protect, haven't you? So I can't allow myself to be blinded by that famous charisma of yours."

"Charisma?" She sounds genuinely bemused.

"Oh, you've still got it, believe me." I bounce one foot. "But I've got to remain objective."

Whatever the cramped dimensions of this little dump, whatever the antique mismatched furniture and the small, furry bedfellows, you can't deny it's got location. The morning sunshine streaks through the window. The window itself peeks toward the sea. In the silence that settles between Lindquist and me, the surf reaches in and says *rush, rush*. I could almost call it magical. I could almost start to like this place, and I've only spent five minutes. But isn't that the point? To make me comfortable. To make me woozy with contentment. She's no fool, Irene Lindquist. She brought me here for a reason, just as I've come here for a reason, and the question is, who will find out the other one's secrets first?

Lindquist stands and watches me with those stiletto eyes. Her silvery hair is still damp from the sea. The scar is on the shadowed side of her face, and the other side is taut and perfect. She glances at her watch, then the window. "Well, make yourself at home. Should be breakfast in the kitchen still, just ask Lani to make you up a plate. I'll be back in an hour or so."

"Are you heading back out on your surfboard or something?"

She smiles and reaches for the doorknob. "No. Just a very important errand. And when I get back, you'd better be ready to answer some questions."

As soon as the door closes, I jump from the bed and head for the window. Irene strides across the grass, all long legs and purpose, to greet a pair of towheaded children in prim school uniforms, streaking toward her from some back door, dragging their satchels. One is a boy, one a girl. I suppose they're about seven or eight years old, but then I'm not all that familiar with children. Lindquist kisses their blond heads and takes each little hand. She appears to be answering questions as she leads them to the Buick in the driveway. Children do ask questions, I know that much.

How nice, I think. A new brother and sister for Leo.

Another thing nobody bothered to mention to me.

AVIATRIX

by Eugenia Everett

(e x c e r p t)

March 1928: California

DURING THE DRIVE back to Santa Monica, Irene asked Sam Mallory question after question. She wanted to know about the mechanics of flight, how it was possible that so heavy an object as an airplane could get itself aloft and stay there.

"It's called lift," he said. "If you look at a wing sideways, it's not flat, is it? It's shaped like—well, like a teardrop. A teardrop, all stretched out. The wind flowing over it has to go faster than the wind underneath. So if you're going forward fast enough—pushing enough air around your wings—you get this force called lift."

He was driving with his left hand, which held a cigarette, and gestured with the right hand, curving his fingers and thumb to demonstrate the sideways shape of an airplane wing. Irene stared at the hand but also at Sam's face behind it, his animated eyebrows, his blunt nose, his hair whipping about in the draft.

"And then what?" she said

"Why, then you keep on flying. You keep on pushing against that edge."

"Which edge?"

"Between lift and gravity."

"Which pulls you back to earth."

He laughed. "Does it ever."

"Aren't you scared?"

"All the time. If you're not scared, you're not really alive, are you?"

"You're not dead, either."

"I don't know. There are a lot of ways to be dead," said Sam.

On Irene's lap, Sandy curled in a ball, purring so loudly that the vibration tickled her legs. They were coasting down Laurel Canyon all by themselves, and the air smelled of cigarettes and gasoline. Already the sun was dropping behind the hills. Irene thought maybe she should ask him about the war, about the various ways you could be dead, the various things that could kill you. But that wasn't what he meant, was it? Anyway, he didn't want to talk about the war. He didn't want to talk about the past, his or hers. So she asked about the future.

"And that's it? You're just going to fly stunts all your life, to keep yourself from getting bored?"

He crushed out the cigarette against the side of the car. "Until something better turns up. I guess I am."

For the rest of the drive, he was silent, or almost silent, answering Irene's questions with such a minimum of words, she gave up and played with Sandy instead, until they pulled up along the stretch of road where Irene's Model T had sat all day. The surfboard was still there, tethered to the roof, too heavy to steal. Sam asked if she needed any help with the spark plug, and she said no thanks, she'd changed a hundred spark plugs. But he stood by anyway, propped against the side of the car, playing with Sandy. The kitten had found a loose button on his shirt. When Irene straightened from the engine, Sam straightened too. She wiped her hands on a rag and said that about does it.

Sam took his handkerchief and wiped at some smudge on her cheek. "You're a real grease monkey, aren't you?"

"When I have to be. Thanks for all your trouble. And the spark plug."

"It was my pleasure," he said gravely.

"No, it was mine. It was—it was something else."

Over Sam's shoulder, the sun melted into the ocean. He tucked the kitten into the crook of his elbow and took Irene's hand. "I want to show you something."

He led her right to the edge of the ridge, so that the dunes piled up at their feet and the ocean spread wide. A couple of surfers met the waves that tumbled over and crashed into the continent.

"That," he said.

"That what?"

"*That's* what I want to do."

For an instant, she doubted him. She glanced sideways at his profile, which reminded her of a bird, the oceangoing kind, except that it was colored by the gold of the melting sun. Then she understood. "You mean Hawai'i again?"

"Farther than that."

"Australia?"

He nodded. "California to Sydney."

"You'd have to stop along the way."

"Yes, of course. I've got it all mapped out. All I need is the airplane and the dough."

"How do you get your hands on those?"

"Why do you think I keep flying stunts, Foster? Take up thrill seekers at five bucks each? Teach all those dumb accountants which way is up?" He set the kitten into the dune grass and lit a cigarette. "I've been testing Rofrano's new ship. It's just what I need. I mean, it needs some modifications, but it's the right ship, all right. The only problem is, it's going to cost thirty-five thousand dollars. Then you need the fuel and the equipment and all the permissions. So I need a sponsor."

"You mean somebody like George Morrow."

"Yes," he said slowly. "Somebody like Morrow."

"You know, I'd have thought Morrow would jump at the chance. You're a national hero, aren't you? He said it himself, it's the publicity he wants, that money follows publicity."

"But it's got to be the right kind of publicity," he said. "I didn't make it to Hawai'i. I washed up. Anyway, the public wants something new. That's what Morrow said to me, anyway."

Together they stared at the settling sun. Irene's palms were damp. She knotted her fingers together.

"I guess your wife will be wanting you home," she said.

For a moment, there was nothing but the sound of the ocean, crashing below them. A couple of screeches from a diving seagull. When Sam finally spoke, he seemed to pick the words with care.

"My wife lives up in Oakland. She hates Los Angeles."

"Oh."

"It's what she wants."

"Well, what do you want?"

Sam finished his cigarette, dropped it in the sand, and turned to her. "I want to see more of my daughter, I guess."

Irene stared at those serious blue eyes and thought, *Sam Mallory*. But it didn't match, this face and that one, the one in the newspapers last summer. She tried to remember what Mrs. Sam Mallory had said in those interviews. Irene was pretty sure it had been something fulsome. She remembered thinking that Mrs. Sam Mallory rather liked being Mrs. Sam Mallory, mother of Sam Mallory's small child, and played that role to its fullest. Something tickled her ankle. Tiny sharp teeth. The kitten. She thought of the white walls of Dr. Walsh's office where she worked as a receptionist, the air that smelled of antiseptic, the way the doctor brushed up against her in the dispensary. She thought of Sam's airplane rising to the sun.

She shaded her eyes and said, "I'll tell you what would be new."

"What?" he said.

"A woman."

II

▶ ▶ ▶

I decided that if I could fly for ten years before I was killed in a crash, it would be a worthwhile trade for an ordinary lifetime.

—CHARLES LINDBERGH, *The Spirit of St. Louis*

HANALEI, HAWAI'I

October 1947

THE POST OFFICE in Hanalei is the kind that does all kinds of business, including the sending and receiving of telegrams. After breakfast, with no sign of Lindquist spinning back up the road in her cherry Buick, I discover a bicycle in the shed and head into town.

I've already met the woman behind the counter, whose name I forget. The ancient nameplate on the counter reads LANALEE, if you look closely. I smile and ask if there's any reply to the telegram I sent yesterday. She doesn't smile back but she fetches the yellow envelope. Before she hands it to me, she says I'll have to sign for it.

"Of course," I say.

She pulls out the list of telegrams—it's not long—and I scribble my initials next to the entry at the bottom.

"Miss Eugenia Everett," she says. "I hear you're staying with the Lindquists?"

"Since five minutes ago. How did you know?"

"My brother is Mr. Lindquist's cousin by marriage." While I try to work this out in my head, she continues in a voice that grows more threatening by the vowel. "So Mr. Leo is my second cousin, you see?"

"I see."

"He's a fine boy, Leo."

"I'd have to agree."

"The Lindquists are good people. You're lucky to be staying with them. Mr. Lindquist, he went right out to Oahu on the morning boat to take care of poor Kaiko." She gives me this look that seems to lay all the blame for poor Kaiko's accident at my feet.

"How *is* poor Kaiko?" I ask.

"He has a punctured lung," she says, shaking her head, as if it were some form of incurable cancer and they might as well dig Kaiko's grave this minute. "Probably Mr. Lindquist will stay in Honolulu for some time. Mr. Leo too."

"Doesn't Leo have a job?"

"Family is family, Miss Everett. There's nothing more important. Here in Hanalei, we are all family. We would do anything for each other." She holds out the yellow envelope. "Here is your telegram."

"Thank you."

"Will there be a reply?"

"Probably not," I tell her, by which I mean *probably not here*, because I have the feeling that whatever ethics govern the sending and receiving of personal telegrams elsewhere in the world, they don't apply in Hanalei. At least that's what I understand from Miss Lanalee. (By now, I've read the nameplate on the counter.)

ABOUT A MILE UP THE road, I stop the bicycle and tear open the envelope. The telegram was sent last night from this fellow I know at the Associated Press.

SENT HONOLULU CLIPPINGS AIRMAIL STOP ARRIVE DAY AFTER TOMORROW HANALEI POST OFFICE CARE OF YOU STOP COST MINT STOP THIS HAD BETTER BE GOOD STOP BILL

I swear aloud, stuff the telegram back in my pocket, and climb back on the bicycle.

BY THE TIME I RETURN to the white house called Coolibah, Lindquist has returned from taking the children to school. She sits in a wicker chair on one of the porches—lanais, they call them—with a large pot of coffee. I set the bicycle against the railing and climb the steps.

"You're perspiring, Janey." She gestures to the other chair. "Would you prefer water or coffee?"

"Coffee's all right, thank you."

"How was your telegram? Good news, I hope?"

My hand, pouring the coffee into the cup, veers off to the left. Lindquist clucks and reaches for a napkin. I blot the spilled coffee and fill my cup.

"I won't be boring and ask how the devil you knew about the telegram. That rat Miss Lanalee, I guess."

"She's very protective. They all are."

I sink onto the wicker sofa. "I have a friend at the AP who's helping me with research, that's all. He doesn't know what it's about, never fear."

"Are you sure of that? Never trust a newsman, I always say."

"Well, you *would*, wouldn't you?" I reach for the cigarettes in the pocket of my slacks. "I asked him to pull some clippings on your flight to Australia. It's always useful to read the news as it actually unfolded."

"Not all the details in those newspapers turned out to be true, you know."

I hold out the cigarettes. She shakes her head.

"But before we get into all that," she continues, "I wouldn't mind knowing who snitched on me. It's just not possible you tracked me here without somebody to point the way."

"Haven't you heard? A journalist never reveals his sources."

"But it *was* a person, wasn't it?"

I finish lighting the cigarette and take a long drag. "It was both. A wee birdie told me about a certain airplane that made its way out of Spain in May of 1937. It was up to me to figure out where it flew."

"Was this the same birdie that told you where to find Sam's wreckage?"

I zip my lips. "Enough about me and my birdies. I'm here, that's all. I tracked you down, and frankly I'm surprised I was the first. It was all there, once you knew where to look. Spain to Paris to Newfoundland. Across Canada. Once the trail went cold in Vancouver, why, I just had to use my intuition."

"And your intuition said Hawai'i?"

I held up my hand and ticked off the fingers. "It's remote. It's got some of the best surfing in the world. And it's got sentimental value for you, doesn't it? Your first flight together. Hawai'i's where it all began."

"My flying career, you mean."

"Not just your flying career. You and Sam." I reach for the ashtray, and her eyes follow me keenly. "Am I right?"

Lindquist sets down her coffee cup and rises from the chair. She walks to the edge of the lanai and holds her hand up to her brow, as if she's looking for something out to sea. Her hair is dry now, curling softly around her ears. She sticks her other hand in her pocket and says, "You know, I never did understand why people cared more about this idea of romance between me and Sam than about the flight itself."

"Don't be naïve. Of course they did. Sex is what makes the world go round. The human species wouldn't survive without it. And when one of the parties happens to be already married . . . well. You can bet those newspaper editors were rubbing their hands with glee."

She turns and moves her hand to the side of her face, fingering the scar. "Well, they were all wrong. I wasn't in that airplane because I was in love with Sam. I was in that airplane because I wanted to fly, and Sam was the best pilot in the world."

I stub out the cigarette, even though it's only half finished. "You're fooling yourself, sister. I've seen the photographs of the two of you. You're goofy for each other."

"Of course we had feelings for each other. We had a partnership, a friendship. But he was already married. He had a family. I understood that."

"You might have understood that," I say, "but I don't believe Mallory did. He was always a bit of a ladies' man, wasn't he? That poor wife of his."

Lindquist props her hands on the railing behind her and crosses her ankles. "Yes," she says flatly. "His poor wife."

"You don't agree?"

She looks out to sea again and back. "Miss Everett, I wasn't the only one who showed a different face to the world than the one I showed in private. Sam Mallory hid more of himself than I ever did. He *gave* more of himself, until he lost who he was, and I will never forgive myself that I cared so much about what the world thought, I let him go. I let him go to wander alone, right when he needed me most."

Again she puts her hand to that scar on her face. *Finally,* I think. Finally we're getting somewhere.

"But first, there was Hawai'i," I suggest.

Lindquist pushes herself off the railing and walks back to me, except this time she plops herself right down on the wicker sofa, so close our knees knock together. I stare in horror at this point of incidental contact.

"I am going to tell you a story," she says. "A story about a man and a woman who both married the wrong people."

AVIATRIX

by Eugenia Everett

(e x c e r p t)

July 1928: California

I N SUMMER, THE ocean current was considerably warmer, and dawn tumbled over the distant San Bernardino Mountains at about half past five o'clock. Irene liked to arrive at the beach before Sam did, though it took some discipline. Sam was an early riser, and he lived only a short way up the coast, in a tiny house overlooking the water.

But on the morning of the thirtieth of July, when Irene pulled over onto the shoulder of the road next to the beach, there was no yellow Nash parked there before her. When she emerged from the wooden shack in her surfing costume, it still hadn't appeared. Nor did Sam arrive down the cliff path while she rode the waves, or when she came off the water and headed back up the hill into the full force of the sun, and Irene understood that he wasn't coming this morning. Sometimes he didn't. Some days he rose and drove straight for the airfield. Still, she would have liked to have a private moment with him, on this particular morning. She loitered another minute or two before she changed back into her dress and drove home.

By six thirty she had turned off Wilshire Boulevard onto Selby Avenue, where she lived with her father—when he was around—in a modest bungalow that encompassed two bedrooms and a clipped, rectangular lawn of tough grass. Out front, there was a lemon tree, on which Irene lavished most of her love and care. The houses on Selby all looked alike to Irene, so she aimed for the lemon tree and turned left into the short drive so she could park the Model T in the lean-to garage she'd built with her father last year.

This morning, however, the garage was already occupied. Irene reached down for the brake lever just in time. She stared at the curved rump of the car in front of her and rattled her thumbs against the steering wheel, until the engine, starved of fuel, started to sputter and miss its beats. She shut off the ignition and climbed out. The surfboard she removed carefully from the back and set in its place at the back of the garage, next to the workbench.

She entered through the side door, which wasn't locked. "Dad?" she called out.

"In the kitchen, pumpkin!"

Irene smoothed back her hair and turned right into the kitchen, where her father sipped coffee at the wooden table. Mr. Foster stood up and opened his arms. Irene stepped into his embrace and kissed his cheek, then turned her own cheek to be kissed.

"This is a nice surprise," she said. "You must've set out early from Victorville."

"I wasn't in Victorville. I was out in Nevada. Reno way. Drove through the night so I could eat breakfast with my best girl." He sat. "Weren't out surfing, were you?"

"Sure, I was. Nice morning like this one." The blue enamel coffee-pot sat on the stove behind him, keeping warm. Irene had already taken a cup and saucer from the cabinet. She poured her coffee, added a tea-spoon of sugar, stared at the swirling liquid as she stirred it in. The heat felt good on her fingers; she didn't realize how cold they were.

"How were the waves?" asked Mr. Foster.

"Waves were good. Big, slow rollers, coming in northwest."

He nodded. "Could maybe join you tomorrow, if you like."

"Maybe," Irene said.

He motioned to the other chair. "Sit down a bit and have coffee with me."

"Can't. I've got to be at work in an hour. I can fry you an egg, if you like."

"Why, I'd love an egg or two," Mr. Foster said, as if the idea never occurred to him.

So Irene fetched the eggs from the pantry, fetched the bread to make toast. Mr. Foster made no move to help, although he could make his own breakfast perfectly well, when Irene wasn't around to do it for him. He made conversation instead, that was his contribution. He told Irene about this fellow in Reno, how he might want to buy Mr. Foster's new idea, the patent for the thingamajig—Irene wasn't really paying attention, hadn't really kept up with her father's latest gadget—for possibly a lot of money, Mr. Foster wouldn't say how much, didn't want to get her hopes up. But the fellow was pretty serious. Bit eccentric, lived all by himself in a ranch way out of town, rich as Midas.

"How do you know?" asked Irene. "How do you know he's that rich?"

"That's what people say."

Irene slid her father's eggs on the toast—over easy, that's how he liked them, yolk gushing all over the place as soon as you pricked them with your fork—and handed him the plate. He reached for the salt.

"Go on," said Irene, so she wouldn't have to talk, and Mr. Foster went on. He told her about the drive, how he figured to save the money for another night at the motor lodge and set out at nine P.M. over the Sierra Nevada, tire went flat right away in the Truckee Pass, another tire blew out near Modesto. But oh, it was a beautiful night to be out driving. The air was clear and dry, so you could see the whole Milky Way spread out in the southwest sky. Not another soul on the road, not until the sun poked up and the ranchers started their rounds. "And the smell, Irene, you know that smell. The sweet, dry grass and the dust and the sage."

"It's a good smell," she said. By now, she'd come to sit at the table across from him, drinking her coffee. The sound of his voice, it was the sound of her childhood, and it wasn't all bad. Hank Foster could spin a good story. Whatever his faults, he could make you smell the air and taste the fried chicken and laugh at the poor sucker at the drugstore, whether or not any of those things had actually existed.

Her father pulled out a pack of cigarettes. "You mind?"

Irene waved her hand. Her father pulled out a cigarette, lit it with a match from a matchbook that said Lincoln Motor Lodge, and took a drag or two. Irene went into the sitting room and brought back an ashtray.

"Say, now," said Mr. Foster. "Here's an idea. I hear there's an air show in Burbank this afternoon."

Irene dropped the ashtray next to her father's coffee cup and stared at the end of his cigarette. "*What* did you say?"

"An air show. In Burbank. Fellow's gone and laid out an airfield there, just the other side of the Hollywood Hills. They'll be testing out some new planes, flying stunts. You should come with me."

Irene snatched her cup and saucer from the table and took them to the sink and turned on the faucet. The water streamed over her fingers and swirled around the blue leaves of her mother's second-best china. "I have to work," she said.

"Call in sick, why don't you."

"Anyway, you should sleep. Driving all night like that."

"Oh, I can stay awake a few more hours. I was just thinking, out there on the highway, I don't spend near enough time with you. Leave you all alone for days. Who knows what kind of trouble you might be getting up to?"

Irene thought she might be having a heart attack. Her hands shook as she washed out the cup, the saucer, and dried them with a dishcloth, one by one. She heard the clink of cutlery on china, the mouthy noises as Mr. Foster chewed his eggs and swallowed.

"Said in the newspaper, that fellow Sam Mallory's going to be demonstrating his new airplane, the one he's flying to Sydney, Australia, next week."

"Is that so?"

"That's so. You remember that business, last summer. The fellow who crashed his airplane in the open ocean, flying to Hawai'i in that pineapple derby, and they picked him up eleven days—"

"I remember," said Irene.

"Well. Now the poor sucker's going to fly to Sydney. What do you think of that?"

"I think it sounds exciting. I wish him luck."

"That cup's about dry, I think."

Irene took the cup and saucer to the cupboard. Her father drank his coffee and wiped his mouth. "Say. Have you heard he's taking a woman with him?"

"Is he? Well. That's news, isn't it?"

"Said so in the newspaper. She's going to be copilot and navigator. The funniest thing. Her name's Irene Foster."

Irene shut the cabinet door.

"That's some coincidence, isn't it?" her father said.

"I guess it's a common enough name."

Mr. Foster had finished the eggs. He took a last corner of toast and swiped it on the plate to gather up the last streaks of yolk. Popped it into his mouth and winked at her.

"You know something, pumpkin? I always did think airplanes would be right up your alley."

AFTER BREAKFAST AND A BATH, Irene drove her father to Burbank in his car, a green Model A, not because he'd been drinking (though she was pretty sure he had) but because she knew he liked her to drive. He had taught her himself, once she was thirteen and could reach the pedals. He dozed most of the way to Burbank, even though Irene put the top down in the heat and allowed the scorching California wind to blow right through him. His eyes opened just as Irene swung the car into the row of vehicles already lined up in the airfield parking lot.

"This is it?" he said.

"It's not much, but it's home."

He raised his eyebrows at that. Irene expected him to ask a dozen questions, how long had she been flying, how had she found the place to begin with, who had taught her to fly, why she'd kept the whole business from him all these months. But he only nodded, as if he understood perfectly, and reached for the door handle.

The airfield was already filling with people. They had billed this afternoon as the first public demonstration of the new Rofrano Centauri, but in fact Sam and Irene had already made several test flights. Without fanfare, they had flown it together down to San Diego and back, Sam in the cockpit and Irene in the navigator's seat just behind him, while the earth lay flat and fascinating as a map beneath them.

But nobody else knew anything about that. The fanfare, the crowds now gathering at the airfield, they had nothing to do with the inside of the Centauri's revolutionary aluminum fuselage, which contained only Sam and Irene.

IRENE SPOTTED SAM RIGHT AWAY. He stood next to the hangar, hands on hips, grinning his wide-mouthed grin before a semicircle of newspapermen and airplane fanatics. The California sun blazed away on his hair. His face had tanned bronze to match. As he spoke, he caught sight of Irene, hurrying past with her father, and his eyebrows went up. Irene shrugged and continued on to the cafeteria, where she sat her father down with a cup of coffee.

"I thought I was going to see an airplane," he said.

"You'll see it, all right. I can't let you in the hangar, that's all."

"Your own father?"

"Rules are rules. A hangar's a dangerous place if you don't know what you're doing."

"Now, pumpkin—"

"Drink your coffee, all right? I'll let you know when the excitement starts."

WHEN SHE RETURNED TO THE hangar, Sam still held court outside. She nodded to the security guard and slipped in by the side door. There were no windows on this building, nothing to allow passersby any glimpse of the machine that lay inside. Irene flipped on the lights, and out of the blackness appeared this beautiful silver bird.

Now, it's easy for the modern reader to forget what a revolution the Rofrano Centauri caused in American civil aviation. These days, she hangs by cables in a gallery all her own of the California Museum of Flight in Sacramento, viewed and photographed by thousands every year. Her iconic lines decorate any number of books and articles and motion pictures on the history of airplanes. But in July of 1928, nobody had seen anything like her before. Irene thought she looked like a giant winged bullet. Her fifty-four-foot wings were molded directly on the aluminum skin of a fuselage thirty-eight feet in length. There was not an edge or a corner on her. Her two enormous propeller engines threw blades the length of a grown man. She could hold three hundred gallons of fuel in her regular tanks, and another hundred in an auxiliary tank. On paper, the Centauri could fly for over three thousand miles at a hundred and fifty miles an hour before she had to land and refuel.

Of course, flying in the air was not like flying on paper. You had wind, for one thing, blowing you this way and that way according to its own unpredictable formula, and you had navigational error. Hidden under Irene's bed at home were several books on navigation, both by sea and by air, dead reckoning and celestial and radio methods. (The Centauri was equipped with a two-way radio and a backup receiver, as well as an emergency beacon.) She had studied them all, had practiced them over and over during those flights to San Diego and to Oakland, out to sea and back again, and Sam said she was a natural, that her mind had an intuitive grasp of the geometric logic that was navigation.

Still, the Pacific Ocean was a gigantic landscape, a third of the distance around the globe itself, barren and featureless without end, and one tiny airplane was like an ant adrift on the Sahara Desert, looking for islands the size of rocks. A mistake of a fraction of a degree could send you hundreds if not thousands of miles off course.

The door rattled behind her.

"Who's the fella?" asked Sam. "Looks a little old for you."

Irene hesitated a second or two. "My father."

"No kidding! Why didn't you introduce me?"

"Because we have work to do."

"Where'd you stash him?"

"In the cafeteria, putting himself on the outside of a cup of coffee. He's what you might call the worse for wear."

"I see."

That was another thing about Sam. You didn't need to explain yourself; he let you decide just exactly how much to tell him, or not. He didn't force you to share your sorrow. He didn't force you to share his. He laid his hand on the skin of the Centauri, near the seam of the cockpit door, and said, "Weather forecast looks about right."

"What about the ship?"

"I spent two hours this morning with Rofrano, looking over every inch of her. Not a hair out of place. She's ready."

"And you?"

Sam crossed his arms and turned on his side, leaning against the plane. "I've been ready for months. You?"

"Course I'm ready."

"You don't sound sure about that."

"Of course I'm sure!"

"Not turning yellow on me, are you?" He said it with a grin, as if to say *Of course you're not yellow, you of all girls.* "Anyway, you brought your old dad to see you off."

"That was an accident. He turned up this morning from some kind of business trip, high as a kite. He'd seen the papers. I couldn't leave him home."

"Jehosephat, Irene. You haven't told your *father?*"

Now Irene crossed her arms. "I wrote a letter, is what I did. You can say things right in a letter. I figured I'd mail it right before we take off."

"*Irene Foster,*" he said, shaking his head, "you've got more sand in you than any man I've met. You're going to fly across the entire Pacific Ocean in a metal bird in the sole company of a bum like me, and you don't care to tell your own father about it?"

"I don't, no. I didn't want him anywhere near this place, and especially not those newsmen out front. Now it's too late, I guess."

Sam turned his back against the fuselage. Irene stared at his cheekbone, his closed eye, his tense jaw, his matted hair, and asked if he had slept here in the hangar last night. Without moving, he said he had. Nerves, he said. Me too, she told him. So he cracked open one eye and lifted up one corner of his mouth and asked why she hadn't joined him?

Irene could have answered this question all kinds of ways. Plenty of people already thought that she and Sam were having a love affair, after all. The newspapers hinted it so brazenly that the history books, written in the years to come, would take some form of romantic entanglement between Irene Foster and Sam Mallory as fact. Could you blame them? Put two attractive, red-blooded people, man and woman, adventurers both, together inside a closed cockpit, and naturally some form of chemistry was bound to brew between them. Stood to reason! Anyway, you could just tell, when they were together. That banter, for one thing. The way they looked at each other. And that time she picked a piece of lint from his sleeve? That was the kicker. Everyone in the press room agreed this was something a woman would only do to a man with whom she was intimate.

Then there was the matter of the wife. No sane newspaperman was going to print anything to besmirch the sanctity of the American marriage, but that Mrs. Samuel Mallory was something else. She would sit down for an interview in her prim, middle-class parlor in Oakland, arranging herself and her small, angelic daughter, whose hair was like a cloud of pale gold, on the sofa in their white dresses and ribbons. She was a handsome woman, there was no doubt about that, dark haired and almond eyed, but you could see at a glance that she must've been ten years older than her husband, and those ten years had begun to tell.

She would relate to some reporter how she'd been the widow of one of the other pilots in Mr. Mallory's squadron, and how she and Mr. Mallory comforted each other after the war, and how that friendship grew into love. What was that? Did she *trust* her husband? Of course she did! She trusted him absolutely! She believed Miss Foster was a woman of integrity, passionate about flying, and Mr. Mallory was a man of honor. She had no objections whatsoever to the proposed flight. Mr. Mallory always carried a navigator on these adventures. If that navigator happened to be a woman, why, these were modern times, weren't they? A man and woman could surely labor together as friends, without allowing any base inclination to intrude between them.

The reporter would nod earnestly and take all these words down in his notebook, which he repeated verbatim, without a hint of irony, in his story the next day. It was for the reader, after all, to make of Mrs. Mallory what he would. It was for the reader to determine whether a man should fly all the way to Sydney, Australia, in the company of some doll he wasn't married to, and whether his wife was a fool to let him do it. Frankly, the newspapermen didn't care, one way or another. The story made good copy, that's what they cared about.

As for Irene herself, she hadn't even met Mrs. Mallory. In all those weeks since March, when Mr. Morrow had first agreed to finance the Sydney expedition—all those weeks while she and Sam had planned and trained and flown together in almost daily proximity—Sam's wife hadn't once come to visit. Instead, Sam flew the repaired *Papillon* north to Oakland once every month or so, in order to keep their affairs in order, and to spend time with their daughter, Pixie. He stayed for two or three nights at a time. As for what he did there, Irene never asked. She didn't feel she had the right to ask.

Which was why, when Sam cracked open one eye and lifted up one side of his mouth and asked Irene why she hadn't joined him in the hangar last night, she just turned away to inspect the line of rivets along the wing.

"Figure we spend enough time together already, Sam Mallory," she said.

AT ELEVEN O'CLOCK ON THE morning of the thirtieth of July, 1928, the doors of Hangar C at Rofrano's Airfield in Burbank, California, drew open and the Centauri rolled out like "a giant silver torpedo," as the *Orange County Register* phrased it. The metal sides flashed in the sun. The photographers swarmed her, bulbs popping. Mr. Rofrano appeared out of nowhere in a pale suit and a Panama hat and spoke to the reporters. Irene watched all this from the window of the cafeteria, where she was sharing a final, anonymous cup of coffee with her father. The air was hot and filled with grease, with the clatter from the kitchen, but Irene didn't mind. To her it smelled like home.

"That's your ship, is it?" Mr. Foster whistled. "Mighty fine bird."

"You see that man in the Panama hat? That's Mr. Rofrano. He's the one who designed her."

"The moneybags?"

"No. Mr. George Morrow, the publisher, he put up the money for the airplane and the flight expenses."

"Say, where is he? I'd like to shake his hand."

"You can't," said Irene. "He's on a steamship. On his way to Australia to meet us."

"You must be setting off soon, then."

"As soon as we can."

"That's swell. You be sure to tell me the big day. See you off in style." Mr. Foster swirled the last of the coffee in his cup. He fiddled the cigarette between his fingers. The sun was nearly overhead, and the light came like dust through the windows, so he didn't look as haggard as he had that morning. Irene remembered when he was the handsomest man she had ever known, when he filled any room with magic. Now his hair was gray and thinning and his skin had begun to sag. He talked too loud. He made grand, clumsy gestures as he spoke. At some point, he'd developed this habit of sticking complicated words into conversation, so that strangers would understand he wasn't just any old drunk, he was a smart drunk. He was so conscious of his own dilapidation, so ashamed of himself, and until this moment Irene hadn't even realized. She was too busy being ashamed of him herself. She laid her hand on his arm, and he looked at her in surprise. Even as a child, Irene had never just touched a person for no reason.

Irene hadn't finished her coffee, but she set the cup in the saucer and drew her other hand away from her father's arm. "I'd better be off, I guess, before they send a posse out for me." She leaned in and kissed her father's cheek. "I'll see you around, Dad. Don't go poking your nose into anything, now."

Mr. Foster, a little dumbfounded, put his hand to his cheek and sank back in his chair. "All right, then. You have yourself a time out there, pumpkin."

SOPHIE ROFRANO MET HER JUST outside the cafeteria door. "Irene! There you are. I've been looking all over."

"Is something the matter?" Irene asked.

"Not *matter,* exactly. I just wanted to warn you in time."

"Warn me? About what?"

"Bertha's here."

"Bertha? Who's Bertha?"

Sophie hissed in her ear. "*Sam's wife.*"

"Oh, right. Well, she's got a right to come, I guess. He's her husband."

Sophie stopped and turned Irene to face her. "Now, listen to me. I haven't said anything because I didn't think it was my place. It's your affair, not mine."

"*Affair?* That's a funny word to use."

"My dear," said Sophie, full of sympathy, "anyone can see how it is, between the two of you."

"We're good friends, that's all. We've got a rapport, like friends do."

Sophie still held Irene's upper arms, just below the shoulders. She stared into Irene's eyes for a moment or two, frowning, until Irene shrugged and the hands fell away and Sophie crossed her arms over her chest. "All right. Whatever you say. I'm sure you're just as pure as Ivory soap, the two of you. But you need to know a little something about Bertha Mallory, Irene."

"What's that?"

Sophie tilted her head in the direction of the Centauri, where the crowd of reporters and photographers milled about under the blazing sun. "What she says to those fellows, those newspapers? What she says to you or me or anybody?"

"Yes?"

"Don't believe a word of it, that's all."

WHEN THEY REACHED THE AIRPLANE, Irene spotted Bertha Mallory. You couldn't miss her, really. She stood right next to Sam, as light and feminine as a fairy, resting her arm through the crook of his elbow. She wore a white dress that swished a few inches below her knees, white shoes and stockings, a straw cloche hat with a navy blue grosgrain ribbon around the crown, and no cosmetics at all except for a swipe of cherry lipstick. Though she wasn't tall, she held herself straight, as if still balancing that schoolgirl book on her head. The cloche hat cradled her face just so. Her eyes were dark and lovely, especially as they turned toward her husband and glowed with pride, while the little girl held tight to her other hand.

". . . simply couldn't be any more proud of him," Mrs. Mallory was saying. "Flying's always been his life. We're just a poor second, Pixie and me."

"Now, that's not true, darling," said Sam.

"Yes, it is. And it's perfectly fine! When you're married to a genius, gentlemen, you have to understand that his work *must come first*. You have a duty to the world to give his ambition full rein, to take care of hearth and home and let him do all those great things the Almighty means him to do."

Then Mrs. Mallory squeezed her husband's arm and smiled at him worshipfully, while he offered a small, tight grin to the cameras. Irene stuck her hands in the pockets of her trousers. She had changed into her flying costume, similar to Sam's, which was military in style, a khaki tunic and a Sam Browne belt over cavalry-style breeches, long golf socks, shiny leather shoes. Her hair was scraped back in a snug bun at the nape of her neck. She and Sophie stood at the fringe of the crowd, arm in arm.

"All right, all right," said Sam. "You've got your snaps. We've got a flight to prepare for. Has anyone seen Miss Foster?"

"Oh, yes," said Mrs. Mallory. "Miss Foster. Where is she? I'm so eager to meet her."

"She's right here!" Sophie called.

The reaction was like a frenzy. The details of Miss Foster's identity had been kept so carefully quiet until now, she was like the lost city of Eldorado. Nobody in the press had ever spoken to her or even seen her. A few of the older, more cynical hands in the newsroom had figured she didn't even exist, that she'd been created for publicity purposes, or was actually a man after all. So you can imagine the fuss when Irene waved her hand and said *Good morning, gentlemen!* It went something like this, except the questions came all at once:

Miss Foster! Miss Foster!

Any thoughts on the upcoming flight, Miss Foster?

Is it true you're only just meeting Mrs. Mallory today, Miss Foster?

All right if we take your photograph, Miss Foster?

"Why, yes," she said. "I don't see why not."

A dozen flashbulbs exploded around her. She looked right between them all and found Sam's bemused face and smiled at him, so that all those photos that appeared that very day in the afternoon and evening editions showed a cheerful, happy face framed by a leather aviator's cap, far more pretty than anybody expected. Underneath these photos, Miss Foster was quoted variously about how excited she was to travel across the ocean, how impressed she was with Mr. Mallory's skill and tenacity as a pilot, how eager she was to prove herself, how proud to represent the ambitions and capability of women everywhere. Just about everybody reading a newspaper that evening or the next morning thought that Sam Mallory was either the luckiest man alive or else the unluckiest, depending on his or her opinion of the sanctity of marriage.

When Irene was done answering the questions of the reporters, Irene made her way to Sam Mallory and his wife. Mrs. Mallory smelled of some delicate, floral perfume that Irene didn't recognize. Sam said, "Irene, I'd like to present to you my wife, Bertha. She wanted to join us here at the airfield today to see what the fuss is all about."

This introduction was clearly meant for the reporters clustered about, taking down every word. Irene took Mrs. Mallory's hand and said, "I'm so pleased to meet you at last, Mrs. Mallory. You must be awfully proud of Sam."

"I am." Mrs. Mallory squeezed Irene's hand, just tight enough. She stared into the space between Irene's eyes. "My goodness, aren't you the prettiest thing! Sam, isn't she just lovely?"

The reporters laughed. Sam said gallantly, "Not only lovely, but a fine pilot and navigator. Miss Foster has the coolest nerves you've ever met."

"I can see that." Mrs. Mallory released Irene's hand. "Of course, I have every faith she won't need them, not with Sam Mallory at the controls."

"We'll be flying eight thousand miles across the open ocean next week," said Irene. "I naturally expect every hazard to come our way. But I am confident we will overcome the difficulties of such a challenging voyage and prove to the world what modern aviation is capable of."

The reporters nodded and scribbled in their notebooks.

"You can see why I feel so fortunate to have Miss Foster as my flying mate," said Sam. "Having her aboard is no publicity stunt, gentlemen. You won't find a better partner for a trip like this one, man or woman. What she lacks in experience, she makes up for in courage, natural skill, and the instincts of a born pilot."

Mrs. Mallory wasn't looking at Irene any longer; she gazed serenely across the assembled reporters and took up her daughter's hand again. She spoke as if reciting from a prepared script, which probably she was: "I am grateful that my husband has secured the assistance of such a single-minded professional for his endeavor. I know Miss Foster understands how much Pixie and I depend on her skill and endurance. Our very hearts and lives are at stake."

"Believe me," said Irene, "so are mine."

More laughter.

"All right, all right," said Sam. "I think it's about time we gave you gentlemen the dope on what this bird can do. I don't know if you've noticed, but our mechanics have been busy fueling the plane while we've been shooting the breeze out here. Our equipment's aboard, ready to go. Miss Foster? Do feel like heading up in the air and taking a turn above Los Angeles?"

"I certainly do, Mr. Mallory. I couldn't be readier."

Sam turned to his wife and kissed her good-bye—more flashbulbs— and then bent to lift Pixie in his arms. Sam's daughter had a round face and a light sprinkle of freckles across her nose, like any cherub. She put her small arms around her daddy's neck and cuddled his face against hers, and how those photographers loved her for it! Sam whispered something in her ear, and she nodded her bright blond head. Irene turned away when her eyes started to prickle.

There at her elbow she found Sophie, who enveloped her in a hug.

"Safe flight, my dear one. Where's your father?"

"Still inside the cafeteria, I think." Irene reached into the inside pocket of her tunic. "Here. Give him this. I meant to mail it, but since he's here in person . . ."

Sophie took the envelope. "You'd better hurry inside that airplane, then. Before he reads it."

"I will." Irene turned to Sam, who was showing Pixie how to wave to the photographers. "Are you going to quit mugging for those cameras and get us in the air, or what?"

The crowd laughed. One of the photographers called out, "Aw, come on, Miss Foster. How about one of the two of you?"

Irene checked her watch—eleven fifty-six—and lifted her chin to judge the distance to the cafeteria. "Just a minute or two, I guess."

So Irene stood next to the gleaming ship with Sam, first waving, then looking at each other, then hands on hips casting each other the old challenging gaze—a novelty pose, they called it—and finally Irene sitting on one wing, in between engine and fuselage, while Sam stood next to her knee. That was the shot that made most of the papers, the shot that made the history books and the encyclopedias. Sam propped his elbow on the wing's edge, right next to Irene's leg, and they looked sunny and at ease with each other, like they were setting out for a picnic instead of the final test flight of a prototype aircraft they planned to fly across the Pacific Ocean together.

At last Irene nudged Sam, and Sam said, "All right, boys. You've had your fun. Now it's time we had ours."

He put his hands around Irene's waist and slid her back to the ground, and nobody took a photograph of that. In those days, a respectable newspaper simply wouldn't publish it.

BY THE STANDARDS OF 1928, the Centauri was a large, powerful aircraft. Still, it was not luxurious, certainly not in comparison to the modern passenger airliner. For one thing, when you were traveling thousands of miles over the ocean in 1928, you didn't carry so much as a pound of unnecessary weight. The main deck was made of aluminum and left bare. The seats had no cushions. The air was hot and smelled of oil and gasoline. It was a special grade of fuel made especially for airplanes, and Sam and Irene weren't planning to waste a drop of it.

The enclosed cockpit of the Centauri was larger than that of most existing airplanes, but not wide enough to accommodate both of them. Irene sat behind Sam, in the navigator's seat, which had its own window and communicated with the pilot by means of a pulley cable they called the clothesline, even though their seats were only a yard apart and she could reach out and touch him if she wanted. This was because the two giant engines threw off so much racket, you couldn't hear anything else inside that airplane but the relentless beat of gears and propellers. Nor did you want to. Without that noise, you were in trouble.

Irene checked her box of notepaper and pens. She checked her charts and equipment, her compasses and sextant and smoke bombs that measured wind drift, her celestial maps, her Mercator projections of the North Pacific and South Pacific, ocean currents indicated, prevailing winds noted. She had recalibrated all three of her magnetic compasses an hour ago, but she checked them again now, because a mistake of a sliver of a degree would mean missing those volcanic specks known as Hawai'i by hundreds of miles. She turned on both radios and settled her headset over her ears, tuned the agreed-upon frequency and announced herself into the transmitter. A crackle came back from the transmitter in the airfield's control tower, then Mr. Rofrano's baritone, eternally calm. *Rofrano tower. Centauri, acknowledge.* Another voice joined them from the United States naval station at Long Beach. Everyone in place, everyone at his designated mark. A whole legion of supporting actors in this drama, the choreography of which had been arranged by George Morrow.

In the cockpit, Sam started the right engine, then the left. The propellers thudded, measured at first, then faster and faster until the thuds all merged into a noise like a colossal insect. The ship faced north, so there was no glare from the sun to disturb their preparations. Not a word passed between them, by air or by paper. Sam knew exactly what she was up to, and Irene knew what Sam was up to, almost as if her own hands performed his tasks and her own eyes looked through that cockpit window and surveyed the airfield, the sky, the landscape, the wind sock that drooped atop the control tower.

As they pulled away from the hangar area and onto the landing strip, Irene couldn't help looking out the window at the crowd that followed them, forming and re-forming in a swarm, like ants. Already Irene felt detached from them. They belonged to the earthbound world. The slim tube of the Centauri contained Irene's world. Everything that was real and important.

ELEVEN MINUTES LATER, THE CENTAURI lifted off from Rofrano's Airfield in Burbank, California, on an east-southeast bearing, banked south, and crossed directly over the city of Los Angeles before reaching the edge of the Pacific Ocean in the sky above Long Beach. Irene saw Catalina Island crawl past on the left, surrounded by a hundred tiny white scratches, the wakes of motorboats. She informed the Long Beach naval station of their position, altitude, and heading.

Once they reached eight thousand feet, Sam leveled off and turned his head to wink at Irene, as if they'd just gotten away with something mischievous. The radio crackled. Irene turned her attention to the receiver, while Sam turned his attention to the controls. It was the Long

Beach naval station, acknowledging her transmission and wishing them Godspeed.

Because the Long Beach naval station already knew what Mr. Rofrano was now announcing to the reporters gathered in the makeshift press room of the airfield cafeteria, while they ate their grilled cheese sandwiches and smoked their cigarettes, passing the time before the scheduled return of the Centauri from its test flight.

The Centauri would not return to Burbank that day, after all. Sam Mallory and Irene Foster had just begun their historic flight to Sydney.

HANALEI, HAWAI'I

October 1947

WHAT I DIDN'T tell you about that Spanish fellow, the one who told me where to find Mallory's wreckage, was that we were lovers. Or maybe you've guessed? I mean, it wouldn't be out of character for me, and in times of war we are all prone to do reckless things, like take lovers we know will probably die.

We met at an airfield outside Paris, not long after the Allies retook the city from the Nazis. Those were heady days. The journalists all found digs at the Hotel Scribe (and they say the press doesn't have a sense of humor) where we proceeded to drink the bar dry. That's another story. I did try to refuse the assignment to photograph Allied airplanes landing and taking off from this French airfield, which only last week belonged to the Luftwaffe, but that didn't work out so well and Raoul Velázquez de los Monteros was the officer assigned to show me around.

Naturally I was curious about the name. It turned out he'd flown for the Republican Air Force during the civil war in Spain, and when the game was up in early 1938, he fled over the Pyrenees to France and offered his services to the French air command, vowing revenge on Fascists everywhere. Two years later, when the Fascists overran France, he was forced to flee again, this time to join the Royal Air Force, and that was more or less how he wound up escorting an American photographer around the Orly Air Base, ten miles southeast of Paris, on a beautiful early September day in 1944.

You will comprehend that Velázquez did not think much of lady journalists and even less of lady photographers. Moreover, he had been seconded to this American base as a kind of liaison officer after surviving an improbable number of combat tours and was not especially happy in that role. He was gruff with me, which I found endearing. He was not exactly handsome and not exactly tall, but he had this oddly graceful stockiness to him, and a brusque, efficient manner that softened by degrees as we toured the hangars and the tower, and he told me what I could photograph and not photograph. At the time, I wore my brown hair cropped short and no cosmetics at all—maybe a swipe of lipstick, when I could find any—and I must have looked like a different species from the sumptuous Polish mistress he kept in London. (Although possibly she kept him; I was never quite clear on that point, and tellingly he had no money except his RAF pay.) Still, despite all that military bristling we ended up sharing dinner at a cheap little café near the air base, where the delighted proprietor kept refilling our glasses with all these magnificent vintages he had kept hidden from the German occupiers for four long years—resistance takes many forms, you understand—so that one thing led to another and we ended up in bed. *C'est la guerre,* as the French say.

I was so pleasantly surprised! Not only was Velázquez a generous lover, he had the gift of stamina, even on the outside of two or three bottles of wine. We met often over the next several weeks. I used to snuffle the fur on that barrel chest of his and soak up the pungency of him. My Spanish bear, I called him. He taught me the Spanish phrase for that, which I forget. Anyway, one night I mentioned to him that I was breaking a rule of mine, sleeping with a pilot, and he demanded to know why I wouldn't sleep with pilots when after all they were the best lovers in the entire world, and eventually we got around to the subject of Sam Mallory. He went quiet and reached for his Gauloises, a habit he had picked up when he fled to France, and smoked without speaking for some time. I had far better sense than to interrupt him. When you've been chasing photographs as long as I have, you know when your subject is about to reveal some vulnerable secret.

"I knew Sam Mallory," he said at last. "He taught me how to fly at the beginning of the war, at the fighter school in El Carmoli on the southern coast of Spain."

AT THREE O'CLOCK IN THE afternoon, Lindquist breaks off to go collect the children from school. She seems to have forgotten that I'm not to be trusted, or maybe she thinks that these things she's told me, these confidences, have won my loyalty. Before she leaves, I ask if I can take her picture, and she doesn't even hesitate. *Go ahead,* she says. She's vain enough to turn the right side of her face to the camera, however.

When she leaves, I turn restless. I read the notes I scribbled in my notebook. I rise from the wicker sofa on the lanai and return across the short stretch of lawn to the cottage, which has been faithfully cleaned by Lani, the housekeeper. I toss the camera and the notebook on the bed and take the key for the suitcase from my pocketbook. The key fits; the lock clicks. But when I lift the lid, I know right away that someone's been inside, someone who has been very careful to leave everything as she found it.

Nothing's missing. My clothes are all there, my underthings, my few vanities. I am not so foolish as to keep anything valuable in this suitcase. I've been to war, I've lived in various godforsaken corners of the world, some lawful and some not, and the first thing I do when I come to rest in a new lodging, I find a hiding place for what's important. And you see? Wasn't I right?

I close the suitcase and go to this hiding place of mine—I'm not telling you where it is—and reach inside. To my relief, all is where I left it. The leather diary, thank God, and underneath it, the smooth, cool handle of my pistol.

HER LAST FLIGHT   115

LINDQUIST'S CHILDREN BARREL ACROSS THE lawn an hour later, making straight for the kitchen door and the cookies on the other side of it. Lindquist calls on them to stop and say hello to Miss Everett, our guest.

At the word *guest*, they pull up like a pair of ponies and turn to me with amazed expressions. "We've never had a guest before," says the girl, who's an inch taller than her brother and presumably the elder.

"No doubt." I stick out my hand. "Janey Everett. I'm a photojournalist."

"Is that a journalist who takes pictures?" the girl says.

"Exactly right. I've always said the kids are quicker than the grown-ups."

"I'm Doris." She shakes my hand. "And this is Wesley. He's only seven."

"Oh, he'll grow out of that soon enough. Hello, Wesley. Come along, my hand's not going to shake itself."

Wesley giggles and shakes my hand.

"They are handsome specimens," I say to Lindquist. "You must be awfully proud. Do they do anything interesting?"

Doris says, "I play the piano and jump my pony. Wesley's pretty dull, though."

"I ride horses too!"

"Not very well, and you can't jump yet."

"Chip off the old block, isn't she?" I observe to Lindquist.

Lindquist shoos them toward the kitchen door. "All right, all right. Go get your cookies and change into your swimsuits. We're going to take Miss Everett down to the beach and teach her to surf."

"Don't worry!" I call after them. "She's only kidding around!"

A HALF HOUR LATER, I'M standing in the sand with a surfboard while Doris and Wesley demonstrate the essentials of surfing to my thick understanding.

"You see? It's easy!" Doris calls from the top of a wave.

"Come on out! The surf's low today!" adds Wesley, just as he spills gracefully from his board into the water.

"Aren't you worried about sharks?" I ask Lindquist.

"Oh, the sharks always gather where the fish are, near the upswells. We don't see any around here." She lifts her surfboard under her arm. "Not often, anyway."

The water, I'll admit, is delicious. Most of my experience with oceans has been of the frigid kind, and it's a nice surprise to stick your toe into a tropical bath instead. I don't know much about the mechanics of waves, how they form, what physical features of headland and reef and island shelf, what fickle variations of wind and tide and current turn some ordinary ripple into a behemoth worthy of riding into eternity. I do understand that each beach has its own particular wave, like a voice or a signature that might vary in each iteration but still presents a form anybody can recognize. The waves rolling on this beach are happy, gentle waves. Not the kind to set your pulse racing, unless you're a beginner like me.

"All right," says Irene. "The first thing is to swim out just past the breakers, where the waves form."

It occurs to me, as I choke and stroke my way through the surf—yes, actually *through* those giant breaking waves to get to the relative peace on the other side—that Lindquist might actually be trying to kill me. If some landlubbing photographer dies while attempting to surf, the local authorities will deem this incident a foolish, unfortunate accident, won't they? There will be some inquest, some noises of regret and humility in the face of nature's might, and everyone will go on with her life. Except the dead photographer in question, of course.

The board is heavier than I expected, an awkward thing to drag along as you paddle and gasp and paddle some more, as you eventually start paying attention to the rhythm of the waves, so you can make your progress in the gaps between them, and then gather your fortitude and dive straight through the arc of water as it breaks over you. I hear the children laughing somewhere, Lindquist calling out some motherly instruction. My head reeks of brine. Then I emerge from the other side of an especially big *nalu*—that's the Hawaiian word, the children have informed me, smug little bastards—and the world is blue and calm, the waves mere swells, the sun hot and white above us.

"Now get on your board," Lindquist says. "Just straddle it, that's right, like a horse. Paddle a bit, so the current doesn't carry you out too far. There's not much rip on this beach, so it's good for beginners."

I don't quite understand the meaning of this word *rip*, but it does sound menacing and best avoided. The paddling I could grow to like, however. The ocean rustles like a living creature underneath me—and here I look downward, to make sure there's not *actually* a living creature underneath me—and carries me on its back. Ahead lies the white beach, the jungle, the pale buildings on the ridge. Above it all, the sky without a cloud.

"Watch the shore," calls Lindquist. "That's how you get your bearings. The waves will carry you one way, so it's up to you to counter the drift."

I think I understand her. The board rises and falls with the incoming waves. I lie down on my stomach and rest my cheek against the slippery wood, so that my whole body moves in this delicious rhythm, surging and then idling, the sun baking me from above. Some small effort's needed to keep from wandering off, but even that's beyond me. Haven't I struggled against the current all my life? Haven't I fought and scrapped and survived? And all along there was another way. To lie on a strip of wood and allow the ocean to determine my course; to simply exist, lulled by the infinite strength of nature. Probably this is the meaning of heaven. You search and search, you think you glimpse it from time to time, in the aftermath of lovemaking or the bottom of a bottle of good champagne, and always it eludes you. Until now, perhaps? Here on the surface of a pacific ocean?

A round of screeching from the tadpoles. I lift my head and see a wall of approaching water. Lindquist yells something. *Just hold on to your board,* or something like that. *Start paddling.*

I look to the kids, who lie on their tiny stomachs like me, brown arms paddling for Jesus, sweet little lungs screaming out delight. I do what they do, except my screaming is not delight. It's just terror. This monster rises up behind me and gathers me up in its mighty jaws and spits me to shore in a jumble of board and bone and hair and salt water, and somewhere in the middle of it, I lose the desire to live. I just figure I'll die, and what I know and all I've seen will die with me, and maybe that's what God intended all along.

AVIATRIX

by Eugenia Everett

(e x c e r p t)

July 1928: Hawaii

THE ISLAND OF Oahu lies about two thousand five hundred and sixty miles by air from Los Angeles, assuming you travel the shortest possible route over the curve of the globe. (That's a hundred miles farther than New York, for reference, although a thousand miles shorter than Lindbergh's historic flight to Paris.) The average cruising speed of Octavian Rofrano's revolutionary new twin-engine Centauri was about a hundred and forty miles an hour, which represented a 30 percent improvement over the single-engine Lockheed Vega, considered the fastest plane aloft in the middle of 1928. Divide one by the other, subtract three hours to account for the rotation of the earth, and Sam and Irene could expect to arrive in Honolulu at six-thirty the next morning, or approximately eighteen and a half hours after taking off.

Eighteen and a half hours is a long time to spend in an airplane, especially without stops along the way to stretch your legs and smoke a cigarette. Moreover, the Centauri was flying over the Pacific Ocean, which presented the same featureless, mirage-inducing landscape as a desert. The monotony was not improved by the weather that day. Shreds of fog appeared about a half hour out of Burbank, which soon turned to a bank of cloud so high and thick, Sam pulled back the stick and sent the Centauri climbing all the way up to twelve thousand feet, which was as far as they could safely go without requiring additional oxygen. They now flew above the clouds, but without the ability to drop smoke bombs to measure the wind drift, Irene couldn't rely on dead reckoning to determine their position. Instead, she tuned the radio to the frequency on which the navy broadcast its navigational beacons. As long as the pings came back in a steady rhythm—as long as Irene could still hear those pings—they were on course.

To pass the time, she wrote a note to Sam.

Radio beacon steady. Hold course.

He wrote back, *Nice weather we're having.*

Here at twelve thousand feet in the air, the temperature was cold, about twenty degrees Fahrenheit. Both Irene and Sam had already put on their scarves and their fingerless gloves, and still Irene's fingers were almost too stiff to hold the pencil and scratch out a reply.

First she wrote, *Nice to meet your wife at last.* She crumpled that up and threw it in the wastebasket.

Next, she wrote, *Improvement expected. Clear skies currently in Hawai'i.* She crumpled that up too.

Finally: *Your daughter takes after you.*

Sam pulled this note from the clothesline and held it between his finger and thumb for some time. Irene looked over his shoulder. There was a photograph stuck into the instrument panel, a snapshot of a small, towheaded girl wearing a large bow in her hair. Irene couldn't tell if Sam was looking at her note or the photograph, or both at once.

After a minute or so, Sam picked up his pencil and wrote on the back of Irene's note.

Better she turns out like you.

IN A WELL-BUILT AIRPLANE LIKE the Rofrano Centauri, ably piloted in decent weather with adequate navigational guidance, fatigue was the chief danger. Every pilot had his own method of dealing with this condition. Most favored coffee. Others appreciated the stimulant effect of chewing gum. Singing was popular, or (among the pious, anyway) the recitation of Bible verses, or (for the mathematically minded) the solution of complex equations. In the account of his famous Atlantic crossing, Lindbergh claimed to resort to propping up his own eyelids.

Now, Sam and Irene were fortunate to share this burden of staying awake during their audacious voyage across the Pacific. They had filled several Thermoses of coffee and packed some sandwiches, though not many because nothing sent you to sleep so quickly as a full stomach. Since Sam flew the airplane, it was Irene's job to supply cup after cup of java, and also to look the other way when this gluttony reached its inevitable conclusion. (A pair of milk cans, if you have to ask.) She was also supposed to pass notes every ten minutes, to which Sam was supposed to answer back. After six hours of steady and uneventful flying, however, Irene had run out of both technical observations and small talk.

She wrote, *Good idea to tell press this was test flight.*

Sam replied, *Live and learn* and handed back his empty coffee cup. Irene filled it and passed it on, then poured herself a cup of coffee and wrapped her frozen hands around the mug. Sam had told her about the start of the Dole Derby, about Lindbergh's flight and the chaos of departure. The throngs of press and spectators that nearly caused disaster. He'd insisted on this misdirection, and he'd been right. Why, the excitement over the supposed test flight was nutty enough; imagine if all those reporters had known they were leaving for Australia that very day! It was unnerving, the idea of all that mass attention directed on the two of them.

Irene set down the cup and leaned down to retrieve one of her maps from its case on the floor. But her hand didn't encounter the metal edge of the map case. Instead, it sank into a nest of warm, soft fluff.

The fluff moved, jumped into Irene's lap, and started to purr.

By now, Sandy was maybe seven or eight months old and had grown into a large cat, a diligent mouser, who considered Hangar C her personal dominion and Sam Mallory her personal servant. She looked up at Irene and stretched one lazy paw over the side of her lap. She had a narrow, pointed face and a pair of tawny eyes, which conveyed both affection for her human subjects and an insuperable right to occupy whatever space she pleased.

Irene reached for the notepaper and wrote: *Stowaway*. She clipped the note to the clothesline and ran it forward. Sam glanced left in surprise; the next note wasn't due for several minutes yet. He read it, frowned, and looked back. His mouth made a round, panicked hole.

Sandy, on the other hand—Irene could have sworn the cat grinned back at him. It was a love affair between the two of them—unequal, naturally, in the face of Sandy's obvious superiority of status—but a love affair nonetheless. From Irene's lap, Sandy jumped to her accustomed place on Sam's shoulders and started to lick his leather cap. Then she draped herself comfortably and went back to sleep.

AS DAWN APPROACHED, THE CLOUDS thinned and then disappeared altogether. The black ocean spread beneath them, split apart by a cold white moon. Irene's head was now intolerably heavy. She thought about Lindbergh propping open his eyelids. She took her pencil and dug it into the back of her hand, just to create some sensation, any kind of stimulation to her nerves. The airplane began to dive. Irene looked at Sam and saw that Sandy was gone and Sam's head was bent to his chest. She lunged forward and grabbed the stick.

"Wake up!" she yelled in his ear, but she couldn't even hear herself. Still, the jostling woke him. Sam took the stick back and shook his head a little. Irene sat back in her chair and hunted for the Thermos of coffee, but it was empty. There was only one Thermos remaining. Irene opened it and poured some coffee into Sam's cup, although it wasn't that hot anymore, just warm. She nudged it into his hand and he drank. His eyes were wide and staring. Sandy wandered up, having completed a routine patrol of the premises, and sniffed at the box of sandwiches. Irene unwrapped one and fed the cat a few delicate bites of chicken. She poured some water into a coffee mug so that Sandy could drink.

When the cat was satisfied, Irene put her headset back on and turned the volume as high as it would go. Faintly the pings of the radio beacon came to her, just a hair off. Irene wrote a note to Sam: *Adjust bearing two degrees south.*

Sam nodded. The ship banked slightly and righted itself.

Irene calculated their position. They were now only three hundred and seventeen miles from Honolulu, or should be. She wrote another note.

Two and half hours left.

Then, *You OK?*

Sam handed back the empty coffee cup and read both notes. Sandy was back on his shoulders now, grooming her long fur in preparation for another nap, cleaning Sam's leather cap. He glanced back to Irene and lifted his left fist, thumb pointed upward.

THEY RAISED OAHU WITH STAGGERING precision, at a quarter past six in the morning. Sam saw it first. He nudged a nodding Irene in the shoulder and pointed out the cockpit window. Irene saw a smear on the horizon and rubbed her eyes. When she looked again, it was still there, surrounded by the salmon-pink reflection of the sunrise behind them.

Together they stared at this miracle, this mountain rising out of the ocean. Of course, Irene could not yet confirm that this was Oahu itself, instead of one of the neighboring islands—Kauai to the north, or Molokai or even Maui to the south—but that didn't matter. They had plenty of fuel left. They had found Hawai'i like a speck of dust on the great Pacific. When at last the distinctive shape of Diamond Head grew clear from the window, she wrote a final note to Sam: *Diamond Head sighted to south-southeast. Begin approach to Rodgers Field.*

HANALEI, HAWAI'I

October 1947

WELL, I'M ALIVE after all. Coughing and sputtering, drenched and tumbled, on my hands and knees where the foam washes up, surfboard missing, swimsuit almost torn from my body, but I guess that counts as living, since I'm aware of it. *Cogito ergo sum*, as the philosopher said.

My stomach heaves, and out comes about a quart of the Pacific Ocean.

A pair of long, elegant feet appear to my right, then the bottom edge of a surfboard as it plants in the sand. Dimly, I hear the laughter of children.

"Well done," says Lindquist, without irony. "Now get out there and do it again."

LINDQUIST IS THE KIND OF mother who believes in routine, which means dinner at six o'clock sharp. The children are sent to the kitchen to help Lani prepare the food and set the table. I wander into the library in search of Olle's liquor cabinet—Lindquist, it seems, doesn't touch alcohol—and discover several bottles of fine old Kentucky bourbon whiskey, which gives me a new affection for old Olle. While I'm savoring a sour, I hear some commotion from the driveway, the putter of a small motorcycle and Lindquist's voice calling out to somebody, who answers back in a voice not unfamiliar to me.

I look out the back window and consider the distance to the guest cottage.

"Janey," says Lindquist, when she appears at the library door a moment later. "Look who's come for dinner."

MINDFUL OF MANNERS, LEO'S BROUGHT a couple of bottles of wine to dinner at his stepmother's house, even though he knows she doesn't drink. "You and Janey can share them," she tells him. "I'll just stick to water."

Naturally, the children adore him. He's their brother, after all, and they've known him all their lives. They pepper him with questions about Uncle Kaiko.

"Aw, you know Uncle Kaiko," he says. "He woulda checked right out of the hospital this morning if Dad hadn't held him down. He likes the morphine, though."

"I thought you were going to stay there overnight," I say.

"I thought so too, but the fellow who was supposed to cover for me ate some bad clams at lunch, so I had to take the afternoon boat back after all."

"What a shame."

"I thought so too."

"Did Olle say how much longer he means to stay in Honolulu?" asks Lindquist.

"Surgery went all right, but the doc wants Kaiko to rest up a few more days. I guess we'll see. Dad might come back early, though, if Kaiko drives him crazy enough. But enough about all that. Kiddos? How do you like having a houseguest around here?"

Doris leaps at the opening. "We taught Janey how to surf!"

"Miss Everett," says Lindquist.

"Oh, you can call me Janey. We're practically related, since you just about killed me this afternoon."

"Aw, I'll bet you were a natural," Leo says.

Wesley jumps from his chair. "A big wave took her under! You shoulda seen it, Leo! She about drowned!"

"Sit down, Wesley," his mother tells him.

Wesley sits, sort of, but his arms keep demonstrating the massive arc of the wave that was nearly the death of me. "It came over like this! She missed the top and just went head over—head over—" He's laughing too hard to go on, the little brat.

"She looked like a drowned rat," Doris says helpfully.

Leo looks at me. "You all right?"

"Perfectly fine, thank you."

"So?" he says to Doris. "Then what happened? Did she pick herself right back up and get back in the water?"

"Yes, she did," I tell him.

"Only because Mama made her," Doris says.

"Like riding a horse," says Lindquist. "You fall off, you get straight back on again. And then she did very well. We'll make a surfer of her yet."

I drink the wine. "I'm afraid I'm not planning to stick around that long. But I appreciate the thought."

Leo falls quiet. The conversation turns to school, about which I have some opinions, because it's awfully satisfying to have opinions about other people's affairs, don't you think? Lani brings in dessert, which is some kind of pound cake dressed in pineapple sauce, and then Lindquist shoos the children off to help clear the table and bathe and change for bed. As I said, a mother who believes in the healthfulness of routine, or else she has another design in mind when she exits the room on some motherly errand, and Leo and I are left alone to contemplate each other across the table.

He rises and divides the remaining wine between my glass and his.

"Not staying long, you said?"

"I'm here on business, I'm afraid. Isn't that the very first thing I told you, the other night? *Are you here for business or pleasure,* you asked me, and I said *Business,* plain as day."

"Irene says you're writing a book."

"Well, Irene's right. I'm writing a biography of Samuel Mallory. The pilot? He taught your stepmother how to fly."

"Yes," Leo says. "I know."

"I should hope so. He was one of the greatest pilots of his time. So I've come to talk to your stepmother about him, since—well, since I suppose you could say she knew him best. Didn't she?"

Leo pushes away his wineglass and leans forward to fix his eyes on mine. "So listen. I think it's time we got something straight between the two of us."

"I think that's a fine idea."

"I don't hold it against you, sleeping with me to get to my stepmother—"

"To be fair, I didn't know she was your stepmother."

"Doesn't matter if you knew or not. You wanted something out of me, and you got it, and no harm done. We both had a real nice time. No hard feelings. I just want to make things absolutely clear, though, for the future. If you do a single *thing* to hurt Irene, I mean if you cause her the smallest amount of misery—"

"Don't be ridiculous."

"Because she's been through hell already, and she's got the kindest heart in the world, and I know Mallory meant the world to her. I don't want her having to relive all that. It's in the past."

"I appreciate your concern for her, Leo. I really do. But she agreed to speak to me. I wouldn't be here if she didn't. I told her exactly what I wanted from her, and she said yes. She wants the story told. She wants the truth told. And sure, sometimes it stings a little, when you bring up all the old memories. Like lancing a boil, as they say. But in the end, we all feel better when the truth is out there in plain sight. Nobody likes a secret."

"That's a cute speech, Janey. But you didn't answer my question."

"I didn't realize you'd asked one."

"Can you promise me you won't hurt her? And I don't mean lancing some damn boil. You know what I mean. If you use her the way you used me—"

"Believe me, I won't do *that*. Not unless she invites me, anyway."

He brings his fist down on the table, hard enough that the wine sloshes in its glasses. "You tell her the truth and nothing but the truth. So help you God. That's what I'm saying. You come to her clean. She gets to decide what she tells you and doesn't tell you."

I spit in my palm and hold it out to him. "Promise."

He stands up and clasps my hand. "All right, then."

His grip is strong. He doesn't pull back, and neither do I. We stare at each other across the table. From somewhere upstairs comes the sound of a child calling *Maaaama!*

"You're staying in the guest cottage, is that right?" Leo says.

"That's right."

He nods and releases my hand. "I'll walk you back."

IF YOU'RE THINKING LEO HAS any designs on me, now that we've reached our little accord, you'd be wrong. We walk across the lawn in silence, though I'm crackling with electricity. When we reach the door, he stops. He must have gone home first before he came to dinner, because he's changed out of his sea uniform and now wears a white shirt and pressed trousers, a navy blazer, a plain blue tie, none of which I can make out in the darkness. Just the reflection in his eyes of the lights from the main house.

I touch his fingers. "I don't suppose you had time to stop at the drugstore, while you were in Honolulu?"

He pulls the hand away and gathers it inside the palm of the other one, behind his back. "I'm afraid I didn't have time. Good night, Janey."

He turns and starts to walk back across the lawn.

"You were lying, then," I call after him. "You do have hard feelings."

He stops and turns back to me. "I wasn't lying to you, Janey. I understand you better than you think. I just think it's best if I stand back a little, from now on. Sometimes you have to keep watch from a distance or you don't see things as clear as you should."

So he walks away, and it's strange to see. It wasn't supposed to hurt.

AVIATRIX

by Eugenia Everett

(excerpt)

July 1928: Honolulu

WE FORGET, DON'T we? We are seduced by the ease of airliners today, the punctilious way they make their rounds, like milkmen. We forget what a feat it was to cross the Pacific from California to Hawai'i, what a test of equipment and ingenuity, of mechanical skill and navigational skill, of pure luck, of courage most of all. We forget how dazzled we were by those with the guts and the ability to make these flights. How we worshiped them as heroes, and by worshiping warped them into something else. Poor Irene. Poor Sam. By the time the Centauri's wheels kissed the Hawaiian ground and rolled to a stop, it was already too late. They could not turn back. They could not foretell that in that instant, their old lives had been picked up, side by side, by a giant wave that was hurtling them onto an uncharted shore.

TWO KNOWN PHOTOGRAPHS STILL EXIST of the gala dinner in Honolulu on the night of July 31, 1928, celebrating the safe arrival of Sam Mallory and Irene Foster on the first leg of their landmark flight to Australia.

In the first photo, Sam hands Irene out of the rear seat of the Hispano-Suiza limousine that delivered them from the Moana Hotel.

He's wearing a tuxedo, she's wearing the evening gown provided for her by George Morrow, a long, pale, gauzy confection made especially by a Hollywood costume designer, whose name is now lost to history. Sam's left hand holds her left hand, and his right hand disappears at the small of her back. Despite this physical contact, there seems to be no particular intimacy between them. Their faces point toward the crowd, to the various municipal officials and local business bigwigs, not toward each other. Sam Mallory is simply a gentleman helping a lady from the back of an automobile. This photograph was reprinted in hundreds of newspapers across the United States and even around the world, and nobody had the nerve to suggest—at least in print—that there was anything untoward about their association.

In the second photo, which was recently discovered in the archives of the Associated Press, Irene stands at the podium, flanked by the territorial governor on one side and Sam on the other. She speaks into the giant microphone. Her expression is both passionate and exhausted. Her eyebrows form sharp, eager peaks. Her hands grip the lectern on each side. To her left, Sam Mallory stares up at her with an absorption that might be interpreted as surprise, or rapture, or merely an intense interest in what his flying partner had to say that evening. Whatever this expression meant, however, it wasn't indifference. It was not gentlemanly concern. If you were Mrs. Sam Mallory and opened up your early-edition newspaper on August first to find *this* photograph instead of the one that actually appeared there, the one taken outside the Hispano-Suiza, you would have excellent cause to drop your cup of morning joe and say to yourself, *Uh oh*.

But while a photograph may tell a thousand words, it doesn't tell the full story. It's an instant, a snapshot, a single frame of a lengthy motion picture. A sentence lifted from a novel. Irene, of course, had no idea what emotions painted Sam Mallory's face as she made her speech in the hotel ballroom that evening. She was exhausted, and she still couldn't hear very well, and hadn't even imagined she would be called on to speak. She had done her duty already! She'd shaken all the hands and said nice things to everybody about Hawai'i and the hotel. She'd expressed amazement at the suckling pig, the sweetness of the pineapple. When the speeches began, she sat back and figured her work was done. Sam rose and delivered a spirited address—or so it seemed, though she couldn't make out the words—which she dutifully applauded while checking her wristwatch.

It was Sam who nudged her shoulder on his return. "Irene? Your turn."

"Me?"

"They want you to speak."

Irene opened her mouth to say, *Aren't you the one who's supposed to speak?* But the room was silent, everyone was looking at her, there wasn't time to argue. Sam rose and helped her out of her chair. She made a quick, nervous gesture to smooth back her hair, to straighten the lei on her chest. As she approached the podium, the vibration of applause met her ears, if not the sound itself. She smiled and laid her clasped hands on the edge of the lectern. Everyone was smiling. A flashbulb went off in the corner of the room. She thought, *What in the devil have I got to say to these people?*

IN THE OLD DAYS, WHEN Irene's mother was still alive, when Hank Foster's drinking was just a feature of him and not the ruination of him, Irene's parents used to have friends over for dinner. Hank Foster was very good at dinner parties. (Irene's grandparents would say that dinner parties were about the only thing their son-in-law excelled at.) Irene sat at the top of the stairs in her white flannel nightgown and listened to the goings-on in the parlor and at the dinner table, and it was clear that Dad was the star of the show. He wasn't the only one who spoke—the best actors know how to play off the supporting roles—but he was the one you wanted to hear, he was the one who made you listen and laugh and think and sometimes cry, who sent you away at the end of the evening with that warm, well-fed, optimistic buzz that said, *Now that was a darned good party.*

Still, Irene was an analytical child, then as now, and as she got older she started to wonder how he did it. What was the secret to his style, how did he keep everyone pitched forward and engaged? Irene compared her father to her teachers at school, who just rattled on about facts and figures, names and dates, and nobody gave a damn. So why did you give a damn when Hank Foster spoke? Because he didn't explain his ideas in *lectures.* He explained them in stories. He made everything human. He made you *experience* his ideas. She asked him about it over breakfast the next morning, and he laughed and agreed. *Tell 'em a good story, I always say.*

Now it was Irene's turn. She stood in front of two hundred and twenty members of Honolulu's best bigwigs and their tanned, expectant wives, everyone straining to hear what this remarkable woman, this aviatrix, this Irene Foster had to say.

Tell 'em a story, Hank Foster said in her ear.

So Irene opened her mouth and talked about that first day surfing with her father, and how it was terrifying at first and then you started to learn the rhythm of the ocean. How, on the way home, her father spoke about the great Hawaiian kings and how you couldn't rule over other men unless you could master the giant waves of Waikiki and Kahalu'u. So these feats, which some might consider quixotic, are in fact vital to humankind, she said. Someone has to go out there and do them, to prove that they can be done, to plant in every breast, man and woman, the yearning to surf, to fly, to dream.

She spoke for less than ten minutes, and since she still couldn't hear very well and hadn't rehearsed anything—hadn't even imagined she would be called on to speak—she remembers babbling on about the importance of aviation to the future of mankind, and her gratitude to Mr. Mallory and Mr. Morrow for this exhilarating opportunity, and her hope that women around the world would take some inspiration from this flight and consider flying as a possible hobby or even career.

She was shocked, later, to read accounts of this short speech as an "electrifying prophecy" and a "call to arms for those who believe that womanhood's best days are ahead of her." Shocked at the thousands of letters she received from women and girls around the world, the tears, the gratitude, all of which seemed addressed to someone else, some public icon who was not Irene at all.

AS FOR SAM, HE RODE back to the hotel with her in silence. Irene figured he was tired. She was tired too; she was thoroughly exhausted. She had forgotten the flight, she had forgotten Sam's wife and Sam's little daughter, she had forgotten just about everything she ever knew. They parted in the hotel lobby—their suites belonged to opposite sides of the Moana, somebody's pointless notion of propriety—and Irene hardly took time to undress before she staggered into bed, where she slept for an untold block of hours before opening her eyes to stare at the ceiling fan that dragged in circles above her and wonder where the hell she was.

Then she remembered. She was in Hawai'i.

She sat up. The room was dark, the curtains shut tight. It might have been any hour, it might have been noon the next day, but some instinct told Irene the sun hadn't yet risen. The air was warm and damp and smelled of flowers. Irene should have left the window open to the breeze coming off the ocean. She reached for her watch on the nightstand and discovered it was half past four in the morning. No wonder she was awake! In Los Angeles, it was half past seven. Her brain jumped and sizzled like an electrical circuit. Her body felt as if she'd been overturned by a bulldozer. There was no hope of returning to sleep.

She swung her legs out of bed and staggered toward the window that overlooked the beach. When she drew open the curtains and raised the window sash, she saw that dawn hadn't yet arrived, wasn't even a promise, and the old familiar moon still spilled its light across Waikiki Beach and the ocean beyond.

Not so deserted. Irene rested her forearms on the ledge and allowed the breeze to whisk along her skin, and when she opened her eyes again she saw a man on a surfboard atop a ridge of phosphorescent foam, soaring toward shore.

AS IRENE HURRIED DOWN THE empty stairs and corridors, out the doors to the terrace and beach, she told herself that this surfer was probably not Sam. This was Waikiki, there were plenty of surfers, and Sam ought to be asleep after a day like yesterday. But that was just logic. She knew it was Sam; of course it was Sam. She'd recognized his figure from four stories up. She knew his hair, and the way he moved his board, and the way he positioned his arms. She also knew that he liked to surf early, before the sun came up and the people with it.

She reached the sand just as he came out of the waves, carrying the massive board under his arm like a piece of kindling. His hair was wet; his arms and shoulders ran with salt water. He shook his head and noticed her, and to her relief he grinned.

"Shouldn't you be sleeping?" she called out.

"Shouldn't you?"

"I just woke up. Anyway, I'm not the one flying the airplane."

Sam walked right up to her, and for a second or two Irene thought he might drop a kiss on her cheek or even her lips. Instead he planted the end of the board in the sand and flung himself down.

"You can, if you like," he said.

She sat down next to him. "Can what?"

"Fly the airplane. I've been thinking. Staying awake so long, it's not safe. We should take turns flying the bird, so the other man can catch a few winks." He turned his head to the side to look at her. "What do you think?"

"I'm game."

"I know you're game. That's why I asked you along. Say." Now he rolled the rest of his body on his side so he was facing her, up on one elbow, his wet head propped up on his hand, a yard of pale, moonlit sand between them. "That was some show last night. You were terrific."

"At the dinner, you mean?"

"When you gave that speech. That was something else. I didn't know you could put on a show like that."

"Baloney. I couldn't even hear my own words."

"Honest Injun. You socked it to them. I'll tell you, they loved your act a hell of a lot more than they loved my sorry efforts."

Irene held up her hand. "Wait a second."

"What's that?"

She closed her eyes and fell back on the sand. "I can *hear* you!"

He laughed and rolled on his back again. "Same thing happened to me when I woke up. Realized I could hear the waves outside the window. Then I figured I might as well ride a few of them, since I wasn't going back to sleep."

"I thought we weren't supposed to bring any extra weight."

"Nah, I borrowed the board from the bellhop. You want to take a turn?"

"I can't. I've got my pajamas on under this thing." She fingered the sash of her dressing gown.

"So what? I won't look."

"Sure you won't."

"Well, I might. But it's only me, right? Your old pal Sam."

To the left, an indigo light had begun to outline the shape of Diamond Head. The waves thundered quietly toward Irene's feet. The stars, which had spilled across the black sky so generously a moment ago, were dying off. Irene untied the belt of her dressing gown and sat up.

"All right," she said.

She'd lied about the pajamas. Pajamas were so much unnecessary weight! Under the robe, which had been provided by the hotel itself, she wore only her drawers and her camisole. She didn't look back to see if Sam was watching, not because she didn't want to know but because she didn't want to care. The surfboard stood at his feet, stuck in the sand. She lifted it with some effort.

"Watch for the sharks," Sam called out behind her.

Oh! It was good to plunge in the salt sea again, good to feel the muscles of the ocean tossing her about. The same current, the same water she and Sam had crossed yesterday, thousands of miles of it. She attempted two waves and foundered on both of them, filling her nose with salt, but she just grabbed the board and swam out again, a little farther this time. The sky grew lighter by the minute; now she could make out the buildings lined up along Waikiki, the great gray Moana smack in the middle. To the right, Diamond Head made a crisp silhouette against the golds and pinks of the rising sun. Another wave surged up beneath her. She lay on the board and paddled her arms, looked over her shoulder to judge this thing, monstrous, all the world's energy thrumming inside. The glow of the sunrise blinded her. She closed her eyes and felt the wave instead, discovered its rhythm, paddled to keep up with it, right on the sweet spot, higher and higher, oh it was a beauty, wait and wait and *now*! Scramble to your feet, perfectly balanced, knees bent, soaring forever along a diagonal line to the beach until you skimmed straight into the foam, you sucked every ounce of momentum from the water and then jumped overboard and laughed for joy. Hauled up your surfboard and scrambled up the sand, looking for the fellow who waited on the beach for you.

But he wasn't there. The beach was empty.

Irene came to a stop where the water washed around her shins. She spun around and there he was, stroking toward her, a few yards away. In another second he caught up and snatched her against his chest.

"Goddammit, Irene! Didn't you hear me yelling?"

"Yelling! Yelling for what?"

"Shark," he gasped.

Sam's legs gave way and they sank kerplop into the undertow. The water whisked away and left them bare. Sam's heart thundered in her ear, his arms wouldn't let go.

"I didn't see any shark," she whispered.

"Big silver fin about six feet away from you. Just before you caught the wave." He flopped them both backward to lie on the wet sand, Irene on top, while another wave washed up to his ears. "I thought you were a goner."

They lay another minute or two while their flesh molded and their wet clothes glued together. Irene slid a few inches down along his left side; her right knee rose to cross his thighs. Her arm curled atop his breastbone, rising and falling. Her breathing slowed, and so did his. The surfboard bobbed away. Dawn broke at last, and the sky turned pink.

Three stories above them, a man stood at the window of his hotel room, opened the sash, lifted a camera equipped with a special long focus lens, and snapped a few photographs.

HANALEI, HAWAI'I

October 1947

WHEN I RETURN to the house a half hour later, I carry a thick manila envelope from the lining of my suitcase, which I toss on the sofa table in front of Lindquist.

"You missed this."

She looks up at me, brow furrowed. "I don't know what you mean."

"My suitcase. Never mind, that's not important right now. *This*." I press my finger on the envelope. "I want to talk about this."

Though the sun fell below the ocean long ago, the air remains balmy. Lindquist has settled back outside to the lanai, where you can hear the surf beat upon the night sand. She drinks a glass of lemon water, iced; I've fetched something stronger from Olle's stash. It's just the two of us, and the absence of any male spirits in the atmosphere is both peculiar and tranquil.

Lindquist leans forward in her wicker chair to examine the envelope. "May I?"

I remove my hand and she takes the envelope and opens it. One by one she removes the photographs, examines them, and lays them on the table.

"Where did you get these?" she asks.

"Here and there. You'll notice the AP owns the rights to most of them, so I've pulled favors and had prints made. You don't get the same detail from a newspaper clipping."

"That's true."

She pulls out the last photograph and lays the envelope to one side while she studies them. You would think the sight of these images might inspire some kind of emotion in that face of hers, but she's just lost in thought, fingers knitted together and pressed to her bottom lip. I light a cigarette and stare over her shoulder.

There are a dozen of them, although I've got many more stored at the Los Angeles bureau office where I was conducting my research. I chose each one with care. Here's Irene Foster standing next to Sam Mallory and his wife, while he holds a towheaded cherub in his arms. Here's Foster and Mallory posed before their Rofrano Centauri, just before they depart on their landmark flight to Australia. Foster and Mallory, tired but triumphant, waving from the airplane door on arrival in Oahu. Foster delivering some speech in Honolulu, Hawai'i, while Mallory looks on. Lindquist points to that one.

"I couldn't even hear my own voice," she says. "The noise from the engines in those days, it was deafening. Literally deafening. That was my first speech."

"First of many."

"I didn't even know what to say. I didn't know I was supposed to speak at all. I thought that was Sam's job." She chuckles. "I remember standing there and wondering what my father would say. He could always hold an audience. He was a terrific raconteur. Also a drunk."

"Wasn't everybody's dad a drunk?"

"You too? Then you know what it's like." She shakes her head. "Those marathon flights, they were murder. All strung out on coffee and nerves. And all the same, that was the best part. It was just you and the airplane and the landscape around you, and the rest of it didn't matter, the speeches and interviews and newspaper articles. You knew you were doing something special, something nobody else had done before, and that first flight . . . Sam there in the cockpit with me . . ." She reaches for her lemon water. Her other hand finds the calico cat that sleeps on a cushion at her feet.

I wheel around the wicker chair to prop myself on the arm, right next to her. My own glass is empty, but I'm not about to leave her for the sake of a little more bourbon. Photographs. They have an effect on people, don't they? Show somebody a picture from some particular moment that means something to her, some *person* who means something, and you can just about hear the noise of suction as she's drawn back into the past. As she becomes the person she once was. It's a technique I've used before, not least on myself. I stare at her long finger, which taps on another photograph, also taken nineteen years ago in Honolulu, in which she and Mallory step from the back of some giant limousine, and he's just turned away from her to face the camera and hasn't yet put on that face you wear when you're being photographed.

"That expression," she says. "In the other ones, he's just posing for the camera. When I remember Sam, this is what he looks like."

I FIRST STARTED TAKING PHOTOGRAPHS when I was small, maybe eight or nine. My father gave me one of those Brownie cameras for my birthday one year, and such was my adoration for him, I accepted this present as you might accept diamonds. He showed me how to use it, and even today, when I'm messing about with cameras, I sometimes recall my father's scent, deep in the cavities of my head, that flavor of cigarettes and shaving soap and perspiration and engine oil and whiskey that set him apart from everyone else. I hear his rumbly voice as he explains how it works, the principles of light, the mirror inside the camera that places an upside-down image on the film in the split second of the shutter's opening and closing. Then he talks about subject and composition and shadow, and I listen so earnestly because this is my father, who knows everything, who is capable of anything.

Sometimes I think about the time he took me out for a drive to look for things to photograph and how we stopped for lunch at some little roadside diner, I don't remember where, and how we both ate grilled cheese sandwiches while he told me I shouldn't listen to a word he said about subject and composition, I should photograph only what I wanted to photograph, and how I wanted to photograph it. I said I wanted to photograph *him*, so he sat back and smiled, posing, and I told him not to smile, I wanted him to look exactly as he really was and not some grinning stranger. So he stopped smiling and looked out the window, and I took a photograph with my Brownie, kind of blurry because I was too close, just across the table. But I still have that photograph. I wouldn't trade that photograph of my father for all the gold in Fort Knox, because in that moment we were happy, in that photograph all our happinesses are contained.

Afterward, on the way home, he told me I ought to be a photographer someday. He said I had the instinct for it, because here I was, only nine years old, and already I knew how I wanted to photograph somebody: not as mere fact but as truth.

"WHAT ABOUT *YOUR* FACE?" I say to Lindquist. "What are *you* thinking in that photo?"

She laughs. "As I recall, I'm thinking I'd much rather be back inside the airplane."

But she's not in the mood to say more. Sometimes photographs have that effect as well; you're drawn back into yourself, your own reflections on the past, and you don't want to share them. That's fine too. I figure she'll go to bed thinking about what we've just seen, about that monumental flight to Australia with Sam Mallory, the flight that changed her life, and not only will she wake up remembering all kinds of details she's long buried, she will want to unburden them to somebody.

BECAUSE OF ALL THE BICYCLING and surfing, I have no trouble falling asleep as soon as I crawl between the fresh new sheets of that bed. My battered, exhausted body can do no more. Not a single clear thought, not a twitch of muscle. For a few blessed hours I am plunged in the deep, and then I burst back out, panting, just as fast as I went down.

I consult my watch. Twenty-six minutes past one o'clock.

As I know from experience, there's no point in lying flat on your back, or tossing and turning in some vain attempt to get back what you have lost. I throw off the covers and walk naked (I don't wear pajamas, but maybe that doesn't surprise you) to the carrying case that holds all my photographic equipment.

The dark of night, I've learned, is the perfect time to develop film. In the first place—well, it's *dark,* which is a necessary condition for the process. In the second place, making photographs is good for the soul. There's a routine to it, a series of precise maneuvers on which you must concentrate all your attention. Once, back at the Scribe bar in Paris, Bob Capa told me that he took a hundred and six photographs on the landing beach on D-Day, the best photos he ever took, priceless, historic, irreplaceable, and some goober in the photographic lab back in London mishandled the film and destroyed all but eleven of them. So you see, you can't let your attention wander. You can't let any other ideas distract you. For a blessed hour, you can think of nothing else.

So I find a light socket for my red bulb. I lay out the trays, pour in the chemicals. Unroll the film from its casing, clip the ends, load the reel. Another thing I love about developing film at night, nobody bothers me. As much as I enjoy company—a certain kind of company in particular—I prefer to be alone. Answer to nobody, pretend nothing, expend not the slightest effort to entertain, to cajole, to argue your cause. To manipulate the inanimate is so much easier.

Not all the negatives are worth the effort of turning into photographs, mind you. I inspect each one thoroughly, and in the end I find only six I want to print. As I pull each one from its bath and hang it to dry, the way a housewife might hang her laundry, I feel a sense of perfect accomplishment, as if I've done all I could. I wash out the trays, put everything away. I unplug my red light from the wall and wind the cord around it. Then I switch on my penlight and gaze at each print in turn.

There is Lindquist with her short silver curls, her graceful, unscarred neck, the firm line of her jaw, although I would have liked her to gaze a little more toward the camera lens, because her eyes are astounding when fixed upon you.

There are the cherubs at play in the surf, goddamn them. Lani in the kitchen. The cherry-red Buick, which looks in motion even when it's at rest. And last, there is Leo. I pull the photograph from its clothespin to examine it more closely. I realize I've forgotten what a perfect specimen he is, how like a drawing from an anatomy textbook. He lies on his stomach in the squalor of a sinful bed. One sheet twines around his ankle; another streaks across the small of his back; he clutches a pillow under one arm. The camera finds the left side of his face, exhausted and happy.

I replace the photograph on the line and climb back into bed. On the nightstand is the leather diary, and tucked inside are a few photographs dear to me. The blurred, sepia snap of my father is one of them. There are a couple of others. But the one I remove from the pages is the photo I took of Velázquez, just before he was reassigned back to his squadron in some RAF forward air base in The Netherlands at the end of October. Unlike Leo, he's awake. He stares at the camera, naked and exasperated, because he wants to get back to what we were doing before, which you can imagine. His plain, wide face bears some shadow of stubble along the jaw and above his thin upper lip; his chest is dark and furry and shaped like a barrel of wine. One arm stretches toward me, as if to take the camera from my hand. His mouth is open a little, because he's telling me that he hates having his photograph taken.

AVIATRIX

by Eugenia Everett

(e x c e r p t)

August 1928: Pacific Ocean

THEY WERE ABOUT nine hundred miles north of Samoa when Irene, who was piloting the Centauri at the time, noticed the fuel level was a lot lower than it should be. A minute or two later, while she was troubleshooting the problem, the right engine stopped. She swore and turned her head.

"Sam! Engine's out!"

He bolted up from the makeshift cot, a couple of yards away. Sandy, curled up against his ribs, leapt away and scurried underneath to hide between the kit bags. "What?"

"I think something's wrong with the fuel line! Right engine!"

Of course he couldn't hear what she was saying. He staggered up and looked over her shoulder at the cockpit dials. Then he staggered over to the window on the right-hand side and peered at the engine, which was illuminated by moonlight. Irene wasn't sure, but she thought he swore. Then he went to the navigator's table. A moment later, while Irene struggled with the sagging airplane, a note came through on the clothesline: *Baker Island, 102 miles bearing WSW.*

She nodded and started to bank for the turn.

Behind her, the radio crackled over the noise of the remaining engine. The longwave frequency, as Sam tried to raise Samoa and the men assembled there to assist their arrival. George Morrow had arranged it all. He had negotiated the itinerary and the logistics with the navy, had confirmed the frequencies over which the Centauri and the vessels lined up along her route would communicate with each other. Had also sat for hours with Sam and Irene and a naval officer at a table covered by charts of the South Pacific Ocean. They'd dickered over islands and currents and prevailing winds and weather patterns. They had settled on the official landfalls—Honolulu, Samoa, Sydney—and also alternatives, should some mechanical fault occur, should some storm arise along their path. So Irene already knew about Baker Island. She could picture it on the map, nineteen hundred miles southwest of Honolulu, a thousand miles north-northwest of Samoa, an expired volcano colonized by coral and shaped like a potato chip. There wasn't much in the way of vegetation, just sand and grass, which was why it made a likely spot to land an airplane in a pinch.

Irene glanced again at the fuel gauge. This was certainly a pinch.

Sam had made no move to replace her at the controls. She looked over her shoulder and saw he was busy at the navigation table, radio headset covering his ears, fingers busy at the dials. Though the engine noise was now diminished by half, she still couldn't hear the pings of Morse code, or whether he'd been successful in contacting the navy. Sam had nearly reached the end of his scheduled two-hour nap; he'd been due to replace her within minutes. A quarter of an hour, and Sam would have sat at these controls, Sam would have possibly noticed the anomaly sooner; Sam with his experience and expertise might have been able to do something about it. Now it was too late. The sun wasn't due to rise for another couple of hours. How were they supposed to find a few hundred acres of sand in the dark of night? How were they supposed to land on it? They had the cold, clear moon; that was all.

All of these thoughts shot across Irene's mind one by one, without stopping for consideration. She didn't have time to think. She had an airplane to contend with, an airplane that could putter along with one engine, as long as the pilot made the constant, necessary adjustments. Still Sam didn't tap her shoulder, didn't make her rise and return to her old seat. Irene kept flying. She got the knack of it. She glanced at the compass every ten or fifteen seconds, glanced at the altimeter (six thousand two hundred feet) and the speedometer (ninety-six miles an hour, much slower now) and the fuel gauge (eleven gallons remaining, dear God) in a continuous rotation. Each piece of information fed her brain. She felt preternaturally alert, as alive as an electrical wire, aware simultaneously of a dozen different things. A moment ago she had had to pinch herself to keep from dozing.

A note dragged into view on the clothesline: *Maintain heading. Superb flying.*

Irene was too busy to be shocked, but she felt the shock nonetheless, erupting down below somewhere, her stomach maybe. Sam wasn't taking over. Irene was going to fly them to Baker Island on a single engine. She was going to land the airplane by moonlight on a coral island in the middle of the South Pacific, no airstrip or anything, no beacon, nothing but moon and stars.

Thank God for the full moon. Thank God for the clear air.

Irene kept one hand on the stick and scribbled on the paper with her other hand: *Miles?*

He replied, *86.*

But that was just dead reckoning, she thought. They couldn't know for certain. She hadn't taken a celestial observation in two hours, and while the radio beacon in Samoa had insisted they were on course, it couldn't tell them how far away they were, where precisely they existed on that curve drawn on the globe between Honolulu and the landing strip on Samoa. So these eighty-six miles were a guess. An answer worked out on pencil and paper. And on that estimate of distance depending the accuracy of their compass heading, and on the accuracy of that compass heading depending their ability to find Baker Island at all.

Still she flew. She had no choice. There was nothing to do but fly.

Fly and calculate. If they maintained speed at ninety-five miles an hour, they should reach Baker in about fifty-four minutes. They should glimpse the island sooner, maybe forty or forty-five minutes, depending on its visibility in the moonlight. In three-quarters of an hour, Irene and Sam would know whether their calculations were accurate.

If they weren't?

Now that Irene had shut off the line to the right engine, they weren't losing fuel at a disastrous rate. Still, if they didn't sight Baker on time, if they had to start making sweeps in search of it, they only had about an hour left to do this. An hour, and the ocean was so vast! They might have miscalculated the tailwind out of Honolulu, they might be a hundred miles north or south of this dot on the map they had imagined themselves. What if—

Another note. *Reduce altitude to 1500 ft.*

Irene nodded and brought the airplane carefully down. Her heart beat in enormous, steady strokes. She felt them in her neck. Her head ached from the keenness of her attention. The air smelled of salt and oil and pungent aviation fuel. She realized she was thirsty.

She scribbled, *Coffee.*

Half a minute later, Sam pushed a cup into her hand.

She drank swiftly. It was hot, but not too hot. In the thicker atmosphere at fifteen hundred feet, they had slowed to ninety-two miles an hour, and they were burning a little more fuel. But they were closer to the surface, and they could more easily spy any telltale interruption in the dark ocean beneath them. Irene's armpits were wet; the sweat trickled down her sides and gathered between her legs, and yet she was cold. She handed the empty cup back to Sam. She had stopped wondering why he hadn't taken the controls. He hadn't, that was all. Maybe he figured it was more tricky to find Baker than to land on it safely, and that was why he remained at the navigator's table, communicating on the radio, taking the speed and heading of the Centauri every five minutes, making the calculation, laying the ruler flat along the map and drawing a neat line that meant absolutely nothing, might be a hundred miles away from their actual position.

Still she flew.

Twenty minutes passed. Thirty.

The cockpit window, high and narrow, didn't afford much of a view. She scribbled another note to Sam, which was probably unnecessary: *Start looking.*

Thirty-five minutes.

Forty.

Irene's eyes hurt from straining into the moonlight. A white square appeared to her left. She ripped it from the clothesline and read: *Reduce altitude to 1000 ft.*

She tipped the nose down carefully. It was so disorienting, flying at night. Sometimes you had this wild, irrational feeling that up was down, and down was up, and the vast textured blackness beneath you was actually the sky. And even though the full moon lay within view, edging downward now toward the western horizon, Irene experienced an instant's panic that the white disk in the sky was not the moon itself, but its reflection on the water.

But the altimeter needle dropped obediently. Twelve hundred feet, a thousand. Irene eased the stick back again and leveled the airplane. Her hands were clammy and slipped a bit on the rubber grip. Ahead of her was nothing, just the same black moon-speckled landscape, not the slightest interruption. She glanced at the altimeter (nine hundred and eighty feet) and the speed gauge (ninety miles an hour). Then the clock, which showed that four minutes had passed, that if their calculations were perfect, Baker Island should be thrusting up from the ocean any second now.

Forty-five minutes.

Fifty minutes.

Irene glanced over her shoulder at Sam. It was dark inside the cabin, lit only by the moonlight and the bulb attached to the navigator's table, and in that glimpse she couldn't tell if his expression, as he stared out the small, ovoid window, was grim or just flat.

She scribbled, *See anything?*

He replied, *Box compass.*

OF COURSE THEY HAD DISCUSSED what to do if navigation failed, if a certain mass of land did not turn up when and where it was supposed to. There was no need to panic, at least not right away. On an ocean so vast as the Pacific, using navigation methods that relied on natural variables and imperfect human observations, errors would occur. You simply tried to keep the margin of that error within reasonable—that is to say, survivable—bounds.

So Baker Island had not turned up exactly where it was supposed to. It must still exist somewhere in the vicinity. According to the laws of geometry, from a point one thousand feet above the earth's surface, the human eye could find the horizon across thirty-nine miles of open ocean in each direction; if you flew your airplane in four straight lines of forty miles each to form a square—boxing the compass, as they call it—you stood the best chance of detecting your objective before you ran out of fuel. At night, of course, your visibility wasn't so exact. If the moon was bright and the weather was clear, as it was now, you might still have a hard time detecting some imperfection upon the ocean's surface that might or might not represent an island. Still, you had to try. Sam and Irene had practiced this very maneuver atop the California desert over and over, by night and by day, and while Sam had always flown the airplane as Irene worked the navigation, still she'd passed him the necessary commands, she'd figured out which direction and for how long they should make their passes over the sand. Why, she'd had the tougher job! She knew what to do. She had just about expected this message from Sam, scribbled in block letters on a piece of square white notepaper.

She banked the airplane and began the first side of the square.

BEFORE FLYING, IRENE HADN'T GIVEN the moon much thought. She knew it guided the tides, of course, which were of some importance in surfing, but she didn't pay attention to the how and why, to the actual progress of the rock in question. Her prior ignorance now stunned her. How could she not have noticed, for example, that a full moon rose exactly at sunset, and set exactly at sunrise? That a new moon—if she could actually see it—did exactly the opposite? The moon was her companion. It shed light on the black ocean. It occupied a predictable place in the sky, a landmark, a beacon. As she swept above the water, searching for some scrap of an island, the moon lit her way. If she found Baker, she would find it by the reflection of moonlight on a patch of sand.

Or else Sam would. He had taken off the radio headset and lifted a pair of binoculars to his eyes. The temperature was getting a little warmer, because they were so close to earth, or possibly because of the anxiety packed tight inside the airplane, and he had stripped off his thick, sheepskin-lined leather jacket and stood now in his flight suit, not moving, fixed on the landscape outside the window. A landscape on which no interruption appeared. Nothing. Water and more water, all the way to the horizon. The minutes ticked by. Ten, fifteen. The needle in the gauge of the main fuel tank hovered just above empty.

Irene scrawled, *Switch to aux tank soon.*

The note took ten or twelve seconds to write. While she was writing it, she was seized with certainty that when she looked back up, when she strained her gaze through the cockpit window, she would see Baker Island. She would see some silver ridge amid all those delicate white threads and curlicues that constituted the moonlit Pacific Ocean, and it would grow larger and more prominent and it would be Baker Island. She knew this like she knew the shape of her own hand, the rhythm of her own breath. She chucked the pencil stub in its can and clipped the note, one-handed, to the clothesline, and turned to the window in triumph.

Nothing.

The Centauri wobbled. Maybe it was the air, maybe it was her hand on the stick. She glanced at the fuel gauge and the clock. They had traveled nearly forty miles now in the first side of the square. Nearly time to bank and turn. Behind her, Sam was moving. Switching the fuel lines. The auxiliary tank held another sixty gallons. If Irene flew the Centauri with perfect efficiency, she could squeeze another hundred and twenty miles from those sixty gallons.

She made the turn. Started down the next side of the imaginary square. Surely Baker Island would turn up any second.

TWO MORE SIDES.

Eighty miles.

No island.

WITH SIX GALLONS OF FUEL remaining in the auxiliary tank, a note appeared on the clothesline. *Descend to 200 ft. Prepare water landing.*

She scribbled on the same square of paper: *YOU.*

He didn't answer. The left engine droned on, oblivious to its imminent death.

Irene started to descend. Her pulse punched against her throat, closing off her breath. Her hands shook on the stick. A hand came down on her shoulder. A finger appeared in her field of vision, jabbing at the window. Irene raised herself an inch or two and followed the line it drew across the water, right toward a tiny patch of white at the extreme southern end of the horizon.

THERE IT IS, Sam yelled in her ear.

Not a panicked yell, no fear at all, just loud and confident so that she could hear him above the noise of the engine.

BUT THE ISLAND, AS IT grew in size and came into focus, was not shaped like a potato chip. More like a dill pickle, or a banana.

Irene couldn't send any notes now. She had to fly, she had to look at this scrap of land by the light of the moon and figure out what it was made of, how to land on it, *could* she land on it. And all the while her heart was beating so hard and so fast, she thought her ribs would break. She couldn't breathe. This white mist seemed to be filling her brain. All those times she had practiced landing in an emergency, landing on the sand in the desert, landing without an engine, but she hadn't practiced this. Landing on some unknown piece of land in the middle of the ocean. The shape of it grew and grew. She couldn't see, she couldn't tell if those dark patches were grass or scrub or trees or what have you.

She couldn't do it.

She flung out an arm behind her and grabbed hold of some part of Sam, his shoulder. She turned and looked at him, and the panic must have burst right into the open, because he took her hand off his shoulder and shouted in her ear, *You can do it!*

I CAN'T! she yelled back, and this time she rose from the seat and let go of the stick.

The Centauri pitched and dove.

Sam slammed her down on the seat, grabbed her hand, and set it on the stick.

LAND THE GODDAMN AIRPLANE, he said in her ear. I'M RIGHT HERE.

She was shaking, she was dizzy. Sam's hand covered hers on the stick. The airplane jerked and rattled as they brought it back under control. She thought, why? Why had he subjected her to this? He was the senior pilot, the better pilot, the stunt pilot who had performed a thousand improbable aeronautical feats, who had cheated death over and over. Why hadn't he taken control the instant the engine stopped? Why make Irene do this impossible thing and kill them both?

But his arms were right there. His face stood firm next to hers. STEADY, he shouted, so she could hear him, so she could smell his hair, his familiar skin. His confidence poured from his palm and into the back of her hand.

THAT'S IT. His voice was firm, not worried at all. KEEP YOUR SPEED UP.

Irene's heart chattered away but her mind cleared. Her vision made a tunnel of the path before them. It was like the roller coaster when she was eleven, the whole world narrowing to a single corridor, to the patch at the end where you landed.

The airplane fell softly. The silver ground rose and grew before her. There was no wind to rattle her, nothing to think about but the descent of the Centauri to earth. The island was flat and covered with sand and grass, as near to a landing strip as you could ask for on an uninhabited island in the middle of the ocean. YOU'VE GOT IT, Sam shouted in her ear. His hand lifted from hers. He stepped back and buckled himself into the navigator's seat. It was like any other landing, like that time Sam shut one engine off and made her land in the Mojave Desert. The earth came up to meet them. The still, dark grass and the brush and *BANG!* The wheels slammed into the ground, bumped and slammed again, tore through bushes, sand and leaves flying up around the windows, spinning and bumping and coming at last to rest in the long, quiet night, an hour before dawn.

HANALEI, HAWAI'I

October 1947

Because olle's away in Honolulu, trying to keep his brother-in-law Kaiko from climbing out of his hospital bed, Lindquist has to cover his flights for him. She doesn't fly the airplanes often, she explains to me, as we drive to the airfield—first because of the risk of some cosmopolitan tourist recognizing her and second because most people would rather eat rabbit droppings than take off in an airplane piloted by a woman.

"So you see," she says, "it was all for nothing, everything I did. All those flights, all those speeches and books, the endless publicity. George used to say that we had entered the age of woman, that people were fascinated by women breaking free to do adventurous things, but look around you."

"I'd say it's a hell of a lot easier for a woman to do what she wants today than fifty years ago."

"But she has to work twice as hard and be ten times as good at what she does."

"It's better than not being allowed to try."

"And when she fails," Lindquist continues, pulling into the long drive from the road, "God help her."

WE BRING THE CAT ALONG in the back seat, because Lindquist doesn't like to leave it alone all day, at that age. *What age?* I ask, and she answers, after a moment's thought, *Nineteen*.

Well, color me impressed. I didn't even know cats could live that long. Lindquist says that's because Sandy's a survivor. Mallory found her on the beach one day, the day Lindquist met him, as a matter of fact. She stowed away on the flight to Australia.

"No kidding?" I look to the feline with renewed admiration. "You mean she survived the crash and everything? The weeks stranded on the island?"

"Lucky for her, the place was lousy with rats. They used to mine those islands for guano, back in the previous century, and naturally all the guano ships were overrun with rats. She must've gained five pounds."

We've reached the airfield cafeteria, where I'm to wait while she takes a planeload of tourists and locals back to Oahu. I observe how she's in competition with her own stepson, and she says not really. Some people like to fly, some people like to sail.

"Count me among the second clan," I tell her, as I settle myself at the lunch counter with a cup of coffee.

"You'll be all right? I should be back in a couple of hours."

"I'll be just fine."

She looks to the cat before she leaves. "Keep an eye on her for me, will you? Don't let her get into any trouble."

THOUGH I TRIED AND TRIED that autumn of 1944, I could not get Velázquez to tell me anything more about Sam Mallory. He said he had promised Mallory never to reveal what he had done in Spain, and he—Velázquez—had already broken that vow for my sake, which was unconscionable and must not be repeated. *You have a way of disarming me,* he said to me, *but now I am on my guard.*

As September passed into October, however, I went on meeting Velázquez. I told myself this was because I still had some hope of disarming him again, and because the strain of war on one's nerves required some carnal release, which nobody understood better than Velázquez. Sometimes he would join me at the Scribe in Paris, when he could get a few hours' leave from his duties at the airfield, which were largely administrative; sometimes I would travel out to Orly and meet him there. In the beginning, the terms of our association were clear and simple. Since we had the good fortune to share an electric physical attraction and libidos of roughly equal strength, we should screw each other silly, as often as we could arrange to meet.

But as the weeks went on, we began to spend time together that was not entirely devoted to sex. We would go on walks or drive a Jeep into some village and look at the local cathedral, if it still stood; after making love, instead of getting dressed or falling asleep, we would have these conversations about art and politics and ethics. I was surprised to find that despite his cynicism Velázquez was an idealist, a believer in fate but also a devout Catholic, even though the Republicans in Spain had hated the church; he did not understand how I, a nonbeliever, could adhere to any moral code at all, and he was deeply worried for my immortal soul. Velázquez spoke in precise, beautiful language, and our discussions had this transparent quality, this clarity of expression, so that you could perceive each thought in the same way you could observe an object with your eyes. I remember I would watch his mouth as he spoke, or the bridge of his nose, or the wisp of smoke from his cigarette. He used to trail his other hand along my skin, to draw some diagram with his fingers to illustrate a point. Often he would turn on his side to fix me with a serious expression and ask me some question that stopped me in my tracks, that required me to walk back all the way along some path of logic and start again, in a new direction I hadn't imagined, while he listened intently. Then we would make love again, and the texture of him was somehow different, and the texture of me.

In October he took me to the opera. I wish I could remember which one. I didn't understand a word, though the music stirred me. Sometime near the end, as the soprano lay dying yet miraculously sonorous, Velázquez snatched my fingers with one hand and wiped his eyes with the other. Afterward he apologized for this weakness and told me about his childhood in Spain, how his parents owned a great estate that was lost during the war, and how they used to take him to the opera in Madrid when he was a boy. He first saw this particular opera we had just witnessed when he was twelve, and it affected him deeply, so that he could not help but respond with emotion tonight because of all he had lost since then. He hoped this had not distressed me.

All this he explained as we sprawled in bed in the tiny room in the Hotel Scribe to which I had been assigned. We had started to make love inside the elevator, because the mechanism was so slow and this was wartime, and finished hard against the headboard an hour later; Velázquez was a disciplined man and always made sure I came at least twice (sometimes more, if he had gone to confession recently) before he finished off. He used to say it was the man's duty to give the woman satisfaction, because a woman who was not sexually satisfied was liable to cause trouble. I saw no reason to argue with him about this.

A few days after the opera I was sent away on some assignment for a week or two, and it was only when we reunited that I realized that matters had gone too far. We devoured each other like a pair of desperate animals, driven by some lust out of all proportion to the length of our abstinence, and after Velázquez rose to dispose of the condom, he settled himself back on the bed and lit a cigarette, which we passed back and forth. An air of quiet despair settled between us. Finally he turned on his side to face me. "You will not like what I'm about to say, but I will say it regardless. I think I am in love with you."

"Don't be silly."

"No, I'm afraid it's true. Listen to me. I had word today that I am to be reassigned back to my old squadron, to conduct some reconnaissance over Germany."

"But I thought you were finished with combat missions. Haven't you flown enough already?"

"Well, it seems they have run short of experienced pilots. It is careless of them, of course, but that's the English for you. I will not ask you to be faithful. That is like asking a cat not to catch mice. But I believe we are going to win this war, we are going to beat the Fascists at last, and when it's over I would like to marry you."

I was so shocked, I nearly tumbled off the bed.

"Me? You're nuts. You should marry some girl from home. You know we won't suit. You'd want me to give up my freedom, and I'd never obey you, which would make you miserable, because you love to be obeyed."

He picked up my hand and held it to his lips. "The girl I was going to marry is dead now. I have no home left to me. For many years I said I would never marry at all, that the world was too terrible a place to bring children into it, and I was too poor in any case. But now there is hope. There is some possibility of a future. And though I am too gruff for you, and autocratic, and ugly—"

"You aren't ugly at all."

"But you are beautiful, and I have no right to you. Still, I promise I will make you a good husband. I will do my best to make you happy. All I ask is that you consider what I say. Then when the war's over, the day Hitler surrenders, I will come back to you and ask again and again until you relent and become my wife. What do you think of this idea?"

"I think it's nuts. You'll want a dozen kids, for one thing."

"That's not true. Three or four would suffice."

"What about your mistress in London?"

"I will keep her, of course," he said gravely. "Every man needs a little variety."

That was the night I took that photograph of him, while he was trying to pin me down, as it were. I then put down the camera and performed an act on him that made him howl, made him curse all my ancestors, made him collapse at last on the sheets and swear the most exquisite vengeance on me, to which I replied that it was a woman's duty to give her lover satisfaction, because he was otherwise liable to cause trouble. Then I laid my head on his thick, furry chest and listened to the thud of his heartbeat through his bone and skin until we both fell asleep.

But I'm afraid I didn't promise to marry him, or even to consider his proposal. We met only twice more before he transferred to his old squadron, flying reconnaissance out of some air base in The Netherlands, and I never saw him again after that, because he was shot down over Cologne in January. When I heard he was dead, I wept with rage, because I thought now I would never find out what had happened to Mallory. I wept and raged and wept until there was nothing left of me.

THOUGH I'M SUPPOSED TO BE looking after this cat, it seems to have the opposite idea. It settles on the counter, about a yard away from my coffee cup, and stares at me. Its movements are stiff, and its eyes are rheumy, and its fur seems to be missing a patch or two, but other than that, Mrs. Lincoln, you'd never guess it's nearly two decades old. I mean it can still leap from floor to stool, and from stool to counter, and I don't for a minute imagine *I* could do that.

"So you were Mallory's cat first," I observe.

The cat makes some adjustment of its forelegs that might be a shrug.

I reach for my pocketbook and light a cigarette. "Believe me, I know how you feel."

The bell dingles on the door. I look over my shoulder to inspect the newcomer, and what do I see but Irene Lindquist in some kind of plain, neat uniform, sliding a pair of gloves over her long fingers.

"Ready?" she says.

"Ready for what?"

"I'm afraid I told you a lie. The passengers canceled last night, when they learned about the pilot change."

"What the devil? Then why did you—" I catch sight of her steely expression. "Oh, no. Not on your life, Lindquist. I don't fly."

"You will today."

"I will *never*. That's final. It's nonnegotiable. It's the one single incontrovertible fact of my life."

WHAT I'M TRYING TO TELL you is that Lindquist allows me an entire bottle of Olle's best Scotch whiskey—he keeps a supply in the airfield cafeteria for nervous passengers—on board the airplane, although she won't allow me to smoke. The other terms of our arrangement aren't worth mentioning. She drives a hard bargain, that's all, and the next time Leo tries to tell me his stepmother's got the kindest heart in the world, oh my, sweet as pie, wouldn't hurt a fly, that stepmama of mine . . .

At which point I realize I'm singing these thoughts aloud, so I clam up before anything else escapes me.

"Oh, I've heard worse," Lindquist says cheerfully.

Even to my inexperienced eye, this airplane isn't exactly the raciest piece of metal aloft. It's designed to carry tourists over the Hawaiian islands or else locals desiring a more snappy form of transportation than the ferries, and what you want for such purposes is an airplane that reassures passengers they'll hit the ground again safely. It's a chunky, sturdy beast of two engines and eight seats, not counting pilot and navigator, and what strikes me as I fasten the straps, taking care not to jostle the bottle in my lap, is that the pilot can't exactly see out the cockpit window.

"Yes, I can," says Lindquist.

"Not very well."

"It's better once we're airborne, and the plane levels off."

"Oh, believe me, I'm not complaining. The less I see the better. Are you sure I can't have one little smoke?"

"Only if you let me take the bottle away."

"Why am I *here*?" I wail. "What have you done to *me*?"

"I have a better question. What makes you think you can write a book about Sam Mallory without ever having flown in an airplane?"

"It is called *imagination*, Lindquist. You literal types wouldn't understand."

She puffs that away and continues doing whatever it is you do, when you're preparing a machine to fly in the air. I hear the noise of engines like the buzz of angry insects. The air smells of gasoline and engine oil. Lindquist fiddles with her dials, scribbles something in her log, that kind of thing. I close my eyes and recall the way the water surged gently beneath my surfboard—no, hold on. That ended in disaster. Better to think of a ride that ended well, like Leo the other night. Leo before Uncle Kaiko. Leo before the fall. Leo—

The airplane moves. My eyes pop open. I suck down another mouthful of Scotch whiskey, and doesn't it run smooth against the thump of my heart? The airplane turns. The engines spool to a roar. Build and build, until that ramshackle fuselage shakes under the pressure of so much power held in check, until the whole world rattles, something's wrong, it's an earthquake, it's the end of the universe.

Then we go. Tear along at some godawful speed while the scream climbs up my lungs. No. *No. NO!* It's too late, I'm strapped in this goddamn chair like an execution, I can't get out, I can't make her *hear* me through all that racket, my God, I can't make her *understand* that I've changed my *mind*, I want to *stop*, I want to stay *safe on the ground*, now faster and faster, until I close my eyes again and give it all up. I say to myself, never mind, what does it matter, if I die I die, this is how Velázquez died, I will die as he died, I will know what he knew, I will feel as he felt, I will maybe see him somewhere—not in heaven, sinners as we are and unashamed, but somewhere warmer—and I'll tell him maybe I might have married him, if he had lived, because it seems I had become a little attached to him after all, it seems I still keep the memory of him tucked deep beneath the glassy surface of that organ most people call a heart. And while I'm thinking all these thoughts, one after the other, experiencing this strange revelation, something happens.

We rise in the air.

All that rattling melts into something like peace.

And I think, *Lord Almighty. I'm flying.*

I lean forward and tap Lindquist on the shoulder. "Where are we going, anyhow?"

"Just a little island out to the west," she says, "where we can be alone."

AVIATRIX

by Eugenia Everett

(e x c e r p t)

August 1928: Howland Island

T HE ISLAND WAS shaped like a pickle instead of a potato chip not
because of some cartographer's error, but because it was not Baker
Island. It was Howland Island, thirty-two miles to the north, and they
had only just caught sight of it at the extreme southern edge of the
horizon. So Sam and Irene had narrowly made landfall at all.

The Centauri wasn't in bad shape, all things considered. There was
no apparent structural damage. The engines and the wheels had come
through the hard landing fine, except for a blown tire. The only destruc-
tion came to the longwave radio antenna, which had broken off, leaving
them unable to communicate.

"But they know we're here," said Sam. "That was my last transmission, that we had sighted land and were headed down."

"To Baker Island. And they'll sail on over to Baker Island and find
no trace of us, and they'll think we ditched at sea and drowned."

"Baker's not so far away. We'll see a ship and signal. Anyway,
they'll look for us here, if they don't find us on Baker."

"You're sure of that?"

"Positive."

It was almost noon. After landing, they had crawled out of the ship and taken their bearings, had drunk some water and settled under the shelter of a wing and slept several hours, while the equatorial sun rose at last and carpeted the landscape in heat. Irene had woken first and shook Sam. Now that it was light, she saw that he had cut his forehead, which was smeared and crusted with dried blood. They had gone down to the beach and washed it with salt water, and now they were staring at the empty horizon.

"I'm sorry," she said again.

"Sorry for what?"

"Panicking."

He lay back in the sand and shaded his eyes. "You did just fine."

"But why did you make me do it? We could have been killed."

"Because I knew you could do it. You're a natural. Anyway, I figured you needed the practice."

"The *practice*?" She hit his shoulder. "The *practice*?"

He opened one eye at last and squinted at her. "One day you're going to be flying solo, and you're going to have to crash some bird somewhere, and I want you to know how to do it. I want you to live."

I want you to live. Irene looked up at the hot sky. She wanted to say something, but her throat was stiff and dry. Sam lay back in his flight suit, tanned and relaxed, hair damp, one blue eye squinting in her direction. As if they were on some kind of vacation! The air was hot and dry and smelled of the ocean. Irene heaved herself to her feet and strode back to the airplane.

According to the charts, Howland Island was about twice as big as Baker, a thousand acres or so, made of coral sand and surrounded by reef. Nobody lived there, except birds. You couldn't live there. The surface was flat and nearly barren, just scrub grass and a few trees huddled atop a small rise near the middle. Irene had a dread feeling that there was no fresh water of any kind.

At least its desert qualities made it easy to land on. The Centauri had dug ruts into the sand and grass, but it hadn't spun or crashed or been damaged by trees. Just an intact shell of an airplane with no fuel.

Irene ducked under the tail and kept walking westward. The sun was high above her, beating down on the brim of her hat. The ocean rushed against the reef. The tide was low, exposing the shallows, and Irene thought they could probably catch some fish there, some crustaceans or something.

Water was a bigger problem. Irene had packed a makeshift distilling kit among her equipment, but distilling seawater was a lot of work for meager reward. Still. Enough water to keep them alive, if they needed it.

If they *needed* it?

My God, they were *marooned*! They were shipwrecked on a deserted island! They were alive. They were lost! They were not lost. They were only stuck.

She stopped and folded her arms and stared at the western shore. The waves washing up and tumbling around the coral. No surfing here. Sam came up beside her and stood too.

"You should get out of the sun," he said.

"How long, do you think? Until we're rescued?"

"Shouldn't be long. A few days."

"What if it's longer?"

She meant survival. But as they stood there together, side by side, watching the empty ocean, gathering sunshine, nothing but grass and sand and rocks and salt water and the two of them, the question took on something else, some untoward quality. Some intimacy that answered itself.

BY THE SUMMER OF 1928, the Pacific Command of the U.S. Navy had grown accustomed to assisting American flyboys on their harebrained adventures. After all, it was in the nation's interest to promote aviation and thereby encourage the development of the world's best airplanes and pilots; you never knew when another war might break out and such things would be required without delay. Last year there was the Dole

Air Derby to Honolulu—what a circus *that* was—and before that you had several individual attempts to span the Pacific from San Francisco to Hawai'i, some of them foolhardy and some of them heroic, and some of them both at once. So the navy knew how to communicate with men in the air, and it knew how to fish them out of the water.

Tracking them down on some scrap of an island in the middle of the Pacific, now. That was a new one.

As it happened—and this should come as no surprise to those familiar with the pattern of threads linking just about every paid-up member of the American Anglo-Saxon aristocracy with all the others— Admiral John Smith, the officer in command of the South Pacific fleet in the middle of 1928, was an old friend of Mr. George Morrow, the two of them having prepped together at St. Paul's in the first decade of the century. They had worked closely together in the arrangements for the landmark Mallory–Foster flight to Australia, and when the first garbled Morse code came through to the USS *Farragut* at 0323 local time on the morning of the second of August (something about an engine, possible detour) Admiral Smith immediately sent a relay on to Mr. Morrow, who had been delivered to Sydney by ocean liner a day earlier.

We can only imagine Mr. Morrow's true feelings as he received this message in the middle of the Australian night, from the comfort of his hotel suite overlooking the harbor. History records only his official reply to Admiral Smith, which was sent nearly two hours later, sometime after Sam and Irene had landed on Howland Island:

COMMENCE SEARCH WITH ALL AVAILABLE RESOURCES STOP INFORM IMMEDIATELY OF ANY DEVELOPMENTS WHATSOEVER

It's also worth noting that the Sydney *Morning Herald* had, during this period of time, somehow obtained the details of the accident and duly broke the news in its early edition, which carried the following headline:

PILOTS MISSING OVER PACIFIC!

Aircraft Disappears During the Night
U.S. Navy Sends All Available Ships in Search of Flying Pair
Possible Crash Landing at Sea; Rescue May Take Weeks
Australian Navy Gallantly Offers Assistance

The news electrified the world.

BACK ON HOWLAND ISLAND, THE Flying Pair at the center of all these radio transmissions and newspaper headlines were busy unloading cargo from the fuselage of the Centauri, which was heating rapidly under the scorching sun. They made an inventory of supplies. There were five gallons of drinking water in a lightweight aluminum canister, specially designed by the Carnation milk company in exchange for promoting the many nutritional properties of Carnation condensed milk, of which they also carried a dozen cans. (Mr. Morrow had made this arrangement, of course.) Before their departure from Honolulu, the head chef of the Moana Hotel had personally prepared two dozen Hawaiian ham sandwiches, with his compliments. Sam and Irene, pausing for lunch, each ate one and pronounced it delicious. *That's some ham,* Sam said, licking his fingers, and in fact this became the slogan for the Hawaiian Canned Ham Company after the whole affair was over, except that Irene's photograph appeared in the first advertisement, tanned and smiling as she held up a sandwich. (The terms of this deal were also negotiated by Mr. Morrow, on Irene's behalf.)

Beyond the water and the condensed milk and the sandwiches, there wasn't much in the way of emergency supplies. Difficult decisions had had to be made as regards that all-important trade-off between comfort and weight, and once they'd committed to carrying a radio set equipped for both short- and long-range transmission, they'd had to sacrifice other items. Already they'd drunk the remaining coffee in the

Thermos containers, which had turned lukewarm anyway. They had a bottle of concentrated lime juice, as recommended by an expert on diseases of nutritional deficiency; two pounds of chocolate, supplied by the Hershey Company; two pounds of powdered eggs; five pounds of ship's biscuits, courtesy of the navy; and a can of peanut butter from the Pond Company, made according to a new process that churned the butter smooth and kept the oil from separating. Irene had never tasted peanut butter, but Sam said it was delicious, rich in protein and vitamins, a fine choice for emergency rations.

"I'll take your word for it," said Irene.

Sam shrugged and held out the tin to Sandy, who sniffed it delicately and thoroughly before lashing out her pink tongue for a sample. "Sandy likes it," he said.

"That's because she's hungry."

"You might be pretty hungry yourself in a few days."

"In a few days, we'll be on our way to Australia."

Sam covered the tin of peanut butter and set it back in the food locker, which was made of the same lightweight aluminum as the water cans. "I certainly hope so," he said.

"Hope so?"

Sam brushed a little sand from his clothes and stood and stretched. Sandy wound around his legs, sniffing for more peanut butter. Irene stared at his profile while he reached into his pocket and drew out a pack of cigarettes—among their emergency rations were a dozen cartons of same—and lit himself up. He strolled to the beach, and Irene rose to follow him.

"Tell me something," she said. "That race to Hawai'i last year. How long were you out there floating on the ocean, before they found you?"

"Eleven days."

"Why'd it take so long? They knew where to find you, more or less."

"Because it's a big ocean, Irene. If they pick the wrong spot to look, why, you're on your own. But you already knew that, didn't you?"

Of course she knew that. It was just something you didn't want to admit to yourself, didn't want to think about when you were starting on your journey, deciding what to pack and what to leave behind, making all these plans and calculations. Now here they were. It wasn't the worst that could have happened, not by a long shot. They were still alive and uninjured, except for a couple of scratches. They were on solid ground, a charted island known to mariners. Undoubtedly the navy was on its way to rescue them. It was all just a matter of staying alive! Irene folded her arms and stared at the reef, bubbling and frothing in the rising tide.

"Anyway," said Sam, exhaling smoke, "at least we've got each other. We're not alone. That's something."

The sun beat fiercely on the crown of Irene's hat. Birds squawked overhead, looking for lunch inside the coral. Beyond the reef, the water was calm and blue without end, the horizon perfectly flat. Sam's shoulder was round and sturdy next to hers.

"That's everything," she said.

NIGHT FELL SUDDENLY, THE WAY it does in the middle of the ocean. One minute they stared, stunned, at a monumental sunset, and the next minute they were sunk in darkness. Sam lit a cigarette that flared bright orange out of nowhere.

"Does it ever seem to you like an article of faith," he said, "that we'll see the old thing again tomorrow morning?"

Irene laughed. "That's not very scientific."

"There's more to life than science, Foster." He stretched and lay back in the sand. "Look at all those stars. You don't see stars like that in Los Angeles."

Irene lay back too. They'd spent the afternoon taking apart the right-hand engine, trying to find the source of the trouble, and she was tired enough to fall asleep right there, in the open air. Sam was right about the stars. They were dazzlingly profuse, a spill of diamond dust. Behind the crown of Irene's head, the moon rose gracefully from the eastern horizon.

"What we need right now is a bottle of champagne," said Sam. "There's nothing like an ice-cold bottle of champagne on a beach at night."

"I wouldn't know. I don't like to drink, on account of my father."

"Aw, I'm sorry. I didn't mean——"

"Don't worry about it. It's nothing."

"It's not nothing. It's who you are, right? Your childhood and everything. That's what the shrinks say, anyway."

The smoke curled around the two of them. Until she met Sam, Irene had always disliked the smell of cigarette smoke. Now it was familiar and safe, the scent of Sam; not when he was flying, because he didn't smoke when he flew, but when he was unwinding after. When he was unwound. After a moment of contemplation, he added, "You never had a drink? Not once?"

"Never."

Sam put his hands behind his head and said, "Bertha drinks."

Irene thought, *Bertha? Who's Bertha?* Then she remembered.

"A lot?" she asked.

"You could say that. It's hard to say how much. She hides it."

"That's a bad sign, hiding it."

"Don't I know it."

Something brushed against Irene's foot, her leg, winding its way upward. A cat's fur, clean and fluffy. Irene reached down to pet her, but Sandy had already disappeared to transfer her caresses to Sam. She climbed onto his chest and started her rasping purr. Sam stroked her back and said, "I come up to visit her and Pixie, and there's bottles in the trash, empty bottles in the cabinets, behind the books in the bookshelf."

"What about your daughter?"

"Oh, she takes good care of Pixie, all right. If she didn't, now . . . if she laid a hand on my girl . . ."

Sandy was now purring like a propeller engine under his hand, almost delirious. Because the moon was still low in the sky, somewhere behind them, it didn't yet illuminate much, just the outline of Sam's head and Sandy's fur.

"You have to understand," he said. "When we met, Bertha and me, I was a kid. War'd just ended. Everyone else who started out in my squadron got killed, except me and Rofrano. So I came out west. Picked up an old Jenny and started barnstorming to make some dough. Then I remembered about Bertha. Her first husband, he was in the squadron, got shot down a month before the Armistice. Good fellow, friend of mine. I knew he'd lived in Oakland. So I thought I should look her up and pay a duty visit. See if there was anything I could do for her. And she—well, I can't even say how it happened. I didn't come for that, I swear. I wasn't in love with her or anything; I didn't even like her that much. She was just *there*, is all. She didn't ask for anything back, just me coming by to—to keep her company. We hardly even talked. I didn't know much about women. I was in the middle of it before I realized what she was up to. Stupid kid that I was. Then she told me she was having Pixie."

"And that's when you got married?"

"We got married real quick, ten-minute ceremony at the registry office, just the two of us and some witness from the building permit office upstairs. Nice lady, curly hair, spectacles. I had the sense she felt a little sorry for me. Afterward, we went straight home to Bertha's place in Oakland and set up housekeeping. Painted the nursery myself. And Bertha set about trying to domesticate me."

"You can't blame her for that, though."

"No, I can't. Can't blame her for wanting a nice tame husband. She said I should quit all the barnstorming and find a real job in an office someplace, and maybe she was right. She had this idea that she could make me into an accountant or something. That's what she wanted, to be an accountant's wife with a fancy house and a daily maid and a nice piece of tin parked out front. And I wasn't that man."

"No, you're not. Not a bit."

"I tried, Irene. Honest, I did. But you know how it is. Flying's what I do, it's my blood and heart, the only thing keeping me sane, the only thing I can do better than the other man. Better than just about anybody. *You* understand, don't you? How you feel when you're up in the air, and the earth's laid out below you, and nothing to tie you down."

"Yes, I understand."

"Well, Bertha didn't. She hated it. She hated that I cared about airplanes more than I cared about her; she couldn't understand why I needed to fly. Especially once Pixie was born. She started having these rages. Then the drinking. She'd always liked the bottle, sure, but it got to be a habit. She'd get a couple of different doctors to prescribe the booze for her nerves or something, buy it all at the drugstore in town that looked the other way. Made everything worse. She'd hit me, throw things, break the dishes, enough to make you think those drys are maybe on to something. Later, she'd calm down and explain how very sorry she was, but I had driven her to it, I'd made her do all that. It was all my fault." He stroked Sandy for a minute. "One night—must've been about a year ago—I figured I'd had enough. Said if she kept on like this, I'd leave for good, I'd take Pixie with me and go."

Sandy got up suddenly and nipped Sam's nose. *Ouch*, he said, laughing, and Irene sat up a little and took the cat in her arms and buried her nose in the clean-smelling fur. "So what happened? Did you leave?"

"Leave? Nah. I was just trying to shape her up. I didn't want a divorce. I couldn't do that to Pixie, take her away from her mother. But I swear to God, I never figured Bertha'd do what she did."

Sandy jumped from Irene's lap and stalked off into the darkness. The whites of her, enamored of moonlight, vanished last. Irene realized her palms were damp, her heart was thumping. She said daringly, "Well, what did she do?"

Sam sat up and took out another cigarette, and while he was lighting it, while he held the cigarette in one corner of his mouth and snicked the flame from the lighter, he spoke from the other corner of his mouth.

"I had a show down in Vacaville the next day. I drove there, checked into this motor inn, like I always do. Got up in the morning, did some flying, had some dinner with a friend or two, came back in the evening. Manager said there was a parcel for me."

The cigarette was now lit. He stuck the lighter back in the pocket of his flight suit and removed the cigarette from his mouth and just sat there, dropping ash into the sand, staring at the salt froth that shimmered atop the reef.

Irene sat up next to him and gathered her knees in her arms. "So?"

"She'd cut off her pinky toe—the left one—and sent it to me in a brown cardboard box, lined with tissue. And a note saying she'd slit her throat if I didn't come back."

THE NEXT MORNING, IRENE GOT up early and did the next best thing to taking a bath. She went swimming in the clear, salty water of the island's leeward shore. The reef dropped off quickly, so she stayed close to the island's edge, stroking back and forth as the sun rose from the opposite horizon. Then she plunged underwater and opened her eyes. She had seen pictures of coral reefs, but nothing could prepare you for the reality, for the colorful, intricate explosion of life. When she came up gasping, the barrenness of dry land amazed her.

There was no sign of Sam. The airplane had come to rest on the other side of the rise at the center of the island, and he was probably still sleeping under the shelter of the right wing. Irene crawled onto the beach and let the warm air dry her skin. When she rose and put her clothes on, she thought she saw a flash of movement in the grass, which might have been a bird or might not. Otherwise, the world was still, and for the first time Irene felt the enormity of those hundreds of miles of ocean surrounding them on all sides, those billions of cubic feet of salt water. The insignificance of this speck of land on which they had perched.

She headed back to the airplane.

Sam wasn't in the hollow where he had slept. Irene rummaged in her kit bag until she found her tortoiseshell comb and sat on a rock to untangle her wet hair. As she sat there, swearing, Sam sauntered up from the north, wearing nothing but a pair of khaki trousers, shaking the droplets from his hair.

"What's the matter?" he said.

"My damned hair!"

He cocked his head to one side. "Why don't you cut it?"

"My mother always said—before she died—" She stopped short.

"And how long ago was that?" Sam asked.

"When I was eleven."

Sam nodded. "That's an awful long time ago, though."

He held his crumpled shirt in one hand and seemed unaware that his chest remained bare, unaware that Irene was aware. She kept her gaze on his face, but the chest remained at the periphery, pale to the neck, ridged on each side with hungry ribs. When they were little, Irene and her cousins used to swim all the time in the pond at her grandparents' house, and she hadn't paid any attention to the boys' chests, except to envy them for their shirtlessness. Now she tried to summon the old nonchalance.

"I don't have any scissors," she said.

"I've got a pair in the toolkit."

She set down the comb. "All right."

Sam went to fetch the scissors from the toolkit. Sandy stalked up from nowhere and licked her paws with an air of worldliness. Irene peered closer and saw a smear of blood on the white fur of the cat's chin, and she thought about the large black rat she'd seen scurrying between some clumps of seagrass yesterday afternoon.

Sam returned with the scissors and held them out to her. Irene looped her fingers through the handle and seized a fistful of hair, matted and wet from the swim, uncombed since the morning they left Honolulu.

"Well?" said Sam. "Go on."

She handed back the scissors. "You do it. I don't have a mirror."

"I've never cut a woman's hair before."

"Neither have I, and at least you can see what you're doing."

"All right. Turn around."

Irene turned around on her rock, and Sam went down on one knee and looked this way and that around her hair, brow furrowed. *Well?* she said, and he replied that it was an awful lot of hair, and how much did she want cut off, anyway?

"To the ears, I guess."

"The bottom of the ears, or the top?"

"Start at the bottom."

Sam took a piece of hair that grew next to her temple, stretched it out, examined it, and lifted the scissors. Irene closed her eyes and heard the soft whisk of the scissors closing, felt the tug of the blades cutting through the strands. She opened her eyes. He took another piece and did the same thing, then proceeded methodically around her head, picking and slicing, picking and slicing. Irene remained absolutely still, her hands folded on her lap. The hair piled up in giant drifts on the sand around her, though she didn't look down until after it was over. Until Sam sat back and surveyed his work.

"Now, I'm no expert, but I think I'd better comb it through first and then sort of trim it all around," he said. "You all right?"

Irene handed him the comb. "Oh, yes."

Now he combed the shortened hair, and it was much easier. He was gentle too. Slow, because they had all morning and all day, there was no hurry at all. Sandy took an interest in the shorn hair, then became bored and wound between Sam's legs. The sun climbed higher. Sam's fingers worked their way through Irene's hair, and already it felt different, lighter somehow, freer. He picked up the scissors again and trimmed carefully. The curls sprang away from the blades, possessed of new, exciting life. When he was finished at last, he stood up and took her hand and pulled her up.

"How does it feel?" he said.

Irene shook her head. The damp strands flew around her face and stuck to her cheek. She touched her fingers to her hair in wonder. "It feels . . . I don't know. It feels like somebody else. How does it look?"

"Sensational."

"Don't kid me."

"I'm not kidding. Come on, have a look."

Sam got his shaving mirror out of his kit bag and held it out in front of Irene. She stared back at this woman who was not her, who could not possibly be Irene, modern and tousle-haired and freckled and sunburnt and liberated, her eyes such a pungent shade of blue they might have been pieces of sky. She couldn't take her eyes off those curls. She lifted them one by one and held them to the sun.

"You see?" said Sam. "Sensational."

MEANWHILE, THE REST OF HUMANITY was working itself up into a state of unprecedented frenzy over the fate of the lost pilots. In the space of forty-eight hours, thanks to the miracle of the modern newswire, Sam and Irene had become just about the most famous people on earth. Members of the press had camped out in their dozens outside the Oakland home of Mrs. Samuel Mallory, who stayed indoors with her daughter and had her food brought in so she wouldn't have to speak to anybody.

The press didn't have to camp out outside the home of Mr. Hank Foster. Irene's father obliged them by joining the hoopla himself. He chewed the fat with the newsmen, he shared stories and photographs of Irene, he made optimistic, colorful comments about the likely fate of the pilots that were quoted around the world. Meanwhile, the Sydney *Morning Herald* issued regular statements from Mr. George Morrow, on behalf of the pilots and the navy, in which no detail was too small, no speculation too outlandish, no possible mention of the sponsoring corporations unmentioned.

In later interviews, Irene would insist that she never dreamed that the world was holding its breath as she and Sam awaited rescue on Howland, and in view of her natural modesty, she was no doubt telling the truth. Despite having experienced the vast outpouring of interest in Sam Mallory's disappearance and miraculous resurrection the year before, Irene was the kind of person who simply couldn't imagine such a magnitude of fuss being made about *her*. She hoped that a ship or two might be dispatched in their direction, and was embarrassed to occasion even that much trouble. When that longed-for ship hadn't appeared by the fourth day, she just assumed it was because the U.S. Navy had more important priorities than a couple of lost pilots, whose misfortune was their own doing. Maybe she was right. Despite countless interviews and research through official and personal correspondence, nobody's yet established just why Sam and Irene were left marooned on Howland for so long, when any fool with a map could see that they might be found there.

Nobody can pinpoint a reason why the world—and the pilots themselves—were left in suspense for so long.

DESPITE CAREFUL RATIONING, SAM AND Irene ran out of sandwiches and condensed milk on their seventh day on Howland Island. Irene suggested they look for crabs. She used to go crabbing all the time when she was younger, and her father would take her down the shore for the day.

Sam and Irene set out together on the leeward side of the island in the late afternoon, carrying one of the empty water cans. They wore swimming costumes, which they'd both packed in their kit bags because a swimming costume didn't weigh all that much, and they'd certainly expected to go swimming once they reached Australia. Irene's was a plain, modest suit of navy blue serge; Sam's was nearly identical except larger and less copious on the chest. The water was warm and clear and remarkably calm, just lapping against the pale sand while the sun glittered on top. Irene marveled at the sight of her feet as she waded out. From the other side of the island, they heard the soft, steady crash of the surf, but here there was nothing but peace, and the fish that nibbled curiously at their toes, and the bright red strawberry hermit crabs that crawled along the reef, scooping up all the smaller creatures. Life grew abundantly here, in the nutrient-rich waters that swelled up the walls of the extinct underwater volcano on which they were perched. Irene plunged her hand in the water and lifted out a wriggling crab.

"Here you go!" she said. "Dinner."

Sam waded over with the empty can. "Blow me down."

Irene dropped the crab inside and said, "Now it's your turn."

"Me? I'm just looking out for sharks."

"You're not scared of the claws, are you?"

"Don't be silly."

"You are too. Come on, here's another one. Just put your hand in and grab him from the top."

Sam made a fed-up noise and dropped his arm into the water. When it came out, a red crab dangled from his fingers. "Dinner," he said.

He dropped the crab in the can, and the pair of hermits scuttled over and under each other. Sam peered in, expression of wonder.

"I can't believe you've never been crabbing," said Irene.

"I grew up in Kansas, for God's sake."

"Still. You've lived in California for years."

"Never went crabbing, though. You have to start young with these things. Your dad has to teach you."

"Well, now I'm teaching you," said Irene.

Sam looked up from the water can. The sun was heading down. Sam's face, already deeply tanned, had turned to gold in the horizontal light. He was grinning. He grinned all the time now, like they were on some kind of exotic vacation instead of marooned together on a barren island, supplies running low. Irene smiled back, because you couldn't help smiling back at a grin like that, Sam Mallory's grin.

"You're teaching me a lot of things, I guess," he said.

THAT NIGHT THEY COOKED THE crabs in the small pit they'd excavated from an old guano mine, a scar left in the ground by the American

Guano Company some fifty years before. Inside this pit, they made the tiny, efficient fires that distilled seawater into something potable, and now they boiled the crabs in the seawater—the fresh water was far too precious—and it turned out all right. For fuel they dried handfuls of tough sea grass and bound it into sticks. Irene could build a decent fire, too, but Sam seemed to have some elemental connection with the whole business, from first spark to dying flame to ember.

After dinner, they lay in the sand and stared at the stars, as they did most nights. There wasn't anything else to do when the sun went down, nothing to see by, so they talked and watched the night sky. Sam was intimate with all the constellations, but Irene hadn't paid much attention to the stars at all until she started learning the principles of celestial navigation.

"The same stars that guided Magellan," Sam pointed out.

"We're just a star ourselves, after all. Who knows, maybe we're guiding some other traveler on some other world."

"That's blasphemy, Foster."

"God's infinite, after all. Why should He content Himself with one little earth?"

Sam didn't reply. Irene listened to the rumble of Sandy's purring from the patch of sand next to Sam's ribs. After a while, she turned her head. The moon was a sliver of a thing now, setting already, but she could pick out just enough of Sam's face to see that he was asleep.

MEANWHILE, AS THE DAYS SLID into weeks, they worked on the Centauri. They both wanted the ship to be ready to fly as soon as help arrived; they desperately wanted to finish the journey in triumph. Sam had figured out that the engine itself was undamaged, that all the trouble came down to nothing more than a broken fuel line, so all he needed to do was to repair it. Except he had no extra hose, nothing to splice the old ends together again. Irene shaded her eyes and frowned at him.

"Don't know why you're bothering with that. They'll have a fuel line for us."

"Who'll have a fuel line?"

"The navy. Once they find us. They'll have a brand-new fuel line you can install in half an hour."

"It's something to do, isn't it? So I don't go nuts." Sam jumped down from the wing. "What's for dinner?"

"Cockles and mussels, alive alive oh."

"Sweet Molly Malone," he sang, thick Irish baritone, and snatched her hand to whirl her around. "As she pushed her wheelbarrow, through streets broad and narrow—"

Irene broke away. "You're in an awfully good mood, for a fellow keeping alive on shellfish and distilled seawater."

"And peanut butter."

"Peanut butter's almost finished."

He squinted at the sky. "I keep telling you we should shoot down a bird or two."

"Like how? Make a slingshot? Anyway, we hardly have enough fuel to distill the water, let alone cook a full-sized booby."

"We'll find a way," he said. "We could live here forever, I'll bet."

CERTAINLY IT WAS STARTING TO seem like they'd lived on Howland forever. The dawn had marked their twentieth day since landing on the island, with no sign of any life upon the surrounding ocean except the occasional pod of bottlenose dolphins. A traitorous corner of Irene's brain was starting to think the unthinkable, that nobody was searching for them, that Sam and Irene were presumed lost, or had simply been forgotten among a thousand more important world affairs.

This was not the case, of course. An exhaustive search was still under way, no hint of giving up, no sir! Hundreds of men combed the Pacific for some sign of the missing pilots, and thousands more wrote and reported and speculated on their whereabouts, and hundreds of millions more gobbled up every crumb of news cooked up by the preceding. The only trouble was, they continued to look in the wrong place. After turning over every stone and blade of grass on Baker Island to the south, the navy had begun trawling the waters to the east, under the assumption—so George Morrow announced to the waiting press—that Sam and Irene had run out of fuel on their way to Baker and made an emergency landing on the water. Mr. Morrow reminded reporters that Mr. Mallory had stayed alive for eleven days on his floating airplane last year, so he was experienced in the techniques for survival. He and the U.S. Navy continued to harbor every expectation for a happy outcome.

So the USS *Farragut* drew its solemn, methodical lines across the open ocean, while Sam and Irene fished for hermit crabs and gazed at the stars from their pile of coral sand some hundred miles to the northwest, and it seemed this state of affairs might continue indefinitely, or at least until some bright spark in the navy, or perhaps Mr. Morrow himself, should have the clever idea to expand the search to include the few additional islands in the larger vicinity.

As of the twenty-second of August, however, Sam and Irene had received no hint of this unprecedented search under way to the south of them, to say nothing of the ballyhoo gripping the globe. Their horizon remained empty. Their radio remained inoperable. So far as they could hear and see, they were the only two people on the face of the earth.

IN THE END, IT WASN'T Mr. Morrow at all who got the clever idea to look for Sam and Irene on Howland Island. It was Hank Foster who checked out some maps from the library, some old navigational charts, and hovered over them with compass and ruler and magnifying glass. On that day, the twenty-second of August, he shot the usual breeze with the reporters gathered in the café at Rofrano's Airfield, where he spent most of his waking hours nursing cups of coffee that might or might not have contained a little something extra. "Boys," he said to them, "I'll tell you what, I don't know why they haven't looked for my Irene on Howland Island."

Within hours, most of America and a good part of the rest of the world had learned not only the name of Howland Island but its exact longitude and latitude, its proximity to the other features of the Pacific Ocean, its history, its geologic composition, its native flora and fauna, its boobies and terns, its guano pits and Polynesian rats, its poverty of fresh water, and its general capability for supporting human life for various lengths of time.

Within a day, the U.S. Navy had dispatched a ship north-northwest at full steam, along with a reporter and a photographer from United Press International, on the express orders of Mr. George Morrow.

AS EVENING FELL ON HOWLAND Island, the twenty-third of August (Howland squatting there on the other side of the International Date Line, remember), the USS *Farragut* plowed through the ocean a hundred and fifty miles away, and Sam and Irene lay side by side on the sand of the island's windward side, listening to the surf—there seemed to be some weather out there on the wide blue sea, somewhere—and watching the stars. They returned to the question of whether they would ever be rescued, whether they would live out their lives on these thousand acres.

"God forbid," Irene said. "Think about your daughter."

"Except for Pixie, sure."

"And flying. Sure would be nice to go up in the air again."

"That too."

This evening there had been none of the usual banter between them, keeping up spirits. Irene busied herself with the distilling apparatus. Sam cooked the crabs in their shells. They ate and drank almost without speaking, because food and water were now precious things, in short supply, and required some concentration. As the sky darkened, Irene had thought Sam looked like a shaman, poking his stick into the glowing ashes, not saying a word. Eventually he settled back in the sand.

When the last ember died, Sandy stalked between them, washed herself thoroughly, and curled up next to Sam's ribs.

Finally Irene spoke. "Did you see that pack of dolphins swimming to the north this afternoon?"

"Pod. Pod of dolphins. Yep, I saw them." He laid down the stick and looked at her. "They'll catch up with us soon. The navy, I mean, not the dolphins."

"Oh, I know they will. It's just funny they haven't shown up yet, that's all. It's not like we're hiding or anything."

"Yeah, it's funny, all right. Won't be too much longer, though. We'll be on our way, back to civilization."

"A hot bath would be grand. Chicken dinner, mashed potatoes. About a pound of butter melting on top. Tall glass of cold lemonade, all you can drink."

"All of that," he said, "but I'm sure going to miss these stars. Won't you?"

Irene looked up at the spangled sky. "Yes."

"It gets you thinking, a universe like that. You start to figure how small you are. How short your time underneath the sky."

"Sam—"

"Irene, I'm going to do it. I'm going to divorce her. Soon as we get back stateside. Before you ask, it's got nothing to do with anything but me and her. I just can't go on the way things are."

"But how? Won't she do the same thing she did before?"

"I've been thinking about that. I figure I should clear some dough from this little adventure, once we get back. Write a book, make some speeches. I'll make her an offer she can't refuse."

"What about your daughter?"

"She can't keep me from Pixie, no matter how she tries," he said, with determination. "I'll hire the best lawyer around to see to that. If I have to, I'll take Pixie myself. I don't like to take a girl from her mother, but a mother like that . . . I don't know. What do you think?"

"I think a girl's going to love her mother, whatever happens."

He put his head in his hands. Irene reached out to cover his knee.

"Sam. You know if there's anything I can do."

"Anything you can do?" He lifted his head and looked at her. "You know I'm in love with you, don't you? You know if I could wave a wand and it would be the three of us, you and me and Pixie—"

"No, don't."

"—I'd do whatever I could to wave that wand. Because that would be heaven for me. To have you both. I'd give up anything for that."

"No, you wouldn't. You wouldn't give up flying."

"If I had to, though?"

"I'd never ask you to," Irene said, without thinking, and Sam turned and seized her hands.

"What are you saying?" he said. "What are you telling me, Irene?"

"Nothing! You've got a wife, Sam."

"Then just tell me you care. Say that I'm not the only one of us lying here at night, burning up with love for somebody who isn't mine."

Well, what could Irene say to that? She wasn't the kind of woman who could lie outright. She wasn't the kind of woman who could move in on another woman's husband, either. She was stuck. Stuck in more ways than one, remember, since it was just the two of them on an island in the middle of the Pacific, no one to know or care what went on in that particular moment, whether they kissed or did not, confessed their hearts or did not, made love in the darkness or did not. Just Sam and Irene and whatever God was paying attention at the time.

Well, let's be honest. In fact, there were plenty of people who cared what was going on, and moreover figured they knew, all right. Millions! As Irene sat in the sand with Sam, holding hands, thinking about how to reply, housewives and bus drivers and secretaries and farmers around the world were right then imagining that scene between the two of them, people *just like you* imagining what would happen if *you too* were marooned on a desert island with some man or woman with whom you were secretly enamored. The more cynical among you might call this an old story, a chestnut, but chestnuts have their purpose, don't they? They allow us to imagine some all-too-human aspect of our condition on this earth, some thought or fantasy or conundrum we share in common, we flawed and yearning animals, we complicated and contradictory beings. That was why the world was transfixed with the story of the lost pilots. Sam and Irene, *c'est nous.*

If you were Irene, what would you say?

If you were Sam, what would you do?

AT 0431 LOCAL TIME THE next morning, the *Farragut* dropped anchor about two hundred yards off the rim of Howland Island. Once dawn broke, the captain dispatched a boat containing himself, an oarsman, and the reporter and photographer from the UPI, to survey the atoll for any sign of the lost pilots.

The news crossed the wire at 0603.

HANALEI, HAWAI'I

October 1947

L INDQUIST TELLS ME to look out the window at that glorious sight below, and I tell her to stick her glorious sights in the world's darkest cave. I ask her what was the real reason she made me come up here with her today. Is this some kind of murder plot? Are we going to crash on this island of hers and end our miseries?

"Of course not," she yells, over the noise of the engines. "What a waste of a good airplane."

"Maroon us on the island, then? Deliver me the full Foster and Mallory experience? The crabs, the peanut butter, the saltwater distillery? Listen up, dame. The desert island survival story, that's a dime a dozen. All variations on a theme of building campfires and eating shellfish and getting sunburnt. Who cares anymore? You know there's only one thing people *really* want to know."

"Oh? And what's that?"

I lean forward. "Did you or didn't you?"

TRY AS I MIGHT, I don't remember how I knew my father was running around on my mother. It seems to me it was just a fact of life. She never tried to hide it from me. As far back as I could recall, she would talk about *your father's little girlfriend*, in this scornful tone of voice, or *that hussy of your father's,* in the same way as you might refer to his beloved automobile or his stamp collection. Sure, I would hear her cry at night when he was away, presumably with some paramour, which was another word my mother favored. But I was just a kid, and I sometimes cried at night, so I didn't think this was especially strange. I adored my father. I thought my father was the most wonderful man alive, handsome and brave and smart, and I knew he loved me more than anything else in the world. He would come home and lift me in the air and call me his best girl, and he would take me out for milkshakes at the drugstore, just me and him, and tell me stories about his day. Of course I loved my mother, but I *worshiped* Dad; I gave him all my secret loyalty. I looked at my mother and felt an awful, guilty, childlike sense of superiority, because Dad certainly wasn't running around on *me*. I was the apple of his eye. Nobody more dear to him than his Janey.

Not until I was older did I realize the truth. Not until later did I understand how much grief my father's sins caused my mother, how it felt when you were betrayed by somebody you loved that much. Because eventually my father left my mother. She came to me one day, when I was about thirteen or so, and said that Dad had left us for good this time, and soon after that Mama met my stepfather and we moved away and that was that. Mama said we were dead to Dad and he was dead to us, and I should just forget all about him and look upon my stepfather as my new father, my real father, a man I could trust.

BUT ALL THAT IS HISTORY. My point is this. As you might have deduced already, I'm fascinated by the subject of sex in general, and infidelity in particular, and have been ever since my father deserted my mother for another woman. In my one year of college, I studied some anthropology and some psychology in an attempt to understand this concept of monogamy and why most human beings will stake their all on one mate, will find themselves cruelly disappointed when that mate proves untrue, when most animals will happily mate with whomever they want. When a stallion, for example, will impregnate every mare in the herd because he has won the right to deposit his superior seed wherever he sees fit, and nobody blames him for it. He's a stallion, for God's sake.

Then I parted ways with college, as you know, and pursued my studies elsewhere, but when the fate of Samuel Mallory began to intrigue me, when I decided I wanted to learn more about this fascinating public figure, I couldn't help searching for clues about his relationship with Irene Foster. If you plunder the newspaper archives for all the articles and interviews covering the Flying Lovebirds' rescue from Howland Island—and there are many, believe me—you'll find that neither Foster nor Mallory lets drop a single hint about the nature of their personal relationship, and yet it stands to reason that a healthy, attractive, red-blooded male would naturally want to fuck a healthy, attractive, red-blooded female, if they were given a chance like Howland, a chance in a million. Stands to reason Mallory would forsake the forsaking of all others and betray his wife; stands to reason Foster would be unable to resist a strapping young demigod like that.

But I want to hear it from *her* mouth. I want to hear from Lindquist what they did, and when, and how often, and whether they gave a damn about poor Mrs. Mallory, left at home with that innocent towheaded tot. I want a real answer. Because nobody's going to read a book about Sam Mallory unless that answer lies inside, right?

Only Lindquist won't answer the question.

She points to her ears. "Can't hear you so well with this racket. We'll talk after we land."

"How long will that be?"

"Not long. It's only about thirty miles away. I'll have us there in a jiffy."

I sit back in my seat and stare at the metal wall. She's got a point, after all. Call me stupid, but I never considered that an airplane would be so damned noisy inside. I guess I just imagined the silence of death.

But believe me, those propellers don't just whirl around quietly. The pistons of those engines don't thrust without friction. The noise goes on and on, and for the first time I wonder how she and Mallory didn't go crazy, listening to that racket for twelve or eighteen hours without pause.

TWENTY MINUTES LATER, THE ENGINES change pitch, and gravity pulls us downward. I still haven't looked out the window, and I don't intend to. What's there to see, anyhow? Down we plummet, *down down down* while my stomach drops in pursuit, my head gets all dizzy, the black spots appear before my eyes. Lindquist, perhaps sensing my decline, glances back over her shoulder and points at my seat. I look underneath and find a paper bag. I'm not sure if I'm supposed to breathe into it or vomit, but my stomach decides for me. Luckily there's not much, just coffee and Scotch. What a waste.

Because I'm not looking out the window, the landing surprises me. We're rattling along, and then bump, and then another bump, and then the continual bumping of wheels on turf.

"Here we are!" Lindquist says cheerfully. She brings the airplane to a stop and I sit there awkwardly with my bag in my hands. The bottle fell out of my lap some time ago and rolled down the aisle to the tail. I unbuckle my straps and stagger after it. Bottle in one hand, bag in the other, I ask Lindquist where I can dispose of my little problem.

"You'll just have to hold on to it until we get back," she says. "There's nothing else here except us."

Naturally I think she's kidding, but when she opens the door and the fresh air rushes inside, I see nothing but green grass and jungle, and the ocean off to the right.

"Isn't it beautiful?" Lindquist says. "I come here when I want to be alone. That's the best thing about flying. It gives you the freedom to leave the rest of the world behind you. Hop down, now. I've packed a picnic for us."

MY LEGS ARE WOBBLY AND something seems to be wrong with the way my head is attached to the rest of me, but I hold myself upright and follow Lindquist along the grass and scrub, through some trees, until we emerge on a cliff above a flawless white beach. A large wave thunders onto the rocks below. Lindquist sets down the picnic basket and puts her hands on her hips. She's wearing her usual uniform of tan slacks and white shirt; she's taken off the navy jacket and the gloves and put a straw hat on her head—to save what's left of her skin, she says, as if she weren't just the kind of irritating woman who can carry off a wrinkle or two and only look more alluring.

She turns her head to me. "Well? What do you think?"

"I hope you're not expecting me to surf, that's all."

"Of course not. Only a daredevil would surf this wave. Give me a hand, will you?"

I help her spread the blanket and unpack the sandwiches and the bottles of lemonade and the orangey-pink fruit she calls papaya. She removes her hat and eats in silence, legs tucked up against her chest, watching the waves form offshore. The sun is hot, but there's enough breeze to keep us comfortable. When we've finished the sandwiches and the fruit, Lindquist tells me there's a cake inside the basket, and could I fetch it out and slice it up with the knife. I do as she asks. As I sink the blade through layers of frosting and sponge, I feel as if she's watching every movement, every tiny gesture, like this is a test of some kind. I hand her a slice. We eat. I say this would be a grand time for a cigarette.

"I'd rather you didn't," she says.

"Well, I've thrown up all the Scotch, so I'd say you owe me a cigarette."

She opens her mouth and stops herself.

"What?" I say.

"Nothing." She stands up and holds out her hand. I allow her to draw me up. The ocean stretches out before us, all the way to the Orient. The wind tumbles my hair. Lindquist speaks so softly, I have to strain to hear her, and yet I have the feeling that this is why I'm here, this is why she brought me here, the flight, the Scotch, the island, the picnic, this particular stretch of ocean before us: all of it in preparation for this moment, some grand speech.

"Samuel Mallory had his faults," she says. "We all do, I guess. But he was an honorable man. He was a good man. He always wanted to do the right thing, even when he fell short. He loved me. He loved his daughter. Everything else came second. He would have died for us both. If you're going to write this book of yours, you have to make that clear, because unless you understand that, you can't understand Sam at all."

"What about his wife? Didn't he love his wife?"

This brings her up short. She studies the question for some time. So long, in fact, that I start to wonder whether she means to answer me at all, whether we will ever get to the heart of the matter.

I continue. "Men, you know. They talk all the time about love and fidelity, but in the end they just follow their own inclinations to populate the earth, and who suffers? The wives and the children they leave behind. And that's something I take personally, because the same thing happened to me. My father left my mother for another woman, and I wound up getting myself in the kind of trouble that a girl often gets into when she loses a father, the kind of trouble she never recovers from, the kind of trouble that haunts her all her life."

"I see," she says. "What kind of trouble, if you don't mind my asking?"

"Ah, but we aren't talking about me, remember? We're talking about you and Mallory and what really happened in that space of time between Los Angeles and Sydney, Australia. Not what the newspapers reported. Not what the photographs showed, God knows. The truth."

Lindquist crosses her arms and kicks a tuft of grass and stares out to sea. A gust of wind dares to tangle her famous hair, the hair that Mallory first cut for her on Howland Island.

"All right," she says. "I'll tell you the truth. I just don't know if it will be enough for you."

ONE LAST THING, THE MOST important thing, though I've never told a soul until now. Remember that fellow at the law firm, the married law-yer who impregnated me? That was my stepfather.

AVIATRIX

by Eugenia Everett

(e x c e r p t)

August 1928: Australia

IRENE HAD SOME inkling what to expect when they touched down in
Sydney, a little more than forty hours after their rescue from Howland. The captain's briefing, the radiograms from Morrow, had all made
clear the worldwide sensation their disappearance had caused, how
everybody in America and around the globe had followed the story with
utmost interest.

Still. When the crowd surged forward to encompass the Centauri,
almost before it had come to a stop on the runway at Sydney Airport,
Irene stared out the window in a state of shock. Nothing could prepare
you for that, nobody could explain what it was like to sit in the focus of so much concentrated attention. In those days, when things like
syndicated newspapers and radio and moving pictures were only just
beginning to exert their power over the mass imagination, fame wasn't
yet something to be afraid of, something that could take over your life
and habits and change your psychological composition. Only one man
in the world really knew what celebrity meant, and that was Lindbergh. As Irene witnessed this evidence of fame, as she was made to
understand what a crowd of fifty thousand people actually looked like,
she didn't feel any sense of elation or triumph. She felt the opposite.

She felt dread. Her life was about to change; her daily existence, her sense of herself—Irene—had just been obliterated and replaced with something she didn't recognize. There was nothing ahead but fog and darkness.

THE FIRST MAN THROUGH THE hatch was George Morrow. Boy, was he beaming! Irene couldn't understand a word he said, but she had the unsettling impression that he was a Broadway manager, and she was an actress who had performed her part perfectly, though she hadn't even seen the script. First he kissed her hand and then he shook Sam's hand. Then he noticed the cat, crouched behind Sam's ankles.

"What the hell?" he said.

Sam picked up Sandy. "Stowaway."

"I'll be damned. That's brilliant!" Morrow exclaimed. "Press'll love it."

A car was already waiting, motor rumbling, to whisk them into town, to George Morrow's suite at the Harbour Rocks Hotel. There, a doctor examined them both thoroughly and pronounced them in excellent health, except for some lingering exhaustion and dehydration, in addition to the temporary loss of hearing, which the doctor expected to subside soon. Morrow and the doctor then bustled outside to announce this happy news to the waiting press, and Sam and Irene were left alone with Sandy, who curled up in an armchair and went warily to sleep.

There was no point in talking yet, because of the deafness, and of course they expected Morrow back any second. Sam got up and walked to one of the giant windows that looked out over Sydney Harbor, and Irene joined him. They didn't touch. Nor did they hear George Morrow when he bustled back inside and came up behind them. They both started when he took each of them by the arm and informed them, loudly, that he was going to escort them by the back stairs to their suites, where the hotel chambermaids were waiting to draw their baths and ready them for an afternoon nap.

"You'll want to get some rest," Morrow said. "Tonight there's a ball in your honor."

POSSIBLY NOTHING IN IRENE'S LIFE until that point felt quite as immediately good as that bath. For one thing, the bathroom itself was a large, luxurious cave of marble and porcelain and soft Turkish towels. The water was fresh and warm, drawn for her by a reverent, wide-eyed chambermaid who added oil from a glass decanter and didn't say a thing, not because of professional politeness but because her heart was too full for words. Then she left, and Irene sank into that tub like you might sink into heaven.

When she emerged, wrapped in a dressing gown, she was taken aback to find George Morrow at home on her sofa, smoking a cigar and nursing a glass of whiskey. He rose at once and asked if he could pour her something. Champagne, perhaps? It was legally available here in Australia, after all, and would help her sleep.

"No, thank you," she said. "I don't touch intoxicants."

It came out more prim than she intended, and Morrow had the grace to set aside his glass. He urged her to the sofa, settled himself in the nearby armchair, and apologized for intruding.

She cupped an ear. "I'm sorry. You'll have to speak louder."

"Of course!" he barked, leaning forward a few inches, and repeated himself.

"You're not intruding at all, Mr. Morrow. We couldn't have made the trip without you," she replied.

"Believe me, Miss Foster, the honor of sponsoring this historic journey was all mine." He paused to beam. Like the rest of him, his dentistry was perfect and whispered of prosperity. "Of course, like the rest of the world, I'm only happy you're alive and well. *Alive and well,*" he repeated, more loudly, because Irene was squinting with the effort of making him out.

"Oh, I guess it will all die down soon enough. I'm just an ordinary girl, after all, and I don't much care for all the fuss."

"An ordinary girl? Miss *Foster.*"

"It's true, I'm as plain as could be. I just like to fly, that's all."

"*Plain?*" He laughed. "Don't you see yourself at all? Plain? *Ordinary?* You're *extra*ordinary. By God, you're the biggest sensation since Lindbergh. Those crowds out there"—he flung his arm to the window—"are here for you."

"And Sam."

"Sam, of course." Mr. Morrow leaned back and set the cigar in an ashtray. Irene couldn't help staring at his immaculate fingernails. It was funny how you forgot certain details about civilization, like how immaculate fingers could be. Now he laced them together and looked at her. He made a couple of false starts before he spoke again. "Miss Foster. Can I be candid with—"

Irene cupped her ear again. "I'm sorry."

Morrow cleared his throat. "Can I be—oh, damn. Never mind. I only wish to say that I see a very bright future ahead for you. You've captured the imagination of the world. Books, lectures. You'll be *bigger* than Lindbergh."

Irene couldn't hear every word. She wasn't sure she understood him properly. Write books? "Sam's going to write the book," she said. "He already said so. He's going to write a book about all this, and use the money to—to—well, to take care of his family."

"People want to hear from *you,* Irene."

"I don't see why."

"Because you're a woman, Irene, and the world's fascinated with women. Women with a sense of adventure, women who can take on men at their own game. The emancipated woman, she's the spirit of the age." Morrow lifted his cigar from the ashtray and pointed it at

Irene's mouth. "*You,* Irene. People want to hear from *you.* They can't get enough of you."

Irene was so exhausted, she didn't want to argue. She couldn't think through an argument, couldn't put together any kind of complex thought or sentence. "But I just want to *fly,*" she said again.

Morrow reached to tap the ash from the end of his cigar. He rose from his chair and approached the window, which looked out over a sunny, chilly Sydney Harbor. It was winter here, after all. Morrow braced one hand against the window frame and gazed out across the sun-dappled water. He wasn't wearing a suit jacket, just his trousers and stiff white shirt and waistcoat, neatly buttoned, conservative dove gray. The blue smoke of his cigar trailed around him. Its rich scent was altogether different from Sam's cigarettes. Irene, sitting on the sofa in her dressing gown, felt woozy with the need to sleep. Morrow seemed to disappear into his blue fog. Her eyelids sank downward. Just as she began to doze off, Morrow appeared next to her on the sofa, so close their knees almost touched.

"Miss Foster, I don't mean to be importunate—" He stopped, coughed, and continued in a louder voice, close to her ear. "And I realize it's none of my business, as a mere friend. But as a *manager*—as your business manager—I feel it's incumbent upon me to ask . . ."

Irene picked at the edge of her robe. "Ask what?"

"Whether there's anything you should tell me, about you and Mr. Mallory."

"I'm afraid I don't know what you mean."

"Irene, they're going to ask, those reporters. Maybe not in so many words. But the whole world's dying to know—a man and a woman, stranded on an island together—don't tell me you don't understand my meaning."

Over on the armchair, Sandy lifted her head and licked a paw. Irene set down the hem she'd been picking and smoothed it over the bump of her knee.

"No," she said. "I've got nothing to tell you about Sam and me."

Morrow held her gaze for a second or two, just to see if she'd back down, she thought. So she didn't. He turned away and stubbed out his cigar in the ashtray. "All right, then. I can see you're tired. Get yourself some rest. We'll discuss all this in the morning over breakfast."

"You and me and Sam."

"Of course."

Morrow's jacket lay over the back of the armchair. He rose and hooked it with his finger. As he picked up his hat, he looked Irene's way and smiled.

"I like the new hairdo, Miss Foster. It suits you."

THE HAIRDO, OF COURSE, WAS to become iconic: a symbol of the age and the women who peopled it, of this daring new generation of females. To millions of admirers, those short curls meant freedom and courage. Certainly they attracted attention. In the many photographs that survive from the press conference after the Centauri's miraculous arrival in Sydney, Irene Foster's hair seizes the camera's fascination: a riotous gold mop glimmering under the lights like some kind of beacon for the brave new world.

Naturally, the reporters wanted to know how and when and why she had cut her hair. And Irene—who was still exhausted, remember, who had napped only briefly before Morrow knocked again on the door of her hotel suite to summon her to her public—let down her guard for a single sentence, the only sentence. She glanced at Sam, who sat at her side; Sam glanced at her, and they shared a smile. "Sam cut it for me, on our third day on Howland," she said. "Long hair just gets in the way of everything, doesn't it?"

The photographers present that day were not stupid. A cavalcade of flashbulbs and camera shutters captured that shared smile, which was reproduced on millions of sheets of newsprint within twenty-four hours, was thrown up on thousands of newsreel screens within a week, was printed in countless magazines and books over the years, was later expanded to gigantic proportions for museum exhibits and popular art. It became, in the collective imagination, a visual shorthand for two separate though related aspects of twentieth century life: for the unique and private connection that exists between two people deeply in love and for a moment in history when an equal standing between man and woman—the possibility for adventure shared, for genuine partnership—became possible.

Humans being as they are, of course, the fact that both Sam and Irene married other people only made it all the more intriguing.

FOLLOWING THE PRESS CONFERENCE, THERE was a gala dinner, then a tour of the city the next day in the company of the mayor, in which Sam and Irene (accompanied by George Morrow) appear to have met at least half the civil servants in the entire province. There was a luncheon with the Sydney Ladies Auxiliary, a military ball given by the Australian Flying Corps, a private lunch at the new Government House in Canberra with Lord Stonehaven, the governor-general of Australia, followed by a formal dinner with the prime minister and senior members of government, along with their wives. Various additional public appearances filled in the gaps of this bruising schedule.

To Irene it all passed in a blur, or rather a jumble. She felt like a doll, dressed up—Morrow had ordered an entire wardrobe for her—and paraded about at event after event, saying the same things to an endless receiving line of people, giving variants of the same speech, more or less, she had delivered to the panjandrums of Honolulu. What she did not experience was time to herself. Each day, Morrow left her at her hotel suite at midnight and rapped on her door at half past seven, so that she had neither time nor energy to do anything else except stumble to bed and sleep deeply, dreamlessly, for the hours allotted. Not only was she never left alone with Sam, they had no opportunity to arrange a private meeting. It was Morrow, Morrow, Morrow, all day long.

On their fifth night in Australia, Irene rang up the switchboard and asked to be connected to Sam, but the operator told her she was unable to put through any calls to that suite without permission. Irene explained that this was Miss Foster, room 205. The operator apologized and said it was still impossible. The next morning, when Morrow's attention was momentarily distracted, Irene told Sam. "I tried the same thing," he said. "With the same result. I'd have marched right down the hall to see you, but Morrow's got guards posted outside my door and yours."

"That's for protection from the public," said Irene.

"Sure it is," said Sam.

When Morrow returned to the breakfast table a moment later, Sam said, "What gives with the telephone lines? I can't get a call in to Irene."

"Of course not," said Morrow. "Because any operator on that switchboard could listen in to your conversation, and every word would appear verbatim in the next morning's papers."

"Baloney," said Irene.

Morrow shrugged. "An operator could earn a year's pay selling that story."

"Couldn't you sue the newspaper?"

"Maybe. But the story'd be out by then." Morrow reached for his coffee. "And I don't think either of you would appreciate your private intercourse being made public."

"That's an interesting choice of words," said Sam.

They were sitting in Irene's suite, where they usually met for breakfast together, since they attracted too much attention when eating in hotel dining rooms. This particular morning that suite was located on the fourth floor of the Hotel Windsor in Melbourne; they were due to leave for the aforementioned visit to Canberra by private rail car in two hours. Outside, the weather was dry and cool, a few clouds skidding across the southern sky. A pair of radiators simmered under the giant windows overlooking Parliament House. At seven thirty precisely, a pair of waiters had knocked on the door and wheeled in this

round table, set for three, with coffee, eggs, toast, bacon, sausages, kip-
pers, grilled tomatoes, grapefruit, an entire pitcher of freshly squeezed
orange juice, and a dish of cream for Sandy, who was now famous in
her own right. The eggs were soft boiled; Morrow ate his from a silver
egg cup, knocking off the tops with a spoon, while Irene and Sam both
emptied theirs on slices of buttered toast. Sam had already drunk four
cups of coffee and smoked three cigarettes. He was in a fighting mood.

Morrow replaced his cup in the saucer. "Of course the nature of your
personal friendship is none of my business, or anyone else's. But you
must be aware of the insinuations made by the more scurrilous members
of the press. Any evidence, or supposed evidence, that your association
is anything other than purely platonic—"

"Is none of anyone's business, except mine and Irene's."

"And your wife's," said Morrow. "Let's not forget about Mrs. Mallory, at home in Oakland with her daily newspaper."

Irene set down her fork and wiped her fingers on her napkin. She
looked at Sam; he was looking at her. Sandy, who had finished her
cream and now curled on Sam's lap, lifted her head and blinked her eyes.

"And your daughter too, of course," added Morrow.

Sam picked up his cigarette and shifted back to Morrow. "All right.
I take your point."

"On the level, now. I don't give a damn what happened between the
two of you on Howland Island," Morrow said. "We're all human. I don't
think there's a man alive who would blame you for letting nature take its
course, in a situation like that. But now you're back in civilization, and
the eyes of the world are watching you both, every second. I advise you
not to stick a fork in your chance for fame and fortune with some foolish
indiscretion. Are we square?"

Sam's face was white. He sucked on his cigarette, crushed it out in
the ashtray, and poured himself another cup of coffee. "As I said, I take
your point."

Morrow turned to Irene. "Well? Irene?"

"I understand perfectly," she said.

BY THEN, OF COURSE, MORROW'S admonitions were too late. Two weeks ago, the owner of the camera that had opened its shutter on what appeared to be a tender sunrise embrace between Irene Foster and Sam Mallory on the Waikiki beach, arrived by steamship in San Francisco, where he proceeded to the offices of the *San Francisco Chronicle* and offered to sell the newspaper the entire roll of film on an exclusive basis.

Now, the *Chronicle*, being the respectable kind of newspaper, none of your scurrilous muckraking yellow journalism sullying its pages, did not deem this particular news fit to print. The subjects, after all, were presently lost at sea, perhaps dead, as far as the frantic world knew. In fact, Sam and Irene were almost certainly dead, heroically so, dead in the sacred cause of human advancement, and you simply had to draw the line of decency somewhere, didn't you? Even in the face of the kind of stop-the-presses scoop for which most newspapermen waited their whole lives. Sorry, sonny. No can do. Anyway, how do we even know for sure that's Foster and Mallory on the beach together? Could be any man and woman who bear a passing resemblance.

Nothing daunted, the photographer then proceeded to the offices of the other newspapers in town, and those down the peninsula and across the bay. The *San Jose Mercury-News*. The *Oakland Tribune*. Still no takers. He bought a train ticket to Los Angeles and visited the *Times*, the *Orange County Register*, and so on down the circulation tables, and still he could not find a single buyer for his sensational photographs. *Denver Post*? Nope. *Chicago Tribune*? Don't waste my time, you goddamn louse. *Cleveland Plain Dealer*? Go stick your photos where the sun don't shine, and what kind of American are you, anyway.

You see the pattern. Not until this enterprising fellow reached New York City on the morning of the twenty-fourth of August, to discover a world made delirious with the news that Irene Foster and Sam Mallory had just been rescued intact from some spit of an island smack in the middle of the Pacific, did his luck finally turn. So electric was the atmosphere in the newsroom of the *New York Sentinel* that the photographer was able to waltz straight past reception and make his proposal to some harried green-shaded copy editor, who happened to be on the last five minutes of a drop-dead deadline. To demonstrate his annoyance he hauled our Peeping Tom straight to the office of the managing editor, threw him in, and yelled, *This fellow says he got a snap of Foster and Mallory fucking on some beach in Hawai'i!* The managing editor and the five or six reporters crowding his office turned and stared, and it would be fair to say that the hackling of journalistic instinct in that room was thicker than the smoke of the seven or eight cigarettes they were presently smoking. *No shit?* said the editor, and the photographer said, *Got it right here, sir. If it ain't the real deal, you can kiss my mother.* (Except he didn't say *kiss*.)

There followed some agonized conferring about ethics, and the publisher himself was called in from some lunch at Delmonico's, reeking of martinis and cigars and beefsteak. But the conclusion was foregone. Yesterday, Sam and Irene were martyrs, whose memory must remain unsullied, as was decent and necessary to American morale. Today, they were mortals, and the whole world wanted to know what they'd got up to on Howland Island for three weeks, and now the *New York Sentinel* had the answer, right there in incontestable photographic negative. You could call it muckraking, you could call it scurrilous, but you had to call it news. And once you stopped quibbling about principle, the only thing left to quibble about was price. (Ten thousand dollars for exclusive rights, as it turned out, which set a record for the time.)

Of course, once the formalities were complete, you had to wait a few days, until the public was bored and restless and eager for something new, but hadn't yet turned its attention elsewhere. So it wasn't until the first of September that the photographs—five were chosen from the roll—duly appeared on page three of the early edition, because you couldn't print a thing like that on the front page, over the fold where anybody could see it, and within hours the newsrooms and editorial offices of the world found themselves struggling with what you might call a dilemma.

Keep in mind, even in those days, the *New York Sentinel* was the kind of paper that staked its profit on the low human greed for other people's beeswax. You might argue that our Honolulu shutterbug couldn't have wandered into a more providential newsroom in America on that particular morning, the morning Sam and Irene were resurrected from the dead. The *Sentinel* had the ethos and the heft and the credibility—just barely—to make those photographs the talk of the town. Newsstand sales set a record that day. So what were all the other dailies and weeklies and monthlies to do? Hold firm to the high ground and watch their readers flock to some other, less persnickety publication?

The solution was obvious. Of course you couldn't just print those photographs by themselves, as a piece of news! Worse than prurient, they weren't even news anymore. So you did what every newsman does when he misses the scoop: he writes a story about the story. You know the kind I mean. *Honolulu Photos: Has the* Sentinel *Gone Too Far?* and that sort of thing. In doing so, it was of course necessary for these Timeses and Picayunes and Tribunes to publish said photos themselves—quietly paying the *Sentinel* its royalty fees—so that the reader could decide for himself if the *Sentinel* had gone too far. You see how this works?

And bang! There you have it. That was how the image of Irene Foster and Sam Mallory embracing on the sands of Waikiki spread right across the world's newsprint like the Spanish flu in the days following their safe arrival in Sydney, Australia, such that you couldn't walk outside without catching it.

Needless to say, it was not much longer before some curious reporter turned up at Mrs. Mallory's door with a copy and asked if she had any comment to make.

AT THIS POINT, GEORGE MORROW might have made a strategic error, depending on your view of the matter. Having proceeded from Melbourne to Canberra and hit it off with the governor and the prime minister, the three of them were invited by the PM—Stanley Bruce, a thorough-going Australian sportsman—to join him for a few days of rest and restoration at a sheep station in central Queensland, owned by a friend of his, a Mr. Howard Hounslow. Possibly Morrow thought this expedition could be turned into a publicity advantage of some kind; possibly he was just too flattered by the invitation. In any case, they agreed, and a day later—just as Mrs. Mallory opened her newspaper and saw the photographs of her husband caught in flagrante on the sand with his lithe navigator, clad only in her wet drawers—the party trundled dustily down a hundred miles of unpaved road to a private residence with no switchboards, no security guards, no separate wings, no physical safeguards of any kind against the natural instincts of two people passionately in love with each other.

The house itself had been built in the last century by some hard-bitten ancestor of Mr. Hounslow, and quarters weren't what you might call luxurious, especially after you'd experienced the pampering of Australia's grandest hotels. But at this point in the week, privacy was the greatest luxury of all, and Irene couldn't get enough of it. On the second morning, she woke at half past five, bathed and dressed, went to the kitchen to cadge a mug of coffee from the surprised cook, and marched outside to watch the sun rise, all by herself, under the shelter of a coolibah tree. (Really.)

We already know that Sam Mallory was just as determined an early riser, so it should come as no surprise that he also woke early, bathed and dressed, and while fastening his cuffs happened to look outside his window, just as Irene strode across the grass with her cup of coffee. He found her sitting under the coolibah, almost invisible in the fragile light. He said something about being careful of the snakes.

"Oh, they don't bother you, so long as you don't bother them."

"American snakes, maybe. The Australian ones are a little hungrier, I've heard. Where'd you get the coffee?"

"Sweet-talked the cook. Sip?"

He took the coffee and drank and leaned his head back against the trunk of the tree. The sun rose by millimeters above the distant horizon.

The ground here was flat, the hills stunted, the land dry. You could breathe deep and taste all the delicate perfumes of the grasslands.

"So the way I figure it," Sam said, "we've got another two weeks of this circus before we board that ship back for California. Three weeks to cross the ocean. I'll break the news to Bertha right after we get back, I mean there's no point trying to soften the blow."

"You're sure?" Irene said.

"Couldn't be more. It's you I'm worried about. They'll call you a home-wrecker and worse, they'll call you all kinds of things."

"Well, I am. I am a home-wrecker."

"No, you're not. Bertha and I, we couldn't be worse for each other. From the beginning, we made each other miserable. Our marriage has been over since long before I met you. The only fine thing we ever had between us was Pixie."

Irene sat up. "But you wouldn't be divorcing her if it weren't for me. So that makes me a home-wrecker."

Sam set down the coffee cup and reached for her. "Irene, don't. You're not doing a thing. It's not your fault I'm crazy for you, can't think of anything but you, don't want to spend a single hour except with you . . ."

Irene let him pull her back down into the grass. He put an arm around her and drew her right up against his side.

"But I won't have them saying a word against you," he went on. "So we're going to lie low for a bit. Strictly professional. The divorce might take a year or so, done right."

"What about flying?"

"Why, that's the best part. We're a team, aren't we? We'll just hold our heads up and fly in every derby, every exhibition, every air show that will pay us. Take the high ground, don't talk to any damned reporters—"

"I like the sound of that."

"Write a book together, go on a lecture tour. They'll flock to see us."

"Will they? Even after all this dies down?"

"Sure, they will. They'll love you. You're America's Flying Sweetheart, remember? Between the two of us, we'll be able to buy our own ship within a year. Buy a nice house somewhere to settle down and shut the damned world out. You wouldn't mind having Pixie around, would you?"

"Of course not."

"Because I can't let Bertha raise her alone. She'd break that child like she tried to break me. Pixie needs a mother like you. Someone true and brave, someone who knows how to love another person."

"I'll do my best for her. You know that."

"We'd teach her to surf, wouldn't we? Wake up mornings and hit the water first thing."

"Yes," said Irene. She played with the buttons of his woolen waistcoat. It wasn't cold, but it was still winter, after all, and the morning air was cool on her hands and face. The sky had turned gloriously pink. She was drowsy and happy, listening to Sam's heartbeat through the wool, listening to his rumbly voice. His hand found hers and wound their fingers together.

"Maybe one day we could have a kid of our own," he said. "Raise it with Pixie."

"Is that what you want?"

"More than anything in the world, except you. What do you think?"

"I don't know. I haven't really thought about kids."

"Well, we've got all the time in the world for you to think about it. You just tell me yes or no when you've decided."

Irene raised herself on one elbow. Her eyes were blurry, but she could see his face, all right, lit up by the sunrise. "Sam Mallory," she said, kind of raspy, "I have never loved anything on earth so much as I love you."

"Not even flying?"

"Not even flying."

"Surfing?"

"Not by a long shot."

He reached for the back of her head and kissed her, and a little while passed before they said anything else. Even then, they didn't say much.

THEY RETURNED SEPARATELY TO THE house. Irene felt like the sun, so full of heat and light she couldn't help shedding it all around her. In the kitchen, she filled her cup back up with coffee and asked the cook if anyone else was up. The cook told her that Mr. Hounslow and Mr. Bruce were out riding, and Mr. Morrow was in the dining room eating breakfast.

Irene realized she was hungry and went into the dining room, where the breakfast dishes were spread out on the sideboard. She heaped her plate and sat down across from Morrow. He'd already said good morning and was studying the newspaper. Since arriving in Sydney, Irene had been avoiding any kind of newspaper or magazine. She was afraid of seeing herself in it, some photograph that looked like her but was not, some quote attributed to her, some description that matched a person who looked and sounded like Irene but wasn't really, not the real Irene, Irene as Irene understood her. But now, sitting in the dining room of this fellow Hounslow's house in the middle of nowhere, skin aglow, mind sharp, Irene felt some curiosity about that newspaper on the table. Not for news of herself! The *rest* of the world, the *real* world, business and politics and baseball. So she asked Morrow if she could read this newspaper when he was finished.

Morrow looked up and smiled. "Do you know what I think? I think you should take a vacation from the news."

"What's that supposed to mean?"

"It's just the same damned thing over and over."

"I don't know. I'd like to know what's going on. I don't even know who's running for president! Did Al Smith win the nomination after all?"

"Yes, he did. The Democratic sacrificial lamb. Hasn't got a chance against Hoover."

The door opened. Sam walked in, whistling. "Who? Al Smith?" he said.

Morrow folded up the newspaper and tucked it under his plate. "They've got to field somebody, don't they? Why not some Irish wet who'll scare the dickens out of the Southern Baptists and raise the hackles of the do-gooding bluebloods. Say, you ought to try the hash."

Sam carried his brimming plate next to Irene and sat down. Under the tablecloth, his leg tangled with hers. "Wouldn't mind taking a look at that newspaper, if you're done with it."

"I was just telling Irene that it might not be a bad idea to take a little holiday away from the news. As we're doing now."

Sam looked at Morrow; Morrow stared back at him. Irene noticed the pause and looked up, but by the time she realized there was some message passing between the two of them, both men had returned to their breakfast. The new-risen sun tumbled through the window. From somewhere in the house came the sound of human activity, Hounslow and Bruce, probably, returned from their ride. Irene slipped off her shoe and caressed Sam's ankle with her toe. He choked a little on his hash and reached for the coffee. The door burst open.

"Morrow! There you are. Some fellow just came in with an express telegram for you." Hounslow thrust out his hand, which held a familiar yellow envelope. Morrow leaned forward across the table and took it. "Fine weather this morning, isn't it? How's breakfast?"

"Breakfast is terrific," said Irene, who was watching George Morrow's face as he read his telegram. "We appreciate the hospitality."

"Why, it's no trouble at all. Bruce here said the two of you were looking a bit peaky with all the fuss. That's the beauty of this place. Nobody can be troubled to find you here." Hounslow clapped his hand on Mr. Bruce's shoulder. "Isn't that right, Prime Minister?"

Morrow rose from his chair. "If you'll excuse me, gentlemen. Mr. Mallory, might I have a moment of your time?"

Sam wiped his mouth and rose. "Certainly."

AT THIS POINT, MORROW HAD said nothing about the matter of the Waikiki photographs. He would later explain to Irene that he was protecting the two of them from unnecessary distraction, that he was using his influence behind the scenes to discredit the images, to shame the publications that printed them, to contain and quench the firestorm all by himself. Reporters were given strict instructions not to ask the pilots about the photographs or face eviction from any further events or interviews; guests and officials were warned not to mention the matter. Newspapers, magazines, all were held discreetly out of sight, and Morrow kept the two pilots so busy with engagements, they didn't even notice.

So Irene had no inkling something was wrong until Morrow read that telegram at breakfast. She saw it in his face—a flash of shock, then dismay, then calculation. His gaze had flicked back and forth, Irene and Sam and Irene again. When he rose and asked to speak privately to Sam, she felt a tremor of foreboding. But she never imagined why; in a month of guessing, she never would have predicted the contents of that telegram, and how it would change her life. Later, she found herself wishing that somebody would invent some kind of warning light, like in an airplane cockpit, that flashed on when a great catastrophe was imminent.

IRENE NEVER REMEMBERED THE SUBSTANCE of her conversation with Mr. Hounslow and the prime minister of Australia over breakfast that morning. She has some vague recollection of the Olympics, which had concluded while she and Sam were marooned on Howland, so it's possible the two men brought her up to date on who had won and lost, which countries had made a good showing. Her mind, of course, was elsewhere. Her mind had followed Morrow and Sam, wherever they had gone for their private conversation. After a decent interval, she excused herself and went looking for them.

The house wasn't especially large, but she found no sign of either man, Morrow or Mallory. She went outside for a walk, thinking that would pass the time or that she might encounter them outside, but the landscape around her remained bare and empty, the wide Australian countryside containing nothing but what God had created Himself. The sun grew hot, and Irene returned to the house. She heard voices in the library, but they turned out to be Mr. Hounslow and Stanley Bruce, so she climbed the stairs and went down the corridor to Sam's bedroom. Before she reached his door, however, George Morrow appeared around a corner and stopped her.

"Irene! There you are. I've been hoping to speak to you. Do you have a moment?"

"Of course," Irene said.

She followed Morrow to his own room, which was larger than hers and had a sitting area, already laid for coffee. Morrow motioned her to the settee. There was no sign of Sam.

"Coffee?" Morrow said, and Irene replied yes. By now, he knew how she took it, and added the single spoonful of sugar without asking first. When they were both settled, he spoke again. "What a circus, eh? I'm glad this offer of Bruce's popped up. I think it's just the thing for you. A few days of quiet."

"It's been hectic, all right." Irene sipped her coffee. "What were you and Sam talking about?"

"A private matter. No doubt he'll tell you all about it, when he can."

"When he can? What's that supposed to mean?"

"I mean when he's able. It's a private matter, as I said."

Irene was trying not to shake from nerves. Of course she couldn't press Morrow. She couldn't imply she had some right to know Sam's personal affairs, that she was intimately involved in them. "I hope it's nothing serious," she said.

Morrow replaced his cup in his saucer and spoke carefully. "As you know, Mallory has a family of his own, which requires his attention from time to time. A family's a great responsibility."

"Of course it is. I hope—"

"You, on the other hand, don't have any such distractions. It's a real advantage, when we consider your career."

"My career?"

"You've got a bright future ahead, Irene. Your name, your face— why, you're the most recognizable woman on the face of the earth. Better than some actress, even, because you've got *credibility*. You've got *substance*. Everybody admires you. I've got so many offers for you, I can't even read them all. Books, syndicated columns, your own show on the radio. Chewing gum. Hair shampoo. Cigarettes."

Irene caught the last word. "But I don't even smoke!"

"Who cares? They'll offer you a pile of money. Enough so you can buy your own airplane. You can fly solo, you can amaze the world, as you were born to do. And I'll stand right by you, never fear. I won't do a thing without your say-so."

"I fly with Sam. We're a team."

Morrow set his coffee aside. "Irene, would you mind if I speak to you candidly?"

Irene clutched the sides of her saucer. Morrow was leaning forward now, hands gathered in the gap between his knees, a pose that reminded her of Sam. "What are you getting at, Mr. Morrow?"

"It's just this. I like Sam Mallory. He's a first-rate pilot, maybe the best pilot in America. Maybe the best pilot in the world. But he's—well, I want to say this the right way. *Impulsive*. He's a little impulsive, which is not a bad trait in itself, mind you, but as a business manager, you become anxious. You don't know what he's going to do next. You can't count on him, to put it bluntly."

"I disagree. I'd say Sam Mallory's the most trustworthy person I've ever met."

"And I'm sure you believe that, and I'm not saying he's not. But you've led a sheltered life, Irene. I know you think you haven't, but you have. I've got twenty years on you, twenty years spent in the business world, and Sam's been to war and everything *that* means. He's got a wife and a kid. He's been around the block more than once." Morrow paused and peered at her, expecting some response.

"Just say what you mean, Mr. Morrow."

"Look, I'm only saying that you might want to reconsider this idea of partnership. On your own, flying solo, you could conquer the world. You don't need a man flying the ship for you. You can be in charge. Look around you. Your time has come. You're the *future*, Irene. You should show all those girls growing up out there what they're capable of. You should give them something to look up to."

"I thought I *was* doing that. Anyway, I don't see why I can't do that with Sam. He's an expert pilot with years and years of experience, and I'm still a novice. I've got a lot to learn from him."

"Irene. Irene." Morrow stood up and walked across the room. He stood by the window and crossed his arms, looking out across the eternal landscape, and then he returned to sit next to her on the old-fashioned settee, with its lion feet and its Victorian humpback.

Irene knew something was coming. Even if she didn't feel the warp of her own instinct, she certainly noticed the signs of George Morrow's own agitation. His thumbs circled each other. She noticed the whiteness of his cuffs against the tan of his wrists and hands. He was a fit man; he played tennis and swam and did all the fashionable new callisthenic exercises in a gymnasium he'd recently built at his own estate in Greenwich, Connecticut. Always Morrow gave off a racket of immense energy contained inside those well-tailored clothes, and maybe it was this energy that was so attractive, and maybe it was his attractiveness that made her hold him at a distance, made her fumble his first name whenever she tested it in her mouth.

Anyway, she knew something was coming, all right. She thought she was ready. She screwed her thumbs together in her lap and lifted an eyebrow to Morrow, as if to say, *Out with it, then*.

He made a movement of his hand, starting toward hers and then thinking better of it. "Now, what I'm about to tell you, I maybe should have said something earlier. I wanted to protect you. I thought the whole thing would blow over. But it hasn't. And it's time you know about some photographs out there."

"Photographs? What kind of photographs?"

"By any chance," he said, staring up at the ceiling, "by any chance did you and Mr. Mallory spend some time on the beach, while you were staying over in Honolulu?"

"Honolulu?"

"Early in the morning, I think. Just the two of you."

Irene couldn't speak. Morrow turned his attention from the ceiling to her face, and she saw that he was not kidding around, he was dead serious.

"You should know that someone took a couple of photographs and sold them to a newspaper," George Morrow said.

She whispered, "It wasn't how it looked. I was surfing, and Sam was on the beach, and he saw a shark out there. He thought it was going to get me. He was just relieved that I came in all right."

"Listen, Irene. I don't care. I can only tell you what it looked like. It looked like the two of you were—well, that you were actually . . . in the act of . . ." He shifted a bit, glanced to the window, overcome by the Puritanism that was stamped in his bones. "Embracing," he said.

"But that's not what happened. Not at all. Everyone's got the wrong idea. I can make a statement—"

"Not now, you can't. Right now, you have got to remain absolutely silent. You have got to remain right here in this house and not speak to another soul outside it."

Irene stood up. "Where's Sam? I want to talk to Sam."

"Sam's gone, Irene."

"Gone? Where? Call him back. We're a team. We—"

"Irene." Morrow stood up and grabbed her shoulders. "Get a hold of yourself. Listen to me. Sam's gone back to Sydney."

She tried to pull away, to run for the door, but Morrow was stronger than she was and held her back, facing him, his eyes versus her eyes.

"Listen! There's been a terrible accident. He's got to go home."

Irene stopped struggling and stared at Morrow's kind, paternal face. She opened her mouth to say *What's happened*, but the words remained stuck in her lungs somewhere, trapped and unable to rise.

He answered anyway.

"Mrs. Mallory's in the hospital, Irene. She saw those photographs in the newspaper and tried to kill herself. Swallowed some pills and slit her wrists with a kitchen knife. The kid found her on the bathroom floor."

HANALEI, HAWAI'I

October 1947

W
HEN LINDQUIST AND I return to Coolibah, I do something I haven't done since I was a child. I crawl into bed in the middle of the afternoon and fall asleep.

A knock awakens me. It takes me some time to come to myself; I look around the darkened room and can't quite remember where I am, or why I'm there, and the first thing I recall is the sea cliff and the picnic. Then the flight and the drive back to Coolibah, during which the cat unexpectedly curled on my lap, purring like one of those propeller engines on Lindquist's airplane.

The knock comes again, a little louder. "Janey? It's Leo."

I swear and roll out of bed. The cat, which was apparently napping at the small of my back, startles and jumps. My shirt and trousers lie in a heap on the floor. I pull on the shirt and stagger to the door.

"Everything all right?" he asks cautiously.

"Why do you ask?"

"You're kind of . . . rumpled."

"I was taking a nap."

He looks up at the sky. "Mama sent me to tell you it's time for dinner."

"Oh, she did, did she? And did your sweet stepmother tell you what she did to me today?"

"She told me you flew out to Ki'ilau together."

Some fur twines around my ankles. I nudge it away. "Is that what it's called?"

"One of my favorite spots. Used to sail out there as a kid and kick around on the beach all day." He props one hand on the doorframe and tilts his head to one side. "If she took you there, she must really like you."

"If she does, she's got a funny way of showing it. Now if you'll excuse me, I'm going to put some clothes on."

I shut the door in his face, and I have to tell you, it feels pretty good.

AFTER DINNER, WE PLAY GODDAMN charades. It's a Friday, so the children are allowed to stay up an hour late, and apparently this is what the little delinquents like to get up to for mischief. Lindquist makes cocoa. Leo pops popcorn. Because Olle's still in Honolulu with Uncle Kaiko, Lani comes in from the kitchen to even the numbers. Lindquist, Lani, and Wesley make up one side; Leo, Doris, and yours truly make up the other.

Leo hands me my mug of cocoa, which is piled high with whipped cream, and leans to my ear. "Added a shot of bourbon."

I lick myself a hole through the whipped cream in order to make sure he wasn't kidding. (He wasn't.) "Well, thank you kindly, bartender."

Now, apparently charades are big in the Lindquist household. They keep a big china bowl in the living room filled with scraps of paper, on which members of the family scribble down ideas throughout the week in preparation for Friday's extravaganza. (I swear to God this is all true.) As guest of the house, I'm given the honor of drawing the first charade, which is

PEANUT BUTTER SANDWICH

in a childish scrawl that surely belongs to Wesley.

"Well, that's easy," I say. I stand up and mime spreading peanut butter on a piece of bread.

"Bread and butter!" screams Doris.

I fold my imaginary bread into a sandwich.

"Book?" says Leo.

I roll my eyes and take an imaginary bite from this mother-loving imaginary peanut butter sandwich, and as I chew my imaginary lunch, I wonder what sin I've committed that can possibly be so mortal as to condemn me to this purgatory.

"Fried chicken?" says Doris, apparently forgetting about the spreading of the butter, and I may kill myself.

"I know! I know!" Wesley jiggles up and down like he has to pee.

"You're not on our team, dummy!"

"Doris, your brother is not a dummy," Lindquist says.

I look helplessly at Leo, begging for relief, and although I can just about *read* the words *peanut butter sandwich* on his face, he only shakes his head and smiles, the bastard.

I set down my imaginary sandwich and unscrew an imaginary lid from an imaginary jar of peanut butter, and some fraught time later Doris screams out *PEANUT BUTTER SANDWICH*! at goddamn last and I crumple to the ground.

"I knew it! That was my charade!" Wesley says.

Doris is sulky. "I don't even like peanut butter sandwiches, that's why."

Wesley jumps up and runs for the charades bowl. "My turn!"

And so on and so on for another hour or two, until Wesley's curled up asleep on my lap and my cocoa's finished, and Leo bends down to lift the limp carcass and carry it upstairs. *Careful,* I mutter.

Doris trips along after them, chattering about something. The bourbon's gone to my head and I'm feeling a little reckless. When Lindquist stands to follow the ankle-biters upstairs, I say, "Not so fast."

"Oh? Haven't you got enough out of me already?"

"Just one question, really. I was mulling it all the way home."

She crosses her arms and frowns. "What, then?"

"This thing you've told me about Mrs. Mallory. How she tried to kill herself. That wasn't in the papers. I mean, this is the first I've heard of it."

"George was always an expert about managing the press."

"But that didn't matter, did it? Wouldn't have changed what happened, if the newspapers knew all about it and made Mallory out to be some philandering daredevil who drove his wife to suicide. Because his goose was already cooked."

"Why do you say that?"

"You had already eclipsed him. You were the star now. Morrow made sure of that, didn't he?"

She looks to the stairs and back again. "Yes. He wanted to make me a star, and he did."

"Because I've been thinking about what you said, the way he managed everything in Australia, and you know what? I think it was all part of his plan. He wanted to separate you and Mallory, so he could get control of your career, and Mrs. Mallory's little temper tantrum just fell right in his lap, didn't it?"

"You could look at it that way. Or you could conclude that he was just doing what he thought was best for me. He thought Sam was reckless and impulsive, and I would be better off on my own."

"Not *alone*. With him. With Morrow."

Lindquist shrugs. "It seemed like the logical thing to do at the time. And we were happy. George took care of all the details and salesmanship I hated. He was considerate and faithful. You might say he was the ideal partner for me."

I climb from my chair—not altogether steady, you understand, on account of the bourbon—and walk right up to her. "You know something? I don't believe you. I don't believe for one moment you were in love with Morrow."

Lindquist glances at her watch. "I'm going to put the children to bed now. We'll discuss all this in the morning."

She starts up the stairs in smooth, elastic movements. Even for dinner, she doesn't wear dresses, just these long, flowing, wide-legged trousers made of silk or sometimes crepe de Chine, set off by some delicate blouse or another. She's got style, Irene Lindquist, even if she pretends to be above such things.

I call up after her. "One more thing?"

She sighs and turns, one hand on the railing.

"Was it true? Did the daughter find her like that?"

Lindquist stares at her hand. The lamplight slants across the scar that blooms from underneath her blouse and over her neck.

"Yes," she says softly. "Poor thing. They say she was hysterical."

"How awful. How awful for her."

Lindquist turns and continues up the stairs. "It was awful for everybody," she calls down behind her.

SOMETIMES I THINK ABOUT WHAT might have happened if some German antiaircraft gun hadn't got the better of Velázquez in the winter of 1945. The war was nearly over, after all, and he might well have survived those last few months of it.

By May, I was in the Obersalzberg, photographing the advance to Hitler's mountain retreat. Velázquez was right about one thing; I had not been faithful, either to him or to his memory. Even before his death, I had picked up a lover or two, as the occasion presented itself. I had also struck up a friendship with a certain American general—four stars and married, another breach of the rules, but this fellow was an incorrigible philanderer so I felt I was not corrupting anybody, and anyway the wife had made her bargain long ago. This energetic and purely physical affair proved fruitful for my career. No longer was I given stupid assignments to photograph the revival of the Paris fashion houses in the wake of liberation; here I was on top of the world, the very front lines of the front lines as American troops liberated all the wine in Hitler's cellar, to say nothing of the silver. I don't know, maybe you've seen a few of those snaps yourself. One of them won the Pulitzer a year back.

Anyway, as I said, I was in the mountains of southern Germany when news of victory reached me. The Fascists had been defeated at last! Japan remained, of course, but everybody knew that was only a matter of time and blood. I took some dutiful shots of the jubilation among the GIs, and then I requisitioned a Jeep and drove into Berchtes-gaden and drank myself senseless on the cheap local liquor.

By the end of the evening, I was addressing the empty bottle, which had become Velázquez in my mind. I told him I was awfully sorry about the general and the UPI reporter after Dachau and that sweet, virile, ecstatic GI from St. Louis in the back hallway of the tavern just now, and I assured him that he, Velázquez, had been a better lover than all three of them together (although that idea was also tempting). I said we've done it, we've beat the Fascists, we've got your revenge on Hit-ler for Guernica and Madrid and your parents and your sister and the girl you should have married. You would feel so vindicated! You would maybe wrangle a pass in the next month or so and come to visit me, and we would not leave our room for two days, and *maybe,* in the joy of that moment, victory and reunion and postcoital gratitude, when you sometimes confuse the intense, satisfied lust you're feeling for true love, I might have made the mistake of saying *yes, yes,* I will marry you, Velázquez, I will become your wife and have your children and live a quiet little life with you in some quiet little house in some quiet little vil-lage in the country. I would have promised you this and maybe I would have done it too. Or maybe not. We'll never know for certain.

I don't remember how I spent that night. In disrepute, probably. In the morning, I drove the Jeep back to the quartermaster and went on with my work, because what else can you do? You cannot call back those you have lost, however much your bones ache with missing them, however giant and mysterious the holes they leave behind.

LINDQUIST DISAPPEARS AROUND THE CORNER at the top of the stairs, to put her children to bed for the three thousandth time or so. The voices and thumps drift downward, Leo and his little siblings, joined by Lind-quist. I head for the library and Olle's liquor cabinet to add another splash of bourbon to the dregs of my cocoa. When I'm on the outside of that, I help Lani clean up in the kitchen, and at last I step outside, where the air is dark and fresh and smells of blossoms. I think how lovely it is to smell blossoms in October. They mingle with the bourbon fumes to produce something new and alluring that I believe I shall always associate with Hawai'i and Coolibah, after I've left this place and moved on to the next.

I haven't taken more than five steps across the lawn before somebody calls my name. I consider pretending I don't hear, but then I find myself craving some company. So I stop and turn.

"O captain, my captain. What brings you outside on a night like this?"

"Do you have a moment?"

"I've got a whole lifetime of moments. The question's whether I should spend any more of them with you."

He smiles through the darkness. "Would you? Please?"

"I should warn you," I say, wagging my finger, "I'm a little the worse for bourbon."

"I guess I've handled a drunk or two in my time. Come along. Find somewhere to sit down."

"I think that would be wise."

He laughs in reply and starts walking in the direction of the sea. He doesn't touch me, doesn't seek my hand or my arm or anything. The moon has risen, three quarters of a clean white pie, just enough light to see by. By and by we come to some kind of gazebo, all by itself, surrounded by nothing but bushes bursting with flowers. You can't tell what color they are because it's too dark, but you can see their petals reflect the moonlight, and you can smell their perfume. I follow Leo up the steps into the shelter of the gazebo and lie down on a bench. He sits nearby, gripping the edge with his hands, and stares at me.

"I just wanted to apologize," he says.

"You brought me all the way over here to say sorry?"

"Wanted some neutral territory, I guess, in case you were going to throw something at me. I was kind of a bozo the other night."

"You had a stepmother to defend. I admired you for it, I really did. No hard feelings, as someone once said to me."

"All right, I was sore. I admit it. I thought you liked me."

"Oh, I *do* like you, Leo. I like you *very much*. I am deeply, deeply attracted to you. That tip you gave me was just the icing on an awfully delicious cake."

"I see," he says, husky.

"It's funny, you're not a bit like him, though."

"Like who?"

"Like this fellow I knew during the war. Velázquez. He was gruff and short and hairy and plain, and I can't ever seem to stop thinking about him."

"Where is he now?"

"He's dead, Leo. He died in the winter of '45, in a bombing raid over Cologne."

"I'm sorry."

"So am I." I raise my head. "Have you said everything you wanted? Because I'd like to go to bed now."

He rises and helps me to my feet. I keep hold of his hand, because we're friends again. We walk to the cottage through the flowery air. The moon glows above us. When we reach the door, I stop and turn to face him, and the air just expires from my lungs. Having watched his face all evening, contorted into all kinds of expressions, I've forgotten how simply alluring he is, how alluringly simple.

"Tell me something. How did your father meet your stepmother?"

"It was the airline. She advertised for pilots, and he'd done a little crop-dusting, so he applied. She trained all the pilots herself."

"And nobody knew who she was?"

"You have to understand, we don't care much about the outside world around Hanalei."

I nod. "That's why she landed here."

"I guess so. I think she hated all the fuss."

"And how did you feel? Getting a new mother after all those years? And then your brother and sister coming along."

I observe him carefully. I am not so drunk that I can't pay attention.

I note his hesitation, the brief furrow of his brow as he gives his answer some thought.

"I was just happy for Dad," he says. "And I was happy for her. For Irene. I thought she'd had a rough time, and now she had someone to take care of her, for a change."

"Everyone needs that, I guess."

"Everyone but you. Isn't that right, Janey?"

I put my hand on the doorknob. "Good night, Leo. Pleasant dreams."

INSIDE THE COTTAGE, I POUR myself a glass of water from the tap and swallow a couple of aspirins. Leo was right, I can take care of myself, all right. I know what to do when I'm going to bed a little the worse for Olle's fine Kentucky bourbon.

But I don't hit the sack right away. Instead I light a cigarette and dig out the leather diary from its hiding place—I won't tell you where—and flip to the last few pages. I should explain that this is not some ordinary diary. More like a journal, a bewildering mishmash of jottings and engine diagrams, telephone numbers and map directions, which takes on narrative form only at the end, in which Mallory writes of his ordeal in the Spanish badlands, the anguish of his own injuries and the infinitely worse anguish of watching Irene suffer, while helpless to save her. His devastation that he will never see his daughter again. It's not something I enjoy reading, and yet since I first discovered the diary, these harrowing words have drawn me back to read them, over and over, until they've scored themselves upon my skin. I seem convinced of something essential inside them, some secret to life itself; that if I experience Mallory's agony often enough, I'll discover what it is he's trying to tell me.

I come to the last line:

GM to rescue at last thank God She will live

Every story has a hero and a villain, doesn't it, and if it doesn't—why, we fashion them ourselves. We want to take sides. We want to pledge our allegiance to one person or the other, one cause or another; to atone for our own thousand failings by planting ourselves on the high ground of righteousness, so we can crush some other poor schmuck beneath our heels and feel we are not simply right, but good.

All along, I have figured this story has one villain, and I thought I knew who it was. But maybe I was wrong, all along. Maybe I should have learned by now that nobody is all good or all bad; that hardly any battles are fought between good and evil. There is more good and less evil, or more evil and less good, but the only time I've ever felt the presence of absolute evil was when we opened the gates at Dachau and saw what men had wrought. And I'll bet even those SS guards thought they were doing the right thing at the time. The human brain is capable of all kinds of contortions, all kinds of earnest and precise blindnesses, in order to protect itself from the idea that it might have made a mistake. That it might have taken the wrong side.

That final line, the last words Sam Mallory ever wrote, as he lay injured in his airplane and waited to die: what if I'm wrong about that?

I run my fingers along the ink, where Mallory's fingers left their mark, and tap some ash into the dish beside me.

AS USUAL, I WAKE UP in a sweat a few hours later. To pass the time, I reach for the newspaper clippings my old friend Bill sent me, the ones about Howland and Australia and the scandalous Honolulu photographs that apparently drove Mrs. Mallory to attempt her own life. Eventually I fall asleep again and rise at nine. Lindquist is gone. I snatch some coffee from the kitchen and bicycle down the highway, right through Hanalei, until I reach the village of Kilauea and the post office on the main road, which serves more or less the same variety of purpose here. The woman at the counter doesn't seem to recognize me. I ask if I can send a telegram.

She hands me the form, and I tap the pencil against my lips a few times before I compose the message.

BILL YOU BIG LUG STOP HOW ABOUT PULLING ALL YOU CAN FIND ON GEORGE MORROW STOP SEND TO YOURS TRULY CARE OF KILAUEA POST OFFICE STOP HAWAII BEATS ALL STOP WISH YOU WERE HERE STOP MUCH LOVE JANEY

III

▶ ▶ ▶

Flying with me is a business. Of course I make money. I have to or I couldn't fly. I've got to be self supporting or I couldn't stay in the business.

—AMELIA EARHART

AVIATRIX

by Eugenia Everett

(e x c e r p t)

October 1936: California

I RENE HAD WIRED ahead to George:

LAND BURBANK APPROX 5PM STOP NO PRESS STOP REPEAT NO
PRESS STOP LOVE ALWAYS IRENE

When the airplane rolled to a stop outside Hangar A, however, Irene looked out the cockpit window and saw four or five men in shabby blue suits gathered respectfully at the corner, holding their notebooks and their cameras. A couple of flashes went off. Landon took off his radio headset and turned to Irene. "I guess your public awaits," he said.

"I'm sorry. I told him not to call the press."

"No such thing as bad publicity, right?"

Irene unbuckled the safety strap and reached for her kit bag. "Thanks for the lift," she said.

"Any time. Sorry about the race."

"Those are the breaks. At least the ship's not a write-off."

"She'll take some fixing, though."

Irene ran a brush through her curls and dug out a tube of lipstick. "She will."

The autumn sun was already dipping below the hills to the west. Landon opened the hatch and a couple of flashbulbs went off, a couple of voices called out in greeting. George bounded up the stairs first, tore off his hat, greeted her with an embrace and a kiss, prompting a few more flashbulbs and a photograph that would appear in the *Burbank Daily Review* the next morning, page four, and the *Los Angeles Times*, page eleven. He drew back and held her by the shoulders. His expression was one of fatigue and relief, and for a moment the exhausted Irene just absorbed the familiar air of him, hair oil and shaving soap and a distant note of cigars.

"Welcome home, darling," said George. "How's the arm?"

"The arm's just fine. I thought I said no press."

"Just a few fellows. Hardy and Patrick from the *Daily Review*, Rogers from the *Times*. Ten minutes, tops." He kissed her forehead. "Then dinner. You must be starving."

"More tired than hungry, actually," said Irene, but George was already replacing his hat, lifting her kit bag, taking her hand. They descended the steps together in a routine George had choreographed so long ago, Irene didn't have to think. The newsmen gathered around at the foot of the steps and began their questions in the usual way, to which Irene answered in the usual way.

"How's the arm, Miss Foster?"

"It's all right." (Lifting her left arm.) "It'll be in a sling for a few more days, but there's no fracture. Nothing to worry about."

"You must be awfully disappointed, Miss Foster. Would you care to comment on the crash in Fort Worth?"

"I wouldn't call it a crash, really. We just had a hard landing, that's all. When a squall moves in just as you're approaching the airfield, you have to prepare for the worst."

"With all due respect, Miss Foster, should you have attempted the landing at all, with weather bearing down?"

"It's a race, Mr. Rogers. Flying the Coast-to-Coast Derby's a different matter from making an ordinary journey from city to city, carrying passengers. If you want to win, you have to take a chance or two. You can't let a little weather get in your way."

"But surely it's not worth risking your life?"

"Any kind of competitive flying carries an element of risk. That's why we fly these races, to push the airplanes and the pilots to their utmost, to push back the frontiers of what's possible, so that the common man can get on an airplane in full confidence that the machine and the captain will get him to his destination in safety and comfort."

As she finished this speech, George put his hand to the small of her back and rubbed his thumb against her spine. He did this to convey approval to her during the countless times they'd stood like this over the years, at the bottom of the airplane steps, while Irene spoke to the press and George gazed at her as if she were some kind of goddess come to earth. They used to rehearse at home. George would ask questions and Irene would answer them, and George would tell her how she ought to have answered them, frankly and openly while still communicating some particular message, some theme to which she and George had agreed. Now it was second nature. Irene knew exactly what she was supposed to do. Say what you would about George—and there were plenty of mutterings by the fall of 1936, few of which ever reached Irene's ears—he had a natural gift for publicity. A genius, really. Without George Morrow, there would have been no Irene Foster, at least as we know her today.

Anyway, she appreciated the gesture. It had been a long flight from Fort Worth, and her arm hurt, and she was tired and hungry, and now she had to stand up straight in the midst of this humiliating defeat and answer impertinent questions in a dignified voice, when all she really wanted was to berate herself for her mistake; to demand whether these smug, paunchy reporters thought they thought they could fly an airplane any better; to crawl under the blankets of a soft, warm bed and hide from the world. At a time like this, a hand at the small of your back, rubbing your aching spine, is worth more than treasure.

After exactly ten minutes of questions, George raised his palm.

"All right, boys. That's enough. My wife's going to need some dinner and a good bed, and it's my job to see that she gets them."

WHEN THEY REACHED THE CAR, Irene turned to George. "Can't you drive this time? I'm just beat, I really am."

George dropped her kit bag in the narrow back seat. "You can do it, darling. It's just a few miles."

"George, please."

"But you love to drive." He kissed her cheek and opened the driver's door. "Makes a great photograph, remember? That's how we want people to think of you. Driving off the airfield in your own roadster."

Of course, he was right. He didn't say it, but Irene knew the photos were everywhere, the Fort Worth crackup, Irene's airplane tilted to one side in a grassy ditch, landing gear crushed, rain pouring down, Irene's head bowed and her face crumpled with disappointment. They needed an image to counterpose defeat with triumph. They needed Irene thundering off the airfield behind the wheel of her custom Hudson roadster, husband at her side. She climbed in. The key was already stuck in the ignition switch. She pushed down the clutch and turned the key, and the engine growled awake, and Irene wanted to bawl out her frustration like a baby. But she didn't. She put the car in gear and pushed down the gas pedal and released the clutch, and she and George roared down the driveway against the setting sun, while the photographers clicked their shutters and captured the moment for history.

IRENE DIDN'T SPEAK, AND GEORGE—FOR once—didn't press her. She whipped the Hudson around the hills, faster and faster, relishing all the wind and speed and thunder, while George's white knuckles gripped the door handle and his eyes darted to the speedometer. She made a final ascent around a last bend and reached their home, nestled into the shoulder of a mountain. The windows blinded her. They had positioned the house to capture the view of the Pacific Ocean as it crashed spectacularly into the continent some twenty miles to the west-southwest, and the setting sun now struck every pane of glass, so that she had to avert her eyes and didn't notice all the cars parked outside until she came up the last of the drive and stopped the car in front of the garage.

"What's going on?" she asked. "Who are these people?"

"Just a few friends I've invited for dinner. To welcome you back."

"I don't want to see anybody. That's the last thing I want to do. I want to eat and go to bed."

"It's just a few hours," he said, in the same tone he had earlier said *It's just a few miles*. Nothing at all, dear, you can do it. You're Irene Foster, you have a public, you simply have to do these things whether you enjoy them or not, it's part of your job.

George got out of the car and lifted her kit bag from the back seat. Irene sat and stared through the windshield at the garage door, washed in orange. Her hands still gripped the steering wheel. George came around and opened the door.

"Can I at least bathe and change before saying hello?" she said, and somehow George missed the irony in her voice.

"Of course you can, darling. I'll keep everyone happy with cocktails."

So Irene went around back with her kit bag while George came in the front door and played host to these guests he'd invited over. The master bedroom opened out to its own patio, and Irene let herself in through the French doors. George had filled the bedroom and sitting room with flowers, vases and vases of them, roses and fragrant stargazer lilies, her favorites. He was good at gestures like that. Irene bent to sniff a bouquet on her nightstand. There was a note beneath in George's elegant handwriting. *You're home safe, and that's all that matters. Love, G.*

She thought about that note as she bathed in the giant white porcelain bathtub, taking care not to dislodge the sling provided for her by the doctor in Fort Worth, who had asked for her autograph afterward. *That's all that matters.* Was it really? Because she also remembered George's words on the way to the airfield, the morning of the start of the derby. *You've got to win this, darling. Not second or third. We need another victory, or the new lecture tour is going to bust.* So the state of her health was important, but it wasn't the only thing that mattered, not by a long shot, at least to George. Flying was expensive. They had to fill those lecture halls next month, and to fill lecture halls you needed the public's fascination, you needed to be on the cover of twelve different magazines, looking dashing and triumphant, and gorgeous didn't hurt, either. You needed rapturous column inches and newsreel footage of you roaring down an airfield driveway behind the wheel of a Hudson roadster.

Most of all, though, you needed a photograph in which you waved triumphantly from the cockpit of your silvery Rofrano Sirius, having just beaten the boys to win the 1936 Coast-to-Coast Air Derby.

The bath was heaven, but Irene didn't deserve heaven. She'd taken a risk when she saw the squall moving in over the Fort Worth sky, and it hadn't paid off. Now her beautiful airplane was on a train in Arizona somewhere, on its way back to Burbank for repair, which would cost a stack of money she didn't have, wouldn't have, unless this next lecture tour was a smashing success. And how was she going to fill fifty-nine lecture halls across America when she wasn't news anymore, when she hadn't won an air race in two years, when everybody had already forgotten about her solo flights to Europe and to Hawai'i and Rio de Janeiro, her circumnavigation of the globe?

Well, George would figure something out, wouldn't he? George always figured something out.

Irene rose from the bath after four and a half minutes, dried herself off, dressed awkwardly in a rose chiffon dress that flattered her height and her angular body, her sunstreaked curls and the freckles she hated and Sam had loved. She added a little lipstick, a little powder, a pair of low-heeled sandals. She could hear the noise and laughter of the guests down the hallway and through the sitting room, George's voice above all, relaxed and confident among all those human beings as Irene could never be. But that was one of the reasons she'd married him, wasn't it? He could do these things she could not. He could manage all that for her, so she could fly.

As she passed through the sitting room, Irene spotted a folded newspaper on the lamp table. She tried to avert her eyes, but the headline caught her. *MALLORY PULLED ALIVE* it said, before the rest of the sentence disappeared around the fold.

Irene stood still and stared at the black letters. Her pulse rang in her ears. For a second or two, she thought she would faint.

When she could breathe again, she picked up the newspaper and unfolded it.

MALLORY PULLED ALIVE FROM WRECKAGE.

San Diego Air Show Ends in Disaster.
Flier Taken to La Jolla Hospital, Condition Remains Unknown

GEORGE AND IRENE HAD CHOSEN a young, rising architect to create their home in Burbank, shortly after their marriage four years earlier, and he had designed the house in an open, modern style that made use of the light and color of the California landscape. At the center of the building, the living room had the feel of a baronial great hall, although shorn of any historical froufrou, as George called it. It was twenty-two feet high with giant metal beams and a wall of French doors that seemed to open out right over the edge of the hill and into the sky above the ocean, although in fact they opened out to a stone terrace and a swimming pool. It was here that George and Irene held most of their parties. The doors had already been thrown open and the air was fragrant with cigarettes and perfume. Irene slipped in quietly and tapped George on the shoulder. He turned and took her elbow.

"There you are! What's the matter? You're pale."

Irene said, in a low voice, "Why didn't you tell me about Sam?"

"About Sam? Sam Mallory?"

"I saw the newspaper. What happened?"

He swirled the ice cubes around the inside of his glass. "I don't know any more than you do. I read the article, that's all, right before I went to meet you at the airfield."

"Is Sophie here?"

"Darling, let me get you a drink."

"I don't want a drink. I want to know what's happened to Sam."

"Sophie won't know any more than——"

But Irene was already beetling across the room, searching for Sophie Rofrano's blond head and pregnant belly. She found them on a sofa, positioned in earnest conversation with somebody's wife. Sophie saw her and lurched to her feet.

"Don't do that," said Irene.

"Oh, I'm all right. But *you*! How's your arm? Or are you just absolutely sick and tired of people asking?" Sophie said all this while embracing Irene, kissing her cheek, and Irene felt the strange intrusion of this big lump between them, the baby to which Sophie was due to give birth in a few more weeks, her fifth.

"Sam!" Irene pulled away. "What's happened to Sam?"

Sophie's face fell. "I don't know for certain. You know how he does all these ridiculous stunts at air shows. Octavian was on the telephone with a few people he knows in San Diego. They think it was a mechanical fault."

"Of *course* it's a mechanical fault. Sam would never—he's the best pilot——"

"Oh, darling, stop." Sophie steered her to the wall of windows and pulled out a handkerchief. "He'll be all right. You know he's broken just about every bone in his body by now, and every time he bounces right back. He's indestructible."

"I'm sorry. I'm just tired, that's all, and nobody told me about it, I just happened to see a newspaper on my way in——"

"He'll be just fine, don't worry. Octavian says he's awake, he's moving and talking."

"What else?"

"Isn't that enough?"

Irene stared furiously out the window. She couldn't turn away and face the room, not with her eyes all red like this, her cheeks damp. Sophie's handkerchief was now a ball in her fist.

Sophie said gently, "There's nothing you can do, Irene. You have to let it be."

"I realize that. It's not like a light bulb you can switch on and off, that's all."

"Of course not," said Sophie. "Of course it isn't. Hello, George."

Irene's husband appeared at her elbow, blocking the sunset. "Nice glass of lemonade for you."

"Thank you." Irene took the lemonade and sipped. Her eyes were dry now. It was just the shock, that was all. With Sam, you expected some terrible accident every day, and yet when the news came, as it regularly did, you still felt that somebody had hit you with a sledgehammer. Sometimes Irene wondered if Sam felt the same way about her. If, when she experienced a crackup somewhere, broke a bone or just strained a tendon as she had in Fort Worth, Sam Mallory felt as if somebody had hit him with a sledgehammer.

IT WAS NOW EIGHT YEARS since that historic flight to Australia, eight years since Irene and Sam had sat together under the coolibah tree; six years since Irene had set a coast-to-coast record flying from New York to Los Angeles in her own Rofrano Centauri and then flown solo from Boston to Paris a month later; five years since she had stumbled into a love affair with her business manager, George Morrow, and accepted his marriage proposal with certain conditions. She had been George's wife for four years, and in that time she had set countless records for airspeed and endurance and distance, had flown solo to various points around the world, had circumnavigated the globe with a copilot and a navigator, had cracked up more times than she could count and been hospitalized in eleven of those instances, had gone on eight lecture tours and made one thousand six hundred and fourteen speeches, had designed her own clothing line, had appeared on a hundred and twelve magazine covers and in six motion pictures.

In all that time she had seen Sam Mallory exactly four times. The last time was seven months ago, at a restaurant in Burbank. Irene was having dinner with George and the Rofranos; Sam was there with a film actress in a sequined dress. They saw each other at exactly the same moment, as Irene and George walked past his table to join the Rofranos at the back of the restaurant, and the sight of his horrified face still wounded her. Later he'd come over to say hello, and it was clear he'd had a drink or two to fortify himself. He laughed and joked harshly, and he introduced the film actress, who was beautiful beyond description and didn't seem to know the history of Sam and Irene. She just appeared girlishly starstruck to meet the legendary aviatrix and babbled on about how scared she was to fly in an airplane, how brave Irene must be. Irene replied graciously, without meeting Sam's eyes once. She watched him walk away though, a little unsteady, the actress's arm looped through his. What little she'd seen of his face seemed gaunt. Those ravishing good looks had been hollowed out by misery.

"Poor fellow," said George. "A wife like his."

Octavian said, "Not anymore. They called it quits a year or two ago, didn't you hear?"

Under the table, Sophie had kicked him, and he'd cleared his throat and changed the subject. But it didn't matter. Irene had already heard that news. Of course she had.

AMONG THE GUESTS AT THE party, besides the Rofranos, were a couple of movie executives, the mayor of Burbank, the president of the Lockheed Aviation Company, and the editor of the *Los Angeles Times*. George was nothing if not methodical about his guest lists. They were all sympathetic to Irene. She had to explain the accident five times, had to describe the injury to her arm, had to express enthusiasm for the upcoming lecture tour, had to chitchat over four courses served in the dining room by the housekeeper.

She was used to all this. George and Irene entertained guests three or four nights a week when they were home, and of course a lecture tour meant countless fried chicken dinners with mayors and aviation enthusiasts and the ladies of the town lecture committees and their curious banker husbands. In response, Irene had invented a character named *Irene Foster, Aviatrix,* who could make patient, polite conversation with all these people and win glowing reviews for her All-American character wherever she went. Irene played this character night after night, like an actress in a long-running Broadway play. She played it now, even though she was exhausted and sick with worry about a man she had loved eight years before.

Only Sophie Rofrano knew the effort it cost her. But then Sophie Rofrano was eight and a half months pregnant and her husband was extremely protective of her. They sat next to each other at the other end of the table, where Irene cast envious glances. She had always envied the Rofranos. Without being attached at the hip or anything like that, they were deeply and affectionately in love. Octavian Rofrano was a reserved man, not easy to talk to. His face, as he made conversation with the woman on his left, crinkled earnestly, as if he were in pain. But when his wife asked him a question from his other side, his expression changed. He turned to her and bent his head—Sophie Rofrano was a small woman—and it was obvious that the rest of the room, the rest of the world maybe, held not the slightest pinprick of interest next to what his wife was saying, at that moment.

Then his expression changed again. He stood and walked around the table to murmur something in George's ear, and George jumped up and said *Of course!* Irene looked at Sophie and Sophie looked at her and pointed, smiling, to her middle. Irene rose and went to Sophie, reached her just as Octavian reached her, and together they helped Sophie from her chair, though she tried to brush them away, laughing that she had done this before, she was perfectly capable of walking to the car. The news rippled around the room. Luckily they were just finishing dessert, and the party ended by everyone waving off the Rofranos on their way to the hospital to have their baby, just like they were newlyweds.

It made Irene think of her own marriage, which took place in the town clerk's office, and how she and George had flown away on their honeymoon from Rofrano's Airfield in Irene's airplane, while half the city's press waved them off. Irene had been furious at this publicity stunt and George had promised not to do anything like that again without asking her first. They had spent their wedding night in Yosemite and started a lecture tour the next day, flying together from city to city to make the most of the newspaper coverage, and Irene had been so busy with flying and speeches and George had been so busy with the logistics and the glad-handing that they were bemused to realize, on the sixth day of the tour, that they hadn't yet consummated the union.

AFTER THE ROFRANOS LEFT, IRENE made her excuses and went to bed with the newspaper. She read the article about Sam three times and learned that the accident had occurred on landing, just as hers had, although the cause could not yet be determined. The engine had gone up in flame and Sam had been burned, but not seriously because they had been able to pull him free within minutes of the crash. He was unconscious but had woken up in the ambulance. He remained at the hospital in a serious condition. That was all, except that it seemed he was now seeing some other film actress, a brunette, who gave a tearful statement to the press before going to the hospital to comfort him. Irene set the newspaper aside and reached for the lamp, just as George walked in, removing his necktie. He took off his jacket too and came to sit on Irene's bed in his shirtsleeves. He laid his hand on her leg.

"I thought you'd gone to sleep by now," he said.

"I was reading about Sam."

"Terrible thing. We'll send flowers."

"Any news about Sophie?"

"Not yet." He shook his head and whistled. "Five kids. That's something. A real handful. I guess it's a good thing you're not the maternal type."

"What's that supposed to mean? Who says I'm not the maternal type?"

"You?" He laughed. "Anyway, you don't have the time for babies. You're Irene Foster, remember? You're leaving on a lecture tour in less than two weeks, and after that it's back to flying. Planning the big one, that's next. We've been planning that for years, the solo circumnavigation."

Irene sat up. "What if I'm sick of it all, George? The whole circus. The lectures and the derbies and the stunt flights."

He stared at her. His hand remained on her leg, just above the knee. He had unbuttoned his shirt an inch or two, and unlike Sam he looked fresh and unlined, enthusiastic for life. George had never minded being Mr. Irene Foster. Why, he'd relished it! A few days after the wedding, when the *Los Angeles Times* had referred to Irene as *Mrs. George Morrow*, he had telephoned the editor personally and corrected him. Irene would be keeping her name. She would be keeping her career. She'd gotten married, that was all, and her new husband had thrown himself into the business of burnishing her image, arranging her lecture tours and her flying schedule, her books and articles, her promotional contracts, her everything.

"I'm afraid I don't quite understand what you mean," he said slowly.

"I don't know. I've just been thinking I want a break, that's all. I'm getting too old to be spending every night in a new city. What does it mean? What am I doing here?"

"You're inspiring a generation of American girls, that's what."

"Am I? You've seen the crowds, what's left of them. Aviation's old news. All the frontiers have been conquered. The future lies the other way. Making flying ordinary, as commonplace as driving an automobile or riding a bus."

"You've already tried starting an airline. That was an expensive bust, as I recall."

"Well, we could try again, with a new team."

He sprang from the bed and started to pace. "But not yet. Let's get through this lecture tour first. I'm headed out to New York tomorrow, drum up some publicity—"

"Oh, George, no!"

"I've got to, Irene." He unslung his suspenders and unbuttoned his shirt. "I don't think we've sold a quarter of the tickets. Something's missing. We need something fresh, we need to do something to get everyone's attention back. We had the derby, and then you crashed out—"

"Crackups happen, George. It's part of the business."

"Well, the timing wasn't the greatest."

"Maybe it's a sign. Maybe I should be quitting that game. Half my friends are dead or maimed. Sam's going to get himself killed any minute—"

"His own damned fault. That fellow *wants* to get killed, if you ask me."

"And why is *that*, do you think?" Irene snapped.

George was arranging his shoes in the dressing room. He kept them in neat, straight rows, polished, shaped by wooden shoe trees so the leather wouldn't shrink. In an earlier age, he would have hired a valet to help maintain all this order, but these were modern times and George had this idea that an over-reliance on household staff was bad form. Still, the care and ordering of shoes was important and not to be rushed. Irene's words hung in the air for a moment before George emerged from the dressing room. He spoke calmly, because he always spoke calmly, even when he had asked her to marry him, as if every word must be delivered in a speech.

"That was eight years ago, Irene. The problem's not that Sam Mallory married an alcoholic bitch with a narcissism complex. The problem's what I told you. He's impulsive. He takes risks, and it's only gotten worse as his career's gone downhill, the way I said it would. It's a terrible shame, I don't take any joy in being proved right, but there you have it. He's a lost soul, and there was nothing you could have done to save him, not eight years ago and not now, even if things had worked out between the two of you. You made the right choice, Irene. You wouldn't have had this career if you'd spent the last decade hitched to Sam Mallory." He made a gesture to the room around them. "You wouldn't be Irene Foster anymore. You'd be Irene Mallory."

"Irene Foster is *your* invention, not mine," she said.

George stood in his underwear in the middle of the room and stared at her in bewilderment. "*My* invention? I don't know what you're talking about. I've devoted my *life* to your career."

"Yes, you have. And sometimes I just want to be a wife, that's all."

Now he was astounded. "A *wife? You?* I thought that was the *last* thing you wanted. I thought you wanted to fly airplanes and make a life for yourself. Now you want to set all that aside and become a *housewife?*"

"Of course not. That's not what I mean at all."

George turned around and went back in the dressing room. He emerged a moment later in a pair of crisp blue and white striped pajamas.

"All right, we're not dizzy in love like some couples," he said. "But that's what you wanted, remember? You yourself said not to expect kisses and hummingbirds all day long, that we were free to love other people if we wanted to, and haven't I respected that? I understand about Sam. I don't play the jealous husband."

"Well, maybe I wish you would, once in a while."

"I don't get it. Aren't you happy?"

"I don't know if I'm happy. What's happy, anyway? I just think I need a change, that's all."

"Look," he said. "We've been planning this thing for years. If I can pull it off, this round the world flight, then we can sit down and decide what's next. If you want to quit flying and start a family, why, we can do that. Just tell me what you want and I'll make it happen."

What Irene wanted to tell him was this. She wanted to tell him that she hated going on lecture tours and posing for magazines and manufacturing these so-called landmark flights, in which she was some kind of circus performer doing feats, and each feat had to be more daring and dangerous and record-breaking than the last or nobody cared.

She wanted to tell him that she had no idea what lay beyond this solo circumnavigation that had consumed them both since the very beginning of their professional association. She wanted to do it; there was no question about that. She longed to fly around the world by herself; it was the culmination of everything she'd worked for. But she also felt terrified of it. Because once she had accomplished this last, this greatest goal, what did she have left? What was the point of flying anymore?

She wanted to tell him that this business of being the Aviatrix had become so thorough, the moments of just being Irene so seldom, that she was beginning to feel that the Aviatrix had taken over the rest of her, like she had been painted over and could no longer find the original soul inside, and that even to her own husband—the person whom she should turn to in relief, the person who above all others should see her as a woman, as a person, as her true self—she was the Aviatrix and not Irene.

But George would just say that this was all nonsense, that she wasn't being logical, that she was doing exactly what she had dreamed of doing, that she was doing what other women could only dream of. That this endeavor was too important and too historic to give up now, when it was finally within sight.

So Irene reached for the lamp and turned off the light, and George, probably thinking about what she'd said, thinking maybe his wife just needed some reassurance after a harrowing few days, some tenderness, sat back down on her bed and asked her if she wanted him to make love to her.

Irene stared at the paleness of his pajamas in the darkness. George had always been a good, considerate lover, and he was certainly attractive. But she did not want to make love to her husband tonight. She

wanted something else. She wanted to feel close to another human being, but not like this, and she couldn't explain how.

"I'm sorry, I'm too worn out tonight, George," she said. "Maybe
tomorrow."

"Tomorrow I'm leaving for New York."

"When you get back, then."

He leaned forward and kissed her and said that he loved her, that
he admired her more than anybody he'd ever met, man or woman, and
then he rose from Irene's bed and went to his bed, and they both fell
asleep.

By the time Irene woke up the next morning, George had already
left for New York. He had to drum up publicity for her lecture tour
before it turned into a disaster.

HANALEI, HAWAI'I

October 1947

LINDQUIST ISN'T SHY on the subject of celebrity. "It's a prison," she snaps. "You can't go anywhere. Even in private, with friends, you find yourself putting on the mask you wear in public. Eventually the mask becomes your real skin, and that's when you know you're finished, there's nothing left of you."

"Well, didn't it also give you opportunity? Money? The means to keep flying? There's no free lunch. You can't have anything in life without giving something up. And you had a lot. You had everything you wanted. You had your airplanes, you had money, you had a nice house and nice friends and the admiration of everybody in America. You had marriage to a fellow who was more than happy to be Mr. Irene Foster, and believe me, that kind of husband doesn't just grow on trees."

"I know that. I accepted the cost because I wanted the prize so much. But then it went out of balance. The cost kept climbing, and the prize meant less and less. And I felt I had lost myself."

I scribble all this down in my notebook. "How so?"

"Because I hadn't really earned it, had I? Oh, I was a good pilot. I was maybe a great pilot. But so was Sam, and he didn't have any of those things. He was living hand to mouth in those years, scraping together fees for air shows and stunts and derbies. Crashing for money, I used to call it. It was just the luck of the draw, and the fact that he'd married a different kind of person."

"Was she so different, though? It seems to me that Morrow was using you as much as Mrs. Mallory used her husband. He just had more class."

Lindquist stands. "That's enough for now, Janey. I'm going surfing. You're welcome to join me."

SOMETIMES I JOIN HER AND sometimes I don't. It's been three weeks now, and I can more or less manage a surfboard and enjoy the thrill of a good wave, but it's not in my blood like it's in hers. On Sundays, when Leo isn't piloting the ferry to and from Oahu, he'll join us, and let me tell you, that man is a natural. A sight to see on the ocean blue. When I'm done, I'll just sit in the sand for the pleasure of watching him poised on his board, riding some giant wave as it curls elegantly over and he skims in to shore and jumps off and shakes his wet hair.

That's when I gather up my things and return up the path to Coolibah. I've been doing my writing in the gazebo, which shelters me nicely both from the sun and from the occasional tropical downpour. I can spread out my clippings and my notes and sit on the floor with the typewriter I've borrowed from Olle, tap tapping away like I used to do back at the law firm where I worked one summer.

Today, however, is a Tuesday, and the picturesque Leo floats somewhere in the channel between Oahu and Kauai, and I'm not in the mood for surfing or gazebo. I've got that restless twitch that takes over my spirit from time to time, the one that's bedeviled me most of my life. I pack my notes and clippings into my knapsack and ride my bicycle to Kilauea, where I ask the postmistress if there's any mail for me, any telegrams. She makes a show of checking, as if she wouldn't know otherwise, and returns to shake her head and tell me no. So I climb on my bicycle and head for the airfield cafeteria, which is another place I like to work, and has the additional benefit of coffee, grilled cheese, and feline companionship.

THAT CAT. I DON'T KNOW why, but it's taken a liking to me. Senility, no doubt. As soon as I settle on my stool at the counter and light a cigarette, it jumps laboriously from the floor to the trash can, and from the trash can to the lunch counter, and then marches on over to my coffee cup, sniffs inside, and eases itself down to my lap, from which no amount of jostling or dishes of promised cream will dislodge it.

I've learned to work around the ball of fluff. Uncle Kaiko takes pity on me and refills my coffee, when he's around. I like Kaiko. He's that bachelor uncle who gets into mischief and humiliates the family on public occasions, but he's also the fellow you telephone at two in the morning for a spot of rescue, no judgments. Now, I grant you, he's a terrible pilot. He's been grounded by Olle for the foreseeable future, so he just hangs around, three stools down, sharing an ashtray while he reads the help wanted column in the Honolulu classifieds. His ribs are still bandaged, and he's got casts on an arm and a leg, but at least the stitches are off his face. Anyway, my point is we get along just fine, Kaiko and me, even if he likes to complain about how I make him fetch coffee in his crippled condition.

"How about this one?" he says. "'*Start your career in real estate! Help wanted for top class Honolulu agency, local preferred, must be go-getter, no experience required, excellent pay, we will train you*'?"

"Sounds ideal, if you're looking for a career in rent collection."

"Rent collection? How do you figure?"

"Call it intuition. Say, do you mind? I'm trying to work, here."

"Gee, sorry." A moment later: "So how's it going? That book you're writing."

"Just swell, when I'm not getting interrupted all the time."

"You know, we weren't so sure about you, when you first turned up. Everyone figured you were trouble. Keep your trap shut, that's what Olle told me, and don't trust that dame an inch."

"Olle said that? The little dear."

"That's our Olle. He's a good fella, I'm not saying he's not, but— well, you know. Kind of the wet blanket type."

"I'll say. He keeps me at such an arm's length, he can't even hand me a drink. I'm glad you feel differently, Kaiko. I do like you, you know."

"What's not to like? And you like my pal Leo, don't you?"

"Well."

"I got eyes in my head. You got more sizzle between the pair of you than a whole pig roast." He makes a motion with his hand. "You're not . . . you know . . . ?"

"I'm afraid not. It wouldn't be professional, you know."

"Now, don't take offense, because I mean this as a compliment, but you don't seem like the kind of gal who lets a little business get in the way of a good time with a guy she admires."

"Why, Kaiko. I'm truly flattered. But in this instance, I figure discretion is the better part of amour. You know how these things go. It wouldn't do to ruffle any of my subject's feathers."

He scratches his brow. "I thought you were writing this thing about Mallory."

"Yes, of course. But Irene's such a big part of the story. As you know."

"Say, you going to put me in there too?"

"Well, Kaiko. The thing is, you didn't know Mallory. He was dead before Irene even met you. So I'm afraid your influence in his life is what you might call peripheral. But I promise I'll mention you in the acknowledgments, how's that? *Special thanks to Kaiko Kamealoha, for fetching coffee and keeping my spirits up.*"

"That's all?"

"Strictly speaking, yes."

He stubs out his cigarette and returns to his omelet. I return to my notes and my clippings. When my coffee runs out, I rattle the cup in the saucer, causing the cat to raise its head for a second or two. Kaiko sighs and slides from his stool and stumps over to the percolator. He refills my cup and his and climbs back on the stool and lights another cigarette. "You know," he says, "I got something that might interest you."

"Have you, now?"

"I guess I wasn't supposed to tell you about it, but that was before, wasn't it? Back when Olle figured you were out to pull a double cross or something."

I lay down my pen in the crease of my notebook.

"Kaiko, my darling. When you *know* I'm sworn to uphold the very highest standards of journalism."

BECAUSE OF THE CRUTCHES, IT takes Kaiko quite some time to hobble his way across the runway to the hangar that sits there by itself. Don't think I haven't noticed this building before. Early on, I asked Lindquist what she kept inside, and she said, oh, an old airplane or two. Some spare parts. I went over there myself a few days later, when I could steal off unattended, and confirmed the truth. Nothing but dust and rust and mothballs, a regular airplane junkyard.

Nonetheless, here I am. Following the cripple toward the hangar, notebook in hand, Kodak 35 on its strap around my neck, because he's got something that might interest me, and that's the kind of suggestion that always sets my pulse racing. Lots of times it comes to nothing. On occasion, it comes to everything. And an old, junk-filled airplane hangar is a terrific place to hide something important, wouldn't you say?

We arrive at the weathered siding. Kaiko gallantly reaches for the edge of the enormous sliding door, but I sweep him aside. When I visited last, I entered through the smaller, human door, but this time I want to throw a little more light on the interior. I tug and yank and eventually the thing gives way. A gust of hot, musty air rushes out, reeking of oil and machinery and rodent droppings. Perhaps we should have brought the cat, after all.

I turn to Kaiko. "Well?"

"Right this way. It's in the back."

"Of course it is."

We pick our way around the skeletal airplanes, stripped for parts, and the various heaps of metal. When I poked through here a few weeks ago, I thought it looked exactly like somebody's garage, oily rags and mysterious bits of machines in their haphazard piles, but now my eyes are more suspicious. I consider whether it's just supposed to *look* haphazard. I mean, why would you just leave a propeller blade lying there on the ground? Neither Lindqvist is the type to encourage disorder, even in a junkyard. I pause to finger the edge of a metal pole that looks as if it came from one of those tent kits for Boy Scouts.

Kaiko calls out from the other side of a stack of tires. "Here we go! Come on and give me a hand with this net, why don't you."

I walk obediently around the tires, around the bones of some old crop duster, just sitting there like a picked-over carcass, and there's Kaiko, standing proudly next to a large, sweeping shape covered by one of those dense camouflage nettings they used in the war.

Ka-thump, goes my heart.

Maybe I should have spotted it before, I don't know. But it hulks down in the back corner, covered by this netting that does the trick pretty well, makes a thing just dissolve into the background so that your eye passes right over it, unless your eye happens to know exactly what it's looking for.

I grab another corner of the netting, and Kaiko and I slide it carefully away from the object beneath, the *airplane*, maybe *the* most famous airplane in the world. A shape so iconic, so memorable, you'd have to be an idiot not to recognize it for what it is.

A custom Rofrano Sirius, the one flown by Irene Foster in the Round the World Derby of 1937.

"Ain't she a beauty," Kaiko says reverently.

AVIATRIX

by Eugenia Everett

(e x c e r p t)

October 1936: California

THE AIRPLANE ARRIVED in pieces the next day, by train from Fort Worth to Los Angeles and then by truck to Burbank, where Rofrano's team of mechanics would reassemble it inside Hangar D. Octavian said not to worry about the bill, she could pay it when she was done with the tour. The baby had been born shortly after he and Sophie had arrived at Burbank Hospital the other night, a girl they'd named Clara, and Octavian was in a generous mood.

Irene stared at the bright, wide interior of Hangar D and her airplane in pieces on the wooden floor. There was the silvery fuselage, there were the wings and the tail, the mighty engines, the crushed landing gear that would be replaced by a new one. Tools and rivets and everything else. She wasn't thinking of the latest crackup; she thought about the flight to Rio de Janeiro, the way the city had looked when she plummeted down from the mountains to the landing strip, glazed in afternoon gold. How she had gazed through the window in wonder and remembered why she flew. Why flying mattered, and the rest of it was only the means to fly, the price she had to pay.

SHE SPENT ALL MORNING IN the hangar, discussing the accident and the damage with the mechanics and with Rofrano, how long the repairs would take and how much they would cost, and then she went to the Burbank Hospital to visit Sophie and the new baby.

Sophie was in excellent spirits, as you might imagine. She was one of those women who gave birth like a peasant in the fields, and she was already disobeying the orders of the doctors and nurses by pottering around the hospital room, doing this and that. She carried the baby around like a small white-bundled football in the crook of her right arm. For some reason, this reminded Irene of Sam, who used to carry Sandy around the same way.

"She's been an angel," Sophie said, "although they're generally angels at first, and then they wake up on the third day and turn your life upside down. Would you like to hold her?"

"I'd be afraid to."

"Don't be silly." Sophie thrust the baby to Irene, who had no choice but to hold out her good arm and accept this present. "Open your eyes, Clarakins. That's the most famous woman in the world holding you. And if you're lucky, she might just teach you to fly someday."

"Her father ought to teach her that."

"No, I'd rather she learned from another woman. Octavian's a darling and I adore him, but he can't help condescend a little. He'd call her sweetheart or something, and she'd never learn properly. *You* taught me more about flying than my husband ever did."

Irene thought about Sam, who had taught her to fly and never called her sweetheart. She peered into Clara's face, which was squished shut and somewhat red, not at all like a baby in an advertisement. "Should I be doing anything? Is she breathing?"

"Of course she's breathing."

"How can you tell?"

"My dear," said Sophie, "you just know. Now tell me about the airplane. What does Octavian say? Can it be fixed quickly?"

They spoke about the airplane. Sophie was something of a mechanical genius, knew everything about engines and aerodynamics. She took Clara back, to Irene's relief. Outside the window sprawled Burbank, bigger and bigger every day. Outside the door, the nurses giggled and listened through the keyhole, thrilled that Irene Foster stood on the other side of it. Irene interrupted herself in the middle of a discussion of ailerons. "How did you meet? You and your husband."

Sophie didn't miss a beat. "He was delivering an engagement gift from my fiancé."

"You were engaged to someone else?"

"Not for long." She cuddled Clara to her chest. "Honestly, how could Mummy even *look* at another man, after that?"

"If I told you something," Irene said, "if I told you that I wanted to just disappear somewhere, where nobody knew me and no one could find me, what would you say?"

Sophie looked up. "I'd say, where and when should I bring you your cat?"

OUT IN SAN BERNARDINO, HANK Foster was nearly dead of liver disease. His wife, however, was a dedicated nurse. He had married her three years ago, surprising everybody. Like him, she was an alcoholic. They had met at a drying-out hospital, to which Irene had sent him after an especially bad bender that had required several personal telephone calls from George to the publishers of various newspapers. They had kept the story off the front pages in exchange for a series of interviews with Irene, which took place in the privacy of her own home and offered readers an intimate portrait of her life as an aviatrix and wife. Irene hadn't loathed anything in her life as much as she loathed those interviews. She still hadn't quite forgiven her father for them, although at least it had all led to this woman, Pamela Benson Foster, who seemed to view her present charge—nursing Hank through his final illness—as the single good work that would secure her place in heaven after a lifetime of sin.

"He's having a good day," she told Irene, on arrival. "He sure is happy you're visiting."

"Is he still in bed?"

"No, he's out back, on the porch. His favorite spot. We had some friends over last night, and all he talked about was you. Proud as a peacock."

Irene followed her through the house, which Irene had bought for him after the first book came out, the one she and George had written together on the steamship home from Australia. *Flight from Home* continued to sell respectably well, thanks to the drama surrounding the rescue and all the subsequent scandal, and Irene had signed over royalties to her father, which earned him a decent income. He sat now in the rocking chair that looked out across the San Bernardino Mountains. He had an Indian blanket over his lap, though the air was warm. When he saw Irene, he tried to rise, but she shushed him down and kissed his cheek.

"How are you feeling, Dad?"

"Pretty well, pretty well. Better than you, I guess." He nodded to the sling.

"Oh, it's all right. Looks worse than it is. I can take it off when I drive and everything."

"That's my girl," he said, proud as a peacock.

"I'll just get some lemonade," said Pamela, from the doorway.

Irene settled herself in the other rocking chair and stared at the wedge of blue sky above the mountains.

"So what happened out there?" asked her father.

"Just a squall, really. I shouldn't have tried landing. I should have circled until the thing passed through. I had the fuel. But I figured I had to win that race. I didn't have any minutes to spare."

"Had to win the race?"

"For publicity. You don't get publicity for coming in second."

"You don't need any publicity. You're Irene Foster."

"Well, tell that to George," she said. "No, forget I said that. George is right. This lecture tour, we can't fill the seats. Couple of towns are talking about canceling."

"I can't believe that. Why would they cancel? Who wouldn't want to hear you talk?"

"People who have seen me before. I haven't done anything new since the Rio flight. I haven't got anything to talk about, just all that business I've done before."

"That's some business, though. Nobody could get tired of hearing about that."

Irene laughed. "*You* couldn't, maybe. But you're my father."

He reached for her hand. "I sure am."

Funny, how she had resented him once. She had hated him, and despaired of him, and been ashamed of him. Her father had been a thing she avoided, a carbuncle on the hide of her life. He had been the cause of her misery, he had drunk away all their comfort, he had failed her and failed her. Now he was dying, and it wasn't that all these feelings had disappeared or been forgotten. They lay in a heap on the floorboards between their two chairs. But above that heap, Hank's hand linked with Irene's hand. She clung to that hand. She said, "Remember how you taught me to surf, when I was eleven?"

"That was nuts, wasn't it? You were just a scrap."

"Those were the best moments of my life," she said. "The truest."

"What about flying?"

"Flying's something else, now. Flying doesn't belong to me. But that does. Just you and me."

She didn't add, *And Sam,* even though surfing belonged to her and Sam too. Because where was Sam now? In some hospital room, attended by a starlet of some kind.

BUT SURFING GOT ON HER mind anyway, and when she left her father's house, instead of returning to Burbank, she found herself headed in the direction of the Pacific Ocean.

She wasn't actually going to surf. For one thing, she hadn't touched her surfboard in years, not since she arrived home from Australia and packed it away in the garage. Presumably the moving men had then transported this ancient thing to the new house in Burbank, but Irene didn't know where it was, or whether George hadn't just had it thrown out at some point, while she was away. No, she wouldn't surf. She couldn't surf. She just wanted to see the ocean, that was all.

These days, the beaches were more crowded. So many people had moved to California at the end of the twenties, and then as the crops kept failing in the Midwest and the farmers moved here in their droves. This promised land, California. Even when money was tight, you could still pack up a picnic lunch and your bathing suit and take the family to the beach. The sand and sun and ocean were all free. The smell of brine, the cool breeze off the water, the tide that filled the rock pools. The noise of the seagulls, the tiny, interesting crabs, the way the waves rose and hung and unfurled in perfect arcs—all these miracles could be experienced by anybody for nothing at all, like a birthright, and so they packed the beach at Huntington, at Santa Monica, at Long Beach, and learned to paddle in the cold Pacific current, to swim and to surf.

Irene didn't want to see any of these people. She didn't want to be seen, to be recognized, to be eaten alive and have nothing left of herself. She went instead to the old spot, where Sam had once had a house not so far up that strip of beach, where there was a wide spot in the road on which the surfers parked their cars at dawn. Before she left the car, she tied a scarf around her head to disguise her hair, the sandy curls Sam had cut for her on Howland Island, which were now an iconic symbol of American womanhood and rendered her instantly recognizable. Under a silk scarf, nobody even saw her.

The old path was still there, snaking carefully down the cliffs. Right here, the bend where she and Sam had spoken their first words. The beach was not deserted. People were out there enjoying the surf, picnicking from baskets. None of them noticed her, this lean woman wearing a white shirt and plain dungaree trousers, her hair bound in a silk scarf that rippled and whipped in the gusts of wind that came off the water.

The sun was falling now, and Irene hadn't eaten since eight o'clock that morning. Her stomach was vast and empty. She should return home now. She should go back to the house that she and George had designed and built together.

She turned and started up the path, but instead of walking to where she had parked the car, she walked along the edge of the cliff until she came to the small, weathered gray cottage that had once belonged to Sam. Irene knew the house well. She and Sam had spent hours there in the weeks before the flight to Australia, poring over maps and charts. Sam used to make her cocoa, while he drank coffee spiked with whiskey. She never drank cocoa anymore because it reminded her of Sam, and those weeks and months that marked the territory between Irene's discovery of flying and the world's discovery of Irene. When flying had just been flying, this terrific adventure she was undertaking with Sam, and the future opened before her in bright, grand colors.

Now she stood on the sandy path, ten or fifteen yards from the southwest corner of the cottage, not far from the place where she and Sam had stood after returning from the airfield with Irene's new spark plugs, the day they had met. The house and the ocean had not changed; the sky, the setting sun, the smell of the sea and the warm grass, everything was exactly as it had been that first evening. In fact, the encounter returned to her so vividly that, at first, she took no particular notice of the aging yellow Nash roadster parked outside the front of the house, because it belonged there in her memory. Then she stiffened and put her hand to her mouth. She looked at the small stone terrace, the deck chairs where she used to sit with Sam on sunny afternoons, and saw a man in one of them.

"Hello there," he called.

"I thought you were in San Diego," she called back.

"I thought you were in New York."

She held up her arm. "No, I cracked up in Fort Worth."

They stared quietly at each other. The surf crashed. Sam had a bruise on his jaw, a black eye. A thick white bandage wound around his forehead and the back of his skull. His clothes were too bulky for his lean body, suggesting more bandages underneath. A pair of crutches lay on the stone next to the deck chair. Irene walked closer.

"How did you get out of the hospital so soon?" Irene said, which was a way of asking how badly he was hurt.

"I just walked out. Never liked hospitals. I figure the sea air will cure you faster than a hospital can."

Irene came to a stop at the edge of the terrace. The sunset could not disguise the wan, fatigued cast of Sam's skin. "You look like hell," she said. "Don't you have someone to look after you?"

"I'm not an invalid."

"What are you making for supper?"

"I don't know. Boil an egg or something."

Irene climbed over the low wall of the terrace and put her hand on the lower half of Sam's forehead, the part that wasn't covered by the bandage. "I don't think you have any fever."

"Of course I don't have any fever."

"What about that actress of yours? What's her name? She ought to be here, looking after you."

"I believe she would tell you that's not part of her job description."

Irene stared at Sam, who stared back. They hadn't been this close, or this alone, since Australia. Possibly they hadn't touched, except for a handshake or two.

Irene said, "I thought you'd have sold this place by now."

Sam settled his head back and closed his eyes. "I would never sell this house."

INSIDE, EVERYTHING WAS THE SAME, as if it hadn't been touched since she left it. The single big parlor, overlooking the water. The tiny kitchen. The lavatory. The hallway that led to the bathroom and to Sam's bedroom, which she had never entered or even glimpsed. To the right of the parlor was a small office, lined with bookshelves, where Sam had kept all his books and maps. He had this idiosyncratic method of shelving them. He once tried to explain to Irene, but it just ended in laughter. Somehow he always found what he was looking for.

The windows were open to the sea breeze, and the door to the little stone terrace. The same two deck chairs sat in the same proximity, like the promenade deck on an ocean liner, Sam asleep in one of them. As Irene cooked an omelet, she could see the top of his head from the kitchen window. She had laid a blanket over his legs while he dozed. She thought he had broken an ankle or something; he wore a cast over his foot that went halfway up his calf. When the omelet was finished, she divided it in half and put the halves on two plates; she poured a whiskey and soda for Sam and plain soda water for herself and brought everything out on the terrace, which was now dark beneath a black sky dazzling with stars.

Sam was already awake. The omelet and whiskey amazed him. "Just like we used to make," he said.

Irene sat down in the other deck chair with her plate and her glass of soda.

"I don't mean to imply anything untoward," said Sam, cutting into his omelet, "but does your husband know you're here?"

"He's on his way to New York."

"He didn't get the news about Fort Worth?"

"No, it's about publicity." She hesitated and told him about the flight, the solo circumnavigation. He let out a low, slow whistle.

"That's some flight. But then you always did have sand. More sand than anybody I ever met. Remember how you landed on Howland?"

"That was you," she said. "You were the one who wouldn't let me turn yellow."

He finished his whiskey. "Why did I do that? I don't know why I did that."

Irene took his empty glass and hers and went to the liquor cabinet to refill them both. When she returned to the terrace, Sam had finished his omelet and lit a cigarette. The wind tufted his hair around the bandages. He looked a little bit like a bandit, and she told him so.

"A bandit? That's funny."

Irene said, "I heard about your wife."

"You mean that she isn't my wife? Years and years of refusing me a divorce, and then she splits for Reno with Pixie. Divorce papers arrive in the mail."

"That must make it hard to see your daughter."

"Irene," he said, "Pixie hates me. Sends my letters back unopened. Not that I blame her. I was a chump. I wanted Bertha to hate me enough to kick me out, and I wound up hurting my own daughter instead."

Irene thought of her father on his rocking chair. "You have to keep trying. You can't give up."

"I don't know," he said. "I think I'm done."

"Done with what?"

He took a long drag on his cigarette.

"Have you ever wondered if maybe you got it all wrong from the beginning? That you somehow started off in the wrong direction, and everything you did since, every step, it was all the opposite way from where you meant to go?"

The stars blinked sleepily above them. Irene turned to Sam, whose throat worked and worked. Irene tried to speak too. Sam got there first.

"It's been coming on for a while. Bit by bit, ever since I got back from Australia. Bertha was still in the hospital. I'll never forget the expression on her face. Like she'd won some game of chess or something. Trapped me in a tiger pit. And there was nothing I could do to escape, because of Pixie. Because she was Pixie's mother. Whatever move I made to grasp some straw of joy, she would counter it. I thought, I can't do this. I just can't go on."

"But you kept going. You kept on flying."

"It was the only thing I knew how to do, the only way I could support my daughter. So I flew, because I had to fly, but when I got into an airplane I didn't care if I lived or died anymore. The only thing that kept me alive was Pixie, because she needed me."

"Oh, Sam—"

"I just—I have nothing left, Irene. Nothing. Last weekend, in that air show, I went through my routine, you know, cut everything a little close. Gave them a good show for their money. About halfway through, I just knew. I was through. It was time to either break free or die. And I thought there was only one way to do it so I wouldn't get the chance to back out."

Irene put her face in her hands.

"Not to *kill* myself. Crash the ship, that was all, so I couldn't go up again. I know how to crash, you know. Used to do it all the time for the movies. God knows the crowd loves it. That's what they're really there for, to watch somebody crack up. I did it right at the end, when I came in for the final landing." He finished off the last ounce of whiskey and soda and made a motion with his hand. "Clipped the ground with my right wing, turned a nice cartwheel. Bang."

Irene dropped her hands and stared at him. There was nothing to say, even if she could remember how to talk. Sam raised the cigarette to his mouth, and the end flared orange in the darkness.

"Irene," he said, "it's all right. I'm here, aren't I?"

From the darkened beach came a scream of drunken laughter. Neither of them moved. Irene remembered her soda water. She lifted it to her lips and drank it all, and when she was finished she could speak again.

"So what are you going to do now?"

"I'm going away for a while."

"Where?"

"Maybe Europe. They could use me in Spain, I'm thinking."

"*Spain?* You mean the war? What do you care about Spain?"

"You have to care about *something*. I don't have anything left to care about anymore, nothing I love that's not stolen away. I have to find something, or I swear I'll die."

"What about flying? You care about flying."

He turned his head, and the light from the kitchen burned in his eyes. "*You* care about flying, Irene. I haven't given a damn about it since I walked out of that sheep station eight years ago. Since then, I've just been making a living."

"But you're the best pilot I know."

Sam finished the cigarette and stubbed it out. "You should go home."

"You can't just give up! Fly with me. We're a team, remember? We could fly around the world together, like we said."

"What I'm trying to tell you," Sam said gently, "is that it doesn't matter to me anymore. Flying does not matter. Setting some record, it's pointless. You get yourself killed for no reason at all."

"That's not true."

"If I'm going to get killed, I want to die for a reason. I want my daughter, if she ever gives a damn, to say that her father died for something. For a *reason*, for something that was bigger than his own ego."

"Don't say that. Don't say it like you're already dying."

He lifted his empty glass and held it by the rim. "Irene, we're all dying," he said. "Some of us take longer than others, that's all."

AFTER THE DISHES WERE DONE, Irene put a record on the old-fashioned phonograph in the living room and made cocoa. She helped Sam into the armchair in the living room and sat on the rug, leaning against his good knee while they listened to music. The first record was some sentimental Kalmar and Ruby, "Who's Sorry Now" followed by "Thinking of You." When that finished, and the needle scratched softly on the disc, Irene got up and flipped through the records until she found something without words, a Schubert piano concerto. She put that on and returned to Sam's knee. This time he idled his hand in her hair.

"Remember when I cut it for you?" he said. "Little did I know we were creating a sensational new hairstyle. Copied by millions of women the world over."

"Hardly millions."

"But nobody wears it better than you." He lifted a curl and ran it between his finger and thumb. "It's getting late, Irene. You should be heading home."

"I'm not going anywhere. Someone's got to look after you."

"Your husband might have something to say about that."

"My husband's in New York."

"But he'll be back. Sooner or later."

Irene wrapped an arm around his leg and closed her eyes. "I'm not leaving you alone like this."

THE NEXT MORNING, SHE DROVE back to Burbank to pick up some clothes and a toothbrush. Sandy greeted her at the door, making loud, accusing *miaows*. The housekeeper said that Mr. Morrow had been calling for her. He had reached New York last night and was staying at the Peninsula. Irene packed fresh clothes and a toothbrush into her kit bag and rang up the Peninsula. She asked for George Morrow's room and they connected her right away.

"Where in God's name have you been?" he asked.

"I've been at Sam's house. He left the hospital and needs someone to look after him."

The silence at the other end lasted so long, Irene thought they had been disconnected, except that the static still crackled in the background. Finally she asked if he was still there.

"I'm here," George said. "Can't he hire a nurse?"

"I've got nothing else to do. The mechanics are working on the airplane."

The next silence didn't last quite as long. Before Irene could break in a second time, he said, "All right. If that's what you want. Just remember you've got the first lecture in Sacramento in ten days. And for God's sake, don't let some photographer catch you."

When she returned to the cottage, she told Sam that she'd spoken to George.

"So what did he say?"

"He said to make sure I didn't forget about the lecture tour. And not to answer the door to any photographers."

"Jesus," said Sam.

"Anyway, I've got a surprise for you."

"What's that?"

Irene reached back into the car and drew out a fluffy, bemused calico cat from the passenger seat.

SAM STILL HAD HIS OLD surfboard, and Irene liked to take it out in the morning, just as the sun was beginning to rise, while Sam watched anxiously from the terrace. He was worried because of her arm, but he didn't say so. She would climb back up the path, carrying the heavy board on her shoulder, grinning and wet and shivering, and she would put the board away and straddle his lap and kiss him. He liked to taste the salt water on her skin, to nuzzle her dripping hair. He told her to be careful not to get his cast all wet, and she said she would be very careful.

But they never were.

AFTER THEY MADE LOVE AND Irene showered off all the salt water and washed her hair clean, she would kiss Sam good-bye and put on a scarf and sunglasses so she could buy groceries without being recognized. She brought back lots of vegetables and fruit and meat, in order to build up his strength. "You're too thin," she told him. "You need someone to look after you, not these giddy starlets who only love their own reflections in the mirror."

He would pull her back on his lap and ask what she loved.

"You," she said. "Flying. That's all."

THEY WERE NEVER CAREFUL, NOT once. They made love recklessly, as often as they could because of so much lost time, and when they weren't making love they lay on the rug together, arguing about the future, while Sandy curled in the armchair and watched them with sleepy, predatory eyes. Sam was still determined to go to Spain, as soon as the cast was off. Irene wanted him to fly with her instead. Fly around the world, the way they had talked about eight years ago.

"I told you, I'm done with stunts," he said.

"It's not a stunt. We'd be lengthening the horizon of human possibility. Pushing the boundaries of aviation."

"Save it for the speeches, Irene. You're a decade out of date. Who cares about that kind of thing when the whole world's in the middle of a depression, when villages are getting bombed?"

"There's nothing you can do about that. But you can still show people what airplanes can do, that air travel is the future."

"They already know that. I can't show them anything they haven't seen with their own two eyes." He rolled on his side and wrapped his arm around her waist. "Don't keep risking that sweet life of yours for this nonsense. Come with me instead."

"Oh, and that's not risking my life?"

"I'm not talking about fighting. I've shot down enough airplanes, God knows. I'll be training pilots, that's all. Flying in food and medicine, maybe, flying out the injured. Now that's some good an airplane can do."

"But won't the other side try to shoot you down?"

"They won't catch me. They won't catch you, either. You're a terrific pilot. Come with me. Leave this show behind you."

"I can't. What you're talking about, that's not what I do."

"We've got another chance, you and me. Let's not waste it this time, all right? Let's not leave each other again."

"*You* left," she said.

"You married Morrow."

She put her arms around his neck. "Enough arguing, all right? We have better things to do."

But the next morning, when Irene went out for groceries, she stopped at a newsstand and bought a newspaper. The man gave her change and peered at her. "Say," he said, "ain't you that lady pilot?"

"I don't know what you're talking about."

"You are! Irene Foster. Son of a gun, my old lady's never gonna believe this!"

Irene put the change in her pocket and folded the newspaper under her arm. "People mistake me for her all the time, I'm afraid."

When she returned to the cottage, she put away the groceries and opened the newspaper and started reading about the war in Spain.

FROM THE PERSPECTIVE OF HISTORY, it's easy to see the outcome of the Spanish Civil War as inevitable, and maybe it was. But in the early fall of 1936 the Nationalist coup had only just started to gather steam, and the bombings of Madrid and Guernica still lay in the future as horrors yet undreamed of. You could say to yourself that while Hitler and Mussolini might be supplying Franco, Stalin had thrown the resources of the Soviet Union behind the leftist Republic, and how in the hell did you choose between thugs like those? Even in 1936, before history had revealed them for the monsters they were, had revealed the Holocaust and also the Ukraine famine, nobody could reasonably pretend that either fascism or communism was a nice benevolent system of government. Why did it have to be one or the other?

Still, while the great nations of the world remained officially neutral, plenty of Westerners had decided which side they were on and took action, and most of them sided with the loyalist Republicans. They represented, after all, the lawfully elected government, however leftist, whereas the Nationalists stank of ruthlessness and repression. It's not entirely clear what political views Sam Mallory held—he never expressed them publicly, and few private documents remain—or how he first came into contact with the various American brigades giving succor to the Spanish Republicans. What we do know is that this turning point in Spain's history happened to coincide with a turning point in Sam Mallory's life, and possibly the political question was irrelevant anyway. He was a man searching for purpose, and in the death and horror of a brutal war, he thought he had found it.

Irene wasn't so sure.

"They're bombing everywhere," she said. "They're assaulting Madrid right now. Hitler's sending his own air force."

"I already told you all this. Civil wars are brutal. It's personal, it's not just some fellow you might be friends with if some archduke wasn't assassinated. Everyone's got a grudge. Against the Church, against the Reds, against the rich, you name it. They're killing children over there."

"It's terrible. But it's not our fight. When did Spain ever send help to you, when you were fighting Germany?"

"That's not the point. It's not about keeping score. It's about relieving misery."

"You can't just fly off to Spain to redeem yourself from some imagined sin. Spain is not purgatory."

"It is if you're living there."

"Then don't go," Irene begged him. "Don't get in the middle of somebody's family fight. You know how it is in families. Everybody's desperate for the high moral ground, and they'll all fight dirty to get there. Try to get in the middle of that and you'll end up dead."

"And I thought you were an idealist."

"And I thought you weren't."

"If I'm going to die in an airplane," Sam said, "I don't want to go down in the middle of some ocean, chasing an empty record."

They were lying in bed. It was nearly midnight, and they had been arguing about this most of the day. Arguing and making love and arguing some more. The weather was turning chilly at night, so they fought curled around each other, sharing heat equally, skin on skin. Sandy slept on the bed with them, on a vacant pillow or else tucked into the bend of somebody's knee. Sam was feeling much better; the bruises were already healing. Irene said it was because of the soups she made him, all the strong broth and wholesome food. Sam insisted it was the whiskey and the sex. He lay on his back, because that was more comfortable for his left leg in its plaster cast, and Irene lay on her side with her arm across his chest. Now she propped herself up and looked down at his face in the moonlight—the moon was waxing now, nearly full—and her heart ached because this was how he'd looked on the beach at Howland. So she did what she couldn't do then, and straddled him. Sandy startled and leapt to the extreme end of the bed. Sam put his hands on her hips and grinned up at her, as if he hadn't just spoken about getting shot down over Spain in his airplane.

"Promise me something," she said.

"Name it."

"Promise me you won't die in an airplane."

"I won't die in an airplane."

"Promise me."

He drew her down for a long kiss. "Irene Foster. I swear to God I will die in your loving arms, and nowhere else."

LATER, IRENE WOULD LOOK BACK on those nine days with Sam and marvel at how she could have been so joyful, when she knew this arrangement was short and temporary, when the future beyond it was like a night fog. How, when they ventured out to the beach after sunset, she could have danced in mad swirls on the sand while Sam played records on the phonograph; how they could have made love for hours under the glittering night sky with no regard whatsoever for the possible consequences of uniting yourself sexually with another human being. She could only say that she was drunk at last, for the first time in her life, and didn't realize that when you were drunk—and it didn't matter what you were drunk on, dope or alcohol or danger or passion—you lost all inhibition. You forgot your drunkenness would end eventually in some kind of misery or that consequences even existed at all.

What she couldn't say was that they didn't make the most of those nine days. They might have been nine years, Sam and Irene packed so much into them. They laughed and fought and ate and played and made love, and on the last night, after Sam hobbled up the cliff in his crutches, and Irene followed anxiously with the phonograph and the records, they fell into bed so exhausted, they did not make love at all, for once. They just slept in a tangle of skin and sweat, did not dream, did not stir until a premonition of dawn slid through the open window.

Irene opened her eyes and peeled her skin from Sam's skin. She slipped out of bed and wriggled on her bathing costume and surfed for an hour. When she climbed back to the terrace, Sam had a cup of coffee ready for her, and this morning he wasn't smiling.

"You've decided, then," he said. "You're going to Sacramento."

She didn't ask how he knew. She took the coffee and drank, and when her mug was empty she washed it out and showered in Sam's bathtub, under its rickety shower pipe. He was waiting, towel in hand, when she came out. He dried her off himself, sort of hopping about on one crutch, which made her laugh. Once he had her laughing, he set her on the edge of the chair and made love to her a final time on his knees, cushioned by the rug: an ingenious solution to the problem of the cast, which had bedeviled them all week. When they had both finished, panting like racehorses, wrung stone dry, ruined for life, she hung herself on his wet shoulders and cried a little.

SAM HOBBLED OUT TO THE car with her. He said he wanted to make sure she left safely, which made her eyes roll. "Sam, this is nothing.

Didn't we land that ship on Howland Island by moonlight, with one engine?"

"It's not the big things that kill you, Irene. It's the little things." He raised his hand and caressed Sandy, who nestled in Irene's arms, rubbing beneath her ears as she liked. She stretched out her chin and purred graciously. "Sure going to miss this pussy of yours," he said.

Irene started to laugh in great whoops, so that she had to lean back against the car to keep herself steady. Sam just shook his head and kissed her, and for an instant, the great sky blue above them, the bad thing had never happened, eight years never happened, and they were just Sam and Irene who shared a single joy, a single passion, and that was enough.

"Stay out of trouble, all right?" she said, knowing it was a stupid thing to say, because he was going to Spain, of all places, and she was going to fly solo around the world, and their separate paths were strewn with trouble.

Sam didn't even bother to answer. He grasped the door handle and opened it for her. Irene stepped inside and sat in the driver's seat, dumped Sandy carefully into the passenger seat, and Sam leaned in to kiss her again.

"When you're done with all this, let me know," he said.

"Let you know? How?"

"I'll send a postcard or something. You'll find me."

Irene pushed down the clutch and turned the ignition. The engine coughed once and woke. Sam stepped back and waved her off down the road. As she swept past, she heard him call something, but she couldn't make out the words.

GEORGE CALLED HER FROM NEW York the next morning, while she was eating breakfast in her hotel room in Sacramento. The speech had gone well. She was her old self, animated, bursting with passion for this thing called flying, for the grand possibilities of human endeavor. She did something she hadn't done before, which was to talk about the famous

Australia flight: what exactly had gone wrong with the engine, how they had found Howland by moonlight, how she'd learned from Sam Mallory to remain calm at the moment of crisis, the one absolutely necessary characteristic of a great pilot. The audience—a dinner crowd—had stood and applauded for six minutes and then turned to dessert, which was pineapple upside down cake.

"Had a nice time?" George asked.

"The best."

"Good. I thought maybe you needed a little vacation. A little light-hearted fun, for a change. You weren't yourself."

"Well, I'd have to say I feel like myself again."

"And how's Mallory feeling? Bones all healed?"

"Bones don't heal in a week, George. But I firmly believe he's a thousand times better than he was before I came."

"I'm glad to hear it. Now listen to me, Miss Foster. While you've been resting up, I've been thinking. Kicking around a few ideas with the publicity fellows here. Tell me what you think."

Irene swirled her coffee around the cup. "Think of what, George?"

"The circumnavigation. What if it's not just *you* flying around the world?"

"You mean a copilot? A navigator? I've already done that."

"No," he said, and Irene could hear the excitement in his voice, a vibration she knew well. She imagined him sucking on his cigar, beaming into the telephone, while New York hustled and bustled outside his window.

"What, then?"

"A race," he said. "A race around the world."

HANALEI, HAWAI'I

November 1947

K AIKO LEANS ON his crutches near the airplane's left wing, looking deeply pleased with himself. I duck under the tail section and gaze at the faded letters and numbers with reverent eyes.

"Is this what I think it is?"

"If you think it's Irene's old airplane, the one that vanished from the face of the earth, then you would be one hundred percent correct, Sherlock."

I walk around the fuselage in slow, small, cautious steps. The metal is dull and dirty and curiously fragile, as if you might dent it by pressing a finger against the skin. It's also smaller than I imagined. In photographs, scale is maybe the hardest thing to convey. That's because a camera lens sees the world in only two dimensions, while our miraculous, stereoscopic human eyes have evolved over the eons to see the world in three dimensions. When you compress every object, near and far, into a single flat plane, your eye can't necessarily tell the difference between something giant and something tiny. You know what I mean. You've gone to the Grand Canyon or someplace, you've oohed and you've aahed, you've taken out your Brownie and filled an entire roll of film with magnificent vistas of this monumental work of nature, and you've bounded off to fetch the developed prints at the drugstore a week later, and what a disappointment! That's not how you remembered the

Grand Canyon at all! This is just some pretty landscape. It doesn't stir your heart, it doesn't make your soul grow, the way your soul grows when you actually stand on the vast rim of nature's greatness.

Now, professional photographers have turned to various tricks and expensive equipment in order to create the illusion of what we call a depth of field, but by and large, you can't understand how big or how small a thing might be unless you're standing in its presence, measuring its size against your own, and I always imagined that this airplane, as legendary as it is, as capable of flying all the way around the world, was . . . well, bigger. But she is not big at all. Not an unnecessary ounce of metal encumbers her. She's designed for utility, form following function as the modern designers insist, but what a form. The sleek lines of her, the way her nose tilts just so, the cocky angle of her tail. You can just about hear the soft whistle of the air as it whooshes along her sides. I gather my courage at last and run my fingertips along the curve of her cheek. There is not a flaw on her, not a dimple.

"How did she get here?" I ask.

"She flew in, what do you think?"

"Just flew here to Hanalei? From where?"

"Don't you know all that already? You and Irene, you've been huddled up like sisters."

I examine my fingers for dust. "We haven't gotten to the part about the race yet."

"No kidding?"

"You know her. If she doesn't want to talk about something, she just stops the conversation right there. Don't worry. I'll get it all out of her eventually."

I move around the nose to the wing, duck under the wing and lay my hand on the edge of the door, which is positioned near the tail.

Kaiko shifts on his crutches. "Say . . ." he mutters.

"How do you open this thing?" I ask.

"Beats me. You know something? I think we oughta—"

"Wait a second. She climbed in near the cockpit, didn't she? There's this photo . . ." I turn to the wing. If there's one thing on this airplane that beats my idea of size, it's the engine. There are two of them, large enough to hide a man inside, and the propeller blades stick from the front of this thing, long and curved and what's the word? *Deadly*. I test the wing with my two hands and prepare to hoist myself up.

"Now, wait just a second!" says Kaiko.

"I won't hurt anything, I promise. Just peek inside."

"Hold on! I never said anything about—aw, come on, Janey—stop that, she's gonna kill me!"

I pull the hatch open and drop myself inside. "Don't worry! I'll just be a minute. Take a few photos and . . . and . . ."

For a minute or two, I stand without blinking, the way the Magdalen must have stood inside the tomb of Jesus. Is that blasphemous? But the feeling's the same, I think. When you step inside a space that is sacred, the way the inside of that Rofrano Sirius feels to me. I can't explain it. I can't tell you what queer, otherworldly electricity hovers in the air. As I lift my camera and take the first photograph, I flinch, because I understand I'm transgressing some taboo, I am crossing the boundary between profane and holy. Still I snap the pictures. I must. Because I have no flash, because I wouldn't use one if I had it, I've got to open the aperture wide and hold myself still. *Click, click, click*. Outside the metal skin, Kaiko groans and fidgets. I emerge some minutes later and close the hatch behind me. Climb down from the wing and aim the lens at the exterior. *Click, click.*

"*Now* can we split?" begs Kaiko.

"Like a banana."

"You're not going to send those photos to some newspaper, are you?"

"My God, of course not! That would be a terrible waste."

"Waste of what?"

"This is *gold*, Kaiko. Don't you see that? Pure gold."

We emerge into the sunlight. I grasp the edge of the door and slide it shut. Both of us look this way and that, to see if we've been observed, but the surroundings are quiet and green and motionless.

"Janey," Kaiko says, in a serious voice, "I shouldna done that. You got to promise you won't tell anyone."

I tuck my camera and my notebook into my knapsack. My heart's still thundering, my fingers shake. "Not a soul. You have my word."

But I don't ask him why, after a decade tucked in a shed, Irene Foster's custom Rofrano Sirius should have not a speck of dust upon her skin, inside or out.

THE CAT ENJOYS RIDING IN the basket of my bicycle as we trundle up and down the road from Kilauea to Coolibah, passing through Hanalei in between. Sometimes I check the post office again in the afternoon, before doubling back to Coolibah, but today I cycle straight back and calculate the hours until nightfall, when I can take out my developing equipment and turn that film into photographs. Already the whole episode has the texture of a dream, something my brain cooked up out of fantasy. Did I really just stand inside the cockpit of Irene Foster's missing airplane? Did I really just climb down from its wing and snap a photograph of its snub nose?

So enraptured am I, I hardly notice that the ferry should be coming in about now, has probably already docked, until I'm skidding past the little pier, wobbling my bicycle around the few departing passengers, and hear my name called over the racket.

"Ahoy, matey," I reply. "How was the sea today?"

"Wet and salty, like always. If you can wait a minute or two, I'll give you a lift back to Coolibah."

"What about my bicycle?"

He shrugs. "You can leave it here, if you like. Dad'll pick it up on his way home."

I wait for him to finish putting the boat to bed. The cat does not appreciate this interruption. I remove her from the basket and lean the bicycle against the railing. Leo climbs aboard his moped and I climb behind, one hand holding the cat and the other hooked around Leo's waist.

I soon realize this was a terrible decision. In my present state of agitation, I should be anywhere on earth but straddling an engine with Leo Lindquist, while the Hawaiian afternoon rushes through my hair. I haven't slept with anybody in almost a month, a terrible drought, and here is a fresh, warm body under my fingertips, already proven, smelling and feeling exactly right. When we round the point and start toward the Coolibah drive, I burst out, "Just stop here! I think I'll go surfing for a bit."

"Surfing? *Now?*"

"Why not?"

"It's an hour until dinner."

"I've been working all day. I need a little fresh air."

He pulls the moped to the side of the road, where the path runs down to the beach. Because hardly anybody else ventures so far, the Lindquists keep a few boards in a small wooden cabana. I set the cat in a pile of towels and shut the door so I can change into a swimsuit. It's one of Lindquist's, and it's a bit long, but it will do. I grab a board and open the door, and there's Leo, sans shirt.

"*What* do you think you're doing?" I ask indignantly.

"Surfing. 'Scuse me. Got to find a pair of trunks."

HE TELLS ME LATER THAT he had no designs on me whatsoever, that he was just worried about me surfing alone. I don't know about that. One fascinating detail I learned about Leo in the past couple of weeks—he commanded a PT boat in the South Pacific during the war, and such men are always thinking several moves in advance, however straightforward they appear.

We paddle out together. The surf is gentle, and we coast along without speaking, wave after wave, communicating in that wordless way of two people on the water. One wave rises up, bigger than the others, just as I'm about to head in. Maybe I'm tired, maybe I don't have the chops yet, but I misjudge it completely and tumble into the drink. To his credit, Leo doesn't try to rescue me. He catches up with me as I stagger onto the beach and asks if I'm all right.

"All *right*? Are you *kidding*?" I throw myself on the dry sand and laugh at the sky. "That was just what I needed!"

He laughs too and throws himself next to me. The sinking sun turns his skin to bronze. I lie there and find a curious pleasure in my own restraint, in the uncomplicated perception of his body next to mine, both of us still panting a little, dripping and salty, bound together by a half hour of shared adventure. And while I'm contemplating this innocent enjoyment, congratulating myself even, Leo turns on his side and kisses my lips.

"What was that for?"

"I'm sorry. Lost my head. It won't—"

I reach for his shoulders and kiss him back.

LEO BRINGS ME A FLOWER when he returns to Coolibah for dinner an hour later. His hair is dark and wet from a hasty shower, and the flower is a passionflower. I tuck it behind my ear. At dinner, Doris asks me why I'm wearing a flower in my hair, and I tell her it's from a suitor. Leo grins from across the table. Olle's busy carving the pork roast. Wesley's got his head under the tablecloth for some reason. Lindquist leans forward on her elbows and frowns.

Once dessert is cleared and the children sent to bed, Olle retires to the library and Lindquist sends Leo on an errand. As soon as he disappears around the corner, she turns to me.

"Kaiko made a little confession to me this afternoon," she says.

"It's not his fault. I might have goaded him a little."

"You're doing your job. I understand that. But the airplane is off limits, is that clear? I want that film you took."

I hesitate. "It's in the cottage."

"Then bring it to me at breakfast." She jiggles her wedding ring. "Please."

"But why? I mean, you've kept it, all these years. It must mean something to you."

"Because even if I destroyed that airplane, the parts would make their way into public notice. Someone would find some scrap of wing, some section, match the rivets. It's safer where it is. At least until I'm dead."

"You don't believe that. Not really. You're worried about some scrap making its way into the wrong hands? You can't destroy that airplane, any more than you could cut off your own arm."

She stands.

"You keep it clean, don't you? Not a speck of dust. You keep it in working order."

"Her," Irene says. "An airplane is a she."

"She, he, it. There must be a reason, right? So tell me."

Lindquist reaches down for her glass of soda water and finishes it. But she doesn't sit. She's just stalling for time, she's trying to think. A week ago, she would have walked away, but today—I don't know, maybe it's the passionflower in my hair, a symbol of some kind, marked *friend*—she considers what she should say to me and not say to me.

"Bring me the roll of film in the morning," she says, "and I'll tell you about that airplane."

FOR THE RECORD, LEO AND I did nothing but kiss on the beach that afternoon. On my honor! You never know when a pair of pint-sized ruffians might tumble down the path, for one thing, and for another this was a different kind of kissing from the kissing I was used to. When Leo drew back and stroked my hair with both hands, the way you stroke a cat, I thought about telling him I had never done this before, just kissed a boy and nothing else, but I realized how that made me sound, what kind of person that made me. So I said instead that we should probably head back to the house, before we did something we might regret.

"I don't regret this," he said. "Do you?"

"Yes."

He leaned his forehead against mine and said he was sorry. I asked for what. He said he had got me all wrong, he'd sized me up and figured I was just using them all, Irene and the entire family, that I was some hard, cold villain who would break his heart.

I told him he was probably right, that maybe I was that villain.

"Maybe," he said, "but I'm starting to figure I could take that chance."

The touch of his forehead was warm, the muscle of him, the sanded skin, the breath. I sat on my knees, in the V of his legs, his gentle arms on either side of me, his hands resting at the back of my head. I was surrounded. I thought that I had come to like Leo a great deal, over the course of the past weeks. I had maybe come to like him too much.

I had come to like them all too much.

I kissed him one more time and clambered to my feet.

"Believe me," I said, "you shouldn't take that chance."

FIVE HOURS LATER, WHEN THE black night presses against the windows, I'm regretting this moment of high-mindedness with all my might. My God, what I wouldn't give to have a Leo lying next to me, equipped and willing to give me oblivion.

Instead I climb out of bed and prepare my makeshift darkroom. I move as silently as possible, the way I learned to do when I was small. I remove the film and clip the ends and load the reel; I sink the reel into the tank and fill it with water from the sink and swish it from side to side. Then the developer, the stop bath, the fixer, the rinse. Hang the negatives on their clothespins and clean the trays.

But despite these comforting rituals, I'm still restless. Something nags me. I'm thinking about that airplane I saw today, and about that last flight from Alexandria, and the search for Irene Foster that dragged on for weeks.

I find my way to the little table that serves as my desk, and I pull out the stacks of articles sent to me in batches by my old friend Bill at the Associated Press, in response to my saucy telegrams. He's been a good sport, Bill Cushing, and I owe him a drink or two. I've organized them in neat manila folders, according to subject, and I take out my penlight so I can read the labels. ALEXANDRIA, reads one.

It's now three o'clock in the morning. I climb back into my cold bed with a stack of decade-old newsprint and read without comprehension until my eyelids droop, until I can't go on. I set aside the clippings on the nightstand and that's all I remember, until some erotic dream takes shape in my sleep, as it often does.

But this time it is not Velázquez who fucks me furiously in the grass of some airfield, while a series of propeller engines scream over our heads, one after the other, each louder than the last.

It's Leo.

IN THE MORNING, I BRING the prints and the negatives to Lindquist and set them down on the tablecloth next to her breakfast plate.

"There you are. Now talk."

IV

▶ ▶ ▶

The first lesson is that you can't lose a war if you have command of the air, and you can't win a war if you haven't.

—JIMMY DOOLITTLE

AVIATRIX

by Eugenia Everett

(e x c e r p t)

April 1937: Egypt

H AVING REACHED ALEXANDRIA just before midnight, Irene was now a full two days ahead of the next competitor. She'd been lucky, of course, but she had also flown with the kind of cool, single-minded confidence she hadn't felt in years. The monsoon in Delhi, for example. When everyone else had remained on the ground, Irene had taken off in her gleaming, rebuilt Rofrano Sirius, tore right through the rain and clouds to the calm above, and built a lead that was essentially insurmountable, barring accident. You might even call it a classic Foster maneuver: the gutsy, calculated risk, relying on a thorough knowledge of geography and meteorology, allied with her characteristically precise piloting and sound instinct. The old Irene was back.

Now there remained only the final hop to Casablanca, where George waited for her in a suite at the Anfa Hotel. He had cabled her an hour ago to congratulate her on her safe arrival, her expected victory. The telegram slip lay before her now, on the desk in her hotel room, fluttering a little in the draft from the ceiling fan.

Irene rose from the chair and walked to the balcony, which overlooked some market square. At this early hour, just before dawn, the streets were empty and dark. Still, she sensed the echoes of the noontime bustle, the dust and heat and the smell of manure and hot, spicy meat, and it awakened all her curiosity. That was the trouble with these races, these stunt flights, with barnstorming generally. You sped along from point to point without any regard for what lay between. You cared only about the destination, about reaching some point on a map in the shortest possible time, and never about this vast, fascinating globe you sought to shrink.

At precisely five o'clock, a set of knuckles rapped on the door. Breakfast. Irene was specific about this meal: two eggs poached *firm*— you did *not* want to fall sick on a flight like this—served on buttered toast with a large pot of coffee. In some of the more exotic ports of call, these eggs might not necessarily come from what you'd call a chicken, but that was all right with Irene. The nutritional properties of the egg were more important than its lineage. She took the tray from the waiter at the door and handed him a tip, and then she settled to eat. She didn't rush. She knew this was her last moment of peace until she went aloft.

AS SHE CROSSED THE HOTEL lobby to meet Mr. Fish, the American ambassador in Egypt who would accompany her to the airport, the desk clerk called her name respectfully.

"Another telegram has just arrived for you, Miss Foster," he said.

Irene opened the telegram envelope with the tip of her fountain pen, which she kept in her pocket in case of autographs. It was from George.

GALA DINNER TONIGHT FRENCH AND AMERICAN OFFICIALS STOP FLY
TO PARIS TOMORROW THEN RETURN HOME SS NORMANDIE 2 MAY
STOP POSSIBLE TICKER TAPE PARADE ON ARRIVAL NEW YORK STOP
WILL ADVISE STOP LOVE ALWAYS GEORGE

She stuffed the telegram back in its envelope and folded the envelope into her pocket. "Let's go," she said to Mr. Fish.

IN HER LAST KNOWN PHOTOGRAPH, Irene Foster stands at the door of her Rofrano Sirius and waves to the crowd below, all of whom had risen before dawn to watch her depart. She wears her usual uniform, a loose, shapeless flight suit that looks gray in the monochrome print but was actually khaki, covered by a leather jacket. Knee-high boots like a cavalry officer. A leather cap covering her famous sand-colored curls. Two rows of small, even white teeth gleam from between her smiling lips. Of all the photographs taken of Irene, this one is perhaps the most famous, because it's the last moment anybody could say for sure where Irene Foster was and what she was doing. And everybody loves a mystery, don't they? Everybody wants to look into those pale, thrilled eyes and imagine what happened next.

HANALEI, HAWAI'I

November 1947

THE LAST TIME I saw Velázquez before he rejoined his squadron in The Netherlands, we went for a walk in the darkened Paris streets after dinner. He had tried to obtain an overnight pass but could not, so we had only a few hours before he was required to report to the airfield. We ate at the Ritz, because it was one of the few places you could get a decent meal if you were willing to pay enough money, and Velázquez seemed to think that some ceremony should attach to our last evening together. I drank glass after glass of expensive wine, and Velázquez said I should walk it off for a bit before we returned to my hotel. He took my arm and steered me carefully around the various hazards. It was still quite early, because of the curfew, and I remember thinking it was strange to be so drunk so early in the evening.

To pass the time, he told me more about his childhood. I asked him about this girl he was supposed to marry, and at first he was reticent, saying it was not right to speak of his previous love at such a moment, but at last he admitted that he had met her while visiting some Basque friends from university, that she was the daughter of a lawyer, beautiful and also very clever (*maybe not quite so clever as you, my beloved, but just as beautiful*), and his Castilian parents were not pleased that he had fallen in love with a girl so decidedly bourgeois. *Her* parents, meanwhile, were too intimidated to press the case for true love, because Iberia as a whole retained strong notions of caste in those days. Velázquez solved this impasse by getting her pregnant, but by then the war had already started and he hurried down to train at the fighter school in El Carmoli, in the south, because he had always wanted to fly and felt a duty to come to the defense of democracy. He promised he would return north to marry her before the baby came.

"Then what happened?" I asked.

His face turned bleak. "Guernica," he said.

"SOMETHING'S WRONG WITH THE CAT," I tell Lindquist, when I come in to breakfast. "It doesn't want to get out of bed."

Lindquist shrugs over her newspaper. "She's old. She'll get up when she's ready."

"I don't know. I think you should take a look."

As I said, the cat's grown attached to me, and it's now taken to sleeping on my bed at night, observing my darkroom rituals with an air of disgust such as only a cat can affect. Over the past week or so, I've noticed that it moves a little more slowly and deliberately, hopping down by degrees; that it stays curled for hours in a snug ball in one corner. At first I figured, as Lindquist did, that this was just regular old age, and no wonder. But when I rose this morning, the cat didn't stir. I checked that it was still breathing but I thought maybe it should go to the vet, just to be sure, because Irene thought the sun rose and set on that cat.

I explain all this to Lindquist as she crosses the lawn with me in giant, silent strides. I'm surprised by the tenderness with which she addresses the beast. She strokes its fur gently and bends down to ask it a question, and I don't know what the little furball says to her in reply, but Lindquist lifts her head again with the same white, bleak expression I remember from Velázquez's face, when he told me about Guernica.

"Do you think you can hold her in your lap on the way to the veterinarian?"

IT TURNS OUT, THERE'S ONLY one veterinarian on Kauai and his office is on the other side of the island, in Lihue, and because Kauai is essentially a volcano, we have to motor all the way around the perimeter instead of directly across. Lindquist drives the Buick like a racecar, which would scare me if she hasn't always driven that way, guided by an intuition for her car and the road beneath. The cat sits in my lap, not complaining. The children are at school already.

"Thank goodness," says Lindquist. "They'd be devastated."

Now, I'm no expert, but I'm pretty sure this is what the shrinks would call projection, although I don't say so. Lindquist would rather die than admit sentimentality. I don't say this to criticize; I'm the same way myself. To admit you are sentimental is to admit you are vulnerable, that you are susceptible to emotional excess, and we can't have *that* in this modern age, can we? Lindquist pours out all her sentiment into the road, into the neat, quick curves and short stretches of pure speed, as we race toward the veterinarian in Lihue.

As for me, I'm not worried one iota about the damned cat. It's a nuisance, so far as I'm concerned. I don't understand its affection for me, because I rarely offer food and my lap is not soft. The kids find it hilarious, the way this moggie follows me around and says *miaow* when I leave to visit the bathroom or something. It's a jealous creature too. If Leo brings me a passionflower, as he sometimes does, that cat will shred the petals the instant my back's turned, and more than once it's stalked his hand or his foot when he settles down beside me on the sofa of an evening. Still, despite its distaste for the rituals of human courtship, the cat is an agreeable cat, and I go so far as to stroke its fur as we bend and twist along the Kauai highway, because I don't want it to fret about its condition. The vet will fix whatever's wrong. I repeat this thought aloud to Lindquist.

"He'd better," she says grimly.

I consider delivering some nonsense about how the cat's had a pretty long run, wouldn't you say, I mean I've never heard of a cat living nineteen years. But that's the last thing you want to hear about something you love. It doesn't matter if it's had a long life or a happy life; there's never enough life.

Instead, I say, "Didn't you and Mallory find it together? On the beach or something?"

"Yes. The day we met."

"That's sweet. And who got custody?"

"Mallory had her before Australia. Then I took her home with me after we returned. His wife didn't like cats, and after she—after she came home from the hospital, he thought he should stick around his family more. He should try to be a good husband."

"Poor Mallory. It just wasn't in him." I brace myself around a particularly high-wire turn. "Say. Where did it stay when you were flying around the world?"

"Oh, the Rofranos used to take her for us. They had all these children to lavish attention on her. She loved stowing aboard, but she was better off with them. Especially in Spain."

The puss stirs in my lap. I give it a reassuring scratch between the ears, so it won't get any dangerous ideas. "Spain was no place for a cat, was it?"

She doesn't answer. She won't talk about Spain. Believe me, I've tried every trick. She says it's a topic she won't discuss. I ask her how I'm supposed to write a biography of Mallory if I can't explain his final weeks, and she says I should go to Spain and ask around. I say I've already tried, and everybody's dead. She shrugs and says maybe that should teach me to mind my own business. To which I reply that that minding your own beeswax goes against basic human nature, and besides, I've made a pretty decent living so far off of other people's beeswax, and I can't go back now.

THERE IS A CERTAIN SMELL to a veterinarian's office, animal and medicinal both at once, and the Lihue Veterinary Hospital has it on thick. A man sits with a beagle in the waiting room. The beagle looks worried;

the man looks annoyed. "I don't see why we can't go right in," he tells the receptionist. "She's very sick."

The beagle wags its tail and pleads silently.

"I understand, sir," says the receptionist. "Mrs. Lindquist, hello. Dr. Alba's waiting for you. You can go right in with Sandy."

The man stands up. "Now wait just a minute—"

Lindquist extracts the cat carefully from my arms and marches past the reception desk. One of the doors opens; a man appears in green scrubs, holding a clipboard. "Mrs. Lindquist! What seems to be the trouble with our miracle kitty?"

"What in blazes is going on around here?" the man says. "I was here first! Look at her. She vomited twice this morning!"

"The doctor will be ready for her soon, Mr. Caruthers. I'm afraid you'll have to wait."

"This is ridiculous! Some damn *cat* gets in before my Mollie? We've been waiting half an hour already!"

I crouch in front of the beagle, who wags at me and leans forward to plant a wet one on my left cheek. "Poor Mollie. Who's a sweet, patient girl?"

Mollie licks the right cheek.

I look up at the man. He's forty or forty-five, the kind of fellow who's starting to look middle-aged and doesn't quite realize it yet. He's combed his thinning hair carefully over the bald spot on the crown, and his face is pink. He's wearing a short-sleeved shirt in pastel plaid (if that's the correct description for such a horror) and a pair of rumpled linen trousers. I give him my best smile. "I'm so awfully sorry to keep her waiting. I'm sure this won't take long. It's a pretty healthy cat for nineteen years. Probably just needs another pill or something."

"*Nineteen?*" The man looks back to the door in amazement.

"Nineteen. Can you believe it? So of course the doctor wants to see it right away. We'll just have to keep Mollie happy for a few more minutes." I fondle the soft beagle ears. "Poor baby. Have we got an upset tummy?"

"Vomited twice already this morning."

"Oh, dear! Does she have a temperature?"

"Well, I don't think so. But she's a real sweetheart, our Mollie. I just hate to see her suffer."

I rise and sit on the bench next to Mr. Caruthers. Mollie follows me and lays her muzzle in my lap, God knows why. "Tell me about Mollie, Mr. Caruthers. How old is she?"

"She was two years in August."

"Still a puppy, almost!"

"She'll eat anything, you know. That's why I brought her in. Crazy dog. She's taken a liking to *you*, though."

"Oh, she's just a friendly little baby, that's all. Does she bay?"

"Does she!" He laughs. "She'll just run right off after some rabbit, hollering and hollering. Comes back two hours later covered in mud and ashamed of herself. She's terrific with the kids, though. Got a three-year-old wandered off a few months ago—you know how they are at that age, you turn your back for a second, we were frantic, I tell you— called the police, neighbors out searching, the worst thoughts going through your head."

"I can imagine."

"Worst day of my life. Night came on. Couldn't sleep. Went right out again as soon as dawn broke and what do you know. Found him in the brush, curled up asleep with Mollie. She just looked up at us and wagged her tail. As if to say, *Don't you worry, I would lay down my life for this child of yours*."

"What a good girl you are, Mollie!" I scratch her forehead and she sighs, full of meaning. "A good big sister. You just go on taking care of those kids, do you hear? Give them a nice soft pillow to rest their heads on when life gets a little too much."

Mr. Caruthers leans forward on his knees and reaches out to pat

Mollie on the back. He clears his throat. "This cat of yours? She'll be all right?"

"I hope so. Mrs. Lindquist's had that cat so long, it's like another child to her."

"Gosh. I'm sorry."

"You know how it is. People let you down all the time, they come and go, but she and that cat . . ." I stare into Mollie's eyes, which are brown and soft with understanding. "I guess Mrs. Lindquist was practically a kid herself, when she got that cat. Now it's just about all that's left of the girl she was."

"Ain't that the truth," Mr. Caruthers says softly. "Do you know what's wrong?"

"She's just old, I guess. She takes a pill for her liver and another one for her kidneys. But anything could go wrong, at that age."

Mr. Caruthers hesitates. "I hate to say this, but maybe she just figures she's had enough. She's done all she can and it's time to go."

"Maybe that's it."

Mollie gives my fingers a last swipe with her tongue and settles at Mr. Caruthers's feet, leaning against his legs. From some distant room comes the bark of a forlorn dog in its cage. The receptionist looks up at us, then swiftly back to whatever's lying on her desk.

"You sound like you have a real affection for animals, miss," says Mr. Caruthers. "You must've had a pet or two, when you were little."

"Me? No, I'm afraid not. Well, I brought home strays all the time, but my mother wouldn't let me keep them."

"Why not?"

I reach to straighten Mollie's ear, which has flopped over the top of her head. "According to Mama, taking care of me was trouble enough."

LINDQUIST EMERGES ALONE FROM THE examining room about fifteen minutes later, pale and dry-eyed.

"Well?" I ask.

She glances to Mr. Caruthers and back to me. "Could I speak to you for a moment?"

We step outside, in the shade of a squat palm. She is all business. "I'm afraid there's no hope. It's heart failure. Dr. Alba wanted to put her down right away, but I'd like the children to say good-bye first."

"I can drive back and fetch them for you."

"Would you? Olle's flying right now, and I wouldn't let Kaiko inside my car to park it, even with the cast off."

I attempt a smile. "You're sure you trust me behind the wheel?"

"Oh, Janey. That's the least of my worries, believe me. I'll just wait here with Sandy." She shades her eyes and glances to the door. "Make her as comfortable as I can. God knows she deserves that much from me."

LINDQUIST TELEPHONES AHEAD, SO THE children are waiting in the front office at school, satchels neat and hair askew. As I bustle them into the back of the car, I realize I haven't the faintest idea what to say to them. Tadpoles are mysterious creatures to me. Innocent one second, worldly the next, so you never know what kind of tone to assume. Surely they are familiar with the concept of death, though? I start the engine and glance in the mirror at their taut little faces.

"Everybody ready?" I say cheerfully. They nod.

I let out the clutch, and we spurt from the driveway. Lindquist was right; I'm a crack driver, if I say so myself. I have an instinct for automobiles, the way some people have an instinct for horses; I guess it's in my blood or something, the same element as in Lindquist's blood. The kids don't move as I turn this way and that, until we're roaring down the main highway, ocean to the left of us. We motor through Kilauea, where I glance in the direction of the post office, though of course there's no time to stop. We've traveled eight or nine miles before I open my mouth to address the small fry huddled in the back. Open it wide, since the engine makes a real racket at that speed.

"I want you both to be very brave for your mother. You know how much she loves that cat."

They nod.

Doris says, "Is she dead already?"

"Not yet. But it's time, you know. Every living thing has its time on this earth, and its time to . . . well, you know. Heaven and all that."

"I know." Doris looks away.

I glance at Wesley in the mirror. He looks as if he's holding back a regular Niagara of tears. "Wesley? You all right?"

"Yes, Janey."

"I know it's hard to lose something you love, but—"

Wesley bursts into sobs.

"Now you've done it," says Doris. "Can't you just leave us be? We already *know* all that!"

I shrink back into my skin and focus the rest of my attention on the road. I don't even look back in the mirror. What do I know about tadpoles, after all? I can hardly remember being one myself.

I STOP THE CAR AT the veterinary hospital and open the door meekly for the ankle-biters to hop out. I usher them into the waiting room, where Lindquist sits on the bench. Sandy forms a mound of calico fluff on her lap. Next to her sits Mr. Caruthers, and at his feet lies Mollie, head on paws, who rises and wags her tail as the children approach.

"How's the beagle?" I ask.

"Oh, she's fine. A little indigestion, that's all. I just thought that Mollie and me, we'd maybe stay for a bit and keep everybody company." He gives me this sort of half-ashamed smile, not unlike Mollie's own expression. "She's good with kids, you know. When they're sad."

The children crowd around Lindquist's lap. I start to turn for the door, give them all a bit of privacy, but Sandy chooses to lift her head and blink at me. Her eyes are cloudy and sort of confused. Probably they've slipped her something to make her comfortable. We should all be so lucky. I step forward and reach between limbs to give the old furball a little scratch around the ears, the way she likes, and wish her Godspeed.

Then I head back outdoors and light a cigarette, which I smoke in long, deep drags, staring through the fronds of the palm to the blue sky above.

AFTER OUR LAST WALK THROUGH the streets of Paris, Velázquez delivered me to my room at the Scribe, but he kept his clothes on. He said I had had too much to drink, and would neither enjoy nor remember the occasion properly, and he wanted our last time in bed to be memorable, like it had been four days ago when I had driven out to the airfield to meet him. I asked if he would lie with me until I fell asleep. He hesitated and then agreed.

I remember I put on my nightclothes and swallowed some aspirin with water before I climbed into bed, as was my habit when I was drunk. Velázquez stayed dressed atop the covers, so he wouldn't be tempted, he said. He put his arm around me, however, and I laid my head on his chest. I told him I was sorry about his fiancée, and he thanked me gravely.

"But it was selfish of me to tell you that story," he said. "It's a terrible, tragic story, and I should not have added to your burden."

"Why did you tell me, then?" I asked.

"Because I want someone else to remember her, in case I am killed. I want someone else to know that she was alive, and how she died."

"Don't say stupid things like that. You won't be killed."

He reached for his cigarettes on the nightstand and lit one. He told me to go to sleep, and that's the last thing I remember about Velázquez, his solemn voice commanding me to sleep, and the smell of his cigarette, those pungent Gauloises he used to smoke, the smell of good-bye.

I MAKE STRAIGHT FOR THE cottage when we return to Coolibah. The yellow Ford is parked out front—Olle's come home—and so is Leo's moped, and I can't face either of them, I really can't. I am only just held together by a thread.

I run a bath and emerge an hour later, wrinkled and shivering, to wrap myself in the bathrobe that appeared on the hook one day, no explanation, a typical Lindquist maneuver. I badly want a drink, but to fetch a drink means returning to the main house and Olle's library, and that is impossible in my present condition, so I light a cigarette instead. I lie on the bed like this, in my bathrobe, smoking in long, deep drags as I stare at the dark wooden beams of the ceiling, and I feel this terrible hole in the bed, where the cat used to sleep, and also a terrible hole in my chest, as if someone has reached inside and torn away some piece of flesh. The cavity grows and grows, splitting my ribs apart, until at last I spring from the bed, crush out the cigarette, and sit down in the chair before the desk, where my life's work lies in neat stacks of manila folders, carefully labeled.

THIS IS WHERE LEO FINDS me some time later, when he knocks on the door. I bark, *Come in,* without looking up, and hear the creak of hinges.

"Irene sent me," he says, apologetic. "She figured you might be hungry, since you didn't come to dinner."

Though I'm afraid of the likely state of my face, I turn anyway. Leo's carrying a tray with a plate of food on it, a glass of water and also a glass of something else. I can tell from his expression that I'm not myself.

"Thanks. Just set it on the dresser."

He stares at me another second or two before he steps to the dresser and nudges aside my hairbrush with his knuckles to make room for the tray. "You should eat."

"I know I should. I'll eat when I'm hungry."

"The bourbon was my idea. Thought you could use a drink. Don't tell Irene."

"Is it a double?"

"What do you think?"

I scrape back the chair and fetch the bourbon from the tray. It's a double, neat, as if he read my mind from all the way across the lawn. I thank him sincerely and return to the desk.

"What're you working on?" he asks.

"This and that," I tell him, and then I figure I owe him for the bourbon and add, "George Morrow. I've been trying to figure out what happened to him. After he called off the search, I mean. There's nothing in the newspapers. He's turned into a recluse or something."

Leo shifts his weight from one foot to the other. "I guess he was pretty upset. She was his wife, right? His whole life was wrapped up in her."

"He just ended the search and released this final statement to the press—*The time has come to let Irene go, forever honor her memory, allow me to mourn her in privacy,* that kind of thing—and that was that. Never went out in public again. Sold his house in Burbank to Rofrano."

Leo scrunches his face. "Rofrano."

"Mr. Octavian Rofrano? The Rofrano Aircraft Company? He designed the airplane she flew. They were pretty close, the four of them. Socialized together. Lindquist says they used to keep . . ."

"Keep what?"

I turn back to the yellowing newsprint on the desk before me. "Keep the cat for her, when she was on her lecture tours and her . . . and her . . . ."

"And her what?"

I look up again. "Say. How *did* she get the cat back?"

"I don't know. I wasn't around back then. I mean, I *was*, but—"

"Because if Sophie Rofrano was mothering the cat while Irene flew around the world . . ."

Leo spreads his hands.

"I know, I know. You don't know nothing." I wave my hand. "Thanks for the hooch, anyway. You're a real pal, Leo Lindquist."

"Janey—"

"I'm fine. I truly am. It's just a cat."

"Goddamn it, Janey Everett. Would you just for one *minute* admit that you care about something? *Anything?*"

I continue to stare at the newsprint, although it's starting to blur. "Would you for *one minute*, Leo Lindquist, admit that I'm just passing through? Sure, I liked the cat. I like you. I like your whole lovely happy goddamn family. You're a real nice bunch. But I'm here to write a book, that's all. I'm here to get the facts, and maybe make some conclusions from those facts, and when . . . when I'm done . . . when I'm through . . ."

He lifts me from the chair and sits down on the edge of the bed, while I fall to pieces against his chest, like I have not done in some time, not since I heard that Captain Raoul Velázquez de los Monteros had died of catastrophic injuries in some field hospital just across the German border, two days after his airplane had fallen in flames from the sky.

LEO WAKES ME IN THE night and tells me I was having a dream. I already know this, because the dream still hangs around me, more real than the bed and the room and Leo combined. It was about Velázquez. To make it up to Leo, I snuggle my face into his chest and allow him to stroke my hair, the way he likes.

"When you leave," he says, "I don't want you to tell me first. You should just go."

I can't reply to that. I mean, I could, but it would come out all wrong, and I don't want Leo to be upset with me. He doesn't deserve to be upset, and I don't think I could stand it. So I comfort him the only way I can, in the only language I really know, the only thing I have to offer him, which others may call a sin but to my way of thinking is a gift, this body of mine, this appetite for intercourse, this instinct I have for giving and receiving pleasure. I figure the only thing is to ride him to exhaustion so he goes right back to sleep, and an hour later that's what he does, tucked inside the cradle of my arms and legs, lips still moving like he's trying to tell me something. I've broken another rule, I guess, but by now I've broken so many, it doesn't seem to matter.

I HAVE ONLY A MOMENT or two to hold him close before somebody knocks on the door. I reach for Leo's shirt and pull it over my head. On the other side of the door, Lindquist gives me a withering look. She holds a cardboard box under her arm.

"What's that?" I ask.

"I need to speak with you."

"At this hour?"

"It's the only time we have. I want this to be the two of us."

"What? Why?"

She stares at my face for a second or two. There is some faint light from the porch, and a moon that's nearly full in the western part of the sky, so I guess she can see me all right.

I shift from one foot to the other and cross my arms. "Well?"

"I think it's time to tell you about what happened to your father in Spain," she says. "Pixie."

AVIATRIX

by Eugenia Everett

(e x c e r p t)

April 1937: Spain

FOUR AND A half hours after taking off from the airport in Alexandria, Irene landed in perfect weather at the El Carmoli air base on the southeastern Spanish coast, near Cartagena. Nobody stopped her or tried to intercept her, even though this was one of the major Republican air bases and the location of the high-speed flying school for fighter pilots. It was a landing strip in the middle of the desert, bleak and brown, tufted with long, skinny grass. The airplanes, lined up in motley rows, were years out of date. As she rolled toward a hangar, she felt all the amazed eyes on the airplane's skin, and still not a single soul moved from the buildings or the shadows to stop her. Maybe they were all taking a siesta or something, Irene thought.

She brought the ship to a stop and turned off the switches, made notes in her log. She unbuckled herself from the seat and bounded to the door. Outside, a couple of men in flight suits stared at her, astounded. "Good afternoon," she said, in her best Spanish. "I am looking for Señor Mallory." She made a gesture with her hand, indicating height. "American. Blond hair."

Both men nodded vigorously. "Señor Mallory! *Sí*!"

"Do you know where he is?"

Maybe she said it wrong. Irene had studied French in school, and most of her Spanish was learned in bits and pieces as she navigated her way around Los Angeles. The men looked at each other gravely, and back at her.

"He is in the north," said one of them. "He is in Guernica."

IRENE FOSTER HAD NEVER HEARD of Guernica before that day, the twenty-seventh of April. Not many had, outside of Spain itself, although it was a symbol of Basque independence, where King Ferdinand had stood under the municipal tree in 1476—the famous Tree of Guernica, an oak—and sworn an oath to uphold the rights and laws of the Biscay province, of which Guernica was capital. It was located on the northern coast, right on the edge of the Bay of Biscay, and it had been horrifically bombed by the Luftwaffe the day before, on behalf of the Spanish Nationalists.

All this was explained rapidly to Irene, once she'd identified herself as a friend of Señor Mallory. Too rapidly, because she didn't quite understand the significance of this episode until later. It was war, after all, and bombs got dropped during wartime and killed people. It was terrible, and Irene felt this as a personal horror because bombing seemed to her a perverse way of using this great scientific achievement that was an airplane, that dropping bombs from airplanes was a betrayal of everything she had strived for. As if your beloved brother had turned out to be a murderer. But when she heard the word *Guernica* she didn't feel any particular foreboding. No cold chills down her spine. Why should she? Not yet.

There were many deaths and injuries, said the men, and Irene could tell from their faces that this thing called Guernica was a terrible, wretched affair. Still she did not really understand. Señor Mallory had taken off in one of the larger airplanes late yesterday afternoon, as soon as the news had reached them, and flown north to help evacuate the wounded. One of the other pilots had flown in company with him, a man whose fiancée lived with her family near Guernica. They had heard nothing since from either man.

Nothing at all? Irene asked. They hadn't returned here with their evacuees?

There was no cause for alarm, they assured her. After all, Mallory was not a combatant. Probably he was taking these injured people to Madrid or to Valencia, not to hot, dry, isolated El Carmoli, with scant hospitals nearby. He would be back in a few days, once the wounded were all evacuated.

How do you know this? Irene demanded. How do you know he hasn't been shot down or crashed?

The two men traded glances and said of course there was no way of knowing for certain. That was the nature of war. You simply had to keep faith and wait for news. Señorita Foster could stay here for as long as she liked. The commandant's wife would be happy to accommodate her until Señor Mallory returned.

That was very kind, Irene told them. (By now they were inside the hangar, sheltered from the fierce sun, drinking hot, strong coffee that lifted the hairs on Irene's arms and the back of her neck.) But instead of accommodation, she would prefer a map and a hundred gallons of aviation fuel, for which she would pay in American dollars.

OF COURSE, IT WASN'T QUITE as easy as that. News had reached the commandant of this somewhat embarrassing (although hardly surprising) breach of the airfield's defenses, such as they were, and he came striding in a moment later, demanding to know what was going on. She told him she was here for Señor Mallory.

"Señor Mallory?" he said, peering at Irene. His face illuminated. He switched to English. "*Miss Foster*! You are Irene Foster!"

Irene tried to tell him that this was a secret, but he was already pumping her hand with joy.

"I am a great admirer!" he told her. "I am filled with happiness to meet you! I have spoken about you many times with Señor Mallory! You are like a queen to us! But are you not supposed to be in a race right now?"

"I left the race," said Irene. "I've come to join Señor Mallory."

The commandant's face turned grave. "Señorita Foster, this is no place for a woman. This is war. I cannot be responsible for what will happen to you if you stay. It is quite possible we will be bombed. And what is there for you to do?"

"I can train pilots, for one thing."

"I am afraid that is impossible. This is not America. No Spanish man will take instruction from a woman, certainly not in a matter so serious as flying. Besides, this is a fighter school! Have you ever fought in an airplane?"

Irene had to admit that she hadn't.

"Well, then. My wife will care for you until Señor Mallory returns from Biscay. We will attempt to send him a message, yes? Obtain some news, to make the waiting easier?" The commandant leaned forward, as one who understands the delicacy of such matters. "And your husband? Is it necessary for us to send him a message as well?"

"No, it's not necessary. But I'm afraid I don't intend to stay here, as grateful as I am for your hospitality."

"No? You wish to stay in town instead?"

"I'm not going to stay anywhere," said Irene. "I'm going to go find Sam."

IT TOOK SOME ARGUING, BUT finally they let her go. They even gave her the fuel for nothing, although she offered repeatedly to pay. It had something to do with hospitality, and with the way the commandant admired her. Irene Foster! Sometimes her fame had its uses.

Before she left, the commandant sat her down with the map and went over the terrain, the geography of Spain. He remonstrated with her. The news from Guernica is terrible, he said. There will be frightful wounds, children maimed, the entire town destroyed.

"That's why I'm going," she said. "I want to help. I want to make sure Señor Mallory is safe."

"Do you love him very much?" the commandant said earnestly, as if the immorality of loving a man other than your husband meant nothing to him, or that a woman so great as Miss Foster could naturally love whom she pleased.

"Yes, I love him very much," Irene said, in Spanish, and the commandant nodded, as if the matter were closed.

So she took off at dawn, after a hasty breakfast and more strong coffee, and the last thing Irene said to the commandant was that he must not, above all, tell anybody where she was, or that she'd visited the air base at all. *Even your husband?* asked the commandant, and Irene replied, *Especially my husband.*

This disturbed him, but he wished her Godspeed anyway. As she made her turn at the end of the runway and began to spin her engines, preparing to depart, she saw the fleck of him through the cockpit window, standing by himself to watch Irene Foster take off in her famous airplane from his own air base, what an honor.

THE COMMANDANT WARNED HER THAT as she headed north, closer to the territory held by the Nationalists, she might encounter enemy aircraft, mostly German. They did not, as a rule, go out on regular patrols, but there was still some danger that she might blunder into a bombing group. Nobody had been expecting the Guernica attack; it had occurred in the middle of the afternoon, on a market day, sunshine and stalls and fresh food brought in from the country farms, then out of the clear blue sky came the grind of propeller engines, bombs whining through the air and exploding everywhere. *So keep your eyeballs peeled, Señorita Foster,* the commandant said, proud of his command of American idiom. As

Irene flew northward over the deserts and plains of central Spain, she wondered if he'd learned that phrase from Sam.

Because there was no airstrip at Guernica—or if there was, it was destroyed—Irene flew to Bilbao, which was about ten miles to the west. Four hundred miles separated Bilbao on the northern coast of Spain from the air base at El Carmoli on the southwestern coast, a flight of less than three hours for such a powerful airplane as the Sirius, but Irene would be crossing the frontiers of this war twice, from Republican to Nationalist territory and back again. Later, Irene remembered thinking how remote you were, flying two and a half miles above the earth. You would never have known this country was at war: it just looked like any old landscape. First she flew over the deserts of Valencia, then the hills and valleys of Aragon that grew into the deserts and mountains of Navarre. As she hurried north, the arid blue sky took on clouds. The ground became green and fertile. She passed from Republican territory into Nationalist territory, and there was no change at all. She would not have known the difference. She crossed into the ancient country of the Basques, where the Republicans still held control of a strip of land bordering the sea. Somewhere ahead lay the Bay of Biscay, that graveyard of ships, that cauldron of notorious weather. Five miles from the coast, along a river estuary, grew the town called Guernica, of which Irene had never heard until now: a town of only seven thousand souls, but vast significance to the Basque people. As Irene began descending into Bilbao, she looked east, in the direction of Guernica. She saw only fields, some woods, wisps of smoke, roads crawling with tiny vehicles. There was something there, but you couldn't tell what it was.

BEFORE IRENE LEFT EL CARMOLI, the commandant had promised to send a radio message to Bilbao and alert them that an American airplane was on its way to provide humanitarian aid to the beleaguered Basques. Whether or not this transmission was successful, she met no resistance at all during her flight or landing, from either the Condor Legion—that was the German air force operating for the rebel side—or the loyalist aircraft doing their best to defend the region. When she put on her headset and radioed the Bilbao tower on the frequency the commandant had given her, she was given clearance to land, but there was no one to greet her, no sign at all that she was expected. She jumped down from the airplane. A few men ran past, toward the control tower. She didn't recognize the scattered airplanes on the ground, but she saw at a glance that they were ancient and dilapidated, no match at all for the airplanes of the Luftwaffe, which she had inspected on an overseas lecture tour two years ago. Some kind of hasty grass netting covered each of them, to disguise them from above. Irene felt the sun on her neck and took off her leather jacket, but not her flight suit. She followed the men toward the tower, and just as she reached it, the faint thud of a propeller engine began to grow in the distance, from the southwest.

Irene turned and looked up at the sky. Two airplanes approached like a pair of birds, too fast and too high to land. She put up her hand to shade her eyes. *What the hell are they doing?* she thought, not comprehending at all for some reason. Irene had never in her life encountered an airplane that was not a friend to her. Of course she knew that this was war, that airplanes were now divided into ally and enemy, but it didn't seem real. War was not real. Not until she heard the quick thuds of bullets, not until she saw the dirt spray up in neat, evenly spaced spouts, like a stone skipping over the water, did she realize what was happening.

Somebody shouted in Spanish. An arm fell over her shoulder and dragged her backward, into the shelter of the tower. The bullets thwacked past, the noise of the German engines ground the air. Irene was pinned up against the concrete wall of the control tower, half covered by the body of some thick-chested stranger who stank of sweat and cigarettes. He was shouting Spanish in her ear, curses or warnings, and the sound of his voice grew louder and louder until she realized that was because the engines were drawing away, that the bullets had stopped. Then the grip loosened, and Irene stepped away and turned to thank this fellow who had saved her from her own ignorance. He was a couple of inches shorter, stocky, unshaven. He looked as amazed as she was.

"*Hostia puta*," he gasped, "it's a woman!"

"Yes. I'm looking for Señor Mallory. He flew in last night from El Carmoli."

"Señor Mallory? Then you are—you must be—"

"His friend."

He embraced her and kissed her on each cheek. "My name is Raoul Velázquez de los Monteros," he said, "and I will take you to Mallory this minute."

SAM WAS NOT AT THE airfield. Raoul Velázquez said he'd gone out in the last convoy, to collect wounded and other evacuees. He had made several flights already to take people to the hospitals in Madrid and on the coast—Velázquez couldn't say exactly how many, because he had been making these flights himself and saw Mallory only in passing—but his airplane had been damaged or shot or broken down in the last run and he had gone to help on the ground while the mechanics attempted to repair it.

By the time Raoul had talked them both into the back of an ambulance, bouncing its way down the cratered road into Guernica, the sun had fallen deep in the western sky. The light was at its most beautiful, which made the devastation around them all the more astounding. Irene peered through the small window at the back of the truck and saw the burned-out remains of a convoy that had been bombed; a house made of rubble; a field populated by a herd of dead cattle; all of them coated in a fine, translucent gold as they might appear in heaven.

The closer they got to town, the more ruins they passed, some still smoking faintly. The doctor beside her said the Germans were still bombing, that they were actually bombing the evacuation convoys, the fucking bastards. He was an American, a Jew from Brooklyn, a Communist. He told Irene all about communism as the ambulance jolted and ground its way to Guernica, how this struggle represented the monumental battle of rich against poor, capitalist against proletariat, Church against man, and that when the door of the ambulance opened and Irene saw what fascism had wrought, she would see all this as clearly as he did. Irene loved him for this ferocious idealism, and because he didn't seem to recognize her, even when she said her name was Irene.

Raoul was quiet. As they lurched down the road, closer and closer to the center of the devastation, he did not look out the window. He sat with his back to the cab, his knees drawn up against his meaty chest, his fingers linked together like a bridge across them. He stared into space without saying a word, and looked as if he might be praying. Irene remembered about the fiancée and asked him if he had found her yet.

"No. I have searched for her among the wounded. I have asked everyone. Nobody has any news." He paused. "She is carrying my child. We were supposed to marry next month, before the baby is born."

"I'm so sorry."

"It is my fault. She wanted to wait until we were married. She is a virtuous girl, very pious. But I thought our families would never agree to let us marry, so I seduced her into bed and made her pregnant, and if she dies now, before I can marry her . . . in a state of mortal sin . . . and my child still a bastard . . ."

"God would not be so cruel as that," Irene said.

"No, it is God's will. This is my punishment. My father used to tell me I was too arrogant and too lustful, and God would turn my sins against me."

"This is not an act of God. This is an act of man."

The ambulance lurched to a stop, and the doctor rose and shook Irene's hand and thanked her sincerely. He said she could help carry the stretchers, since she was so tall and strong. She opened her mouth to say that she wasn't here to carry stretchers, she was here to find Sam Mallory, but she realized they were probably the same thing.

IRENE DID NOT TURN COMMUNIST when she stepped out of the ambulance and saw what the bombs had wrought in Guernica. She already considered herself a pacifist; she hated the idea of people killing each other, and thought the official American policy of non-intervention was probably right. But something had to alter inside her head at the sight of so much rubble, spattered with blood. At the sight of human limbs torn off human bodies, and the carcass of some unfortunate donkey, ribs splintered apart to reveal its stinking viscera. It seemed that not a stone was left in place, not a house neglected. The smell was that of a slaughterhouse. The noise was of souls in purgatory.

She thought, *An airplane did this.* You could fill your airplane with bombs and kill a thousand people, without ever knowing whom you had killed, with no more pang of conscience than if you had brought down your boot in the middle of an anthill.

When she found Sam, two hours later, it was by accident. She and Raoul carried a stretcher together and had taken a wrong turn, and were trying to climb over the ruins of a house while the woman in the stretcher, whose right arm was a stump bound in blood-soaked bandages, and whose gut had been laid open in an eight-inch gash, screamed in mortal anguish. Irene had actually forgotten all about Sam, or at least forgotten that she was supposed to be looking for him. She did not want to find him; she thought that if she did find him, he would probably be dead. So they turned some corner and met another pair of stretcher-bearers, and she happened to catch the eye of one of them and it was a blue eye, it was Sam's eye.

It took him longer to recognize her. He hadn't had the slightest idea she was in Spain, here in Guernica looking for him. He thought she was enjoying her triumph right now, feted in Paris with George Morrow by her side. He caught her eye twice, went right past, heard her shout his name and slipped on a rock, dropping the stretcher. Luckily he had been carrying the lower half. Irene kept hold of her own stretcher but she streamed with tears. Sam was dirty and unshaven and exhausted, his clothes torn and bloodstained, his hands blistered raw. She screamed some curse at him, for being here at all. Then she thanked God that he was alive.

THEY SAID NOTHING IN THE ambulance, on the way back to the air-field. Sam fell asleep on Irene's lap. Raoul sat next to them, staring at the wall of the truck. They had not seen his fiancée among the dead or wounded; nobody could remember seeing a woman of her description, seven months gone with child.

By the time they reached Bilbao it was dark, and all the airplanes had been caught in the strafing except Irene's. She said they could load the patients into the Sirius and fly to Madrid or to the coast, and Sam said all right, but they would have to wait until dawn, because you couldn't navigate from the air when all the towns were blacked out. They ate some stale bread rolls and hard cheese in what had once been a commissary, and went to sleep on pallets in the hangar, one blanket each, while the wounded begged for morphine on the other side of a line of curtains.

BY THE GRACE OF GOD, the Germans didn't bomb them during the night. Irene woke first and checked her watch, which had a luminous dial. It was half past four. Sam was heavily asleep next to her. She didn't want to wake him, so she lay perfectly still. The injured had either fallen asleep, or given up, or died, because the hangar was quiet. She stared at the shadow that was Sam's face until she felt him wake, felt him feel her beside him. Felt him start with surprise and then relax.

"Goddamn," he whispered. "So it wasn't a dream."

THE NEXT DAY, IRENE MADE three flights out of Bilbao, taking wounded to the hospitals in Valencia, stopping only long enough to load and un-load patients and refuel the airplane. For the next several days, she and Sam and Raoul flew during the daylight, back and forth, while the mechanics worked to repair their planes at night. When they sat together at night, eating their dinner, Raoul didn't speak, and Irene knew there was no news; he was just flying and flying, to keep himself from thinking about his fiancée.

When she returned from her last flight on the fifth day, the sun had nearly set, and she had trouble judging the runway in the glare. She came down hard, and the jolt knocked the breath out of her lungs. The orderly in the back thought they were going to crash and screamed. Irene felt her last nerve fray down to nothing. She kept her composure until the ship rolled to a stop. Then she put her head on the edge of the instrument panel and cried.

"YOU NEED A REST," SAID Sam.

"I'm all right."

"You're not. You're exhausted. You need to eat and sleep."

"So do you."

"I'll see if I can find you a private room somewhere," he said. "With a real bed. Or a cot at least."

"That's not necessary," Irene insisted, but she was falling on her feet, staggering on Sam's arm as he led her to the commissary and made her sit. He brought her some food and some red Spanish wine and went to speak to the commandant. When he returned, he told her that the commandant had relinquished his own quarters for her.

"Damn you," she said. "You told him my name, didn't you?"

"Had to. Anyway, what difference does it make?"

The commandant's quarters were small and bare, just a washstand and a narrow camp cot, a tiny lavatory attached. Sam said he would sleep on the floor and went to get their kit bags from the hangar. Irene sat on the camp bed and closed her eyes. Her ears felt as if they'd been stuffed with rags, but she was used to that sensation. Silence, that was the only luxury she cared about now. Silence and darkness. There was a blackout curtain hanging in the window; she got up and pulled it shut, then lit the paraffin lamp, just enough to see by. She took off her flight suit for the first time in two days and washed herself as best she could in the basin. When Sam opened the door she turned. He didn't see her right away. He set down the kit bags and the pair of blankets and said something about filling their canteens from the sink. His voice trailed away in the middle of a sentence. In the hollow glow of the lamp, his expression changed from shock to wonder to despair. His mouth gaped open, trying to make words again.

"Does George know?" Sam said at last.

"He does now. I left him a letter."

The room was small, and they were only a few yards apart. Irene stood with her hands straight down her sides, wearing only her underwear, her plain silk undershirt and silk drawers, silk not for luxury but because Irene found it the most comfortable fabric for long flights.

Sam asked if he could touch her. She said of course.

He stepped forward and stretched out his blistered fingers to measure the shape of her abdomen. *How long?* he asked, and she said *Six months,* and he said *No, I mean when will it be born,* and she said *About the beginning of August,* and he started to sob. She gathered him in her arms while he wept into her hair. Between them, the baby jerked and stirred like a grasshopper.

Sam did not sleep on the floor that night, after all. Somehow they found a way to wedge together in the cot. When dawn broke, and Irene started from some dream, she smelled cigarettes and knew he had been awake for some time, turning everything over in his head.

"Well?" she said. "What are you thinking?"

"I'm thinking that if it's a boy, you should name him for your father."

"What about *your* father?"

"I don't remember my father. He left my mother soon after I was born."

"Oh, Sam."

The room was hot and stuffy, and they were both naked, stuck to each other like a pair of coals that had burned out together. Irene loved the way her belly fit into the curve of Sam's side. She didn't want to rise. Every part of her felt heavy and grafted onto Sam. She didn't think she could move. She asked, "So what if it's a girl?"

"No girls. After Pixie? No, I can't take another girl, Irene. I can't take that kind of hurt again. It's got to be a boy. That's all I ask, a son."

"You'll find her again, Sam. She'll come back to you. She will."

"I don't get it," he said. "How could your own husband not know you were pregnant?"

"Because he hasn't seen me naked in months."

"Still."

"Well, the flight suit's baggy. And I'm tall, so it doesn't show that much, anyway. If you're not looking for it, if you don't *want* to see it, you don't see it."

He stubbed out the cigarette and kissed the top of her head. "Fair enough. But all the same, we've got to get you out of here. The sooner the better."

WHEN THEY GOT DOWN TO the hangar fifteen minutes later, they were amazed to find that it was full of children. The Republicans wanted to evacuate them from this strip of war zone bordered by the Bay of Biscay on one side and the Nationalist-held territory to the south. At the ports they were loading children on steamers, bound for England and Mexico and the Soviet Union. But these ships were filling fast, so someone had decided that the children with relatives in the eastern regions—those still under government control—should be transported there by air.

"It's too dangerous," said Sam. "What if some German patrol bumps into us? They won't give a damn that we're a civilian aircraft."

But the Republican officers insisted. Whatever the danger, it was worse here in Biscay, which Franco was determined to bomb into submission and then take by force. Irene just shrugged. "I can fly them to

Valencia in less than two hours. We can take three planeloads in one day, maybe four if we leave right away."

Sam said darkly, "Can I speak to you for a moment, Señorita Foster?"

But Irene got her way. It was her airplane, after all; she could do what she wanted with it. And what she wanted was this: she wanted to fly her airplane for some decent cause, some noble cause like evacuating the Basque children; she needed to work herself almost to death in order to purge this unspoken guilt that she was somehow complicit in the bombing of Guernica because she flew airplanes, because she had, in her naïve enthusiasm, so relentlessly pushed the frontiers of aviation, and it had all led to this, the dropping of bombs, the machine gunning of civilians from the air. Sam threw his fist against the wall of the hangar but Irene crossed her arms and held firm.

"All right," he said. "But I'm flying too. If we both fly, we can finish sooner. And when these children are safe in Valencia, Irene, you're done. Is that clear? You stay in Valencia with them."

"Only if you stay in Valencia too," she said.

"Irene, I have to go back. I can't just desert."

"The only thing left to do is to fight to the death, and you promised you weren't going to fight. Remember? Back in California, you said you'd had enough of fighting."

"That was before I saw what happened here."

"You promised. You swore to God, remember? If you stay here and fight, then I'll stay here and fight, right beside you, so you can keep your promise to me. You can die in my arms."

"Jesus, Irene. How do you remember these things?"

"That's my deal, Sam."

She stared him down, until she could see him weigh the scales in his head: on the one side, his death wish; on the other side, Irene and the small grasshopper they had made together. Finally he shook his head. The grasshopper won.

OUTSIDE, RAOUL WAS READYING HIS airplane to fly, checking the skin for any holes or ruptures, checking the propeller blades and the wheels. Irene noticed that his eyes were red and she stopped to ask him if there was any news, had he heard anything.

"Yes," he said. "They have found her body at last. She was killed in the first wave. A building collapsed on top of her."

"Oh, Raoul! I'm so sorry."

He turned to climb into the cockpit and stopped, with his hand on the edge of the wing. He spoke into space, but just loud enough that Irene could hear him.

"What I don't understand," he said, "is why God should have killed her and the child, when the sin was mine. Why he did not just kill me instead."

"God did not kill them, Raoul. The German bombers did."

Raoul turned to her and kissed her hand. "Good-bye, Señorita Foster. I fly back to El Carmoli now. May God watch over you and my friend Mallory."

ALL THAT WEEK THEY RAN to Valencia without incident, not a single German airplane in sight, though the sky was wide and blue and cloudless. Sam flew the only spare airplane he could find in Bilbao, a French-built Potez bomber that could barely manage a hundred miles an hour. In the air, flying the Sirius next to this ramshackle ship, Irene felt like a Thoroughbred trying to keep pace with a Shetland pony. In the back of the Sirius was a woman who was supposed to be chaperoning the twenty-two children crammed in the fuselage, which was not equipped for the transportation of any animal at all, let alone a human child, let alone twenty-two of them. By the final trip, the woman seemed to be drunk. Irene was so relieved when they arrived safely in the municipal airport in Valencia and handed the children over to some supervisor, she nearly threw up. It was the middle of May and the weather had turned hot. Sam followed her into the ladies' waiting room, which was empty, and waited until she came out of the washroom.

"I have to go back to Bilbao," he said.

"No, you don't. You're done, remember? You promised."

"Well, there was a radio message from the commandant, and another bus full of children just turned up at the airfield. If I leave now, I'll get there just before sunset. Then I fly back first thing tomorrow morning."

"Not without me, you're not."

"For God's sake, you're pregnant! Don't do this to me, Irene. If I lose you, I'm done for."

"No. We fly together, Sam. That's the deal. And if we take my ship, we'll be there and back in half the time."

"Irene," Sam said wearily, "you are the goddamn most stubborn woman in the world."

BUT THE MECHANICS TOLD THEM that some of the Sirius's propeller blades were damaged, and they would need the night to make repairs. They flew the Potez instead and just made it back to Bilbao before sunset, and while the commandant had taken his room back by now, Sam found them a private corner in the hangar, no more than a closet, so they could sleep away from the noise of the children and the pilots. The room had no light at all, and as soon as Sam closed the door Irene took off his shirt, unbuttoned his trousers, and the touch of her fingers on his skin was like the striking of a match. There was no room to make love on the floor, so Irene just braced herself against the wall while the frenzy overtook them both. In less than a minute Sam had finished. As soon as he caught his breath, he apologized. Irene thumped back against the wall and carried his wet, slack body on hers. If she could have spoken, she would have told him that he shouldn't be sorry, that it was sublime to give comfort to your lover when he needed it. That you knew for certain you loved somebody when his pleasure gave you more joy than your own.

SOMEHOW THEY FIT THEMSELVES IN blankets between the walls and fell into oblivion, which ended abruptly in a crash that rattled the floor at eight minutes past three in the morning. Sam bolted up, wide awake.

"What was that?" Irene said, although it was obvious.

Sam just swore and grabbed his clothes. The room was black, and he couldn't find his service pistol. Irene discovered it inside her shoe and gave it to him, although she wasn't sure what he meant to do with it. Shoot bullets at the incoming airplanes? Another crash made the walls shake, and now the children were stirring on the other side of the partition, crying softly, nobody screaming because they all knew what a bomb sounded like, they knew there was nothing to do but hide and pray.

"I'm going to man the guns," said Sam, meaning the three paltry, aging antiaircraft guns atop the control tower. "Get the kids under cover, all right? As best you can."

He took an instant to kiss her and ran through the door. Irene shoved her feet into her shoes and followed. The hangar was chaos. The chaperones were not warriors. They didn't know what to do, whether to hunker down inside or take the children and flee into the farmland. Irene cupped her hands and hollered in Spanish, "Into the cellar!"

Possibly she had the word wrong, but everybody understood when she yanked open the wooden hatchway to the bunker beneath, which had been dug out of the clay some weeks before. Sam had shown her, the first day. It was damp and primitive, nothing but dirt floor and no lights, but it afforded some cover from the bombs that now made the whole building shudder, made such a racket it got into your head so you couldn't think. Explosion after explosion, each one louder and bigger, so you knew they were getting closer. Irene thought she could hear the *rat-a-tat* of a gun, in between the blasts, and she hoped to God it was the Republican antiaircraft guns and not the German strafing.

She kept on shooing children down the ladder. There was only the faintest light to see them. The last one scrambled beneath the floor of the hangar, and Irene set her foot on the ladder, but she couldn't force herself down. She thought, *Someone's missing, I'm sure there's somebody missing, that can't be all of them.*

She called out and heard nothing except the mad detonation of bombs, the roar of aircraft engines, all of which had grown so loud they drowned out the sound of the guns. Irene ran frantically around the hangar, looking beneath airplanes, behind wheels, in corners, but she couldn't see a thing, only shadows that might or might not be objects, might or might not be a terrified child. It was just too dark. She thought she heard a whimper. She stood still and closed her eyes. The hangar rocked around her. She turned left, took four steps, and stumbled over a small, warm, sobbing body.

"There you are," she said, although she couldn't even hear her own voice. She scooped up the child—he was so light, like a bird, underfed and hollow-boned—and carried him in her arms toward the hatchway, from which the tiniest light drew. She set the child on the top step of the ladder and gave a small push, yelled down below that there was another one coming, and then the whole world turned as bright as day, as hot as the sun, as a bomb dropped right on the southeast corner of the hangar, fifty feet away, and detonated.

HANALEI, HAWAI'I

November 1947

I T WOULD BE romantic and fitting, I suppose, to tell you that Lindquist and I fly to Ki'ilau by moonlight inside the Rofrano Sirius that sits at the back of its hangar, shrouded in camouflage netting. But when we arrive at the airfield, Lindquist makes no move to the hangar that harbors the world's most famous airplane. We take the company ship instead, the one we flew a few weeks ago, when we went on our picnic.

I am no more inclined for flight tonight than I was then, but what choice do I have? She's found me out. She knows my weakness, my terrible need. She understands how deeply I require the knowledge inside her head.

I DID NOT LIE TO you. I never said I *wasn't* Sam Mallory's daughter, did I? Since leaving home, I've told only one person, and that was Velázquez. I told him in the last hours I knew him, as we walked around the dusky streets of Paris together. It was my final hope, my single remaining card to play, my ace, and though Velázquez was at first disbelieving, then astonished, and then struck with awe at this evidence of God's mysterious ways, still he wouldn't break his promise. He apologized and explained that it was not his secret to tell.

I forgave him for that. I hope you'll forgive me for misleading you.

It's just that I don't tell anybody who I am. People have a way of making assumptions about you, when they discover you were spawned by some famous person, some person they think they knew because they read about him in a newspaper. And to reveal your true self to another person, that's like taking a knife and paring away a section of your own skin, so that somebody else can see the workings of your blood and muscle for himself.

But here is the truth. When I was thirteen years old, as I said before, my mother told me my father had left us for good this time, had taken up with one of his whores and wanted no more to do with us. She packed me in the car and took me to Reno, Nevada, where you could then obtain the most efficient divorce in America. She told me we would move to a new home in Washington State, containing a new father, whose name she adopted for me. She told me that Mr. Everett would take better care of me than Mallory ever had, and I should take him to my heart. I didn't believe her. I tried to run away and find my father again, but I didn't get far before my stepfather found me and brought me back and whipped me on my naked buttocks with his belt. He told me that my mother had just been protecting my feelings, that my father was actually dead, he had been killed in an airplane crash like the crazy fool he was, and I should forget he had ever existed.

I don't think my stepfather quite realized what kind of effect this statement might have on me. He wasn't a man of much imagination, so he couldn't have understood what it was like when your father made his living in an airplane, flying stunts, flying races, flying for daring distances over water, just *flying*, all the time, every day, so that his daughter would lie awake at night and pray and pray that his airplane would not crash, that her father would return to her and cradle her in his arms *just one more time*, that was all I asked of God. When Mr. Everett told me that my worst nightmare had come to life, that my father's beloved body had gone to earth and been destroyed, I felt not sadness but relief.

Finally, there was no need to worry that he would be killed, because he was already dead.

Except that Sam Mallory was not dead yet. Just imagine my astonishment when I left home and got out in the world and discovered that he was still alive and kicking in 1936, the year before my stepfather popped my cherry on the Chesterfield sofa of his private office. Just imagine my guilt that I hadn't succeeded in escaping that day when I was thirteen, that I might have found my father and saved him if only I'd been more intrepid, more clever, more determined.

Just imagine my fury at the woman who had stolen him from me, who had known him when I had not, who had won his heart and kept it for her own exclusive use.

Anyway, I'm telling you now, better late than never. I was born Eugenia Ann Mallory of Oakland, California, daughter of Samuel and Bertha Mallory. My father was the greatest pilot the world has ever known, and I am here to find out how and why he came to die on the badlands of northern Spain, at the exact moment I needed him most.

LINDQUIST FLIES BY MOONLIGHT AND what she calls dead reckoning, and when we land we make only the softest of bumps before rolling to a stop in the middle of the night grass. She takes me to the same place we had our picnic. The moon stands above the horizon and strikes a luminous path across the ocean before us. Lindquist sits right at the edge of the cliff, and after a second or two of hesitation I join her, even though I'm dead scared of heights. Did I mention that? Something to do with my fear of airplanes, probably. I don't look down, that's all. If I do, the vertigo will overcome me, because I'm already a little dizzy. My heart thumps in my chest like a dynamo. Lindquist doesn't speak, so I pipe up in order to break this terrible silence. I ask her how she figured out I was Mallory's lost daughter.

"Do you remember when I brought you out here a month or so ago?"

"Do I ever."

"Well, I had my suspicions. I couldn't put my finger on it. Your hair's dark, for one thing, and what I remember most about Sam's little girl was her bright blond hair—"

"My mother loved that hair. Started to go dark right after Dad came back from Australia. Stood to reason, I mean she was a brunette herself. But she was real disappointed. She had her heart set on a blonde."

"Did she? I guess I'm not surprised. Nothing that woman could do would surprise me." She crosses her legs, Indian style. "Still, every time I looked at you, I heard bells dinging in my head. You look like him. Your eyes are alike, and you have his jaw, just a little softer, but I only recognized that later. It was your gestures, your way of speaking. The way you sit and look at the person you're talking to. So I thought I'd bring you out here, away from all the distractions. I watched you while you ate and talked. And I just knew. You were like Sam reborn as a woman."

"Except I hate to fly."

"That's no surprise. It must have terrified you as a child, the way he kept crashing and getting hurt."

I pull my cigarettes from the pocket of my jacket. "You'll excuse me."

"That's another thing, the way you smoke like a chimney."

"I do not." I light the cigarette. "I only smoke when absolutely necessary."

"My God." She puts her face in her hands. "My God. I can't do this."

I'm calmer now. My heart has settled back into something approaching its usual rhythm. In my other jacket pocket hangs my pistol. I don't know if I mean to use it. Depends on what Lindquist has to say, or what she means to do with me, Sam Mallory's last remaining issue, as we dangle from this cliff in mutual desperation.

"Can't do what?" I ask.

"I haven't told a soul. That's the only way you survive, you keep it locked away so you can't think about it. If Olle knew . . ."

"Not even Olle?"

"This is off the record, do you hear me? This doesn't go in your book. I don't care how you end it, you can't write this."

I wet my finger and hold it in the air. "Scout's honor."

"I'm only telling you because you're Sam's daughter, and you have a right to know. Nobody else does. Nobody else has the right to know a thing about him."

I flick some ash down the side of the cliff. Below us, the water churns against the rocks.

AVIATRIX

by Eugenia Everett

(e x c e r p t)

May 1937: Spain

IRENE REGAINED CONSCIOUSNESS inside an airplane. For a moment, this didn't seem strange to her. She was aware of pain, but it was a foggy, unspecific kind of pain, as diffuse as it was terrible, and she realized she was drugged. Morphine?

Baby, she thought.

She tried to move her arms, but she was strapped to something, a stretcher. She screamed out, *My baby, where is my baby?* She couldn't feel if it was still there. She couldn't feel her stomach at all. The grasshopper stirrings had gone quiet, but then this human insect of hers went to sleep all the time, went still for hours, so maybe it was drugged, too, on the morphine they had given her.

A bomb. That was it; that was what had happened. A bomb in the hangar. She was badly hurt. She was on an airplane, somewhere above the Spanish countryside, and though she couldn't see anything, she knew it was one of the Republican airplanes, a Potez bomber by the sound of it. Sam's airplane.

She felt her mind slip away again. Sam was alive. Everything would be all right, because Sam was still alive.

THEY WERE LANDING. IRENE FELT the sharp angle of descent. She thought hazily that it was too sharp, they were descending too fast, something had happened. She heard somebody's voice, Sam's voice yelling to her, but she couldn't make out a word of it.

We're cracking up, she thought.

Something was wrong with the engines. One of them had gone out. There was a cough, a sputter, and the other engine died.

No fuel, she thought.

How had they run out of fuel? The mechanics should have filled the tank last night, after they arrived back from Valencia. Maybe the mechanics had forgotten. Maybe they had forgotten to tell the mechanics? Sam was shouting at her from the cockpit. Telling her, probably, to brace herself. As if she could. She heard him better now that the engines were dead, but the thing about coasting, it was still noisy. There was the rattle of the airplane, the roar of the wind around you.

Down, down, down.

When would they hit? Surely it couldn't hurt her as much as she hurt now. She thought she was boiling in oil. She just wanted to die, she wanted to crash already, except the baby would die and so would Sam.

The airplane slammed into the ground. Her last thought, as they skidded along whatever surface Sam had found to crash on, was that this was probably how it was supposed to end, after all. In a crash somewhere, just the two of them.

BY NOW, MORE THAN A week had passed since the disappearance of Irene Foster on the final leg of the Round the World Air Derby, and dozens of aircraft had crisscrossed that stretch of the Sahara Desert where she was presumed to have crashed.

The first headlines expressed shock.

IRENE FOSTER VANISHES OVER SAHARA!

Frantic Search for America's Flying Sweetheart!
Husband Clings to Hope: "Irene Can and Will Survive Any Disaster!"

Across America and around the world, people who had forgotten all about the crash landing in the Pacific eight and a half years earlier, the frantic suspense as the navy combed the ocean for some sign of Irene Foster and Sam Mallory—*and say, wasn't there some scandal about Hawai'i, some dirty photographs?*—now recalled the excitement of those three weeks. They gathered over radios and newspapers, inside barbershops and outside newsstands, and discussed the latest developments, the desperation of poor George Morrow who had dedicated his life and his career to his brilliant wife. Nobody even noticed when the first airplane crossed the finish line in the Round the World Air Derby; today, not even the most ardent student of trivia can name the man who piloted that ship. (For the record, it was Art Landon, who hadn't heard the news about Irene and was shocked to learn that he'd won; he then spent a week with the search team, flying over the desert in search of wreckage.)

All that effort and expense, you might think! All those pilots who put themselves and their airplanes in danger to look for Irene, when she wasn't anywhere near the Sahara! All those newspaper headlines, all that suspense shared by the citizens of the world! How could Irene subject everybody to such an ordeal? Disappear without trace? Surely she knew there would be a search, there would be reporters dispatched to North Africa, there would be millions of dollars wasted on her behalf!

In fact, she did understand all those things, which was why she posted an express letter to George Morrow at the Anfa Hotel in Casablanca, the night before she departed Alexandria. In this letter, she informed her husband that she was irrevocably in love with Sam Mallory, was carrying his child, and had flown her airplane to join him instead of finishing the race. She asked George to forgive her and not to look for her, because she did not want to be found. She thanked him for all he had done for her, and wished him nothing but happiness in the future. She left it to him what to say to the press, but she trusted that he would encourage them to leave her in peace with Sam and their child, and allow her to find the contentment she had sought in vain all these years. (*With love and gratitude, Irene.*)

According to the hotel's records and the testimony of the bellboy who delivered the letter, it arrived in George Morrow's hands the next day while he sat in the lobby, waiting for news of his wife. He gave the messenger a ten cent tip and opened the envelope immediately.

So Irene hadn't given her husband much thought. If there was one thing George Morrow could do better than just about anybody in the world, it was to handle the press. She figured—when she had time to think about it at all—that he had given the world some statement that skirted the truth, that made him out to be a patient, generous husband who wanted nothing for his wife but her happiness. She had, in fact, not the least idea that she *had* disappeared without trace, that she might now be clinging to survival amid the wreckage of her airplane in the middle of the Sahara, that the attention of the world was fixed on her, that hundreds of people were even now employed in a desperate race against the clock to find her. She would have been appalled; she would have been furious with George.

But she didn't know any of this. If she had, she would have broken her silence long before she actually did crash in a desert, not in North Africa but in Spain, about three hundred and fifty kilometers northeast of Madrid.

AS THE POTEZ HIT THE ground, Irene expected to die instantly. She had forgotten that there was nobody in the world who had crashed an airplane so often and so skillfully as Sam Mallory. It was almost as if his entire career had been made in preparation for this moment, when the ship he was piloting—the one carrying the only person left to him on earth, in urgent need of medical care—ran out of fuel because some German bullet had pierced the main fuel tank, which went unnoticed until half an hour into the flight, when he was already over the strip of Nationalist territory between the Basques and Madrid.

The impact was like the end of the world. An almighty bang jolted through the metal frame and everything went flying, except Irene. She was strapped down not just to the stretcher but to the main deck itself, so that she was part of the airplane as it hurtled across the surface of the desert, over rocks and through bushes, bouncing and crashing and skidding until it came to rest at last, tail torn away, landing gear collapsed, propeller blades scattered across the desert floor.

Then silence.

The shock of it numbed Irene's physical pain. She stared at the bare struts that ran along the top of this metal tube in which she was bound, unable to move. She tried to scream Sam's name, even to whisper it, but she had no strength at all, not even that. *Maybe I'm dead,* she thought. A shaft of sunlight poured through some broken window. The pain returned. Her ears rang with it. Her lips were cracked and thirsty. She closed her eyes and thought, *So this is how I die.*

SOME TIME LATER, IRENE OPENED her eyes to sunshine and a desert landscape, a curious rock formation, pain such as she had never known. Something cool touched her forehead. *Sam?* she whispered.

I'm here, he said. The pressure of his hand on hers.

What's happened?

We've crashed. We ran out of fuel. Waiting for help.

Sam?

What is it, Irene?

How bad am I?

He didn't answer right away, and Irene thought that he wasn't going to tell her, and she was angry. She had a right to know what was wrong with her body! She had a right to know what was causing this pain. She had a right to know if she was going to live or die. She had a right to know if her baby was dead.

Then he started to speak. He said that she was burned, on the side of her face and on her back, and that her left arm had been broken by some falling debris. The rest was cuts and bruises. He said she might lose the arm, but not to worry, because he always liked the right arm better anyway. As for her face, why, it just made her more interesting.

Sam? she said.

What is it, Irene?

I can't feel the baby move. Is the baby still there?

There was a fragile silence.

Then: Don't worry about the baby, said Sam.

Why not? said Irene. Why not worry? Is he gone? Is he gone, Sam? Tell me the truth. Is he gone?

Irene, said Sam. Irene.

Irene wasn't crying, but a few tears slid from the corners of her eyes and down her temples into her ears. More followed, until they bled into each other, but she wasn't crying. Her chest didn't move, except in shallow, delicate breaths. A line of water ran from each eye. That was all.

WHEN THEY HAD CRASHED IN the middle of the night, Sam had carried her out of the wrecked fuselage because he was afraid of fumes. Now it was morning, and the desert heat began to take hold. They lay quietly in the shade while Irene dangled between sleep and hazy half-consciousness, and Sam gave her water and stroked her hair. In a moment of lucidity, she asked if he was hurt.

"Oh, just my bum ankle," he said.

"Can you walk?"

"A little."

"You should walk. You should try to find help."

He was smoking a cigarette. She could smell the tobacco, a more pungent variety than the ones he used to smoke back in California. She wanted to turn her head and look at him, and possibly she could have done if she tried hard enough, but her skull felt so heavy and her neck so stiff. So she just imagined him instead, hair askew, smoking thoughtfully against a boulder or something while a blue sky surrounded him.

"Irene," he said, "there's nobody for miles. This is the desert, the badlands."

"You should try."

"Can't leave you here alone. Might be days."

"Then at least you'd save yourself."

"Sweetheart," he said, stroking her hair, "don't worry. They'll send someone out to look for us. Just sit tight, all right?"

"Oh, I'm not going anywhere, believe me."

He laughed and kissed her forehead and said she was the same old Irene, the same good sport, game for anything. What he didn't say was that his bum ankle was actually broken in several places, and that his left ear was nearly torn off, and a deep gash cut through to the bone of his left thigh, narrowly missing the femoral artery. No, he wasn't going anywhere, and certainly not miles out into the scorching desert. Not unless he had to.

STILL, WHEN NIGHT FELL AGAIN, Sam managed to drag her back into the fuselage, which had settled deep enough in the earth that it was not such a great height, just a ledge. In the darkness, she couldn't see the blood, or his mangled face, so she didn't know how much effort this required. She went to sleep, and sometime during the night she dreamed that they were outside, the three of them, alone in the night, Sam and Irene and their dead child, who was wrapped in a bundle in Sam's arms so she couldn't touch him or see him. She tried to scream, to give some voice to her anguish, but the peculiar paralysis of dreams had stiffened her so she could neither move nor speak. The stars twinkled coldly at her grief. Even though she couldn't actually say the words, she heard her own voice ask Sam where they should bury the baby, and he replied that when the sun rose he would dig a hole beneath a boulder nearby that reminded him of a bear.

She realized she was awake. She asked Sam to repeat what he had just said.

"I buried him with my own bare hands in the graveyard next to the airfield," Sam said.

"Him," Irene said.

"Yes. The commandant promised to put up a headstone when the bombing stops."

As he spoke, Sam made some rustling movements. Irene didn't know he was binding up his thigh and his ankle with some gauze in the medical kit. The iodine and the morphine he saved for her, because he knew that burns were the most painful wounds of all, and the most susceptible to infection.

"Did you give him a name?" Irene asked. "Will there be a name on the stone?"

"Henry Foster Mallory. Is that all right?"

Irene couldn't think. She didn't remember that she herself had told Sam, if their baby was a boy, to name their son after her father. Between the physical pain and the morphine for the pain, there was not enough room for memory or even grief. She only felt grief when she was asleep.

But she wanted to feel grief. She wanted to mourn. So she just said, *Yes, that's perfect,* and let herself go.

AFTER THAT, IRENE DID NOT want to live. She could survive the loss of a baby, because women did that all the time, and she could survive pain because she had experienced physical agony so often before. But she could not survive both at once, and when their water began to run out the next day, there was just no point in living, was there? Nobody was going to rescue them. She begged Sam to take his service pistol and shoot her. If she were dead, he could keep the rest of the water for himself; he could go for help, he could save himself.

Sam said that if she were dead, he would have no reason to save himself. He went on changing her bandages. He moved her inside the airplane, to shelter her from the sun, and sat with her, and brushed her hair, and wrote in his diary. He said he wanted some record of events to survive when the wreckage was found. In case his Pixie ever grew up and wondered what had happened to her father.

IN THE MEANTIME, IN THE outside world, people were still obsessed with the mystery of Irene Foster's disappearance, although not so much as three weeks ago because hope of discovering her alive had begun to fade. The Sahara was a harsh, miserable, inhospitable climate, after all. You could not survive long. So airplanes continued to crisscross North Africa, but not so many as before, and interestingly George Morrow was not among them. George Morrow was in Spain.

He had flown from Casablanca a week ago, and while there's no record of exactly where he first landed—so much Republican paperwork was destroyed in the course of war—it's certain he arrived at the government-held airfield in Valencia on the fifteenth of May. Probably he had heard some rumor, or received an anonymous note, because the Foster disappearance had captured attention everywhere, even in the midst of war, and many in Spain did not approve of wives leaving their husbands for lovers. So Morrow came to Valencia and asked to speak to the commandant, and the commandant—after some persuasion, no doubt—admitted that they had recently received word that Miss Foster and Mr. Mallory had gone missing while flying between Bilbao and Valencia, and that one of his best pilots was out right now, scouring the desert in order to find them.

Fine, said Morrow. But if he comes back empty-handed, I'm going to put on a flight suit myself and join him.

ON THE MORNING OF THE fourth day, a noise came from the southeast. For some reason Irene heard it first. She told Sam to wake up, somebody was coming, an airplane was coming. Sam crawled to the emergency kit for the flare gun and went outside. In his fatigue and dehydration, he nearly misfired it. Then it went off and sent an arc of red smoke through the air. The noise shifted a moment later.

"I think he's seen us," Sam said. By now, his voice was like the rasp of a saw. Irene couldn't really speak at all. As she listened, she perceived that this airplane had a single engine, and that it was not in the best of condition. A moment later, the ship came into view through the open hatch, flashing in the sun. Irene watched it approach them in an acute descent. Whoever he was, he was a good pilot who understood the exact limit of the airplane's capabilities. She thought all this without emotion, without any joy, because joy was now impossible. The ship landed two hundred yards away in a roar of propeller blades, a plume of fine desert sand. Seconds later, the hatch opened, and a man jumped to the ground, followed by another man.

At first, Irene couldn't see their faces, because the morning sun struck fiercely on the fuselage and cast halos around them. They were both running. In seconds the halos faded and Irene, struggling upright, could at last see their faces.

The first man was her husband, George Morrow.

The second was Raoul Velázquez.

HANALEI, HAWAI'I

November 1947

B Y THE TIME we return to Hanalei, dawn is breaking to the east be-hind a bank of gathering clouds, and the wind is picking up. I seem to have forgotten my fear of flying, or maybe I no longer care what happens to me. The bumps and jerks of the airplane induce no more panic than the twists of a roller coaster. Instead I stare out the window at the clouds around me, the wondrous, monstrous three dimensions of them, the delicate pattern of wave meeting shore, the infinite beauty of the earth, and I begin to see why man must fly.

We drive back silently to Coolibah down the empty road. When we reach the driveway, Lindquist stops the car and reaches into the back for the cardboard box she was carrying earlier.

"This is for you," she says.

I peek inside and close the lid swiftly. "Thank God. I thought it was the cat."

"Sandy? Good Lord, of course not. I'm going to pick her up at the vet's right now. I wanted her cremated." She puts her hands back on the steering wheel and stares at the pale house before us. "Tell Olle where I've gone, will you? Ask him to take the children to school this morning?"

There's something funny about the way she says this. I sit there by her side, hand on the door handle, not quite ready to open it. She's the one who breaks the silence.

"I appreciate your forbearance, by the way."

"Forbearance?"

"Not killing me." She tilts her head in the direction of my jacket pocket. "I wasn't sure what you meant to do with that."

"I wasn't sure, either, to be perfectly honest."

"I guess you had every right to hate me, growing up. It was either hate me or hate Sam, and I'd rather you hated me."

I open the door and step out. "You've got it all wrong, Foster," I say, through the open window. "The person I hated was myself."

CAPTAIN LEO HAS ALREADY LEFT for the docks. I can tell because his moped is gone from its usual spot, near the gazebo. I march indoors to the noise of the Buick, turning around to head back down the highway toward Lihue. I make straight for the library with my cardboard box.

Now, I forget. Have I described this library? Because it's certainly not in the usual style, if you know what I mean. That masculine leather-and-mahogany atmosphere you expect to seep from the cornices? Why, there aren't even any cornices! The walls are covered by simple shelves, containing nothing but books—Lindquist is not the knick-knack sort of person, she hasn't got the time of day for objects that offer no practical purpose—and the furniture is spare, except for an armchair near the window that looks as if it was meant to sleep in. The liquor cabinet is built into the wall, not far from the desk. You open the door and rummage through all the bottles until you find the right poison. The owner walks in just as I'm walking away with a nice double bourbon.

"Where's Irene?" he demands.

"Relax. She's alive and well. She took me on a little trip last night to unburden herself. Now she's headed to the vet to pick up the cat's ashes. She asked me to tell you to deliver the tadpoles to school this morning."

He nods to the box, which I've laid on the sofa table. "What's that?"

"Some photographs she wanted me to have."

A frown drifts across his face. "Have you seen them?"

"Not yet. I thought they might require a little fortification." I jiggle the glass. "Say, you look as if you could use a little fortification yourself. Can I pour you another?"

We end up side by side on the sofa, drinking a pair of doubles at six o'clock in the morning, as we stare at the cardboard box of photographs Irene gave me. Now, another thing I should have mentioned earlier. For all its grace and homelike comfort, Coolibah is curiously sparse of photographs. Believe me, I notice these things. Most people will have far too many photos cramming the walls and shelves and every available surface; it's the curse of the modern home, in my opinion. All those framed images lined up in rows, like soldiers, and not one of them in twenty shows any regard for form or light or subject or composition, even by accident; they're just jumbles of anonymous, blurred, badly lit, badly dressed people or—worse yet!—that deadly plague, *the landscape*. A photograph should be a thing of beauty, in my opinion, and if it's just there to recall a family reunion or show off some delightful holiday you took to San Diego or remember how Aunt Mildred looked at her high school graduation, why, stick the old thing in an album so it doesn't steal the limelight from something worth looking at.

So it's not as if I don't approve the paucity of photographs in the Lindquist household. It's just *odd*. And I have the feeling the solution to this mystery lies before me, except I'm unwilling to lift the lid that conceals it. I feel as if I have spent the past month approaching a precipice, step by step, and now there's nowhere left to go, the edge lies before me—much as it did on Ki'ilau, as Lindquist described the events in Spain to me in calm, precise, terrible words like the dripping of rain into a barrel. And I cannot take that last step, because where will I go? Right over the edge into nothing.

"Did she seem upset to you?" asks Olle.

"Does she ever seem upset? That's not her style, and you know it."

"I know. But you understand me. Is she going to be okay?"

"She's survived worse. It's just a cat."

"It's not just a cat. You know that." He drinks. I pull out my ciga-rettes and offer him one, and he's grateful. He lights me up first, then himself, and then he adds, "*You* loved that cat."

"Says you. Now, listen up. There's something you need to under-stand. You know her dad was a drunk, right?"

"She's mentioned it."

"So when your parent is a drunk, you learn certain things. You learn to hide what you're feeling. You learn that most people can't be trusted. You learn that if you love somebody, that person is probably going to hurt you, and there's nothing you can do about it but try not to love people if you can possibly help it."

Olle reaches for an ashtray.

I continue. "Of course, some do the opposite. You go around falling in love with every last person you meet, hoping someone will take you in like some kind of stray animal and keep you fed and watered and warm. All depends on the person. But I'd say your wife is among the first tribe."

"Takes one to know one?"

"You bet."

Olle finishes the bourbon and heads for the bottle. He refills himself, tops me up a little, and sets the bottle down on the sofa table next to the cardboard box. He settles himself back down beside me—he's a big man, solid Scandinavian frame—and says, "She won't stop grieving him. I don't think she ever will."

"Can you blame her?"

"I fell in love with her the first time I saw her. I never thought she . . . I never in a hundred years thought I stood a chance with her. The day she married me, I was the happiest man alive. Of course, I knew I couldn't compare to *him*, but I thought I could make her happy. I could be something else to her. She needed someone dependable, a reliable husband after what she went through. I thought I was that man. I thought I could accept being the second place in her heart, as long as I had some place there at all. As long as she was sleeping next to me at night, I thought I could win her over."

"It was a nice thought."

"She never talks about him. I wish she would. I'd know she was getting over him. Well, if you ask me, that fellow was no hero. Always taking risks, doing just what he wanted, never caring about anybody but himself. If you ask me—"

"Careful," I say.

He turns to me and scrunches his eyebrows together, and I realize he doesn't know. Lindquist hasn't told him the truth.

I shrug. "You're not an impartial observer, that's all."

"No, I guess I'm not. I hate the son of a gun and always will. All I have in this world is what he left behind." He rises to his feet and sets down the empty glass. "I better see about the kids now."

"I'm not sure that's such a good—"

But he's already lurching through the door, and I think it just figures, Lindquist would find another fellow who likes his liquor.

I SPEND SOME TIME STARING at the box, finishing my cigarette. I have no further taste for bourbon, for some reason. From upstairs comes the creak of floorboards and the murmur of voices, as Olle wakes the children. He's a good father. I've seen him with Doris and Wesley, and he loves his kids, no doubt about that, plays games and offers hugs and all those things. Life is not divided neatly into good people and bad people, good parents and bad parents. We are all of us human and scarred with sin. We make mistakes, some small and some terrible.

But he *has* drunk two double glasses of fine Kentucky bourbon before breakfast.

I stub out the cigarette and rise. The box can wait.

BY THE TIME I'VE GOT the ankle-biters dressed and fed and delivered safely to the schoolhouse gate, I'm so weary my eyes are crossing. I should go to bed. Instead I pour myself some of Lani's good, strong coffee, light myself another cigarette, and return to the cardboard box in Olle's library. Except Olle is already there, asleep on the sofa, and the pictures lie scattered around him.

I pick them up, one by one, and the funny thing is I don't look at them. I don't believe I want to know what's trapped inside these photographs. But I stack them neatly on my lap, and on the very top—I can't help noticing *this*—there sits a wedding photograph.

Now, it's possible I arranged it on purpose, as I picked them up; that I subconsciously sorted these photographs, without really looking, and crowned the whole stack with this one, to be examined first. Weddings are always the most interesting of human events to capture on film, after all. All those people gathered together to witness the union of two people who belong to them, and who will now belong to each other. How do you tell the story of all those individual stories, how do you weave it all together in a single frame?

This one was taken outdoors, probably on the lawn somewhere. In fact, I can't quite say how I know it's a wedding, because the bride's not wearing white, but I do. Her plain, modest dress that might be pale blue or yellow (I have the feeling it's not pink), and her hat is small and elegant. She's holding a small bouquet of tropical flowers in one hand, and her other arm is looped over the elbow of her groom, in his neat suit of what must be linen, judging by its rumpled texture. It's Irene and Olle, of course. Their wedding day, the happiest day of Olle's life. But they're not alone.

I lift the photograph and bring it close.

Next to her stand two children, aged about four or five. A boy and girl with bright blond hair and uncertain smiles. Doris and Wesley.

"Miss Janey?"

I jump so hard, I nearly drop the photograph. The others scatter to the floor around me, black-and-white images of people I recognize, faces I know, small, tender kaleidoscopes of family life. I bend to gather them back up.

"Lani! You startled me."

She glances to Olle's snoring figure on the sofa. "I'm sorry to disturb you, Miss Janey, but . . . my goodness, are you all right?"

"I'm perfectly fine, Janey, thank you. I was just looking at this wonderful picture of Mr. and Mrs. Lindquist on their wedding day."

"It was a beautiful day," says Lani.

"A year or two ago now, wasn't it?"

"Yes, Miss Janey. About a year ago last September. I'm awfully sorry, but what should I tell Mrs. Rofrano?"

I stare at her, without a single shred of comprehension. "Mrs. Rofrano? *Here?*"

"She's a friend of Mrs. Lindquist. That's what I came to tell you. She's waiting on the lanai."

I MET SOPHIE ROFRANO ONLY once, while I was in Los Angeles trying to pick up the trail of the lost pilots. At the time, I thought if I could only find the reclusive George Morrow, I could squeeze the necessary details from him. The trouble was, nobody could tell me where he lived, nobody had seen or spoken to him in years. It was all false starts and somebody's friend's wife's cousin spotting him at her horse trainer's guest cottage in Rancho Cucamonga, or not. That kind of thing.

And the worst of it was that I couldn't reveal what I knew, for fear of word getting around that I had found Samuel Mallory, or rather I had found his remains and the remains of his airplane. That I suspected Irene Foster had not only survived her famous disappearance in 1937 but that she and her husband had left Mallory to die in the Spanish badlands while they flew off to start a new life together.

But then I went through the property records on the Morrow house in Burbank and discovered that it had been sold to Mr. and Mrs. Octavian Rofrano in the early fall of 1937. I'd written a letter, polite as could be, explaining that I was a journalist writing a follow-up piece on the whole affair, the tenth anniversary of the disappearance looming and all that, and perhaps she could answer a few questions for me. She'd refused, of course, but I have my methods of persuasion, and without getting into any of the details, let's just say we met for coffee a week or two later at a diner near what had once been Rofrano's Airfield, that icon of the golden age of California aviation. The old place was now getting paved over to become part of somebody's studio lot, having been sold to the government in 1942 for the use of the U.S. Air Force, and this diner was all that remained of the era.

As you might imagine, she wasn't much help. Those innocent blue eyes, my goodness. She sipped her coffee with cream and sugar and pecked away at an apricot Danish, and she kept checking her watch because her youngest was due home from school any minute. "Irene met Clara just after she was born," she told me, "which was only a few months before she left for that round-the-world derby, and I'm so grateful she had the chance to hold my baby girl in her arms. We were all such good friends."

That was nice, I said. But what about the flight? Why did Morrow sell his house to you after he called off the search in June? Did he say anything about Irene? Any clue about what might have happened to her?

"Oh, we didn't *meet* George at all," she said. "It was all done through an agent. He was just broken-hearted. He'd poured his fortune into Irene's career, you see, and now he'd lost everything. We bought the house so that he would have something to live on. But we never heard a word from him directly. I always thought he just couldn't go on without her."

Interesting, I said. And you don't have any idea where he went? Where he might be living now? Any chance I might be able to get in touch with him?

Sophie fixed me with those big, appealing eyes and flat-out lied through her teeth. "I haven't the faintest idea, I'm afraid," she said firmly. "I sometimes wonder if he's even *alive* anymore."

OUTSIDE, THE WEATHER'S TAKEN A turn, and the first thing I notice is not Sophie Rofrano but the rain that lashes against the railing of the lanai and the wind that bends the palms. Then a woman turns away from contemplation of the wild weather and startles at the sight of me. She's wearing a pair of slacks the color of mustard and a white shirt, hair tied back by a patterned scarf, pocketbook tucked under her arm along with a newspaper. I consider what's contained beneath that scarf, the knowledge behind those eyes. I ask her what the devil she's doing here. She tells me she's here to see Mrs. Lindquist.

"I'm afraid you've missed her. She's off to pick up a package on the other side of the island. But she ought to be back before long. Something to drink? Lani's bringing more coffee."

"No, thank you."

"You must have just come in off the morning boat."

"Actually, I flew," she says, a little smug.

"Did you, now? Must have been something important."

She regards me warily and taps the newspaper with her index finger. I draw the cigarette case from the pocket of my trousers and tilt it in her direction. She shakes her head. I take one for myself and light it. I hope she doesn't notice the trembling in my fingers, owing to those photographs back there in the study, the images that slide across my imagination, over and over. The sensation of drawing close to some small, hot, irresistible flame that will likely incinerate me.

"You might as well tell me," I say, as carelessly as I'm able. "She's already explained everything. Spilled the whole sack of beans."

"Has she? Everything?"

"Oh, yes." I hold up my left hand and cross the first two fingers. "We're like that, Irene and me. As soon as she realized I was Sam Mallory's daughter—"

"*What?*"

"Oh, yes. Don't you remember little Pixie?" I spread my arms. "All grown up, as you see."

Sophie Rofrano drops into a chair and stares at me. *Agape,* I believe, is the word.

"So if you've got something to say to Irene—"

She pulls the newspaper from under her arm and holds it out. It's a copy of the *Los Angeles Times,* dated two days ago, folded to page four. In the left-hand column, a black headline hovers above a blurred photograph of an airplane in the middle of the desert.

The headline reads:

MORROW MYSTERY SOLVED AT LAST

Wreckage of Reclusive Publisher's Aircraft Found in Spanish Desert
Bones Discovered in Shallow Grave Nearby Belong to George Morrow,
Husband of Vanished Aviatrix Irene Foster

And I have no time to comprehend the meaning of all this, not a single second to do more than read this headline and stare at the familiar image, Mallory's airplane plunged in the earth in the shadow of a monumental desert massif, because Lani sweeps past, sets down the coffee tray with a crash that startles me, and says there's a telephone call for me inside, from the airfield.

"Who is it? Kaiko?"

"A Mr. William Cushing," she says, "from the Associated Press. He says it's urgent."

I PICK UP THE TELEPHONE in the library, where Olle still lies snoring on the sofa, though I cup my hand over the receiver so he stays that way. The call is collect, the kind of cheap trick I usually wouldn't stand for, but Bill Cushing and I go way back, even before the war, when we were both covering the Kentucky Derby for the AP. I was the photographer, he was the writer. As I recall, Gallahadion won the race at odds of thirty-six to one. I soon learned we had a great deal in common—me and *Bill*, I mean, not the horse—from our love of fine Kentucky bourbon to our love for strapping young men. Bill's a fellow you can trust, for the most part, and he has a talent for spotting trouble, which is why his voice, tunneling through the telephone wires, jumps straight on my already jangled nerves.

"Janey, you gorgeous creature! You'll never guess where I am."

"What the devil's going on, Bill? Some kind of double cross? Because I swear—"

"*Double* cross? Hell, it's the *opposite*. I've been fending them off. You've been *scooped*, my dear. Like ice cream in July."

"Scooped? What in blazes?"

"A story ran a couple of days ago—did you get my cable?—ran in the *LA Times,* about George Morrow's body being found in an airplane wreck in Spain, and some schmuck casts his eye over the photo spread and swears he saw a woman he's convinced is Irene Foster, flying some tourist plane in Hawai'i. I'm standing here in this dump of an airfield cafeteria with a half dozen reporters, waiting for the weather to clear—"

"The *weather to clear*? For what?"

Even as I'm speaking, something catches my attention on the lamp table before me, the pile of scattered photographs I left there on my way out to the lanai. Bill's voice drones in my ear at a high, nervy pitch.

"Darling, don't you know? Our mystery woman left half an hour ago, just before we landed from Honolulu. She's in the air right now, headed to some island—that's what this fellow Kookoo says—"

"Kaiko?" I lift a photograph from the pile.

"That's it. He says she's likely headed out to some island to the west. The boys pooled some dough, hired this Kookoo—Kaiko, whatever his name is—to fly us there once this goddamned squall—Janey, are you listening? You know I'm doing my best—"

"Yes, of course," I reply. And I *am* listening. I really am. But this emergency, this imminent invasion of curious newspapermen and, inevitably, the rest of the goddamned world, seems so distant to me, as faint and far away as Bill's own voice.

Because in front of me, between my fingers, I see a photograph of a blond, spindly girl dressed in her first school uniform, unmistakably Doris, and a bewildered towhead in short pants who is unmistakably Wesley.

As for the proud man who holds the hands of these imps before the Hanalei school gate, he is unmistakably my father.

AVIATRIX

by Eugenia Everett

(e x c e r p t)

May 1937: Spain

IRENE COULD SEE from George's expression that the scene was terrible. She knew she had bled heavily; she still didn't realize how badly Sam had been hurt too. So there was blood everywhere, like the remains of some brutal murder. Irene could smell the blood; it hung so thick and coppery in the confined air of the Potez, she had almost forgotten it was there.

George stopped short, looked this way and that, stumbled back outside the airplane and was sick in the sand.

"Thank God you're here," croaked Sam.

"Mother of God," whispered Raoul. "What has happened here?"

"Irene was hurt in the bombing at the Bilbao airfield. I was evacuating her to Valencia but the fuel tank'd been strafed, we didn't see the bullet hole because it was dark, and we ran out of fuel."

George climbed back inside, pressed a handkerchief to his mouth and nose, and knelt next to Irene. "Can you talk, sweetheart?"

"She needs *water,* for God's sake!"

Raoul had already unstrapped his canteen and held it to Irene's lips. "She has had the baby?" he asked quietly.

"Yes," said Sam. "Back in Bilbao. He lived for thirty-two minutes. I buried him with my own hands."

"I'm sorry to hear that," said George, "but it's probably for the best."

Sam stood up on his knees, hauled up George by his collar, and drew back his fist. But he did not punch. His left leg crumpled underneath him, and he collapsed on the metal deck next to Irene.

George straightened his collar and knelt back down. "Darling, we'll get you out of here, I promise. I've got a doctor waiting in Valencia—"

"What about Sam?"

George glanced at Sam. "I'm afraid someone will have to come back for Mallory. The airplane won't take a fourth passenger."

"But Sam's hurt. He needs a doctor too."

"We'll leave water for him. I'm sure this fellow will be back in a jiffy. Won't you, Velázquez?"

Raoul was checking Irene's bandage and didn't answer.

"George, *you* should stay. You're not hurt. Sam—"

"*Damn* Mallory! That—that bastard there, he's the reason you're dying in this godforsaken desert in the first place! The reason you're not safe on an ocean liner heading back to America. He's going to *kill* you one of these days, don't you realize?"

Sam spoke up. "Irene flew to Spain on her own, Morrow. She flew here to escape *you*, as a matter of fact. You and that prison you've built around her—"

"*Prison?* You've got a nerve, you son of a bitch. I've set her *free*! Free to fly on her own, instead of second best to the goddamn magnificent flying ego of Sam Mallory! Do you know how frantic I've been? Held back the damned press, chartered a flight to Alicante, bribed a dozen officials to track her down on the crazy chance that—"

"Gentlemen," said Raoul, "I'm afraid Miss Foster has fainted."

RAOUL CARRIED IRENE ABOARD THE airplane they had flown from Valencia. Mallory watched them go, watched Morrow jump down from the broken Potez and into the sunlight. He dusted off his hands and stuck his head back inside.

"I imagine you already know this, Mallory," he said, in a kind voice, "but there will be no airplane sent back to rescue you. You're on your own. And if you do survive, by some miracle, you stay the hell away from my wife from now on. Is that clear?"

Mallory spoke through cracked lips. "Go to hell, Morrow."

Morrow shook his head and turned away. As he walked across the sand, he called back, over his shoulder, "Just remember, this was your doing, Mallory."

HANALEI, HAWAI'I

November 1947

I N THE SUMMER of 1946, I was in Nuremberg, that half-ruined city of ghosts and lawyers. My hotel was lousy; the food was worse. The daily evidence of man's perfidy accumulated in what I had begun to imagine as sedimentary layers, grotesque upon grotesque, and I meanwhile suffered from some stubborn, unspecific gastric illness that was melting the flesh from my bones.

Miserable and starved, I sat at the bar of my hotel one evening in July, enduring the heat through a succession of whiskey sours and American cigarettes, when a fellow showed up and asked if I could possibly direct him to Miss Eugenia Everett, the photographer. He wore the uniform of an RAF squadron commander, the same uniform Velázquez had worn, so I told him I was Miss Everett, who wanted to know?

He removed his cap and sat on the stool next to me and placed a worn, yellowing envelope on the counter between us, seam side up so I couldn't see the name written on the back. He introduced himself as Captain Alfred Hawley and said that he had flown with a certain Captain Raoul Velázquez de los Monteros of the No. 56 Squadron in January 1945, out of the Volkel airfield in The Netherlands; did I perhaps recall Captain Velázquez?

I said I recalled him very well.

Captain Hawley said he was sorry to have taken so long to find me, but his duties with the RAF had not allowed him to pursue any personal errands until recently. He said that he had known Velázquez well during their time together at Volkel, and that about a week before his final flight, Velázquez took him aside and said he'd had a premonition of his own death, and if he should die and Hawley survive, he asked that Hawley deliver a letter to a photographer for the Associated Press named Eugenia Everett. Hawley had said of course, though he assured Velázquez that they would both survive to toast Hitler's defeat. In any case, there was the letter. Hawley was glad to have found me and discharged his obligation to a brother officer, which had weighed heavily on him during the long, hard months since the loss of Velázquez, a tremendous flier and a damned fine chap.

I thanked Hawley and asked if I could buy him a drink, and after some hesitation he agreed. Lest you think I had any immoral intentions, let me assure you I weighed about ninety-seven pounds at the time, was sick as a dog and wan as a phantom, and fully expected to vomit up those whiskey sours as soon as I returned to the dank, shabby, gloomy garret upstairs that disgraced the name of hotel rooms everywhere. All I craved was some crumb of information about Velázquez and his last days. Hawley spoke for an hour; I won't bore you with everything he said. Just that Velázquez had turned especially devout in his final weeks, had gone to confession almost daily, which made me glad because I did not want Velázquez to suffer long in purgatory because of me.

Anyway, you're not interested in all that, are you? You want to know what the letter said. Here it is. You might as well read the whole damned thing.

My dear Janey,

For some time I have reproached myself for withholding from you certain facts regarding the fate of your father. I told you I had made a

*promise to him. This was true, but I have come to believe that he would
not hold me to this vow if he knew that his precious daughter would one
day come in search of him.*

*Yet you generously allowed me to keep my secrets, and when I reflect
on the greatness of your spirit, I am once more overcome by this love
I confessed to you only once, but which I felt with all my soul from
the very earliest moment of our friendship. You will say in your brisk
American voice that I am a sentimental idiot, but it is my honor and
privilege to be a sentimental idiot on this subject, and to be grateful to
God that He has granted me this final joy when I had thought all joy
impossible. It is the last remaining desire of my heart to reunite with you
after the war is finished, so that I may explain all this from my own
lips, but if God wills that we shall not meet again on earth, I pray this
letter will find you instead.*

*You will find the wreckage of Samuel Mallory's airplane in the
shelter of a grand massif in the Bardenas Reales, in the province of
Navarre, in the northeast part of Spain. Inside this wreckage you will
find a human body, which you should treat with the reverence due to all
God's creatures, and the diary that belonged to Mr. Mallory, which will
shed some light, I suspect, on the events that led to this catastrophe. To
all this I can only recommend that you use your immense cleverness to
gather all these hints into a map that will guide you to what you seek,
because I cannot commit to paper any further confidence, or even reveal
to you how this knowledge came to me.*

*May you discover happiness, my beloved, and may a merciful God
forever bless you.*

Velázquez

I THINK ABOUT THIS LETTER, and the particular phrase *Inside this wreckage you will find a human body, which you should treat with the reverence
due to all God's creatures,* as I pedal my bicycle furiously through the

wind and rain down the highway into town. It's funny how you can assume all along that a sentence means one thing, because of your own particular assumptions, when really it can mean something entirely different if you examine it from a fresh perspective.

When I reach the pier, the ferry is still tied securely to its mooring, and the sign on the gate reads CLOSED FOR WEATHER. But nearby, a fellow's bustling about a smaller, nimbler boat, preparing it to launch. I call out and the man turns, and right away I see from Leo's face that he's heard about the reporters gathered at the airfield, and not only has he heard the news but he's holding me responsible.

"Where do you think you're going?" I yell.

Leo turns away and ducks into the deckhouse. I climb off the bicycle and jump over the railing.

"Don't you dare ignore me! I need to find her *right now*!"

"You don't have the right!"

"I have every right! You lied to me! About your father and Irene!"

He flinches at that. "Because I had to! Irene told me to. And it turns out we were right. Now beat it."

"Where are you going?"

"To Ki'ilau!"

"In this weather?"

"Yes, in this weather!" He reaches for the rope that secures the boat to the piling. "Irene took off from the airfield almost an hour ago."

"And how the hell do you know she went to Ki'ilau?"

He doesn't answer that, just unwinds the rope and prepares to cast off, and a terrible feeling takes hold of me, fear and also anger. A clatter of metal sounds behind me, and Sophie Rofrano's urgent voice. She leaps off a bicycle and runs up the dock to the railing.

"Leo! What's happened?"

"Sophie! Jesus. Thank God."

"What's wrong? Where's Irene?"

"She's flown to Ki'ilau," Leo says. "And she's taken the kids with her."

THE KIDS.

To be clear, I don't give a damn about Irene Lindquist at the present moment, clinging to the railing of Leo's boat as we tear across the water. I don't care whether she cracks up in this tempest or does not, whether she lives or does not. My anger toward Irene has returned at full force, so thick and bubbling it may blow at any second.

But the kids.

About a quarter mile out, the squall starts to die away, but the sea remains rough. Nobody speaks. Leo's busy keeping the ship on the right side of the ocean's surface. As for Sophie, she's as keen as I am. Her delicate profile points into the wind. Her teeth are bared. You get the idea she relishes this struggle, man against nature, and who would have thought that petite, elegant Sophie Rofrano was a fighter? But Sophie was the one who wrangled me aboard, Sophie was the one who took Leo by the shoulders and insisted that Janey Everett was friend, not foe.

Was she right? I don't know. I don't know a damned thing anymore. It seems to me that my fate is not in my own hands but elsewhere, laid out in some grand design beyond my comprehension. The rain spits in my hair. We're near the edge of the squall now. The blue sky beckons just above the charcoal shadow that is Ki'ilau, and I'm made of yearning for that patch of hope. Of all the things I have ever loved, the darlings who have vanished, one by one, only this remains. The weather buffets the ship. We pitch and plunge, heel and dive. What use is knowledge? All you can do is close your eyes, not even pray, because God has already decided what he's going to do with you. God has already decreed whether you will live or not live, die or not die, and you must meet your fate as Velázquez did, stoic and obedient.

AS I MENTIONED BEFORE, LEO cut his teeth in the South Pacific during the war, so I suppose it's child's play to him, bringing this mere civilian craft through a dying squall to the small dock that extends from the beach on the leeward side of Ki'ilau. All the same, the boat twists and lurches at the whim of nature, while the engine grinds us closer. Sophie snatches a coil of rope. At the last second, a wave starts us crashing into the wood, but Leo makes some final adjustment and we kiss the dock instead.

Sophie leaps to shore.

I follow her and fall to my knees, stunned by solid ground. While the two of them mess around with ropes and pilings, I start down the dock to the beach. Leo calls after me. I shift to a jog, into the soft sand to the hills beyond, and the path that leads up to the plateau where Lindquist likes to land her airplanes.

Leo shouts again. "Janey! Wait!"

I don't wait. I scramble up the path, slipping a little because the ground's still wet. Out here in the middle of the Pacific, just about every island is a volcano, or used to be a volcano, or a part of a volcano, and I swear you can feel the soul of it under your feet, in the dark, crumbling rock that was once so mighty. I climb and climb. Now the squall is well past, the clouds are parting. From the east comes a gold sun to burn away the haze. I reach the top of the slope and pause to pant. The plateau stretches before me, covered in grass. In the distance, a flash of silver. Behind me, a male voice shouts my name. I lurch forward toward the silver object, running as I have not run in many years, through the wet grass that soaks right through my shoes and socks, the strips of haze that soak my skin and hair. A half mile, or maybe more, I don't know, and the object takes shape, takes on wings and a tail, a fuselage, a nose that tilts to the clearing sky. A hundred more yards, another hundred, and I come to a stop, heaving for breath, beside the most famous airplane in the world, Irene Foster's silver Rofrano Sirius that vanished into thin air a decade ago.

I TOLD LINDQUIST NOTHING MORE than the truth that evening at Coolibah, after the charades, when I said I had no recollection of my mother trying to kill herself, or of discovering her unconscious as Lindquist claims I did. At the time, I was only a kid, so I suppose Nature took pity on me and buried that memory in some deep, secret place I'll never discover.

What I do remember is when Dad came home from Australia. I recall we were alone, the two of us, and Dad was holding me and wouldn't let go, and I didn't want him to. I wanted my father to hold me forever. When he pulled away, his cheeks were wet, and a little bit rough. I guess he hadn't shaved. I told him he couldn't go away again, not ever, and he promised he wouldn't. He said he would look after us both from now on, Mama and me, and that nothing could take him away from me, or me from him.

Of course, he didn't keep that promise. After all, he had to go on making a living, doing the only thing he knew how to do. But when do we human beings ever keep our promises? We mean so well, and we fall so short. He would leave for another air show, another race, another exhibition, and Mama would turn to me and say, *That concubine's going to take him away from us, just you wait. She'll take everything, and leave us with nothing.*

It was not until later that I understood what she meant. You see, in my innocence, I thought a concubine was an airplane. I thought it was the *airplane* that drew him irresistibly from my side, an airplane that fought me for his love.

Only later did I realize it was a woman, all along.

NOW THE AIRPLANE STANDS BEFORE me, but there's no sign of the woman, or the children. And I have come full circle and understand that my father was not pulled from my life by the airplane or by the woman, each on its own, but by the two of them together in an irresistible passion and also by an equal and opposing force that pushed him away, which was my mother. But that's all past and doesn't matter anymore. What matters is what remains of him. What I might still grasp with my two hands, if only she'll let me.

A streak of sunlight finds the airplane's skin and flashes white. The brilliance blinds me. The following breeze streams in, blowing the haze apart, carrying the cacophonous chime of birds, and as I stand there panting in my wet shoes, my wet skin, blind and afraid, the chime clarifies and becomes human.

I turn and open my eyes.

The tribe of them jogs across the grass, Sophie and Leo and Lindquist herself, led by a pair of scampering sprogs, tumbling tadpoles, as wet as I am, sunlight dancing on hair, alive.

AVIATRIX

by Eugenia Everett

(e x c e r p t)

May 1937: Bardenas Reales, Spain

WHEN MORROW LEFT, Mallory pulled his cigarettes from his jacket pocket. He couldn't walk after Irene; even if he had the strength, his ankle was broken, his thigh split apart, his head concussed. Cuts and bruises lay everywhere on his ribs and arms and legs, stiffened during the long days and nights, so that it was agony just to move. Instead he lit a cigarette and reached for his leather diary and the pen clipped inside. He smoked for a moment, wrote a broken half-sentence while the sound of voices drifted through the hatchway, while the engine of Velázquez's airplane started with a cough and whine.

GM to rescue at last thank God She will live

The diary fell from his hands. He didn't have the will. He wanted to listen to the sound of Irene's going and then slip away into rest, because Morrow was right about one thing. This *was* his fault, all of it. Irene, her pregnancy, her dangerous days here in Spain, the crackup, his own death—all of it was Mallory's doing, the work of the devil on his own shoulder, his recklessness, his death wish.

And now he was going to die at last, here in this wreckage in the middle of the Spanish badlands. He was going to get his wish. But Irene would live; that was the important thing. He had not also killed Irene. Instead of wishing Morrow to hell, he should have thanked him. Morrow would take care of her. Morrow would put Irene back on her pedestal in the center of his life, and he would revolve around her to the end of his days, which would be long and many, because Morrow had no death wish. Morrow was not reckless and impulsive and passionate. He would give her everything she wanted, a home and airplanes and probably children. Away from Sam, Irene would thrive. Like Pixie, who had found another father, a better father, and was better off without him. This was the right end, the just end, the only possible end.

God watch over them both, Pixie and Irene. The two living pieces of his heart. God keep them—

A thump shook the fuselage. Mallory opened his eyes.

"Señor Mallory?"

The thick bull shoulders of Velázquez appeared in the hatchway, framed by the sunlight. He had just laid something heavy on the metal deck, like a sack of flour, and now he climbed nimbly over this thing and grasped it under the shoulders and dragged it next to Mallory, without any apparent effort.

"Jesus Christ," whispered Mallory.

Velázquez shrugged and crossed himself.

"I told the bastard if he tried to get back on my airplane, I would shoot him."

KI'ILAU, HAWAI'I

November 1947

DORIS EXPLAINS TO me that they are here on a solemn mission, to scatter Sandy's ashes on the sea below the cliffs, where her father died. Sandy loved Daddy best, she says. Sandy would drape herself on Daddy's shoulders while he flew his airplane. She would leap on his lap the second he sat down and stay there, purring, for hours. Sometimes kneading her claws into his trousers, like *this* (Doris makes claws of her fingers). So this place is just where Sandy would want to settle a final time.

Irene holds the box as we descend along the path on the windward side of the island, where Mallory sometimes came to surf, because the wave on this particular stretch is legendary. That's the word Lindquist uses, anyway, *legendary,* but to my mind the proper term is something more like *suicidal.* Maybe it's the recent squall, but the surf arrives in giant curls of water that rise from the ocean like gods, sudden and enormous, a quarter mile away. The sight is unreal to me. If it weren't for Wesley's small, damp hand, tucked into mine, I think I might fall from the surface of the earth.

We step onto the beach. The sand is hard from the recent rain. Irene takes off her shoes and motions to us to do the same. Together we step into the churning water, up to our ankles. Doris takes my other hand and squeezes it hard. From the corner of my gaze, I spy Leo, who stands with Sophie next to the pile of shoes and socks, about fifteen yards away, as if to protect our belongings. From what, I can't imagine. Irene opens the box, which is made of wood, about six inches square, and mouths a few words I can't hear. The kids and I hold tight to each other's hands. Irene throws out her arm in a wide arc, and the dust makes a glittering smear in the air, hangs there like a rainbow, before it showers into the surf.

"Good-bye, Sandy!" Wesley calls out, in a boy's soprano, packed with excitement.

AFTER A MOMENT, IRENE TURNS and tells Wesley and Doris to go looking for seashells with Leo and Mrs. Rofrano, because she needs to speak to me. The kids scamper off and Irene sits next to me on the wet sand, Indian style as before, one hand on each knee. A long raincoat covers her usual shirt and trousers, and her back is straight, like a ballet dancer's.

"There's something I want you to know," she says. "I want you to know that he was happy here, as happy as he could be. He did not come here to die. He wanted to live."

"I don't know. I wouldn't surf in that, if I wanted to live."

"But you have to understand that he thrived on that thrill. He needed it. I think it was the war, the things he saw there, the way just about everybody died around him. So he needed to test this thing that had protected him, whatever you want to call it, luck or fate or Providence, to make sure it still existed. Then he could go to sleep at night and feel he would wake up alive." She pauses. "That's what I think, anyway. He never liked to talk about it."

I settle back on my hands and stare at the ocean. "What about you? Were you happy?"

"Not at first. At first I was miserable about the baby, and the burns took ages to heal, whereas Sam was back on his feet in a month. He was my strength. He was the one who flew us to Hawai'i, who found this place, who made contact with the Rofranos and arranged for the sale of the house, so we could have something to live on. He was the one who brought Sandy from California, who held me every night when these terrible dreams woke me, who took me out surfing again when my body could stand it. We bought Coolibah and fixed it up together. Then we had Doris. Every day of that pregnancy was like a torture to me. I was so afraid of losing the baby. I had these nightmares that I was in the desert again, that she was coming out of me. But then she was born healthy and kicking and . . . well, Doris. You know."

"She's Doris, all right."

"Oh, we fell in love with her, right from the start. Sam just adored her with this idolatrous love; he carried her around everywhere with him, wouldn't let her out of his sight. We'd already started the airline. First it was just a charter for tourists, but soon we were running regular flights and taking on pilots. Wesley arrived right after. I was so busy. I learned I could just put everything in a box, everything that had happened, and put that box at the back of the closet, and we were happy. The world had left us alone at last, we were still madly in love after all this time. We had these two beautiful children together, we were flying every day, we could step right outside our house and surf side by side. We were in paradise! But it turned out that Sam couldn't put everything in a box, the way I could. The lid wouldn't stay shut, no matter how hard he tried."

She speaks in a clear, precise voice, as if she's considered all these thoughts before. When I sneak a glance or two in her direction, she's staring straight ahead, without actually looking at anything. Even this pause seems considered.

"You might think," she continues, "that if you love somebody long enough and hard enough, you can make him happy. If you give him a home, and children, and love. If you give him comfort at night, and adventure during the day. And he *was* happy. For weeks at a time, it was so good. It was miraculous. He took this joy in the children, you can't imagine. And then the darkness would fall again. I always knew because he would fly somewhere, or drive somewhere, or surf somewhere." She lifts her right hand and points. "Right out there. You see that wave? That was his favorite, when he was in despair, because he knew it might kill him."

"When? What day was it?"

"Just over three years ago. The ninth of September 1944."

"I was in Paris." I stare in wonder at the horizon and think of the Hotel Scribe, of the journey out to the Orly air base in a Jeep driven by the jittery eighteen-year-old GI assigned to me by the Allied command. I cross my legs together, just like Irene's, and tell her, "I met Raoul Velázquez a few days later. On the eleventh."

"Ah," she says softly. "Ah. Of course."

"Of *course*?"

Irene turns to me. "There was a storm the night before. I remember listening to the wind and the rain and thinking Sam would want to surf in the morning, when the weather had cleared but the waves would be coming in like mountains. And sure enough, when I woke, he was already gone. He left a note to say he would be back in time to take the children to school."

"But he wasn't."

"No. As soon as I saw the note, I had this terrible feeling. I told myself it was silly, that Sam was indestructible, but when he hadn't returned by ten o'clock I knew something was wrong. The funny thing is, I thought he had cracked up the airplane. I never thought the ocean would take him. But when I landed here, his ship was sitting on the grass, just fine. The sun was glinting on the fuselage. I found his shoes and towel and things on the sand. I sat down next to them and waited. Waited and waited. You see, he had promised me."

"Promised you what?"

"That he would die in my arms. Isn't that ridiculous?" She laughs softly. "Ridiculous and sentimental. I thought he couldn't be dead, because he'd sworn to God he would die in my arms, and nowhere else."

We're silent for a moment, contemplating the rhythms of the surf, and then I ask her how long she waited. Whether anything of him ever turned up.

"No. Not a thing. As if the ocean just swallowed him. It was Olle who came looking for me, in the afternoon. He took care of everything for me. I was destroyed. I only held myself together at all because of the children, and because Olle wouldn't let me alone." She laughs again. "So I married him out of gratitude, I think. And maybe because I was so mad at Sam for dying."

"Mad? You were mad at him?"

"Of course I was. Weren't you? I was furious. For throwing himself away like that, when we loved him so much. For making us wake up every morning and find a way to go on without him."

From down the beach comes the sound of laughter, as Doris screeches her delight over some seashell. The sun's come out, but the wind still churns, and the surf arrives in tall, angry, chaotic waves. I think that I would like to be a wave myself right now, to throw myself against a rock and just expire.

AT THE BAR IN NUREMBERG, after Captain Hawley put his officer's cap back on his head and left me alone with my letter, I went upstairs and took off my clothes and lay on my bed. I considered whether I wanted to live or not. It seemed to me that nobody was left alive who mattered to me, nobody on earth left to live for. Velázquez was dead; my father, or so I then supposed, had been dead for years. I might as well have been dead to my mother and stepfather. My own body appeared to recognize its isolation and was now wasting away, day by day. Every morning I trudged into the tribunal courtroom and learned that the world itself was not worth living in, that man was so corrupt and so evil that further existence was pointless, that humanity did not deserve to continue.

You are like Sam reborn as a woman, Irene had said.

I don't know if that's true. In my last memory of my father, I'm thirteen years old and he's taking me out to dinner for my birthday, just the two of us, at some restaurant in San Francisco. He orders turbot and Scotch whiskey; I have chicken and a lemon soda. Over some chocolate cake for dessert, he hands me a box, and inside that box is a necklace on a silver chain, on which hangs a tiny shell containing a tiny freshwater pearl. I'm so overcome by this beautiful object, I burst into tears. Dad fastens it around my neck and says that whenever we're apart, as we must be, I should look at this necklace and remember how much he loves me. That I am everything in the world to him, and always will be. He drives me home the long way and walks me to the door, but he doesn't go inside because of Mama. He just hugs me and kisses me good-bye and walks down the step and gets into his car. He waves out the window as he leaves. I remain on the step until the smell of him drifts away. And that's all there is.

I don't really know why I didn't die that night in Nuremberg. I wanted to die, or at least I didn't want to go on living in this terrible new world in which everybody I loved was dead. But something inside me would not die. I woke twelve hours later and realized I hadn't thrown up those whiskey sours after all, and Velázquez's letter still lay on my chest, right on top of my father's necklace.

I am Perseverance, remember. I am Survival.

EVENTUALLY I RISE, AS I must, and dust off the sand. I turn my face down the beach, where Doris and Wesley are kicking salt water at each other, the little urchins. The small, unexpected offspring of my father and a woman against whom I have lived all my life in opposition, side against side, and now that contested ground has shimmered away like some kind of mirage.

Irene rises next to me and asks whether I can forgive her.

I lift my hands and stare at the palms, and I have the strangest feeling that they don't belong to me anymore, that nothing belongs to me, the whole world is new and strange. I remember something Velázquez once told me about crashing his airplane, how he had survived crackup after crackup and how you never felt your injuries until later. God numbed your pain, he said, otherwise you might lose your head in the aftermath, you might be unable to save yourself, for example, from the burning wreckage.

Between my fingers, something moves. I lower my hands and perceive an object wobbling in the air, next to the faltering clouds. Then the noise reaches me, the uncertain putter of an airplane.

"What on earth?" mutters Irene. "*Kaiko?*"

I turn to face her. One hand shields her face from the glare; her eyes are narrow, trained on the airplane, as if calculating its odds of survival. She's got no idea who's aboard, of course. She took off for Ki'ilau before they arrived: the invading army of my fellow journalists, that necessary nuisance known as the world's press, ruthless guardians of a democratic people's right to know everybody else's beeswax. Hapless Kaiko leading them smack bang into her paradise.

I turn back and loop my arm around her elbow, so we face the onslaught together. "Here's a better question. Can you forgive *me?*"

AND YET SHE RISES TO the occasion. Doesn't she always? She stands her ground as they thunder toward her in their crumpled suits, their sweating collars, white-faced and miraculously alive after the hairiest landing I have ever witnessed. The flashbulbs, the shouted questions. The wind whips her silvery hair. She holds up her hand and they *stop,* my God! I have never seen *that* before. I cross my arms and stand the ground by her side. Bill Cushing avoids my stare with an expression of downcast shame that reminds me of Mollie the beagle.

"Gentlemen," says Irene, in her solemn, clear voice. "I appreciate all the trouble you've taken to find me, and your generous concern for my welfare. But I'm afraid you're too late. I have already contracted exclusive rights to both story and pictures with Miss Eugenia Everett of the Associated Press, and will be unable to answer your questions."

Epilogue

▶ ▶ ▶

It is the easiest thing in the world to die. The hardest is to live.

—EDDIE RICKENBACKER

HANALEI, HAWAI'I

April 1949

THE BOOK'S TAKING longer than I figured. I thought that once I collected all the pieces of this puzzle, it would be a snap—so to speak—to arrange them in place and link them together with a few choice words. It turns out that writing books doesn't work that way.

But I am still here.

Habits are habits, and I often rise at two or three in the morning to work on the manuscript. If the words are stuck inside me somewhere, I'll develop a roll or two of film, or maybe I'll sit and look at the photographs Irene gave me, the ones of my father here in Kauai.

I've heard it said that according to certain human cultures, when you capture an image of somebody you capture a piece of his soul. I don't know if that's true. I think it depends on the image, on the skill of the person drawing or painting or snapping a shutter. Whether that person possesses a particular magic quality of soul catching, and maybe that's why we look in awe upon the great artists, because they catch souls for a living, while the rest of us drive buses and milk cows and add sums in ledgers.

On the other hand. When I look upon these pictures of my father, taken by some untaught finger pressing down on the shutter release of an amateur camera, I have the uncanny feeling that he's looking back at me from his monochrome eyes in his monochrome face. This one, for example. He looks a little sideways at me, eyebrow cocked the way I remember it, and his hair falls on his forehead. He's leaning on a surfboard against a wide, pale ocean, upon a beach I recognize as the one nestled under the cliff nearby, the beach where Irene and Doris and Wesley taught me to surf. In another one, he's holding a baby Doris, and you can't see much of his face because it's turned toward this tiny infant, but that little sliver of him is soft with wonder. There are eleven others, no more, but each one captures him in a different mood, a different moment, a different piece of his soul, so that when I hold them together in my hands, I feel as if I'm holding my father safe and whole.

I NO LONGER LIVE IN the guest cottage at Coolibah but in my own little house on the other side of Hanalei, from which I can bicycle daily to surf with my brother and sister when they get home from school or to greet Leo when he returns from the sea. He comes home with me most nights. Before you ask, we're not married or even engaged, but Hanalei is tolerant of these things. Sam and Irene never married, you know.

This morning is a Sunday morning, so Leo stays in bed while I make coffee. I have my own darkroom and also my own study in the spare bedroom, although I prefer to work in the airfield cafeteria. I like the hustle and bustle, for some reason. I get antsy when it's too quiet. Anyway, Leo thanks me for the coffee and tries to pull me back into bed, but I'm having none of that. Today I have important plans, I tell him.

"But it's my birthday," he says. "What could be more important than that?"

"My gracious, what are you? Seven?"

"Twenty-four," he says with dignity.

I admit he's got a point, and allow myself to be pulled back into sin. Leo is impossible to resist most of the time, and especially on a Sunday morning, even though we have already made love a thousand times in a thousand ways, because there is never enough of this. You do not come to the end of your life and say to yourself, *Gosh, I wish I hadn't slept with my lover so much.*

Although there's another reason, a reason we don't mention as we lie sweating against each other afterward, hearts going *ga-thud* in that familiar slow, heavy rhythm. Tomorrow I leave for another photography assignment, this time on the Yangtze River to capture the evacuation of British refugees, and I don't know exactly when I'll return.

AN HOUR LATER I'M ON my bicycle, pedaling west toward Coolibah, while the breeze tumbles through my hair and the early sun warms my shoulders. I like to tell Leo that it isn't him that keeps me here, it's the weather. I don't know, maybe it's both.

Or maybe it's Coolibah that keeps me here. My father did not leave me with nothing, after all; he gave me a brother and a sister, and the woman he loved, and they're all trooping in from the beach right now, still dripping with salt water. I stand on the lanai and wave.

"Where *were* you, Janey?" Doris demands. "The waves were *that high*!"

"Unavoidably detained by the birthday boy, I'm afraid." (There is a snort from Irene's direction.) "But I'm here now, aren't I? Where's Olle?"

"He's picking up the present right now. Kaiko's trying to start the fire in the pit. Doris! Wesley! For goodness' sake, go around back. You'll get the rugs all wet." Irene turns to me. "You'll help them with the cake, won't you? Doris wants to bake it all herself, but you remember what happened last time. And she has to let Wesley do at least some of the frosting."

"Oh, sure, and I'll just telephone Uncle Joe and convince him to end the Berlin blockade while I'm at it. Can't you at least lay out a few preliminary spankings?"

Irene shrugs. "You're on your own. I've got the pig to worry about."

IN THE END, IT ALL comes together. Nobody mentions that Doris's cake is lopsided, or that Wesley forgot the frosting *h* in *birthday*, which is a miracle because Kaiko's the kind of fellow who comes out and says whatever thought's inside his head. Olle drinks too much, but everybody expects that, and anyway he never drinks *too* too much, if you know what I mean, at least around the children, whom he adores almost as much as their mother.

As for that suckling pig, well. Irene always was the kind of infuriating woman who does things impeccably, and this particular pig is practically perfect, down to the pineapple in its mouth. Kaiko got the coals going, so it cooked all day in its pit and the meat falls apart from the bones whenever you prick it with your fork. Now the fire dances in the night, and everybody's laughing and happy, and it's time to give Leo his present.

Olle does the honors, because Leo's his son, after all, and because he went to the trouble to fetch this present all the way from the other side of the island early this morning, from a certain fellow we know who lives near Lihue with his wife and two kids. Olle sets the box in front of Leo, and the box topples over, and out pops a startled beagle puppy, eight weeks old.

Leo starts to cry.

THE THREE OF US RIDE home on the moped, Leo and me and the puppy on my lap. Leo's named her Frankie and already loves her more than me. We've agreed she should stay at my place, because it isn't right to keep a respectable bitch in a bachelor apartment above a tavern, and as we pull into my driveway, Leo casually suggests that maybe he should just give up the apartment altogether, since both pieces of his heart are living here. I hand him the leash and tell him to walk his dog.

While they're outside seeing to business, I light a few candles and open a bottle of champagne and slip into something less comfortable. The cottage is small, as I said, but Irene keeps coming by with lamps and cushions and books and frying pans to fill it up like some kind of permanent residence. Each time she does this I think of a mother bird dropping worms in a nest. Outside, Leo's talking to the puppy. The thought of Velázquez flashes across my mind and is gone, leaving behind a vapor of peace.

The door opens. Leo says, "I think a newspaper might not be a bad . . ."

I turn around. "A bad what?"

He closes the door and drops the leash. "Nothing."

WHEN LEO IS FAST ASLEEP, I climb out of bed and develop the film from the birthday party. A gentle Hawaiian rain falls outside. Once the negatives are dry, I select a few I like best. There's a beautiful one of Doris and Wesley carrying out the cake; you can't even tell that Doris was yelling at Wesley because he was going too fast. I also caught Irene from the side while she watched Olle make one of his rambling, heartfelt toasts. The fire makes a fascinating pattern on her scarred skin. You can see the affection in her gaze, the tolerance that—it seems to me, anyway—is the heart of any marriage. I sometimes wonder if my father gave himself permission to go because he knew Olle was waiting in the wings, adoring Irene from afar, and that while Olle wasn't perfect, he was kind and true, and he wasn't going to leave.

Or maybe a wave is just a wave, and it was Sam Mallory's time to die.

But my favorite picture is the last one, the one I took of Leo when Frankie overturned her box and made her appearance. If you don't believe in love at first sight, then I recommend you look upon the face of a man who has just met his very own beagle puppy. Once the print's hanging by its clothespin, I gaze at it for some time. He is utterly unaware of the camera; his expression is amazed and radiant. I have always loved the smooth texture of his skin, the elasticity of Leo, the way his face is capable of expressing the tiniest nuance of emotion. Velázquez was the opposite; you could not read a single thing on his face, not a hint of what he was thinking or feeling, his past or his present. That's why I prize that photograph of him in my bed at the Hotel Scribe, because I happened to catch a rare moment of candor, when you could look into his dark eyes and see the real Velázquez, the exasperation and hope, his earthiness and his piety.

One more photograph, on which I don't linger long. Doris took that one, because she's curious about my camera, and I sometimes let her use it. Imp that she is, she snapped one of me. *Me!* When she knows I hate having my picture taken almost as much as I hate flying. Still, it's a good photograph, if you judge it objectively. She's got instincts, my little sister. (I still savor those words on my tongue sometimes, *sister* and *brother*.) I'm looking at Leo—you can just see his face in the corner of the frame—and my brow is furrowed slightly, my eyebrows pointing toward each other, though my lips are just turned up at the corners, as if I'm happy and puzzled at once. My dark hair is pulled back from my face, exposing my Mallory cheekbones, and in fact everything in my face screams of my father. That expression is the expression he's worn in a hundred newspaper photographs, like the one taken long ago in Honolulu, as he watched his Irene deliver a public speech for the first time.

I SET THAT ONE ASIDE and tuck the photograph of Leo into my father's leather diary, along with the others I like to keep with me on my travels, Velázquez and Irene and Wesley and Doris, and of course that old snap of Sam Mallory, from the first roll of film I ever took, staring out the window of that diner in the middle of California. I stuff the diary into my satchel, packed and ready for tomorrow, and at last I lift the covers and gently slide myself into bed, next to Leo.

Except I've already been replaced by Frankie, it seems. The beagle curls in a happy ball between us, breathing twice for each breath of ours, tiny heart beating.

I TAKE THE EARLY FERRY to Oahu the next morning, piloted by Leo. Frankie comes with us; Leo says she might as well learn the trade early. I fall asleep in the deckhouse, and Leo wakes me when we dock. A taxi sits nearby, ready to carry me to Hickam Air Force Base, where I'll board a military transport plane to the Philippines, and then another to the Chinese mainland. Leo knows how anxious I am about these flights, far more than about taking photographs of General Mao's brutal advance. He carries my suitcase to the taxi and tells me he tucked a bottle of Olle's bourbon into my satchel.

"Send telegrams," he says, "so we know you're still alive."

I nod. He kisses me good-bye. As I climb into the taxi and look out the window, I notice the other passengers glance curiously at him, their captain who stands with his back to the ocean, staring at this woman who's leaving him. You can tell by his expression that he's afraid she's not coming back.

I tell the driver to stop the car. I open the door and walk back to Leo. I whisper something in his ear, and whatever I've said—I'm not saying what—I think it helps. His expression turns awestruck and full of hope. We kiss again like we mean it, and I return to the car, and the car continues on its way. I stare through the back window. He lifts his hand and waves, and that's the last I see of him before we turn the corner, a single image printed on the film of my memory: Leo's tanned hand spread against the blue sky.

AUTHOR'S NOTE

THIS BOOK ISN'T intended as a veiled biography of Amelia Earhart, and certainly not as a theory regarding her famous disappearance over the Pacific Ocean in 1937. But Earhart's story has fascinated me since I was a girl, and a few years ago I posed myself a certain *What if?* that eventually reimagined itself and grew into *Her Last Flight*.

As a result, Irene Foster can best be described as a composite character, borrowing certain physical and biographical details from Earhart but also from some of the other extraordinary women and men at the frontiers of aviation. My research took me down all kinds of rabbit holes as I investigated those three extraordinary decades between the Wright brothers and Earhart's disappearance, from the technological details of manned flight to the psychology of its pioneers, to the geography of the vast Pacific Ocean. (All of the locations mentioned are real, except Ki'ilau, which is based on the privately held island of Ni'ihau off the coast of Kauai.)

For those of you interested in learning more about the people who inspired this novel and the early aviation scene in general, I have a long list of books to recommend. Earhart herself—as *Her Last Flight* suggests—wrote several accounts of her famous flights, some of which are still available. The classic of the aviation memoir subgenre, though, is Charles Lindbergh's *The Spirit of St. Louis,* which appeared in 1951 and won the Pulitzer Prize. This is the kind of book you read with one hand while you're stirring the pasta sauce with the other: a lyrical, philosophical action-adventure that holds you in profound suspense *even though you know how it ends.* Not only did I come to understand the technical and human challenges of extreme long-distance flying, I felt as if I'd stepped inside the mind of an aviator.

For more on the derring-do mentality of pioneering pilots—and sheer exhilaration—you can't beat Tom Wolfe's *The Right Stuff.* Winston Groom's *The Aviators* combines the biographies of Lindbergh, Jimmy Doolittle, and the indestructible Eddie Rickenbacker in lucid, breathtaking layers. I relied heavily on Jason Ryan's marvelous *Race to Hawaii* for background and details on the 1927 Dole Air Derby. More fascinating stories and characters emerged from *The Lost Pilots,* by Corey Mead; *Sky Girls,* by Gene Nora Jessen; and *The Airplane: How Ideas Gave Us Wings,* by Jay Spenser.

Returning to Earhart herself, two biographies in particular stand out: the extensive and illuminating *East to the Dawn,* by Susan Butler, and Doris L. Rich's *Amelia Earhart: A Biography.* I was especially absorbed by Earhart's childhood and her brilliant, alcoholic father, who never lived up to his promise; and her relationship with her business manager (and later husband), the publishing scion George Palmer Putnam. Earhart's fans will certainly see shades of Putnam in my fictional George Morrow—created with a wink to my own publisher, William Morrow—but I'm afraid my imagination took over from there. (After Earhart was declared dead in 1939, G.P. Putnam married twice more and died eleven years later in Death Valley, California.)

Beyond all the research, though, I have a host of people to thank for bringing this book into the world, the bookstore, and your hands. Ten years ago, as a mother of four young children with an oversized manuscript called *Overseas,* I met my literary agent, Alexandra Machinist of ICM Partners, and her enthusiasm, persistence, crack negotiating skills, and (most of all) friendship have kept the books coming and the children fed, clothed, and housed for a decade now. I am so grateful to her for seeing us safely through every storm, especially now that those little kids are somehow starting college.

William Morrow has been my publishing home for seven books now, and I will never take for granted the enthusiasm and dedication of the entire team as they turn each manuscript into a real book and send it out into the marketplace. Huge thanks to my tiger editor, Rachel Kahan; to her assistant, Alivia Lopez, who keeps us both on track; to Tavia Kowalchuk and Brittani Hilles, for all their magical works in marketing and publicity; to my branding guru, Kathy Gordon; to the fabulously talented Mumtaz Mustafa, who designs those gorgeous covers; to the copy editor (my savior!), who catches all my errors and omissions and keeps my moon phases straight; and to all my heroes in production and sales.

To booksellers and librarians everywhere, thank you so much for your enthusiastic support of my books, and for fighting the good fight to keep us all reading, reading, reading, amid all the distractions of modern life. You are truly the guardians of civilization.

I'm so fortunate to be part of such a supportive community of women writers and bloggers, whose generosity and commitment to one another sometimes staggers me. To name each wonderful soul would require another page or two, but special thanks this year go to the ever-energetic, ever-talented, ever-thoughtful Kate Quinn, whose heart is as genuine as her terrific books. Of course, my love goes out always to my dear chums and "Team W" writing partners, Karen White and Lauren Willig, without whose friendship and fellowship I couldn't last another day in this crazy business. (And if you liked this book, you should really read the ones I write with the other two-thirds of the legendary Unibrain.)

As always, I'm grateful to my family—husband and four adorable kids—who put up with this writerly life, year after year, and still manage to grow into the kind of decent, honorable human beings who will put away the abandoned shopping carts in the parking lot without expecting thanks.

Last and most heartfelt. Thank you, *thank you* to my loyal readers, one and all, whether you picked me up at the library, the bookstore, the internet (legally, for goodness' sake!), a book club, or from a friend. Your support, your thoughtful reviews, your lovely messages, all sustain and inspire me to pick up my laptop and write the next novel.

ABOUT THE AUTHOR

BEATRIZ WILLIAMS is the bestselling author of eleven novels, including *The Summer Wives, A Hundred Summers, The Secret Life of Violet Grant,* and *The Golden Hour.* A native of Seattle, she graduated from Stanford University and earned an MBA in finance from Columbia University, then spent several years in New York and London as a corporate strategy consultant before pursuing her passion for historical fiction. She lives with her husband and four children near the Connecticut shore, where she divides her time between writing and laundry.